UNDER O

PLEDGING SEASON

ERIKA ERICKSON MALINOSKI

This is a work of fiction. Names, characters, places, and incidents are the products of the author's imagination. Any resemblance to actual persons, living or dead, is purely coincidental.

PLEDGING SEASON Copyright © 2022 Erika Erickson Malinoski. All rights reserved.

Print ISBN: 978-1-7375836-1-5
eBook ISBN: 978-1-7375836-0-8

For Jessica and the rest of the Disrupt the Narrative group. You helped me grow so much.

Chapter One
Ya'shul

Blindfolded, I can't see the dawn, but I can hear it. Drums keep time until the sun rises, their pulsing sound vibrating in my bones and drowning out the noises that would normally reassure me I'm not alone. In reality, the rocky outcrop that serves as the fairground stage is crowded—debuting men kneel at the front, debuting women pound the giant heartbeat drums anchored behind us—but the drumbeats wash all that away. All that's left is the feeling that the entire community is staring at me. I wipe sweaty palms on my pant legs, then catch myself and return my hands to my lap. Somewhere in the audience, my family is watching. I try not to shift as the rock beneath my knees pushes little thumbs of granite into my shins.

A shout cuts through the drumbeats, and their cadence quickens. Another shout, and a last thunderous roll sends echoes reverberating into the distance. In the following quiet, it seems as if all sound has vanished. Even the echoes of drums from neighboring mountaintop cities fade into silent anticipation.

There! A horn sounds, barely audible across the

distance separating us from the capital's mountain. Like a bursting dam, horns on other ridges take up the call, sound cascading across the range until our head priestess sounds ours. The notes fade, and our thousands of voices begin the hymn of thanksgiving sung at every spring equinox. I pour my heart into the traditional words: thanks to the winter rains for giving us food and thanks to the winter darkness for giving us respite from the desiccating heat of the sun. *Thank you, Goddess, that this day is finally here.* At the end of the song, my heart is racing. *Finally. Here.*

A cane taps on stone as Priestess Wekmet shuffles forward. "Welcome to this day!" The priestess's words carry across the crowd, the amplification so subtle that their firm voice seems to come from the mountain itself. "Today, we give thanks for the winter that has nurtured us and prepared us to withstand the summer's heat. We give thanks for our foremothers. Let us not forget their deeds."

I bow my head, as everyone does, and the priestess begins the recitation.

"When the waters of Earth rose, flames and storms scoured the land and drove our foremothers from their homes. They appealed for compassion, for justice, for a place where they could raise their children in safety, but they were cast out. They were cast out again and again until finally their last hope of welcome lay in the space colonies far from Earth. But they did not arrive at the colony that had grudgingly promised to take them in. Instead, they were stranded on this sun-scorched world, this dwelling place of monsters. Marooned, they forged a new life, carving a future out of this hostile planet through their perseverance and talent. For our foremothers, we give thanks."

I try to remain still as the priestess names the founders

of each clan, describing their deeds as they exited the space shuttle five hundred years ago, their descendants' heroics as they battled the waves of solar storms that nearly extinguished the planet's human presence, the lessons they passed down to ensure that the attitudes that destroyed Earth would never take root again. The thumbs of rock under my legs sharpen into talons.

The priestess turns to address the women at their drums. "You each come from a line of women who created life on a hostile planet. Your deeds have proved you worthy to take up their mantle. Are you ready in your turn to generate life? To create the planet's future? To carve the next generation out of your own blood and bone?"

A chorus of assent rises behind me. Bracelets rustle and clink as the priestess anoints their brows from a small bowl of oil. "Be welcomed now to the community of women. Today, you take your place among those who generate life of the body, mind, and soul."

A breathless silence, then cheers and calls from the audience as the priestess anoints the last woman on the stage. The crowd quiets, and there's more clinking as each woman accepts a bowl of holy water. My pulse races.

The priestess addresses the newly proclaimed women. "These men will be your helpmeets as you work to make this world what it could be. They will lighten your load and remove obstacles from your path. Your drums have returned them to the darkness and the heartbeat of the womb. Now help rebirth them into the world of men."

Footsteps scramble over the rocks behind us with an urgency that matches my pounding heart. A warm hand grips my shoulder, and my breath catches. The priestess's charge to us to fulfill the duties of men fades into meaningless noise as I strain my senses for any hint of whose hand it is.

Strong fingers give my shoulder a tiny squeeze, and my heart nearly stops. *Please let it be—*

Water pours over my head, so cold it steals my breath. The invocation is over. The hand leaves my shoulder, replaced by a rough towel mopping at my face. A waft of smell of cinnamon and musk curls around my nose, and I sag in relief. It *is* Nareen.

The towel finishes with my face, then fingers slide up the nape of my neck to push the blindfold free.

"Got you, Ya'shul," Nareen's throaty voice purrs in my ear.

Her upside down face emerges from the blinding daylight. Her short, black curls flop forward as she braces both hands on my shoulders and leans over me, a mischievous smile broadening her round cheeks. Cinnamon drifts over me again, and my mouth goes dry. Everyone in her family wears that scent, but for me it will always be the smell of her.

She lets me go, then steps around in front of me, holding out her hand. It hovers in the air between us, braced by the confidence she always exudes. I set my palm in hers, and her blunt fingers close around mine, the beige of her skin contrasting with the darker ochre of my own. Every finger tingles against my skin as I lean on her to pull myself upright.

She catches me as I stumble, my feet as numb as if they've turned to pillow stuffing.

"Sorry," I tell her breathlessly. I thought I'd managed to keep my legs from falling asleep. Surreptitiously, I shake them out, and the bells sewn into my presentation clothing jingle as I try to restore the blood flow to my feet and toes.

"Not a problem." She slips an arm around my waist, her plump curves pressing against my side, and my mouth goes dry. "Take your time." There's a wicked twinkle in her eye as she glances up at me and snuggles her hip closer to mine.

Heat pools in my groin. Plenty of my cousins have ignored my grandmother's oh-so-traditional insistence that we remain celibate until adulthood—until this festival in fact, when debuting makes us eligible to participate in pledging ceremonies. I, on the other hand, have always held back, priding myself on not being ruled by my passions. Moments like this make me wonder why.

Her fingers flex, then slip down to cradle my hip. I stop breathing. In all the years we've known each other, she's been circumspect, properly respectful of my grandmother's dictates. The heat in her eyes as she looks me over now shows me how much she's restrained herself.

Yes. Please, Goddess. It takes all my will power not to melt against her. I should move away. I should move away before this ends with her pressing me up against the rock wall at the back of the stage. There's still an entire festival to go. An entire festival of negotiations and last-minute alliances to make before the evening's pledging ceremonies seal the deals. *You know her family is going to ask for you.* I know. But they haven't. Not yet. Not for hours. I grit my teeth.

"I—" I take a shuddering breath. "I'm all right now." The words rasp from my throat.

She steps away with a little sigh. Her fingers trail heat across my lower back.

I bury my face in the towel, regaining my composure

while she picks up another and wipes the sweat off her bare torso. When I look up, she's standing in front of me, holding out a pot of scent-infused sunblock.

"My back needs touching up," she tells me as I take it, then she turns away. When I don't move, she glances back at me, eyes crinkling in amusement. I stop breathing.

"Are you *trying* to…" My voice trails off in a strangled choke.

If her grin were any wider, her face would split. "Don't worry," she tells me, "I'll do my front. Besides, picking you means I'm close as family for today, remember." She snags my blindfold, which is soaked in my family's traditional perfume, and ties it in a loose loop. Slipping it onto her arm, she tightens the knot with her teeth and waggles the ends at me.

My eyes feel too big. In the olden days, choosing someone at this ceremony was part of a larger mating ritual. Time has attenuated its meaning into little more than this quaint vestige of a tradition, but a thrill shivers over my skin nonetheless.

Nareen laughs and pushes the short curls of her hair up so that the back of her neck is fully exposed.

Oh Goddess. I'm glad that men are no longer picked from a line at this festival like slabs of meat. I *am*. I'm glad that negotiations between families give me a chance to lobby for who I want to be pledged to. But if I have to wait even ten more minutes…

I dip a shaking hand into the pot of sunblock and reach toward her back. Her skin is warm under my palm as I smooth on the ointment with all the restraint I can muster. The little noise of pleasure she makes as I work my way down her spine sends a shiver through me.

"It's—it's all set." I wipe my fingers on the towel and tug at the neck of my shirt. It was all well and good to have pride in my self-control when I was sixteen and convinced that my debut was less than a year away. But now, three more years have passed, my family deciding each festival that I'm *almost* ready. The delay has left me cursing my grandmother and my pride in equal measure.

"Oh, good." Nareen takes the pot back and turns away to apply the rest of it. Her hand follows the curve of her neck and shoulder, then it's only my imagination that fills in the feeling of smoothness giving way to the puckered scar just below her collarbone as her hand slides lower.

I look away. Around us, the formal ceremony is dissolving into talking and mingling as initiates return to their families. I rub at my new beard. When I lower my hand, the scent of her lingers in the stubble.

***

There's a satisfied smile on Nareen's face as she leads me off the stage and through the crowd toward the back of the fairground, where families have staked out their areas and are arranging low tables full of food for the fast breaking. I shade my eyes. The strengthening sun gives the celebration a determined edge, as if everyone is squeezing the most out of the dwindling time before summer makes it unsafe to venture outdoors without a sunshade. A few more proactive families have already erected canopies, and Nareen steers me toward where my family has claimed a prime spot in the middle.

As we approach, my mother looks up from arranging a plate of food in an artistic spiral. She holds out a hand, and I help pull her to her feet.

"Congratulations!" She kisses my cheek, then turns to Nareen, holding the plate out to her favorite apprentice.

Nareen accepts it with a grateful duck of her head. "To you as well, Viya-lun. I can only hope that my career might be as fruitful as yours."

My mother chuckles indulgently. Even though I knew it was coming, it's still strange to hear my mother receive the honorific *-lun*. Just as Nareen started her initial transition into womanhood at puberty, my mother is transitioning out. In the year since her menstrual cycle stopped, she has been wrapping up her work in the family laboratory and preparing to transition from woman to zoman. Under her serene exterior, I can't tell if she's excited about the next part of the festival or nervous. Her upcoming ceremony isn't just about changing pronouns from "she" to "they;" it's about taking responsibility for all one hundred and fifty people in our family.

Nareen catches my mother's hand. "Come! Now that I've delivered Ya'shul back to you, you *must* accept my family's hospitality. It's the least we can do for all you've given me—and continue to give." She casts me a significant look, then gives my mother's hand a little tug.

"Of course," my mother tells her. Her golden-brown face crinkles with amusement, then sobers as her attention settles on me. "Ya'shul, are your presentation materials still back at home?"

"Of course." There isn't room to store them up here while the fast breaking tables are set up. It's only once those are dismantled that we'll set up the booths where men and women can present their accomplishments to the community.

"You should probably go get them now. Marin-lun

has been asking if you're ready."

I look around warily. My grandmother demands perfection at the best of times, but during festivals, the stress of being the zoman in charge sends their tendency to find fault into overdrive. Negotiating all the alliances between our family and others requires attention to the smallest details.

"Even before I eat?" The smell of frying bread teases my nostrils, and my stomach grumbles a complaint. Surely, even my grandmother wants me fed and comfortable before the day's scrutiny.

My mother gives a sympathetic shrug. "Up to you." The arch of her eyebrow makes clear it's anything but.

I nod, and my mother finally allows Nareen to tow her off into the crowd. This presentation, along with the opening dances, is my last chance to impress Nareen's family. Dodging around my bustling kin, I head toward the far edge of our family's area.

"Where are you going?" My grandmother materializes in front of me with a flash of metal and the wave of an age-spotted hand.

I jump. Like many zomen, Marin-lun is frail enough that they rest in a spider-like mechanical walker whose six metal legs pick a path through the crowd. I have no idea how it's possible to sneak up on people in that thing, but they manage it often enough to keep me on my toes.

"Ah…" I eye the zoman's frown. "Home to pick up the materials for my presentation?"

A glimmer of approval sparks, then dims. Elegant gray eyebrows snap together over the wide-set eyes we all share.

"By yourself?"

I blink. Technically, I should be chaperoned by a

family member, a sign that we're serious about guarding the family genome. For all that things have changed in modern times, they've changed less for my grandmother than anyone else.

"Of course I'm not going by myself," I lie. A flash of movement out of the corner of my eye comes to my rescue. "I'm taking Ya'kinem." I nod to where my sixteen-year-old brother is desperately trying to distract the five-year-old he's supposed to be caring for. At least in this day and age, little brothers count as chaperones.

My grandmother's eyes narrow, but they don't call me out for my lie. "I expect your presentation to be perfect," they finally say, pinning me with a look. "Make your family proud. There's a lot riding on how well we impress people this year."

I'll say. There's always some reason my grandmother thinks that being perfect is The Most Important Thing, whether it's trying to keep our family's seat on the ruling council or simply striking the best bargains for our myriad alliances. But this year, it's personal. Now it's my chance to impress everyone and show that I deserve to be pledged out to carry my family's resources into fruitful collaborations with others.

As unobtrusively as I can, I make my way over to Ya'kinem.

"I need to go downslope," I murmur. "Want to 'chaperone' me?"

His lips twist, and he rubs at the scraggly beard that he finally managed to grow. "Was Grandmother—"

"Ooooh, ooooh!" five-year-old U'kylay squeals, cutting off whatever he was going to say. "*I'll* come chaperone you!"

Ya'kinem looks at the child, then shrugs. "Works for me." A gust of wind catches his sunshade, and he wrestles it back into place before the equinox sun can strike his unusually pale skin.

"This way!" the child says, wriggling between a pair of adults and speeding off toward the low stone buildings that line the side of the fairground. Halfway there, U'kylay veers to the right, darting instead into the gardens at the far end.

"U'kylay!" Ya'kinem calls.

"It's a shortcut!" Spikes of straight black hair, strands somehow already stuck together in disarray, bob behind a strand of rustling grass as the child's deep-brown limbs whisk out of sight.

I turn the corner myself with a pained grunt. We *can* get back home this way, but a shortcut? Hardly.

U'kylay is standing stock-still in the middle of the path, face skyward, wide eyes fixed on something high above my head. My breath catches in my throat as a giant pteradon glides over the fairground. It flares its leathery wings for a landing and alights on the towering, rocky promontory that juts up behind the fairground stage. The beast folds its majestic wings and plants its elbow-hands on the ground, crouching to allow its riders to dismount. The bony red crest on its head flashes in the light as it cranes its impossibly long neck to peer around. A plump figure in garish riding leathers slides down its neck, then turns to assist a thinner figure, this one clad in similarly garish robes. On the ground, their tiny figures only highlight how massive the beast really is. The pteradon tosses its head, and I suck in my breath. No matter how many glimpses of one

I've caught, the beasts are still awe inspiring.

"*I* want to climb up there!" U'kylay exclaims.

The promontory is by far the tallest point in our village, a jagged upwelling of rock that sharpens the tip of our ridge into a rugged prow. Over the millennia, the river that meanders through the mountain range has bent around it, carving cliffs on three sides that plunge to the river below. The view must be spectacular: From up there, the entire top layer of our village would be laid out like a patchwork throw, with stone buildings surrounding the central fairground and bordered in turn by a line of wooden platforms at the top of the northern and southern cliffs. At the far end, the gardens and orchards would be a verdant boundary between our settled area and the wildness of the remaining ridge, whose sides slope steeply off into a mix of trees and grazing land.

I've never seen that view myself, though. Our village's temple to the Goddess is directly under the promontory, and a flock of sacred ptercels, the pteradons' smaller cousins, have been cajoled to roost in the tiny caves that dot its surface. It's not exactly sacrilegious to climb on it, or to land a pteradon on top of it, but it's not far off. Disturbed ptercels wheel around, chattering their outrage.

"Come on, U'kylay, we need to get back home," I say, steering the child onward.

"Besides, you know we're not allowed to climb higher than the stage," Ya'kinem adds.

I glare at him. *Now you've done it.*

U'kylay stops. "*They* went up higher."

The two riders pick their way down as the pteradon flips its wings again and curls up among the rocks, indifferent to the screeching ptercels.

"Well," I venture, "they're Wanderers. They do things differently."

Ya'kinem snorts at the understatement. Most clans escaped the intense solar radiation of this world by burrowing deep into the cliffs and staying there for generations, but the Wanderer families didn't. To this day, they're still nomads, building wooden settlements out in the open and moving them every few handfuls of years.

"But why?" U'kylay asks.

"I don't know. They're merchants. Maybe they need to move around a lot."

"But they make trips here even when they don't live here," U'kylay protests.

"Then ask them," I snap—an error. The last thing we need is U'kylay trying to slip off to the Wanderer settlement that, as of this past year, now perches on the ridge only a short walk away from our village. I rub my forehead. The synthaglove I'm wearing taps the time into my palm. I still need to eat, set up, and change into my dance regalia.

"Or better yet," I say, "maybe *after* we go down and get my materials and *come back up again*, you can go around the festival and see if you can find the ones who just landed." I've never actually spoken to a Wanderer, but with any luck U'kylay will have forgotten the possibility by the time we return.

The child finally starts moving. Slowly.

"I don't have time for this," I mutter. Ya'kinem gives me an apologetic look, and I regret taking my nerves out on him. I know how hard it is to manage U'kylay—and how sensitive Ya'kinem is about whether he's good at traditional manly duties like caring for children.

He nudges me. "Think of it this way," he jokes. "Guiding U'kylay down and back up again ought to give you enough material to add an entire section to your manhood presentation about your caregiving experience."

A laugh almost forms in my throat. "Like I have time to make changes now. Don't scare me like that, Ya'kinem." I run a hand through my hair, then hastily pat it back into place.

"You'll be fine," he tells me. "Just remember—U'kylay! Get out of the dirt, please, you're wearing festival clothes."

U'kylay, a stick clutched in one hand, emerges from under a broad-leafed plant. In the child's shadow, light-blue spots glow against the dirt. I blink, but the blue spots remain—tiny, glowing mushroom caps that have been meticulously arranged into the shape of a vulva.

Ya'kinem snickers.

"Oh, for the love of—" I bury my face in my hand.

"Well," my brother says, patting me on the shoulder, "at least someone appreciates your fungus."

Make your family proud. My grandmother's admonition echoes through my mind.

"What are they?" U'kylay asks.

"Part of Ya'shul's capstone presentation project." Ya'kinem tries to suppress a smirk, but his lips twitch until I glare at him.

"But what are they doing *here*?" My hands clench with the urge to gather them up. They should be in the compost pile where I've been growing my experiments.

"Don't worry about it." My brother pushes my hands down and brushes at my disarranged hair. "There were still a lot left the last time I looked."

"Last time—" My head whips around, and he steps

back. "What do you mean 'last time you looked?'"

He has the grace to look chagrined. "It's not like you were using them anymore. They were just growing and growing and...um...I may have shown them to some people, and they transplant really easily, you know, and...well, they're pretty popular."

"Popular," I echo, heart sinking. I close my eyes, but the glowing afterimage is burnt into my retinas. "I'm going to be a *laughingstock*. Marin-lun is going to *kill* me."

"No, no." He waves his hands. "Making little drawings out of them is only a thing among the younger crowd."

"You made—oh, Goddess." I rub my forehead. U'kylay starts moving again, and I follow, my heels hitting the ground with staccato thumps. "I need people to take me seriously, Ya'kinem, not this!"

He pats my shoulder. "Don't worry, you'll do fine. We all trust that your presentation will be very, very serious." Ahead of us, U'kylay stops next to one of the platforms at the edge of the cliff, swings on the railing once or twice, and starts skipping down the wooden stairs that lead to the family dwellings carved into the cliffs below. "You'll be fine," my brother repeats as we start our own descent. He deepens his voice and begins, "I'm Ya'shul, creator of glowing mushrooms. And glowing mice. And glowing goats. And everything awesome. Pick me!" He gives me an exaggerated frown until my lip finally twitches.

I bump him with my shoulder. "The glowing isn't the point. And the traditionalists who think wearing color is sinful don't like it, anyway."

"Have it your way." His mock sober expression reappears. "I'm Ya'shul, the serious and boring. But at least

I figured out how to stop phosfoz from poisoning everything."

"It wasn't *poisoning everything*; it was building up in the tissues of mammals and making them sickly and less likely to produce milk."

"Like I said."

"Getting the details right matters!"

He makes a face. "That's why *you're* the one who spends all your time in Mother's lab rearranging genomes, not me. A, C, G…close enough."

"No," I insist, "it matters." On this, at least, I'm confident. "Knowing that a common toxic compound on this planet is phosphorescent is the *detail* that made me realize that bacteria in the compost pile were concentrating it. And being *precise* meant that I could splice those genes into fungi when I was younger, instead of wasting all my time on boring practice splices. And that's what made it possible to engineer mice that would concentrate phosfoz in their fur and nails instead of their other organs, which is what taught us how to do the same with goats so that now they don't get sick."

Ya'kinem gives an exaggerated yawn. "Or I could let you worry about all that because…oh wait…you already did. Like I said, your presentation is going to be fine. You've got this."

"You really think so?"

He grins wickedly. "As long as you don't get tongue-tied every time your coauthor's name comes up. Oooooh, Nareeeeeeeeen…"

I rub my beard-roughened cheek, feeling the rising heat. "We're just colleagues," I protest. "We had to work together; they're her family's goats. Improving them is the whole reason they apprenticed her with us in the first place."

Ya'kinem snickers. I retaliate with a brotherly knuckle rub to the scalp until he squirms away, laughing.

"You're just colleagues *for now*." He waggles his eyebrows.

"Oh, would you look at that." I nod to the wooden platform that branches off from the stairs at our feet. "We're almost home."

I shoo him across the platform and toward the deep ledge in the red and gold rock that forms the entrance to our family's caves. On normal days, the ledge would be filled with zomen talking with visitors or conducting business, but today there's only one elderly man sitting and watching the entrance while U'kylay clings to his arm. The child joins us as we enter the main antechamber and turn into the children's common room, where my presentation materials are stored on an upper shelf. I gather them up, pausing to take a last look around. I'd thought I'd feel only joy to leave these rooms behind, but now the cheerful carvings on the stone walls make a lump rise in my throat. The sun shines comfortingly through windows high in the wall where the rock has been carved translucently thin, glowing golden with accents of orange and white and red. Other windows stand open, letting in the breeze. The common room for adults on the other side of the antechamber is even finer, but it's not home in the same way.

Ya'kinem seems to absorb the solemnity of the moment. Quietly, he comes to stand next to me and offers to take part of my bundle. Having the strength to carry large loads is such a key marker of manliness that giving him a portion of my burden, especially materials for my manhood presentation, feels intimate. I want to hug him like we used to do when he was younger, when he would run up and throw his arms around me with so much enthusiasm that I'd have to brace myself not to be knocked over. We're too old for that now, though, so I just hand him my box of specimens with a grateful smile.

On our way out the door, he looks around. "Where's U'kylay?"

I cock my head, listening, then bite back a curse. *Now* of all times for the child to sneak off.

"You search the common areas, and I'll search the sleeping areas. Message me if you have any luck." As we tuck my materials back inside the door, I waggle my synthaglove, then reach over to feel its battery monitor. Unfolding the crank, I start winding the battery back toward full charge while we split up to search.

The family cave system is not *that* large. Our family may be a branch of a wealthy clan, but carving enough chambers into solid rock to house an eventual hundred and fifty people is not cheap. The sleeping chambers are communal and quick to search, but fruitless.

As I hurry down the stairs to the dining and bathing areas, voices and clattering at the entrance announce the arrival of the other members of our family who will present today. I hesitate. More people searching would get us out of here faster, but it would shame Ya'kinem to have lost his charge.

I tiptoe downstairs. The kitchen and dining areas on the middle floor are likewise empty, as are the bathing areas on the lowest. Emerging back up into the dining room, I meet Ya'kinem coming down from above. The dim light filtering through the windows highlights every crease of his frown.

"I asked at the entrance," he murmurs in a low voice. "U'kylay hasn't left the cave, at least."

I scratch my beard. Together, we contemplate the one place we haven't searched: the lightless tunnel where the zomen who rule the family have their private areas. I'm almost certain none of them would be home right now.

A soft giggle gives away our quarry. I listen at the first curtained doorway, then cautiously push the draped fabric aside. The luminescent outline of a child's festival clothing is bouncing up and down on the cushion seat behind Marinlun's low desk. Behind me, Ya'kinem inhales sharply.

"U'kylay!" I hiss. "Get out of there! We don't have time for this."

The bouncing stills, and the arms of the outfit cross belligerently. "No."

How did U'kylay's clothing end up covered in luminescent paint? We don't even have any. That I know about, at least. *Goddess, that had better not get on Marinlun's cushions.*

"Only zomen are allowed in here!"

"I'm going to *be* a zoman, after…after *puberty* and—and men…men uh…*men-uh-pause.* I belong here!"

"Yesterday's lesson from Teacher was on the four genders and their responsibilities," Ya'kinem whispers in my ear. "U'kylay's been going on and on about eventually becoming a woman and then a zoman and then getting to tell everyone else what to do."

I cover my face with my hand. "That's not what 'a zoman has the right and duty to guide the family they gave life to' means."

"I want a gender!" U'kylay whines. "Everyone else has one. I don't want to be just 'en' anymore!"

"You *do* have a gender," I tell the child. Children may be hairless, immature, and unable to reproduce, but they still count as the fourth gender. "And 'en' is a perfectly respectable pronoun."

"I want a *real* gender!"

"When you're older," my brother soothes. "At puberty. You'll grow, and your hormones will change, and your brain will change, and your menstrual cycle will start, and you'll get your adult pronouns. You just have to be patient."

Truculent silence greets this statement.

I run a hand through my hair. "Come out, U'kylay. You're not a zoman, yet. You're not even a woman."

"You're not even a full man. So there."

"I am, too—" I snap my teeth shut. *Almost.* All I need to do is get back up there and present to the community, and I'll be done.

"Here," my brother says in a low voice. "I'll handle this. You go catch up with the rest of the family."

I squeeze his shoulder in thanks and hurry up the stairs.

***

I'm too late. By the time I collect my materials and emerge blinking into the sunlight at the cave entrance, my family is nowhere in sight. Even the man who was watching the entrance has gone inside, leaving me alone among the lacework of wooden walkways and stairs.

Should I wait for Ya'kinem? The time tingling against my hand decides me, and I lug the boxes along the walkway. Marin-lun will never know that I was wandering around unchaperoned. It's a ridiculous expectation, anyway.

I struggle up the stairs, almost bumping into a tall man. He steps aside with an apologetic murmur and edges past me as I rest my load on the railing. The sun has barely risen, but already sweat is trickling down my back. I turn to call after him, but his quick footfalls are already retreating into the distance.

"Need a ride?" a lazy voice asks.

Ahead of me, the stairs broaden into a landing next to the wooden tracks that run straight up the cliff. A mechanical lift is parked there, its upper deck crowded with boxes and struts for booths, and a well-dressed woman lounges against a control panel watching me. She's maybe half a head shorter than I am, built of sculpted muscle that she shows off as she pushes herself upright and strides across the deck. She pulls the gate of the lift open and steps aside, her posture an invitation. A peppery, floral scent wafts from her. I recognize it—her family head comes by to consult my grandmother often enough—but the woman herself is unfamiliar.

I hesitate, and she makes a little beckoning motion. I shouldn't be getting into a lift with a woman I don't know, but the lift has an open deck, and we're in full view of everyone on the cliff face. A burst of masculine laughter rises from the lower deck, and the whole thing rocks slightly. Her family's men must be on the other side, loading the lower deck. I should be fine. And I need to hurry.

"Yes, thank you," I tell her, juggling my materials as I navigate the gap from the stairs to the deck. Our families are well acquainted, at least. A call from below announces that the men are onboard and ready to push the winch that powers the lift.

A heavy-lidded smile broadens her lightly tanned face as she secures the gate behind me.

"Would you like me to help below deck?" I offer.

"No need." She indicates a gap in the pile of boxes where I might stand. I arrange my belongings and tuck myself into the nook as she secures a few bundles more tightly, then squeezes past me to release the anchoring clamps. Her arm brushes against my chest, and I press back as far as I can into the boxes that are roped down behind me.

As she returns to the control panel, she brushes against me again more firmly. I plaster myself against the sharp corners of the boxes at my back. The aisle between me and the next pile of struts is narrow, but not *that* narrow. Surely I left enough space?

The lift shudders into motion, and she turns back to me, settling once more into a languid pose. "You wanted a ride?" She packs innuendo into the last word as she looks me over, her gaze lingering at my groin where my too-tight pants are designed to create an artificial bulge. My breath catches.

Shit. I knew not to do this.

She advances on me and draws a finger down my chest, flicking one of the bells attached to my festival clothing. I try to nudge her hand aside, but she entwines her fingers in mine.

"What's a handsome man like you doing out all alone today, hmm?" Her other hand takes over, tracing a path down my chest until she nears the laces at my waist. I recoil as far as I can, but my pants' fashionable tailoring refuses to signal that I am the opposite of interested. She smiles lazily.

"I—"

Excuses die in my throat. We're in full view of everyone on the cliff and just above her family. If I struggle, if I make a scene, everyone will look, and they won't blame her. Everyone knows men are always panting for sex, and no one expects a woman to resist temptation *all* the time. A respectable man makes sure not to do anything, like having an erection or getting into a lift alone with a strange woman, that could be construed as an offer. I imagine my grandmother's reaction when she finds out that I was seen unchaperoned and being pawed over before the festival is even fully started. Breath going shallow, I clutch at the cargo behind me. *Shit.* A rope digs into my palm.

She steps back just enough to run lingering eyes up and down my body. Her smile widens.

My synthaglove buzzes. A message taps itself against the back of my hand. *Where are you?* It's from Nareen.

Lifts. Help. Without taking my eyes off the woman in front of me, I form the commands for the message, then freeze. What will Nareen think?

The woman leans in and murmurs in my ear. "Too bad it's such a short trip up the cliff. Maybe next time." She tweaks my nipple.

I gasp, but she's stepping away, attention already turning to the controls. As soon as the lift stops, I grab my boxes and tumble out of the gate, shaking and nearly crashing into Nareen. Her firm grip steadies me.

"Are you all right?" She frowns, eyes searching my face. Without letting go of my arm, she shifts to give the woman in the lift a narrow-eyed look.

Words stick in my throat. The lift operator's bland gaze crosses mine. I can imagine what comes next: Nareen's face flushing with outraged protectiveness, her immediate confrontation, the attention it would draw. I swallow. She can't protect me from the gossip that would result. Or from the judgment of our settlement's elders.

"I'm—I'm fine." My words come out broken by a little gasp.

The lift operator's lips twitch in a tiny smirk. I turn away, bile rising in my throat.

With a final suspicious look, Nareen steers me away from the cliff edge, hand steadying my elbow. "What happened?" she asks when we're out of earshot. "Jamerol's not the type I'd trust around men."

"Nothing." The word comes out too quickly, and I grimace. Nareen's too loyal to let go if she thinks someone she cares about might need protection. "I just—I'm just nervous about the presentation." The lie tastes like ashes in my mouth.

"You're sure?"

I make myself nod. *That's all it is. Nothing else happened.* I force my trembling to subside.

Nareen presses gently on my back, guiding me and my load of boxes through the maze of stone buildings between the cliff's edge and the fairground. "Do you want to talk about it?"

No. But there's still a line creasing her forehead. "It's nothing," I repeat. "It's just… I need everything to go right. My grandmother—your family head—I can't afford any embarrassments." Can she hear the apology in my voice? I need this to go away. On any other day, I'd tell her. "It's rare enough that a man who has just debuted gets picked for a pledge. Everything needs to be perfect."

She nods slowly, and I let out a breath. I feel for one of the shallow stone stairs with my foot and take a firmer hold on the boxes I'm carrying. Their weight reminds me of their contents: weightlifting and speed cleaning trophies, testimonials about how well I take care of children, worker-of-the-month certificate from the compost piles, a scale model of the lab extension I helped build, my prize for winning the 100% recycling challenge—all the accomplishments that show I deserve manhood. That's what this day is really about: presenting what I can do for the community. I can do this.

Nareen runs her teeth along her lower lip. "Perfect, yes."

Something in her tone makes me glance over at her. She catches my look and shakes her head. "It'll be fine," she says.

"What will be fine?"

She hesitates. "You've been working so hard on getting your presentation together, I wasn't going to say anything."

My arms prickle even in the growing heat. "Say anything about what?"

For a moment, I think she's not going to answer, but finally she swallows. "Are you sure it's a good idea to boast to everyone that you gave birth to a new scientific discovery?"

I stop dead in the middle of the street. Everything I'm carrying is a sideshow compared to my *real* work.

"What are you saying?" The words come out sharp.

"Nothing," she says quickly. "You just—you were talking about how important it is that your presentation is perfect. You don't want people to think you're exaggerating."

My breath hisses out between my teeth. "I'm not exaggerating!"

"I know, I know." She makes a soothing gesture with her hands. "I was there, remember? *I* know. But other people? Think about it. People are astonished that I pulled it off by twenty-two, and you're only nineteen. You know what they say: The more a man puffs, the less there is to him."

"I would *never*—" I know as well as she does that exaggeration spoils a man's attractiveness. "I'm presenting what I *did*. I discovered the gene. I did all the trial and error to figure out how to splice it in. I know the discovery wasn't entirely mine, and I was careful to give you credit, but the part I'm presenting is the part I *did genuinely discover!*" *How could she think I would*—

"I know. I wouldn't have said anything. It's just that my family head is being ridiculous."

"Ridiculous?" My voice sounds flat to my ears.

"The alliances. Ever since they decided our family should make a serious bid for the council seat that's coming open, they've been renegotiating almost all of them."

My breath goes shallow. "Not the one with my family, surely." They can't be. Not when I have so much riding on it.

She says nothing for a long moment. "Not the major points, but which man from your family will be sent to guarantee the pledge was never officially decided. Orzealun could ask for anyone."

Breathe. "You've been asking for me, though." I fight down the rise in my voice. My family head is supposed to promise Nareen's family support as they establish her new lab. Whoever gets sent to guarantee it won't just be symbolically sealing the deal, he'll be her assistant for the foreseeable future. Orzea-lun and Marin-lun are only altering our families' alliance now because of Nareen's transition to full womanhood. It could be years before they feel the need to change anything again.

"I've been *asking*, that doesn't mean they'll do it."

I'm not going to hyperventilate. I'm not. The boxes shift in my suddenly sweaty palms.

"You think—" I can't say the words.

She shrugs. "I don't *know*. The thing is, giving life to a new idea yourself instead of just assisting with it…it's one of the most feminine things you can do. Normally, it wouldn't do more than raise a few eyebrows, but it's not just my family head. Your grandmother is the one who ultimately decides if you're available for pledging at all. And weren't you complaining to me last week that they've been ridiculous lately about 'how men are supposed to behave'? Is it worth the risk? You have so many other accomplishments."

I pace forward, unable to stand still. "None of those come anywhere even close to this discovery." *I thought you admired what I could do.* "Besides, why did Grandmother delay my presentation if not so I could present this?" Women get longer to debut, but almost all men do so by seventeen. My brother somehow finagled sixteen. *I've* had to grit my teeth until nineteen, pretending not to hear the increasingly snide speculation about what's wrong with me.

She opens her mouth, then closes it again. "Are you sure that's why Marin-lun did it?" she asks softly.

A chill of doubt creeps up my spine. "Of—of course." This is the day that was supposed to vindicate me, to show all of them that the reason that I took longer was because I was doing extraordinary work. Marin-lun's voice echoes back to me. *Make your family proud.*

Nareen says nothing.

"Grandmother ought to be happy to have me present something like this," I say. "Isn't this one of the ways we're better than the Wanderers?" Marin-lun has been insistent on showing them up ever since they moved their settlement here. "They're so sexist that they don't allow men to fly pteradons at all. We're better than that. Here, men can follow their talents."

She raises one shoulder. "There's a difference between what's okay to do and what's attractive to boast about. Family heads want men who will be helpful and supportive, not ones whose egos will be difficult to manage."

Every word strikes me like a blow. "This is my proudest accomplishment." I scrabble for my mental footing as everything I thought was true dissolves under me. "I'm not going to just *not mention* it."

"No, no." She waves the thought away. "I'm not saying you need to take it out entirely, just make it more…you know, helpful."

My carefully prepared materials feel like they've doubled in weight.

"It's not fair, I know," Nareen presses, "but I also know how much you've had your heart set on the alliances turning out the way we wanted." She glances away. "How much we both have."

I barely manage to swallow past the tightness in my throat. I'd thought the future was certain. Nareen would debut and return to her family to head a new lab, and my family would send me as a guarantee of our ongoing support and the closeness between our families. Surely—surely that's still what's going to happen.

"What if I just read over what you're going to say," she coaxes. "Suggest some edits if it seems like something might not work. You can decide later." Her voice lowers to a whisper as we come within earshot of my family. "I'll have time while you're busy with the opening dance."

Centimeter by painful centimeter, my fingers curl into the command that sends my presentation from my 'glove to hers. She gives a tiny wave of farewell and strides off, 'glove already twitching.

At the pile of unassembled booths, I finally deposit my boxes and scrub my hands over my face. My newly grown beard scratches against my palm. I'm not sure I can even force food down right now. *The dance. Just focus on getting through the dance.*

Chapter Two
Andeshe

Auntie Haveo is waiting for me, arms folded, at the base of the promontory. "You landed on the Uplanders' temple, Andeshe!" they tell me as I finish helping Auntie Illeab down the rocky slope.

"Isn't it over there?" I tilt my head toward the jumble of stone pillars just south of us. Normally, when I fly into Ikmeth, I land on the field, but today it's packed with people for the festival.

"That's the entrance," the zoman who heads my adoptive family corrects. "The rest is under the promontory."

"Oh. Do you think it will bother them?" Fizz is sprawled on the rocks most of the way down, her chin plopped on a boulder and her eyes closed. A ptercel lands on her crest, but she doesn't even twitch. "I can send her to the settlement if you like. We stopped there long enough to orient her to it."

"That would be good."

I climb back up the rocks and give Fizz's flank an affectionate thump. She cracks an eye open in mild reproof.

Lazy creature. But I scratch her eyebrow ridges anyway.

"Home, Fizz," I tell her, interlacing my fingers like a nest in front of her eye. "Fly home." She can follow that command without supervision.

She chuffs and raises her wedge-shaped head, scanning the towering mountains that surround the ridge until she settles on a spot to the north.

"No, Fizz, new home." I tug her reins until she turns west, peering past the buildings of Ikmeth toward the scrubby forest that drapes over the middle of the ridge and the clearing that has been carved out of it for our settlement. With a sigh, she heaves herself to her feet and shakes her head, dislodging the ptercel.

"I know," I tell her. It's only my imagination that makes her expression seem mournful. "We'll make the best of it. At least it's not far. Home." I slap her flank again, then step back as she crouches and launches herself upward. Shading my eyes, I follow her flight, noting the stiffness in her wings with a twinge of sadness.

Come on, old girl! She beats at the air, and a memory surfaces of her pushing her way out of her shell all those years ago. She'd flapped awkwardly and tipped forward, but it hadn't dimmed the brightness in her eyes when she looked up at me, a gangly-limbed child on the cusp of puberty. Age catches up with all of us, but twenty is far too young for such majestic creatures to start their decline.

I shake away my thoughts and pick my way back down to the zomen below.

"And where was Andeshe supposed to have landed?" Auntie Illeab is asking, leaning on their crutch and waving their arm stump. "On the Uplanders? The fairground is occupied." Their eyes rove over the crowd milling in front of us.

Haveo snorts. "No, but she could have landed at our settlement, and you two could have *walked,* like we did. We built as close to Ikmeth as we could for a reason. The path along the ridge is clearly marked."

Illeab shrugs unapologetically. "Next time." The unscarred side of their face softens, and they tilt their head. "In any case, is that all the greeting I get after not seeing you for months?"

Haveo's sternness melts into a rueful smile, teeth flashing whitely against the weathered umber of their face. "No, of course not. It's good to see you again." The zoman leans in to kiss their longtime lover, then turns back to me. "Welcome home, Andeshe." They pull me into a hug, the stubble of their shaved head tickling my ear.

I inhale the faint scent of pteradon and summer sun. "Yes, thank you." It is home now. Or it will be.

With a final squeeze, Haveo lets me go, then steers us into the crowd.

"Did opening the caves go well?" they ask.

I shrug. "About as well as you'd expect. We finished early. There were plenty of people working on it." Every family in the clan sent people to help clean and restock the distant cave systems we haven't used in generations. But even the camaraderie didn't make the constant awareness of what we're losing any easier to bear.

Auntie Illeab snorts, sending the beads at the end of their rows of gray-black braids scurrying past their jaw. "About as well as you'd expect with all the youngsters who have never been through even a mild solar flare crowing about how brave they'll be in the face of the solar storms.

I kept telling them that hunkering down in the middle of nowhere for a decade trying to preserve a remnant of the pteradon flock isn't going to be all fun and games, but do they listen?"

"They'll find out soon enough," I say. The year and a half we have before the storm season comes is both too short to prepare and too long to wait in limbo. "The last storms were two hundred years ago. No one alive really understands what it was like to go through them." We know the general outlines—solar flares that punch through the atmosphere and ground long-distance flights for weeks, most of our people going underground with the Uplanders, the rest sheltering with carefully chosen pteradons in the wilderness caves where we can hunt nearby game for them—but no one knows what it will be *like*.

Illeab waves my comment away. "Yes, but some of us listen to our elders, or at least the stories they left us, instead of pouting about not getting to take the first shift in the wilderness. Are you sure you don't want to go, Andeshe? You have a sensible head on your shoulders, and I never thought I'd need to persuade you to spend time with pteradons."

I look away. Around us, Uplander families stand in stiff groups, a sea of bland, beige cloth given only some relief by the tans and browns and pinks of exposed skin. Sidelong glances meet mine, then dart quickly away, their owners not even granting us the courtesy of being honest about their curiosity.

When I don't answer, Illeab prompts, "You know Haveo would give you their blessing. You needn't worry that you'll leave the family in the lurch." At their side,

Haveo nods confirmation.

"Fizz isn't going," I say at last.

The zomen give that statement the quiet witness it deserves. Before the sun's radiation gets too intense, Fizz and I will take our last flight together to release her and most of the flock on the far side of the mountains so they can make their way back to the distant ocean where their ancestors fished for themselves. Without enough game close to civilization, we can't keep them all. Only a core of pteradon bloodlines will take shelter in the wilderness caves. Only ones young enough to rebuild the population after the decade-long season of danger and scarcity ends. I swallow around a lump in my throat. I never thought I'd wish Fizz was the dangerous predator Uplanders think she is instead of a lazy lump who only eats when I flop her meal in front of her like a fish. If she could hunt on land, I might see her again. I might be more confident she could make the long flight to the ocean in the first place.

"I'm sorry, Andeshe," Auntie Illeab says. They shift their weight on their crutch and turn their stump and one remaining palm upward. "I wish I'd been able to find a way to feed them all."

I cover their palm with mine and give it a gentle squeeze. It's not my aunt's fault that all their attempts to corral native prey animals failed, no more than it's their fault the pteradons can't digest anything descended from Earth.

I let my hand fall away and start moving again. "Any word on whether the priestesses will be able to predict solar flares more accurately this time around?" If we knew more precisely when flares would hit, maybe we could risk ranging farther.

Haveo grimaces. "Less, if anything. More and more of the instruments left on the starship are failing. We're lucky they've held up this long with no way to get back up there for repairs." The zoman shrugs. "We make do with what we have."

I take a deep breath and let it out in a long sigh. I hadn't really let myself hope, not when Fizz is so far down the list of pteradons to keep, but still.

Auntie Illeab touches my shoulder gently. "At least we'll be able to visit each other. There should be enough gaps between flares for that."

I reach up and press their stump, accepting the comfort. Illeab is my true aunt, not just called *Auntie* like all zomen are. Even in hard times, we still have family. And as frantic as everyone will be during the brief safe windows trying to squeeze in our normal rounds of deliveries to all the ridges, I know Illeab will visit us as often as possible.

The silence lengthens until Auntie Haveo finally claps their hands. "Well, I don't have a perfect solution, but let me show you the progress we've made while you were gone."

They lead us at a brisk pace across the fairground, detouring around groups of Uplanders who are, as best as I can tell, cleaning up the remains of a meal and assembling booths made of metal struts and large pieces of cloth. As the booths go up, the flat, grassy sward transforms into a maze. There's just enough room to walk, though we have to detour around a dispute between two groups about who should move back to make more room for passersby.

We draw closer to a circle at the edge of the fairground. Auntie Illeab turns to Haveo. "Your family has certainly settled in, haven't you?"

I blink. The people swirling around the circle look the same as any other Uplanders, undyed robes and pants and shirts blending together, but their motions and voices are less constrained than the people in the circles nearby.

"Andeshe! Andeshe!" A waist-high whirlwind barrels toward me, and the strangers dissolve into my own family, abandoning their tasks to engulf me and Illeab in hugs.

At least there's always family. I squeeze a little tighter. As odd as it is to see children and parents and men dressed as and mingling with the Uplanders, it still warms my soul to see them again.

The greetings wind down. Babies finish being exclaimed over, children scamper off, and my cousin Velemeth's one-year-old solemnly deigns to be carried. Child on one hip, I follow a patient Haveo around the corner of the booths to our destination.

My steps falter. A bulbous lump of metal and glass squats on the grass, propped up by a pair of skids. Six propellers jut from its domed body while in the back, a stubby tail ends in a rudder.

"You finished the prototype!" Illeab picks their way around the outside of the craft, peering up at the blades.

"Just in time for the festival." Haveo slaps the craft's nose, pride etching every line of their body. Creating a mechanical means to fly has been their obsession for decades. I can't count the number of sketches and models I've seen over the years, much less the number of diatribes I've heard as Haveo tracked down one solution after another in the starship's databanks only to find that it required some element we can't access; or flammable liquid rock that never formed here; or long, flat stretches of land for takeoff; or some other sort of impossibility. Tentatively,

I reach a hand toward the flier. Like everyone else in the family, I've heard updates on its progress, but I've never seen it, not while it's been tucked away at the workshop some of our Uplander allies have deep in the mountains. The metal is cool and hard under my fingertips. "If this works," Haveo continues, "it won't matter that we can't feed the pteradons. Just park a flier under sufficient shielding during the storms, and it's ready to go as soon as there's a break. This time, we can go to the ground with the Uplanders without having to give up anything at all."

Nothing? Memory comes back to me of Fizz nudging my palm, skin warm and supple as she silently begged for eye ridge scratches. I pull my hand away from the prototype, a shudder creeping up my spine.

Illeab pokes their head in the open door. "Where are the batteries?"

Despite myself, I crane my neck. The interior is far more spacious than it should be, given how much battery power it will need. If even something as tiny as my earpiece requires a bulky battery pack clipped to my waist, then the range on this flier must be miniscule. My spirits shouldn't lift at the realization, but they do.

"That's just the thing." A smile spreads over my aunt's face. "The experimental mine our allies opened? The expansion of the one by their workshop? They struck lithium deposits. Now we have a chance of making the batteries light enough to get something with useful cargo space off the ground."

Illeab whistles. "And they let you have some? What did you promise them? All our men and half the teenagers? *No one*'s been able to find a viable source of lithium." They flick the battery pack on their own belt for emphasis.

Haveo swats Illeab's arm. "It was a joint project. They need a way to fly their people back and forth between their workshop and this ridge just as badly as we need to fly everywhere else. I'm not saying they didn't drive a hard bargain, but we've been allies for decades. That counts for something."

Illeab shrugs. "If you say so." They poke at the interior of the flier again. "What kind of range did you end up getting?"

Haveo tips their hand back and forth in a "so-so" gesture. "It's not great, but it doesn't have to be. Not if we're based here and only need to do short jumps to the other ridges."

Not if we're based here. The urge seizes me to jump on Fizz's back and fly somewhere else—anywhere else. Some place where the windows of the flier don't cast back empty reflections of the sky in a horrible parody of Fizz's inquisitive gaze. My throat tightens. I'd toyed with the idea of maybe piloting these someday, but faced with the lifeless, unresponsive *thing* in front of me, I cannot imagine it.

I turn away, blinking water out of my eyes. Perhaps it's better to make a clean break. There are other options here. I cuddle the child in my arms a little closer.

"Andeshe! You're back!" My cousin Velemeth waves to me from the circle of Uplanders on the other side of the prototype. He picks his way across the grass toward me and gives me an awkward hug around the child, who clings to his shirt as he pulls back. "Did you just fly in?"

I nod, letting the child transfer to him.

"I thought that was you. Have you seen much of the festival yet?"

I shake my head. That's what I'm supposed to be doing. I'm supposed to be looking at what the different families do and coming up with ideas for some sort of apprenticeship I might enjoy after Fizz…goes. As much as I might want to, I can't cling to the past forever.

"They're about to start the dancing on the main stage. Do you want to come watch?"

Anything to stop me from dwelling on this. "Lead on."

His eyes flick over me. "Aren't you going to change first?" He smooths a red-brown hand down the tight Uplander men's garb that outlines every soft fold of his body.

I look down. My flying leathers are worn and colorful, but they're comfortable, protecting me from the elements and supporting the rolls of flesh that pad my short frame. I touch the radiation dosimeter clipped to one shoulder. I could take it off, I suppose. I only need it when I'm far away from the temples and their warning systems.

"Later," I tell him, adjusting the hood against my neck. My fingers brush my close-cropped hair. No matter how much cooler Uplander garb is in the muggy air, it feels too much like being stripped of my armor. The sunshades and ointments people here use to protect their bodies aren't hefty enough to reassure, despite the fact that I've seen such protections work for Uplanders with skin ranging from my own midnight-black to the most translucent pink. "The Uplanders are used to seeing us like this." In truth, women dressed like me are the only ones they're used to seeing fly in to visit. Everyone else stays home. Velemeth's comfort going out among them as a man will take me a bit to adjust to.

Some of my thoughts must have shown on my face because he gives me a penetrating look. "Here it's the men who are sent out to other families, you know." There's an edge of defensiveness in his voice, as if he can't quite believe that he's able to be one of them.

"I know." I've visited plenty of Uplander towns on my trade and delivery routes, but that doesn't stop me from being caught by surprise when my family starts mimicking their customs. "I don't disapprove, it's just…is Auntie Haveo sure about this?" I ask. My hand wave could indicate the flier, the family, or all of it.

Velemeth's eyebrows rise at my uncharacteristic misgivings. Normally, I'm the one who returns from my travels keen to insist that Uplanders are ordinary people just like us and determined to bat down the wild rumors about them that persist among people who have never visited their towns.

"Do you need me to list off the reasons we're settling here?" Velemeth asks.

"No," I sigh. As flying becomes more and more hazardous, we won't be able to live in the places we used to. "I'm just not ready yet."

Velemeth hesitates but finally jerks his chin toward the waiting festival. He passes the child back to the parent who's watching all the youngsters, and I follow him into the crowd.

Chapter Three
Ya'shul

Hands press into my calves, a trio of my uncles bracing my feet on their shoulders as we wait on the stage for my turn. My cousin Se'jan bounces once more on the trampoline in front of us and curls into a backflip before dismounting. The crowd roars its approval. Then it's my turn to be launched into the air, arms spread wide. For one glorious instant I float, weightless, then the trampoline rushes toward me. I bend my legs, straightening at just the right moment to send myself arcing upward again. *Perfect.* The blood roars in my ears. I fight the vertigo of a double spin, bunch my leg muscles against the impact of the bounce, and fly upward again. A laugh bubbles up in my chest as I whirl through the twists and turns of my solo. *This is what I can do.* Even as my body strains to its limits, the cheers of the crowd buoy me until I feel like I can do anything.

I fling my arms wide, and their approval soaks into some always-thirsty corner of my soul. I push myself past the fire burning in my thighs, squeezing in one last flight before I alter my trajectory to take me off the edge of the trampoline. The dismount mat rushes in, and I land with a jolt on the padded ground, turning the impact into a graceful bow. Applause thunders.

I retire to the back of the stage to wait with the others. The audience's attention shifts to my brother as he begins his routine.

"Not bad, eh?" I murmur to Se'jan. I mop at my face. I'm not expecting to fish an actual compliment out of him, but perhaps some of the *light* mockery that's the closest he comes. The crowd in front of us is cheering for my brother, but they cheered for me more.

"With such a superlative example going right before you, I'd expect no less," Se'jan replies, but he gives me a tiny toast with an imaginary glass. Even this soon after finishing his routine, his curls are somehow perfectly back in place, framing the cool olive of his face.

I scan the crowd. Nareen isn't here, but my grandmother is out there somewhere. *See what I can do? Is it too much to ask to be celebrated?* This is all I want, to push myself to my limits while my community cheers me on. When I pick out Marin-lun, however, they are in deep in conversation with a tiny, shaved-headed zoman whose bushy eyebrows exaggerate every change in expression. Both of them are watching me. My smile slips.

Se'jan follows my gaze. "Oh-ho!" he crows. "Marin-lun's negotiating with Orzea-lun, hmm?" He eyes the tiny zoman who heads Nareen's family with interest.

I look away fast.

"You know," he says, bumping my shoulder with his, "it might not be you who gets pledged to Nareen."

I know better than to rise to his bait. I fix my eyes on

the trampoline instead. Ya'kinem dismounts with a slight stumble, and the next trio of supporting men launch their dancer.

"It could be any of us," Se'jan prods.

"I *know*." There's one more man left to launch, then we'll close with the final group routine that we've practiced so many times.

"Orzea-lun might want someone for her who's been pledged out before. You know…someone proven, dependable, steady."

"You're not helping." I wish it weren't too early to edge away from him and take my position for the next dance.

"After all," he continues, "it would be pretty unusual to be picked to guarantee a pledge in your debut year. I wouldn't want you to be too disappointed if it doesn't work out." He jerks his head in the zomen's direction.

Orzea-lun points at the soloist and turns to ask Marin-lun a question. My grandmother's forehead furrows, then they shrug and make some brief comment. My nails dig into my palms. *No! Me!* As if hearing my thought, Marin-lun waves in my direction, and I straighten, heart hammering. I stare at the zomen as if I can will my thought across the distance. Orzea-lun looks me up and down with pursed lips and tilts their head. Their attention shifts to a cousin on the far side of the stage.

No. Argh! I feel light headed. The tiny zoman points again.

"I'd give you the benefit of my wisdom," Se'jan says, "but apparently it's not helpful." He closes his mouth with an ostentatious snap of his teeth.

Of course he'd clam up now. My eyes drift again to

the two zomen. Se'jan may be the most irritating person I know, but he's also the most politically astute.

"What?" The word finally grates from me.

"Who are you trying to persuade?"

I press my lips together. My daydreams about impressing everyone with my work, about getting pledged out two or even three times, congeal into a single image of Orzea-lun's assessing eyes.

"What do they want?" Se'jan continues.

"How am I supposed to know?" It takes effort not to run my hands through my hair. The point of sending men to other families to guarantee pledges is to share *knowledge*, as well as genes and other resources. I'd thought that showing off my discoveries would give me an edge, show that I'm knowledgeable enough to compete with men who started assisting in labs before I was born.

"Have you asked Nareen?"

My heart sinks. Pulling the words out is an effort. "Someone demure. Humble. Masculine. Someone who doesn't puff himself up too much."

"Well?"

I rub my temples with my fingers. "Se'jan, you know I hate you in the best possible way."

He thumps me on the back. "I'm always here for you," he replies. "Ready to wield the brickbat of reality."

I snort, then start coughing.

"Right," I gasp when my breath returns. The cheers for the final acrobatic solo mount to a crescendo, and we separate to take our places for the final number. "Right."

***

My boxes stare at me from the floor of my booth. *Have you*

asked Nareen? Voices from other booths drift in through gaps in the fabric walls, my mother's on one side, Se'jan's soft drawl on the other. My 'glove presses an unread message from Nareen against my arm in a tight knot. Slowly, I open the first box, picking out my trophies one by one and setting them on the table. There's nothing controversial about any of them, only praise for my brawn and speed.

My testimonials are next, carefully arranged so that the brush of a finger projects an audio recording of me working with children directly toward the listener's ear. Too soon, the last items left are the models and samples from the lab. I brush my fingers over the carved diagrams, then arrange them in their pride of place at the center of my displays.

Finally, I can fidget with them no more. I know what I was going to say about them. I've rehearsed it so many times that I have it memorized. What I'm unsure about is if I want to know what Nareen thinks I should say.

Have you asked Nareen?

With a jerk of my hand, I start her revised script tapping against my arm.

It finishes. I stare at my booth. Nothing she would have me say is a lie, exactly. She's careful not to claim my discoveries as her own, and she leaves untouched the descriptions of the experiments I performed, but the symbols she chose to convey each concept are softer, muted. The generative spark of curiosity and insight that should tingle against my skin has faded, vanishing into cracks in the narrative as details are left out and deemphasized. This is not the booth of an ingenious scientist. This is the booth of an eager and helpful *lab assistant* who implemented experiments instead of designing them, and whose long hours were put in out of dedication to supporting his mother's research.

I clench my fist. It takes everything in me not to rip off my 'glove and hurl it across the booth. Instead of standing on my own, this presentation reduces me to the "Ya" in front of my name: the last syllable of my mother's, the tiny sound that gives credit for what I do to the one who gave me life. Nareen shed her matronymic at puberty like all women do. I never will.

A whisper sounds behind me, and I whirl. Priestess Wekmet stands in the opening, leaning on their wife's arm. Behind the couple, Marin-lun hovers in their walker.

What are they doing here? I clink my bracelets together in respectful greeting. It's early. Surely the priestesses aren't circulating yet. Later, they'll judge the presentations, bestowing awards for lifetime achievement and most promising new discovery, but for now we should all be left in peace and quiet to set up.

"Priestess Wekmet." My mother hurries out of their booth to join us. "Thank you for your blessings on my son's debut." To anyone else, they would appear serene, their new zoman robes hanging from their shoulders without a ripple of nervousness, but I can see the tiny lines of tension at the corner of their wide-set eyes. This is their last presentation, their final chance to set their status in the community, to earn one of the coveted awards, before they rise above the competitions of womanhood. My mother surveys my booth, eyes snagging for a moment on the box at my feet. I nudge it under the table with my foot. Maybe the hour is later than I realized. I stand straighter. Everything's basically in order.

"Viya-lun. Congratulations." The priestess snaps their fingers in approval, silver rings glinting against ebony skin. "All your children are presented to the community, now, is that right?"

"Yes." My mother's eyes flick around my booth again, assessing. The "Ya" of my name gives credit to the one who gave me life, but it also apportions blame.

The priestess lets go of their wife's arm and strides toward me. Like all priestesses, their eyes are sealed shut, eschewing the temptations of sight for a blessed, permanent darkness, but their bare hands find the first of my weightlifting trophies without hesitation. They press its carved surface between their palms.

"Mmmmm, nicely done." They put it back and reach for the next one. My mother breathes again as the priestess works their way down the row, drawing closer to the sample of glowing fungus in the middle.

I freeze. *I didn't label it.* I put it in shadow where its luminescence would attract the eye and remind passersby of the goats penned near Nareen's booth.

Priestess Wekmet trails their fingers across the gap between the larger displays, then gropes for the object that must be framed in the space. "What are you presenting here?"

My cheeks burn under the withering gaze of the head priestess' wife. My error has forced Wekmet to ask about something obvious to everyone else present.

"I—" My hand clenches around the text my 'glove presses into my palm. I can't meet my grandmother's eyes. Next to Marin-lun, my mother has a tiny worry-line between their brows. "An early stage of—of what I've been doing to help my mother in the lab. And Nareen. Some bio-engineered fungus. It's nothing."

"Ah." The priestess turns back toward my mother. "Your lab certainly has been productive, Viya-lun, I've heard so much about it." Their voice is warm.

I take a breath.

My mother's shoulders relax the tiniest amount. "I'm happy to discuss the details. My booth is next door."

Priestess Wekmet gives a tiny chuckle. "In a moment." They turn back to me and raise their hand to my face. I close my eyes as their fingers trail over my features. "Congratulations, Ya'shul. This day celebrates you as well."

"Thank you," I whisper.

They pat my cheek, then hold out their arm to their wife. The group of zomen amble around the corner to my mother's booth, heads bent in conversation. In their wake, sound feels muffled, as if a bubble of silence has grown up and pushed the hum of the festival away. One by one, I curl my fingers around the presentation script in my hand. My words vanish, leaving only Nareen's in their place.

Chapter Four
Andeshe

"What about them?" Velemeth waves his hand at a booth for what must be the tenth time. "You like animals."

I crane my neck obediently. The crowd around the woman's booth is so dense that it obscures her, but I can catch glimpses—she has a snub-nosed face and gestures animatedly as she speaks. In a gap next to her booth, a small goat ruminates placidly in a ray of sunshine. I meet its dull eyes.

Pteradons aren't just any animals. I scan the sky to the west. The roosting site next to our settlement is so close, I assume Fizz found her way to it okay. I wish I had left with her.

"Andeshe." Velemeth draws himself up until his eyes are almost level with mine. "You have to pick something. You can't keep pining away for what has been."

"I know."

"I'm telling you, the new fliers are the way to go. For you at least." Velemeth can't quite suppress a shudder. Given his fear of heights, even the single flight from our old settlement to the one we have here must have been excruciating. "Auntie Haveo has been working with one of the most prominent families on this ridge. Take advantage of it!" He shepherds me along yet another twisting path in the maze of booths.

My steps slow as we come back into sight of the prototype. An even bigger crowd has gathered around it.

"Look." He points to the middle of the crowd, where a full-chested Uplander woman rests one hand possessively on the nose of the prototype. "With our help, everyone expects Isel to get the festival prize for most promising new discovery. You know what that means? It means her family practically has a lock on the race for the second seat that represents this ridge on the ruling council." He waves a hand toward the east and Treverel, the mountain that houses the capital. "And that means one of the two most powerful families on this ridge not only is our ally, but they'll owe their success in large part to *us*."

"Where's Auntie Haveo?" I'd have expected them to be in the midst of their greatest triumph, but they're nowhere to be seen.

Velemeth shakes his head. "Only men and women present at the festival, Andeshe. Auntie Haveo is out negotiating alliances." He nudges me. "So let's help find some good ones, yes? We want to be well established when the solar storms come, not scraping for survival."

I sigh and turn my feet down a random path. At one booth, a woman shows off finely made hand tools. At another, an artist displays a mixture of tactile paintings as well as some emblazoned with more color than I would expect given Uplander sensibilities. I know my duty. We need to settle into this community as much as possible before the strain of the storms hits.

Near the stage is a large tent decorated with dried gourds and sheaves of rice. Bland-faced clerks sit at tables within, talking one at a time with an orderly queue of zomen that spills out into the grassy area that separates the tent from the family circles. On the tent's far side, a group of unusually tall people stand in a tight cluster waving signs. I squint toward them, but the signs are too far away to read. Turning back to a final circle of booths, I stop to finger an elegant pottery bowl. Would it be so bad to work on creating things like this? People need them.

I set the bowl back on its stand and turn away.

Velemeth huffs in exasperation. "Or we could just send you to work our head tithe." He jerks his thumb toward the tent.

"What does it involve?" I eye the basket of fruit sitting on one of the tables. In the ache of loss, all options seem equally unappealing, but everyone has to eat.

"Oh, Andeshe." He shakes his head.

"What?" The group with the signs begins some sort of chant, but I can't quite catch the words.

"My point is you *don't* want to be a farmhand, so you'd better find something else."

I scrutinize the tent. "Is it farm labor all year round or just everyone getting together to bring in the harvest?" I still have fond memories of being turned loose in the wilderness with the other teenagers to shake ripe pseudoavocados from their trees. Or, as we understood our mandate, to climb to the highest branches and pelt each other with fruit.

"It's four people per family working major harvests and plantings, but Andeshe—"

I shrug. "If someone from the family has to do it,

ensuring everyone can eat would be more meaningful than some of what I've seen."

Velemeth catches my arm. "No, we don't want that. Listen. Everybody who's anybody here sends their tithe in goods or cash to get their portion of the crop. We didn't work this hard for respect only to turn around and send our people out as common laborers!"

"Fine, then. What are *you* planning to do?"

"Work with the temple."

"The temple?" I turn to him in surprise. "I never imagined you devoting your life to the Goddess."

"I'm not. There are lots of people at the temple who aren't part of the priesthood. Scholars, acolytes, students, even temporary housing for people who need it. It's perfect. It's open to all, but it houses some of the most influential people in Ikmeth." He gestures to the city around us. "For all that the priestesses claim to be neutral and focused on contemplating the divine, you know they're nudging things. Through the data link, if nothing else."

I frown. Part of each temple's mission is to maintain a communication link with the starship and distribute knowledge from its databanks freely. Whenever I've asked for one of the old records, the priestesses who conducted the searches for me have been compassionate and helpful.

"They're not like that."

He raises an eyebrow. "So you've always told me, and I've had to take your word for it because there's only so much I could find out remotely. But now that I'm here?" He shakes his head. "Their stated mission is to disseminate knowledge *and* to help us avoid the mistakes that ruined Earth. Of course they're putting their fingers on the scales. Don't let their political neutrality fool you."

Velemeth has always been quicker than I am to pick up social dynamics, but that doesn't mean he's always right. "Have you always been this cynical?"

He gives me an arch look. "Did you want to survive here or scrabble for scraps after the storms hit? We can't afford to be naive. Come on." He tugs me back into the crowd. "An alliance for you, that's the goal. We're done being outsiders. We're done trading money for everything like a family no one wants to ally with. Let's find you something to earn your keep."

I blink. *Earn your keep.* An Uplander phrase. As if we would ever require someone to justify the food that keeps them alive.

"Velemeth." I plant my feet, forcing him to stop and face me. "Why such a rush?"

"You haven't been here. There's a lot to do, and not much time to do it in."

I hold his gaze until his inertia dissipates and he really looks at me.

"A few hours' grace to think about what I do for the rest of my life is too much to ask?"

He takes a deep breath, then expels it slowly. "No." He rolls his shoulders, and when they fall, they've loosened. "No, it's not. I didn't mean to rush you."

We walk silently for a while. The booths are packed with everything I could imagine and nothing I want. Here, a family that makes and repairs synthagloves is also advertising a new immersion-story. I catch snippets of narration as two blindfolded youngsters grope the air near them and giggle. On the other side of the pathway, a woman with an assortment of blankets and clothing samples talks loudly about plans to weave electronics into a bodysuit. Stone carvers create everything from tableware and decor to models of caves that they've recently hollowed out. I half expect to encounter Auntie Haveo there, negotiating for help building the caves we'll eventually call home, but when we find our aunt, they're watching a smooth-faced zoman present some sort of medical advance to a gathered crowd. Velemeth steers us over, chiming his bracelets in a respectful Uplander greeting.

"Have you found anything that interests you yet?" Haveo asks me as we approach. Their eyes are still on the zoman, and a tiny line has formed on their forehead. When I say nothing, Auntie Haveo looks up, then pats my arm. "I know, it's hard. Let me know if you find anything. Or anything you'd rather avoid. Otherwise, I'll slot you in wherever."

I grasp my forearms in respect. With one last look at the zoman, Auntie Haveo drifts away down the row of booths. Velemeth trails after, asking a question in a low voice.

I eye the family Haveo was watching. Working with medicine doesn't seem so bad, though the crowd around the zoman is too thick to allow me to ask questions. The next booth over is emptier, containing only a young man with a broad nose and a neatly trimmed beard who stands alone in the center of it. His hands are clasped behind his back in seeming serenity, but every so often his eyes dart to the gathering next door. He rubs a palm against one leg and the bells sewn into his clothing jingle. A trio of women turn down the path, and his face lights up, but it falls again as they walk past him without a glance. He adjusts the position of a trophy, looking up again with such hopefulness that, for a moment, I almost believe that the correction will draw the trio back to his booth.

I find myself stepping forward before the twinge of sympathy even registers.

"What are you presenting?"

A smile spreads across his russet brown face. He picks up a wooden carving and holds it out to me, launching into an animated description of how much weight his leanly muscled body can bench press. I turn the carving over in my hands until he plucks it out of them and replaces it with another and then another. Mostly they're for mundane physical tasks—races up the wooden steps on the cliff side, construction projects, more weightlifting—but he describes each with such enthusiasm that it makes me feel even older than my three decades.

Don't the bells mark some sort of coming-of-age ceremony? I think they do. Memory trickles back to me of the day I was finally allowed to make my first solo flight—and yes, I was that enthusiastic, too.

"And finally," he continues, picking up something from the middle of a table, "I help in my mother's lab." He opens his hands slightly. A faint, blue glow emanates from the shadow of his cupped palms.

I squint at it. "Are those...glowing mushrooms?"

"Yes. They don't glow, normally. I engineered them to."

"Engineered?"

His eye catches on something behind me, and he stiffens. Under cover of peering more closely at his cupped hands, I shift to the side and glance back at the pathway. A zoman with unusually bushy eyebrows has stopped to listen to us.

"Yes." His ebullience gives way to an odd sort of

stiltedness. He thrusts the dish of mushrooms into my hand. "This is a sample from the early stage of a project I—I assisted the Uleu Asheveran family with." His eyes dart to the zoman.

"Well, they *look* very pretty." Attempting to soothe his sudden tension, I raise the dish and peer at it.

He winces. "It's not that. This was an early test project. I—*we* spliced phosphorescent genes from bacteria into their DNA in preparation for doing the same in goats."

He tosses off the comment so casually, as if miracles of creation are commonplace here. "You changed the genomes of goats? Yourself?"

His eyes flick to the zoman and back to me. "I *helped*," he says, emphasizing the word. "I wanted…to support, you know, support my *family*."

"With what?"

"Well, there's this compound called phosfoz." He stops and looks at my Wanderer clothing. "Are you familiar with it? It's a—"

"I know of it." My mouth goes dry. Ensuring pteradons have enough of it in their diet is a constant concern. "But go on."

I listen as he explains what I already know from Auntie Illeab. How something about Earth-descended animals turns a vital nutrient into a toxin pteradons can't stomach. My heart hammers.

"What does your family do, again?" The scent-based system they use here marks him as part of a sprawling and wealthy clan that, I'd thought, focuses exclusively on human medicine.

"Gene therapies," he replies. "And tailoring medicines

based on an individual's genome."

"But you work with animals?"

He glances at the zoman again. "Yes. But mainly it's Nareen, my coauthor. Her family herds goats."

"Was it difficult?"

The question seems to trip him up. It's so easy to forget that Uplanders are less direct than we are.

"Nareen did brilliant work." He picks his way around the words, so carefully not looking at the zoman behind me that it takes all my self-restraint not to turn. "It was such an honor to work with her."

That's not an answer. "What did *you* do?"

His mouth opens, then stops, no sound coming out. "I supported Nareen," he says finally. "With—with a lot of the research. And things. I can tell you all about splicing DNA. If you want." He snaps his mouth shut.

I shake my head. "I'm looking for someone who could design a new effort from scratch. Is this Nareen person someone who might assist with projects?" All day I've been looking for some Uplander project I could help with, but alliances can run the other way as well.

"Not *assist*, no. She's expecting to have her own lab soon. She'll be receiving assistance from other people."

"But might—"

I've lost his attention. He's watching the zoman behind me. "In fact," he says, pitching his voice so it carries. "Once she has her own lab, I'm sure that—"

"Orzea-lun!" The call makes the zoman he's watching look up. A thin zoman in a walker rounds the corner. "You should have found me. I would have been happy to accompany you."

"It's no trouble."

"Of course, of course." The zoman in the walker holds their body as straight as their stooped shoulders will allow. "Nonetheless, I wanted to show you something that might interest you. A very exclusive offer, but given our history together..." They wave their hand toward a booth farther on.

The young man in front of me swallows. A bead of sweat glistens on his brow as he watches the two zomen walk away.

They pass out of sight, but he doesn't move.

"Is something wrong?" I ask.

He looks back at me with a start. "No, no. What were you were saying?"

I try one more time. "Is anyone aside from Nareen an expert in bioengineering goats? Changing how they metabolize phosfoz, that is?"

He blinks. "I am. I coauthored the entire project."

"You did? Why didn't you say so?"

"Didn't I?" With the zoman gone, his posture loosens, forehead creasing in a frown.

I wave the miscommunication away. "You'd be able to engineer more modifications, then. On your own?"

"Yes." His voice is sharp. "Of course."

I've made a misstep somehow. I tilt my palm up in query, but he says nothing.

The Uplanders have odd things they won't talk about, but I need to be clear. "Are you available to work on projects similar to this one?" I gesture to his displays. Possibilities hover tantalizingly close. No Uplander would know to search for better ways to feed pteradons during the storms, but with their help, could I?

He nods.

"Thank you." I look him over one more time, memorizing his face, the slight wave to his hair, the wide-set brown eyes a few shades darker than his skin. "Your name?"

"Ya'shul." When I wait expectantly, he adds, "Lefmin Quemzol." He waves at the circle of booths he's a part of.

"Good luck with the rest of the festival."

He blinks, and a tentative smile flickers across his face.

I give him what I hope he'll recognize as an encouraging smile and depart in search of Auntie Haveo.

CHAPTER FIVE
YA'SHUL

Why didn't you say so?
I did say so, didn't I? Surely Orzea-lun knows. It's not like they haven't been tracking Nareen's progress. There's no way they could have missed my work. I straighten my certificate from working to improve the compost piles. Who else would have been mucking around where the bacteria was discovered anyway? Certainly not Nareen. Maybe I didn't shove my contributions in Orzea-lun's face, but surely they're obvious. I've done good work.

I turn back toward the entrance to the booth and wipe my palms on my trouser seams. *Enough fidgeting. Smile, draw people in, be confident.* The traffic has gotten heavier. Across the way, two zomen are hashing out a set of interrelated pledges in increasingly emphatic tones. I straighten as they approach me, but they're intent on talking to my mother.

It went fine, didn't it? I didn't get many opportunities to practice earlier. A decent number of people have stopped to peruse my accomplishments, but most moved on without asking many questions. I added a tag to the base the fungus rests on so that it will buzz basic information to any 'glove that touches it. Maybe that's enough. Not everyone is interested in the nitty-gritty details of science.

Beyond the tent, light flashes off a walker's metallic legs. My grandmother enters the nearest intersection. I squint. *Is that...?* Yes, a pile of cloth rosettes rests in their lap. My mouth goes dry—decision time.

Marin-lun parks their walker next to the first booth in our circle. At the twitch of a lever, the legs shuffle inward and straighten, raising its passenger up and forward until they can affix a rosette to one of the hooks welded into the booth's support pole. My pulse pounds. Curious passersby turn to watch.

The zoman continues down the row, sniffing each rosette before lifting it into place with hands that tremble only slightly with age. One of my uncles is being pledged out. I'm glad; it's been a while. My sister Kiu is receiving four pledges. Unsurprising, given that she's taking over running the lab as my mother retires. I suspect more will trickle in during the day. I squeeze my hands behind my back as Marin-lun stops at the far side of Se'jan's booth. The zoman sorts through the pile of rosettes, sniffing three before picking out one. I bite my lip. I would have expected the son of the woman who holds our family's seat on the ruling council to have been pledged out more than once. I try not to take it as an ill omen. The whir of the motor as Marin-lun stretches upward has never seemed so agonizingly slow. *Don't faint*, I remind myself.

The walker makes its ponderous way toward me. It reaches the first pole of my booth...and stops.

Oh, thank you, Goddess! My knees sag as I suck air into my lungs. My grandmother stretches upward and affixes a rosette in place. They give me an oblique look. My hands are shaking with relief. *It worked! I got pledged!* For this, I'll forgive Nareen for the emotional wringer she put me through.

I force myself to stay still until Marin-lun moves off, then I bury my nose in the rosette—*my* rosette—inhaling the comforting scent of…nothing.

What? I sniff again. Each rosette is supposed to be imbued with the allying family's perfume; the scent of cinnamon and musk should be knocking me over. But there's only a confused muddle of picked up scents, already fading, from the jumble in Marin-lun's lap. There's an undertone of something sort of sharp, almost ozone-like, but whatever it is isn't strong enough for me to be sure.

Se'jan is watching me. His heavy-lidded eyes are sardonic. He opens a palm toward the rosette hanging from his booth, inviting me to smell for myself. But even before I touch it, the smell reaches out to envelop me. Cinnamon. Cinnamon and musk.

My breath comes in pants. I *saw* Marin-lun check each rosette as they hung it. "There must be some mistake!"

His lips twist. Marin-lun doesn't make mistakes, not about something like this. I stare in horror at the man who has been pledged to Nareen.

CHAPTER SIX
YA'SHUL

I *should sleep.* I tip my head back against the wall of the ledge in front of our cave. Gritty sandstone presses against my bare back. I should be wearing more than just my loose sleeping trousers to sit out here, but I can't bring myself to care. In the moonlight, shadows from the railing creep across the walkway. Midnight is long past. There's no one out here except me, watching the night sky.

The second moon rises, dim Iamar's red orb trailing behind Kynthia's brightness. The shadows on the ground in front of my feet split. I close my eyes. If only the clock could be rewound so easily. If only I could turn back time even more. Turn back to the real moment the possibilities split; cold, white reality marching on, overwhelming the gentle glow of other dreams.

Nareen's figure swims in front of my eyes, gesturing in animated explanation the way she did this afternoon while a throng of people crowded her booth, oohing over her collection of rosettes. No one had noticed me at the back of the crowd, desperate for an explanation for Se'jan's pledge, closing my ears as the women next to me speculated about their chances of attracting Nareen's romantic interest.

Me, I'd wanted to shout at them. *She wants me.* I'm the guarantee who was supposed to be pledged to her. The five rosettes hanging on the pole next to her had burned into my eyes, a stark contrast to the single rosette that fluttered its lonely ribbons next to my booth. Five, one for each family pledging to hers, one for each family sending her a man who isn't me. And me? Wanted by one unknown family, one not even proud enough to have a strong scent. Is that better than nothing?

I close my eyes, breathing in the thick night air. Better to focus on the rosettes than on what came next, the moment the crowd parted and I saw what hung lower on the pole—a single bronze disc the size of my hand gleaming in the sunlight. *She won the festival prize.* I thump my head against the wall behind me. The raised sigil in the center of the disc had been unmistakable, the prize for most promising new discovery awarded to her. Alone.

I bury my face in my hands, but blocking out the moonlight only leaves room for a more vivid image to coalesce in the darkness; Nareen at the feast that ended the day, head tossed back in laughter, victory an even headier brew than the oozmert we were both served openly for the first time. I counted the number of times someone refilled her wooden cup. Would I feel worse now if I'd given in and downed as much of it as she had? I'd practiced, sneaking furtive sips from purloined bottles like any soon-to-be man does in order to avoid making a fool of himself the first time he drinks it for a pledge. It's not like its aphrodisiac effects could have made the pain of watching Nareen any worse, not when every toast of her success sent spears through my chest. Maybe the alcohol in the oozmert would have numbed something if I'd let it—but my cup sat on the table in front of me all night, untouched.

I press the heels of my hands against my eyes. *I should go in.* Back to the chamber I share with my brother and cousins, back to the chamber Se'jan slipped quietly into late last night, smelling of sex and cinnamon.

If only—I thump my head against the wall. *It should have been me.* In the moonlight, I can't stop myself from reliving the sight of Nareen rising to her feet amid cheers and ribald suggestions for how her First Pledge should go. The last rays of sun had highlighted the curves of her upturned face as she shook out her curls. I wish I'd had something—anything—to focus on rather than the rustle of Se'jan's clothing as he knocked back the last of his drink and rose. Anything but the bronze medallion Nareen hoisted above her head to a final wave of cheers. Anything but the line of guarantees falling in behind Nareen as the men and their families followed her toward the carved ptercels that watch eternally over the entrance to the tunnel that leads into the mountain's womb.

Don't think about it. But my imagination takes me there anyway, to the cavern at the heart of the temple where the biggest heartbeat drum pounds its eternal rhythm. I should have been the one abandoning the light of the surface world, stripping down in complete blackness for the ritual bath in the antechamber, then emerging clean and freshly anointed with scent into the round, central chamber. I should have been the one kneeling in a semicircle with the other guarantees to offer myself and my pledging gift as a guarantee that my family will support Nareen's. Not all pledges involve this level of ceremony.

Later in a woman's career, a guarantee's role may be little more than a formality—delivering pre-arranged goods here, helping with an odd task there—but a woman's First Pledge is different.

I shift against the sandstone, feeling its roughness through the thin fabric of my pants, wishing the mugginess of the night didn't feel so much like the cradling warmth of the temple. I have never entered the tunnel behind the drum, but I know what's there. In the soft nests in the back of the temple, a consignee's first chance to conceive is holy, honored by the entire community. Our ancestors survived here by mimicking the ways of the ptercels, not only by taking to the clifftops, but also abandoning the wantonness of Earth that left children to starve. First Pledges reaffirm the iron law that *every* family whose sperm might have contributed to conceiving a child will contribute to its rearing. The ptercels do it instinctively, males working themselves to the bone to bring food to every chick whose life they may have helped quicken. Humans require reminders, lest selfishness and carelessness again lead us astray.

Stop tormenting yourself. But I can't stop myself from imagining Nareen ringing the bell, inviting me into the curtained nest. I would have lain back, still hard from the oozmert—no, I wouldn't even have needed the drink—and waited for her to envelop me. Only one slide is required to seal a pledge, but that would have been for the others. With me she would take her time, wringing out of me the quick I wish I could give her.

My assistant. The remembered words shatter my fantasy. The harsh, white moonlight pierces my eyes as they snap open. A snippet of overheard conversation echoes in my mind, someone praising Nareen for being the first to think of the compost piles as a place to find new organisms, as if men didn't spend hours per week monitoring the health of the flora and fauna there. *I can't claim all the credit*, she'd replied. *My assistant was invaluable.*

Her assistant. Not her coauthor. Not the man she thinks of as her equal, not the man who deserves to join her in the holiness of a temple ceremony. I swallow around a lump in my throat. Is that why she toned down my presentation, because she knew all along I wasn't worthy? The lightening sky gives no answer, only the harsh reality of sunlight preparing to wither moonlit dreams.

Iamar sets behind the mountains, its tilted orbit barely pulling it above the horizon before it disappears again. Kynthia dips below the roof of the ledge, its light throwing the carvings on the wall into relief before it, too, vanishes. Somewhere nearby, a window scrapes open, releasing the faint clatter of the kitchen preparing to have breakfast ready before dawn. A waft of spices accompanies it. No cinnamon.

"Ya'shul?" My brother stands at the entrance to the cave, rubbing his eyes. "There you are! Marin-lun wants you in their office. Why weren't you wearing your 'glove? They woke me up to find you."

"I'm sorry." The crepuscular workday is beginning, but it would have been nice to sleep in.

He yawns. "No matter. I'm back to bed." He shuffles inside.

I push myself to my feet. Whatever my grandmother wants can hardly make this day worse.

Chapter Seven
Andeshe

"Andeshe, your assistant is here." Auntie Haveo's voice crackles through my earbud.

I toggle the transmitter on. "Already?" Fizz and I got up early to help move rough-hewn beams and planks into position for the construction that's taking place on the cliff below our settlement. I wasn't expecting any Uplander to show up this close to dawn on the day after the festival. It's not a long walk from their city to here, but the festivities lasted well into the night.

A shout draws my attention back down to the ground. Fizz flips her wings, and the wooden beam she's holding in her beak wiggles. On the cliff's edge, the head of construction looks up at me, shading his eyes against the early morning sun.

"Gently, Fizz!" I tug on her reins, bracing my heels against the stirrups of the riding saddle on her shoulders, until she stills. Carefully, she returns the beam to its position next to the pulley that will lower it down to the boundary between the cliff and the steep hillside. The shiver of her treelike neck is the only sign of her discontent. "I'm paying attention to you." Transferring the reins to one hand, I scratch her vigorously with the other. I tell my aunt, "I'll be there as soon as Fizz finishes with this beam. We're almost done."

There's a long pause.

"Don't take too long," my aunt says finally. "I appreciate you building a connection with the only family we know for sure will be on the ruling council, but it only works if we make a *good* impression."

"I'll come as quickly as I can."

"See that you do." Auntie Haveo cuts the connection.

"She's steady, now," I call down to the workers. "Sorry." Beyond the pulley, a series of wooden beams are anchored into holes in the cliff face, supporting stairs that wind from the top of the ridge down toward the caves that are slowly being chiseled out of the rock for our family's use.

The Wanderers on the construction team start back toward their work, but the tight knot of Lowlanders on the far side of the pulley doesn't move. Only when the beam is secured and the head of construction waves us away, do they slowly return to their places.

She won't hurt you, I want to call to them, but I understand. Using pteradons to move materials for the walkway does speed things up, but it takes time to build trust. I slide down Fizz's shoulder and pick up her reins. It would do more harm than good to charge over to them and explain that the giant peering over my shoulder is merely curious. Instead, I guide her back toward her roost, past the small cluster of buildings on top of the ridge. Carved wooden frames support cheerfully painted leather walls that are rolled up at the bottom to capture cooling breezes. The reclaimed materials from our last settlement look far more permanent than they actually are. Auntie Haveo wants us moved into a cave like the Uplanders as quickly as possible.

Fizz nudges my shoulder with her beak, then cocks her head at me in query. I reach up to scratch her eye ridges. Sometimes, she picks up on what I'm feeling before I do.

"I'm just sad," I tell her. I probe at the tiny ache in my chest. "It's always like this, coming to a new place. Proving that you can be trusted, sorting out the rules for how people treat each other. I'm tired, that's all." I believe in my clan's practice of sending members to foster with other families. It does keep us connected. It does build relationships and trust. But I'd hoped that when I finished my twenties rotations, I could settle down with the family I chose, the family that raised me through my teens. I don't have the same lust for adventure and newness that sends someone like Illeab off on wild adventures for months at a time.

Fizz plops her enormous head onto the dirt in front of me, and I wrap my arms around her neck. A lump rises in my throat. She knows enough to comfort me, but she doesn't know what's coming. I lean into the hug for a long as I can. Perhaps it was folly to think that I knew what was coming, that I could plan a simple, contented future flying delivery routes and mentoring younger women to love pteradons as much as I do.

With a sigh, I give Fizz one last pat and let her go. She paces by my side until we reach the rocky hillside where the flock roosts. I unbuckle her harness, then release her to her favorite dust wallow. Pteradons aren't complicated. I can't say they're not dangerous, not when an accidental swipe with a beak could break a person's spine, but all they require is someone who pays attention to how they're feeling. There are no petty squabbles over status, no politicking, no need to untangle layers upon layers of what their actions really mean.

I shake my head to clear it. Being here is what it is. It's also supposed to be an opportunity. I quash a flare of hope, but it beckons to me like a glowing coal, tempting me and yet certain to scorch my hands if I grab for it. Easier to focus on hanging Fizz's tack in the shed near the roost, running the smooth leather through my fingers in search of any flaws. The science probably won't work out, anyway. Better to think of this alliance as Velemeth and Haveo do: an attempt to tighten our bond with a family that holds a seat on the ruling council.

I brush the dust off my riding leathers and dial Auntie Haveo's channel. "I'm on my way. Do we know what to expect?" We don't normally do formal alliances and pledges. Most of the time we're just taking cuts of whatever other families want transported. Even this alliance my aunt negotiated to last only a season.

"I sent him to the community center. It should be free. Just get him oriented to whatever project you want him to work on. Do you know what that is yet?"

I'd told Haveo I had some ideas about modifying animals, nothing more.

"I have to talk to him," I hedge. "Nothing's concrete." The little coal of hope in my chest flares, and I tamp it down.

"Well, it didn't cost us much. Make sure we end up with a closer relationship, though, not some sort of feud, hmm?"

"Of course." I close the connection. The buildings at

the edge of the settlement loom in front of me. I hesitate. I should take the time to trade my flying leathers for Uplander clothes—at least a version of them, I'm not entirely willing to abandon color—but I've already kept him waiting.

When I get to the community center, the young man from the festival is standing just outside it, staring at the closed door. His hands are clutched behind his back.

"Oh," I hurry forward. "It's open. You can just go in. No one else is using it right now." At least I hope not. With so few buildings built for our temporary settlement, we're all packed on top of each other.

He turns toward me, all the muscles of his slender body stiff with tension.

"You're Andeshe?" he asks.

"Yes, come in, come in." I open the door. "I didn't mean to leave you waiting."

He takes a step forward, then comes to a sharp halt on the threshold. "There's *light*."

The leather wall on one side is rolled up to permit ventilation, casting a band of light onto the edge of the floor. I'd have thought the breeze would be welcome, especially since he's covered from neck to toe in the skintight formal wear of Uplander men. Apparently not.

"I can lower it if you'd like."

Ya'shul turns back to me, wide face strained. "This is your first pledge, right?"

Is it that obvious? "I'm afraid so." I give him a rueful smile. I gave up pretending to be suave and polished long ago.

His eyes dart around the room, lighting on the low desks and cushions stacked along the wall. He swallows and squares his shoulders. "It doesn't matter. Leave it up. Whatever." His voice is husky.

"It clearly does matter," I correct gently. "I'm happy to lower it if that would put you at ease. Or if there's something else…?"

He shakes his head, but his body is still tense.

The contradiction between his body and his words thrums against my senses. *You're not going to make this easy for me, are you?* I turn my palm upward, offering what I can. There must be a way to reconcile this.

He looks from my hands to my face, and his lips compress. With jerky movements, he digs a small, cloth-wrapped bundle out of a bag he's carrying and drops it into my outstretched hand. I blink at him in puzzlement.

"Shall we get on with it?" he asks.

I want to repeat my questions, but I've interacted with enough Uplanders in my travels to know that forcing an issue rarely goes well.

"I—very well." But I hesitate. I don't think he realizes that he's practically plastered against the door, desire to flee written into every muscle. I turn away and pull two cushions from their pile, arranging a place to sit on the far side of the room from the offending light. "Please, make yourself comfortable." I stand back. Perhaps giving him space will soothe him.

He recoils, face suffusing with outrage. "I am *not* doing it on the bare floor!"

Oh, for the sake of the Goddess! But I've handled irritable hatchlings before, and I keep my voice mild: "I can get you a chair."

"No! I want a proper *mattress!* Or…or…" His anger looks like it's about to edge over into tears.

A mattress? I stare at him. To hell with Uplander reticence. "What exactly are you expecting that we do?"

He gapes at me, but I hold his gaze. "You're—" He swallows. "You're supposed to take my quick and use it to make a baby." He wraps his arms around his body.

"*What?*" My voice cracks on the yelp.

"That's how pledging ceremonies work."

"Always?" I knew things would be different here, but there are limits.

He stares at me. "First Pledges, yes. Not the later ones."

Thank the Goddess. I ease back.

Uncertainty crosses his face, making him seem even younger. A hint of vulnerability peeks out from behind his ruffled feathers. "You said this was your First Pledge, right? It's supposed to be special. For you, that is."

I go still. "Not for you?"

He looks away, blinking rapidly. "I'll—I'll be all right." He takes a deep breath, then raises his chin and braces himself.

As if I would do any such thing when you're on the verge of tears. I turn away and seat myself on a cushion. "Here." I wave at the other, shifting mine away from it. "Sit."

Gingerly, he settles onto it.

"You're clearly not interested," I tell him. "And I had no idea it was expected. Consider this a second pledge. You're off the hook."

He barely relaxes.

"Did you want sex?" I ask. Bluntness can hardly make things worse at this point.

His eyes go wide. He shakes his head vigorously, then freezes. Longing is written clearly across his face, but it's not directed at me. I study him. He's young, trying so hard to push back his inner turmoil that he forces it out through the cracks between his fingers. Most Uplanders I interact with are older, their facades hard enough that their true feelings leak out as no more than a vague sense that something is off. Watching Ya'shul struggle to squeeze his feelings into a space too small for them makes my heart ache in sympathy.

I hazard a guess. "You wanted to be pledged to someone specific."

He drops his eyes to the floor. One hand comes up to rub his cheek above his beard, but he doesn't deny it.

"Ahhh." Some longings are universal. "That I can't help you with, but for what it's worth, I'm sorry."

He looks surprised. "Thank you."

I give him gentle silence, letting him sit with whatever is going through his mind. After a while, he stirs.

"I'm sorry." He looks away. "I don't mean to be out of sorts."

"No harm done." With that miscommunication cleared up, maybe we'll be able to work together after all. "Shall we start over?"

Confusion hovers transparently on his face.

I tap my wrists together, though my wrist bangles miss each other as I fumble the Uplander greeting. "I'm Andeshe. It's good to meet you."

The corner of his lip twitches, and slowly his eyes brighten. "Ya'shul." His wrist bangles chime, scattering flashes of light across his hands. "You…um…had a project for me?"

Chapter Eight
Ya'shul

*A*t least *Andeshe has a sense of humor.* I knock on the door of my family's auxiliary lab, using the special code that announces who I am and alerts anyone inside that I'm bringing a guest. Heat floods my face. No one on the other side of that door needs to know how much of a fiasco I got myself into. At least the building we have up here near the fairground isn't as heavily used as the main lab in our cave complex. I don't need to parade past the entire family.

I want a mattress! Did I really say that?

Beside me, Andeshe peers at the building's carefully joined stonework with undisguised interest. I'm not the only one who should feel embarrassed. I knew the Wanderers' settlement was rudimentary, but when my grandmother told me the Wanderers were responsible for the mysterious rosette, I'd assumed the woman I'd be pledged to at least had her own lab. Instead, I've come here to explain the details of bioengineering to someone who barely knows what DNA is.

No message to my 'glove warns me off. I pull the door open.

Andeshe strides inside. "It's cool in here!" The announcement echoes off the thick, stone walls.

"Yes." I drop my voice to the softer tones appropriate for indoors. "It's called air conditioning."

"Terribly expensive, though, isn't it?" The Wanderer peers at a vent.

The gaucheness makes me cringe. "We manage." I'm not crass enough to boast about my family's wealth. "This way." I maneuver us around the work benches clustered in the center of the room to the data terminal next to the corner full of caged mice. At my touch, the terminal's tactile display activates, its surface molding upward. As good a job as synthagloves do replicating the feel of exploring an object, sometimes there's no substitute for a physical model.

My festival carvings rebuild themselves in front of me, the sand of the table obediently returning to the last shape I asked of it. The edge of the table digs into my palm. Was it only two days ago that I sat here, putting the finishing touches on my displays? I shouldn't be sitting here watching a Wanderer poke a tentative finger at the edge of the sculptures, only to pull back when the gesture makes it rotate. I should be on the other side of town, sharing Nareen's excitement as we direct her other guarantees to set up the space we dreamed about, the place where the two of us could stretch our wings and explore all the things my family is too hidebound to be interested in. With the solar storms coming, science can't just repeat past successes. We need creativity and innovation. I thought Nareen believed we were going to do it together.

Andeshe finishes exploring the display and looks ready to get on with it. We came here so I could explain the basics to a novice. I close my eyes. Two days ago—one day ago—that was all I wanted to do. I jerk my hand, and the sand dissolves and reforms. In front of an audience of one, each word of what I should have said pulls itself from me like a knife. The Wanderer is attentive and inquisitive, everything I could have asked for in an audience. Resentment fills me.

At the end, I sag back, spent. Andeshe's questions have wrung every drop of knowledge out of me until I can surrender nothing more. It's not enough. I wanted someone to take all of me. Someone who matters.

A knock sounds on the door. It opens, and Nareen stands on the threshold, blinking into the dimness. She yawns and stretches, daylight gilding the curve of her torso before bursting over her shoulder. For a moment, her silhouette is as distant and untouchable as someone emerging from the sun itself. A band constricts around my chest.

"Oh, Ya'shul." She drops her arms abruptly. "I didn't realize you were there." She steps forward, then sees Andeshe across the table from me and stops. She's neatly dressed, hair freshly arranged, showing no sign of the night's exertions.

I clear my throat, but the polite nothings I should say stick like ash to my tongue. A stool scrapes behind me. The air stirs, and Andeshe is next to me, compassionately squeezing my shoulder.

"Thank you for the explanation." The Wanderer's voice is gentle. Too gentle. "I'll take some time to think over what you've told me, and we can talk tomorrow?"

Heat rises in my cheeks. *Am I that obvious?* The graciousness of the withdrawal only makes my embarrassment worse.

Nareen tilts her head, eyeing the short, plump stranger whose colorful clothing is a cloth version of the riding leathers we've seen visiting Wanderers wear. Were it not for that and an oddly muted scent, Andeshe might have been just someone from across town, but as it is, I feel Nareen's curiosity, the determination to understand everything that has drawn me to her ever since we met.

I take a deep breath. "Andeshe. This is Nareen, my—" How do I describe the woman who has been my best friend since my teens? The woman who is inextricably entwined with all my hopes and dreams? "My coauthor." I hesitate. Saying the next words will make them real. "Nareen, this is Andeshe. She's the—"

"He," Andeshe interrupts.

What? I turn. Andeshe is beautifully short and plump, displaying the roundness that is the hallmark of a successful pregnancy, not the leanness of men who are supposed to look like we've given every spare scrap of food to the children. I look closer. No beard, no matronymic syllable, dressed in a Wanderer's flying outfit. Everyone knows only Wanderer women fly. At least, that's what I've been told. Yet Andeshe is looking at me as if astonished that I could have messed up something so obvious. He tugs the bottom of his shirt in an exaggerated motion. Slowly, the curves I'd pegged as womanly resolve into something more androgynous, his outfit into a colorful and unfashionable version of, yes, men's clothes. The bangles on his wrists chime faintly, their deeper, masculine tuning providing the final confirmation.

Oh, Goddess. My face heats. No wonder Andeshe had no idea what I was talking about when I showed up in my sleep deprived haze expecting what I should have had with

Nareen. Men do sometimes work with men from other families, but they don't receive pledges in the same way, certainly not a First Pledge.

"I'm sorry," I backpedal, "I thought—"

"It's no matter." Andeshe waves my apology away. "Only men go out into other families' homes here, right?"

I nod. There are rare exceptions, but only for families that have an unusually close relationship. I turn back to Nareen. "Excuse me, then. This is Andeshe, *he's* the Wanderer—" I stop. I could have sworn that Marin-lun sent me to meet someone I'd been pledged to, but I must have been mistaken. "The Wanderer I'll be working with." My introduction limps to a finish.

"Welcome!" Nareen taps her wrists together with a musical clink, and Andeshe mimics the gesture.

"Ya'shul is wonderful to work with," Nareen continues. "You're in good hands."

I manage a rictus of a smile.

"Thank you," Andeshe replies. He clinks his bracelets at us both and departs. The door closes behind him with a thump, leaving me alone with Nareen.

Neither of us moves for a long time. She should be gone. For good or for ill, she should be out of my life setting up her own.

"What are you doing here?" I ask.

"Meeting Se'jan. Moving my things." She shrugs one shoulder. "You know."

Of course. I can visualize it all too well. I can visualize my cousin doing *all* the things I should have done.

"He won't be up yet." My voice is too harsh.

"I know."

"He always sleeps late after festivals. He hits the

oozmert too hard, and—" I snap my lips shut. I sound jealous. I know not to sound jealous. We're supposed to have overcome the territoriality of our hormones by the time we reach adulthood.

"Ya'shul." She steps closer to where I'm seated. "I'm sorry." Her arms go around me, and I sag against her, the warmth of her neck pressing against my burning eyes. "I know how much you were looking forward to things being different."

"And you weren't?" I can barely force out the words of my greatest fear, that the respect and desire I thought I read in her has been one-sided this entire time.

"Of course I wanted you." She tips my head up to search my face, brown eyes warm. "How could you doubt that?"

I almost shatter with relief, my lungs aching with a shuddering breath. "I don't know. At the festival, you didn't even acknowledge me. You called me your assistant."

"What?" She pulls back, a tiny line creasing her forehead. "When?"

"When you were presenting. Someone came up to congratulate you, and you said—" I swallow, trying to stop my voice from cracking. "You said your *assistant* helped." The lump in my throat won't go away.

She looks faintly chagrined. "Ya'shul...that *is* your title. I was being accurate, that's all."

I know, but my cheeks burn anyway. "You could have said more, you could have told them about how I did just as much as you did, about how I—" My complaints sound thin to my own ears. The festival is about presenting your own work or your family's. No one is going to promote someone else. Even what Nareen said went above and beyond. "Why did you tell me to tone down my presentation, then?" That was my one chance to speak for myself.

Her eyes stay steady on my face. "There was no chance things would work out otherwise," she says simply. "Some chance is better than none."

The ruthless logic of her statement feels like a box closing around me. "You don't know that," I whisper, but memory crowds in on me. What *did* I get when I marched back from Nareen's booth to mine, scalded with humiliation and determined to present what I could really do? One or two curious listeners, a woman who tried to explain my own discovery to me, and—my cheeks burn. The woman from the lift, Jamerol, had stood at the entrance to my booth, surrounded now by a group of younger women, looking at me as if we shared a salacious secret. I'd fumbled on the table behind me, snatching up the first carving that came to my hand and brandishing it at her. *This is who I am, a scientist.* If only they'd listened. Instead, a second woman had bumped Jamerol's hip, flipped the menstruation chime in her long hair out of the way, and blown me a kiss, her slow perusal of my body explaining better than any sermon why the priestesses preach about the sinfulness of sight.

You're seriously hot. Is that really the one thing she could think to say to me when I told her about my discovery? And even that had been better than the menacing blankness that had swept over Jamerol's face when I'd protested. *Don't be testy, can't you take a compliment?* No. No I can't, not like this. She'd stepped closer. *You weren't so standoffish when I gave you a ride this morning.* Her friends had crowed with ribald laughter, making rings with their hands and squeezing in unmistakably lewd gestures even as I'd protested. They hadn't heard a word, only slapping her on the back when she'd responded with ribald jokes about cocks and how *hard* it was to find the time to envelop them all. I thought I'd felt helpless before. It was nothing compared to how I'd felt standing there, the roaring in my ears thankfully drowning out whatever other awful comments they tossed off as they jostled each other back out into the festival.

Nareen is still watching me, sympathy radiating from her face. A sudden stab of resentment lances through my chest. *You should have protected me.* I quash the thought. She couldn't have known. Words tangle on my tongue, too jumbled to emerge. She should never have said anything about my presentation. She should have known what would entice Orzea-lun to choose me. She should have—I don't even know.

Nareen puts both hands on my shoulders, bracing me. "I know things didn't turn out as we'd hoped, but it was the best shot. Now we have to pick up the pieces and move forward."

"What pieces?" Normally I find her confidence reassuring, the way she faces down problems without flinching and chips away at them with grim determination until they give way. But this? "You won't even be eligible for more pledges until after you've weaned a toddler." I will my voice not to crack. "And me? Grandmother delayed my presentation for *three years* so I could build up a project this impressive for my debut. What am I supposed to do next? I gave everything to this project."

Nareen opens her mouth, then closes it again. She looks away.

My skin prickles. "Nareen?" She never avoids anyone's gaze.

She exhales slowly, then her eyes return to mine. "That wasn't why your debut was delayed. Marin-lun wanted to make sure I had all the support I needed to finish my project promptly."

Her words don't compute for a long moment. "*What?* All this time? Grandmother delayed my presentation for *years* so that you wouldn't lose your assistant?"

"You thought you'd be pledged out at the end, too! That would have been worth it!"

That's what had sustained me all that time, the belief that if I just made these sacrifices, everything would be different afterward: working in a new place—maybe even more than one—being valued for my expertise, finally getting to touch and be touched. Instead, the days stretch out in front of me the same as before. Anger courses through me.

Nareen's thumb brushes softly against my cheek. "Ya'shul... I have to ask. I know what your grandmother's like, but did you really wait all the way until your debut?"

I close my eyes, cheeks heating. When she puts it that way, I feel like an even bigger fool.

She sighs, and her fingers move to brush my hair behind my ear before falling away. "I respect your grandmother's right to set rules for your family," she begins, "but—"

"You didn't wait?" On some level, I think I've known. She's not really expected to. It's those of us responsible for the family's sperm who have to take more care.

"I'm twenty-two," she says. "That's a long time."

The three-year gap in our ages stretches between us. I

push myself up from the stool, restless energy turning into pacing. "Why did I even bother waiting, then?" My grandmother's lectures about the sanctity of quickening children and my solemn responsibility to guard the family's sperm echo in my memory. Am I the only gullible one?

Nareen says nothing, not even to remind me of all her subtle offers that I could have accepted. *Anything that doesn't risk pregnancy.* As if I haven't gotten myself off any number of times imagining the sheer variety of acts that could stop short of making a child.

"Did you ever try anything more?" I don't know what masochistic impulse prompts me to ask. I know the fury that would ensue if I allowed intercourse to turn my quick into a blank check for another family to demand support from ours, but it's different for her. The most she'd get is a slap on the wrist and early acknowledgement as an adult. If that. Between sheathes, testes irradiators, and the many ways she has to turn her cycle off, it's unlikely she'd get pregnant, anyway.

She tilts her head. "Are you sure you want to know?"

I don't, actually. I've always judged my cousins for sneaking out in the night and then back in again, smelling of oozmert and freshly bathed skin. But where has my silent superiority gotten me?

Nareen catches my hand, stilling my footsteps. She draws me forward until I can feel the heat of her body radiating across the hair's breadth of space between us. Her scent wraps around me.

"Do you want me to envelop you?" Her voice is low and soft, lips almost brushing my ear. "Your family is already obligated to mine. We don't even need to take precautions." She brushes her fingers down my throat, and I close my eyes. The fire of her touch trails down my skin until her fingers settle lightly on the first button of my shirt. My breath goes ragged. *That's all I've wanted for years.*

"Yes," I whisper. It's so easy to let my head fall back. Her fingers tug at the button, and it pops free, exposing the hollow of my throat. Her lips brush my skin, and a gasp escapes me. Featherlight kisses trail along my collarbone until I arch up into her touch.

She pulls back and I pry my eyes open, blinking her face back into focus. She smiles and caresses my cheek again.

"Let's get you a little privacy," she says, her voice low and warm. A conspiratorial smile lights her face as she slowly pulls away and crosses to the door of the washroom. Moments later, she appears out of the door to the connected storeroom and draws me to my feet, tugging me through the door and past rows of shelves. In the back of the storeroom, a dim lamp casts a warm glow over a secluded nook that she has padded with towels into a makeshift nest. A jar of lube is carefully positioned near the bag Nareen often carries. Hesitantly, I lower myself onto the towels, crossing, then uncrossing my legs. *Should I lie back?* I raise my knees to my chest.

"Do you want the light on or off?" she asks me, fingers poised on the switch.

"Off." In the dark, I can pretend this is what it should have been.

The lamp clicks off, and I let the wild pounding of my pulse fool me into imaging that the cool air and rough towels are the humid warmth and plush padding of the nests in the temple's womb. Gentle hands push my knees down, then Nareen's weight settles on either side of my thighs. Warm hands cradle my face.

"You have no idea how long I've wanted you," she murmurs, then her lips are against mine. My mouth parts under hers. The buttons on my shirt give way, and her hands are warm against my chest, lingering as if she too can't quite believe this is real. I arch into her touch, and her palms skate upward over the planes of my chest as the breath hisses out of her. I may not know how long she's yearned for me, but I remember the moment years ago when I'd looked up with breathless excitement from an experiment to see her watching me with the shining eyes of a kindred spirit. Ever since then, she's been there whenever I've turned to her, her attention warm and supportive, her strength an anchor I never had to think about.

Strong hands push me back onto the towels. For a moment, all I can do is lie there, years of habitual restraint not yet giving way. Then her breasts press against my body as she devours me with kisses. I raise tentative hands and suddenly their weight is real, heavy in my palms. She purrs deep in her throat and nestles against me.

This is real. The desire to taste and touch overwhelms me, and I raise my head, straining forward. She giggles and slides upward until I can catch her nipple in my mouth, enveloping as much of her as I can. She shifts her weight to the side, and her fingers scrabble at the laces of my pants. I spring free. Cool air slides across my heated flesh. She pulls away and tugs my pants and drawers down my hips until I'm completely open to her.

"Mmmmm, I want to see you." Her voice is rough.

"All right."

With a click, the darkness vanishes, replaced with dusty boxes and a discarded stool listing drunkenly over a broken leg. Nareen's silhouette shifts to block the bulb with her shoulder. Her face is in shadow, but edges of light turn the side of her breast and arm from tan to gilt. She shifts farther, and light spills across my hips. Her breath sighs out of her as she trails her fingers along my inner thigh, hand spiraling up to trace the veins along my shaft as the light throws them into relief. I gasp and close my eyes, sinking back into the sensation. Her confident touches pull me onward until I'm writhing. The sensation changes as she strokes lube onto me, then heat envelops me in one long, smooth slide. I gasp, arching off the floor, as she starts to rock, her back arching in pleasure.

"Mmm." She takes a firmer grip on my ribcage and snuggles her weight into my hips. She bends to the side, and I crack an eye open in time to see her pluck something from next to the jar of lube and nestle it into the space between our bodies. It buzzes, and I jump, but as she resumes her rhythm, I relax again. Her motions become more and more intense, punctuated by little moans, and I close my eyes as fire collects in my groin. She lets out a long groan and jerks above me, waves of shuddering overtaking her until she folds over me, panting. Her pace slows.

Wait. I open my eyes, the tightness of my groin still clamoring for release. The lamp outlines stark edges on the shelves behind her. Her hips circle one more time, then she leans forward and nips gently at my lip.

"I have wanted you so much."

My own need vibrates unfulfilled. This isn't how it's supposed to go.

"Have you quicked yet?" she asks, lips curving.

I shake my head.

"I can keep going." She draws a lingering finger down my chest and starts rocking again.

Oh, thank the Goddess. There's more. This is supposed to feel better than what I can do on my own. Her motion is different, almost a swirl, as if she's leaning into a stretch that feels amazing for her. She picks up speed again, then leans down next to me with a low laugh.

"I don't even need the oozmert to come twice. You're that hot." Silhouetted against the light, her cheeks bunch in a smile.

Something isn't right. I grasp her hips and try to get a better angle, but she shifts back.

"Are you getting close? I want this to be good for you." Her thumb strokes away the furrow that must have formed on my forehead.

"I'm—I've never done this before." It should just work. Aren't my own fantasies supposed to pale in comparison to having the woman I love on top of me, our bodies finally joining?

"Try this. It always works for me." She nestles the vibrator more firmly against our bodies.

It doesn't. My thrusts become more and more desperate as her writhing builds toward its peak again. *I'm not quicking. Why can't I quick?* She throws her head back, light streaming around her curls as a moan escapes her. She tried, it's not that she didn't try. I've heard some women don't, but she did. Do I tell her it didn't work? *What's wrong with me?* Prickles of anxiety run down my back. *Goddess, am I softening?*

Her core clenches around me and she bends forward, shudders arching through her body. *Now. Now's the moment.* Nothing happens. I try to swallow, but my tongue sticks to the roof of my mouth. As her movements slow, I force myself to give two quick jerks and a moan, a parody of what isn't going to happen. She sags forward onto my chest, and I fall still. *I can't even do this right.*

The sweat starts to cool on my body. Nareen snuggles against me, and I wrap my arms around her as if holding her close enough could fill the hollow in my chest. A lump rises in my throat. She levers herself up on one arm to press a gentle kiss against my lips.

"Thank you," she says softly, looking into my eyes, "for letting me be your first."

My throat closes. Slowly, she disentangles herself from me and extracts a towel from the pile. With careful solicitude, she wipes me off, then mops at herself.

"I'll be right back." She kisses me again and whisks back into the aisles toward the door that connects to the washroom.

I push myself up until I'm sitting. *I've had sex. Now what?* Grabbing the towel, I scrub at my groin again. *All this time, all this worry, and I didn't even give anything up.* The roughness abrades my still sensitive skin. I wad the towel into a ball and toss it at the floor. *Am I that useless?* Nothing has changed. Nothing is going to change. I shake out my pants and shirt and pull them on. My fingers fumble with the buttons.

Nareen's soft footfalls sound in the darkness. She reenters the light and pauses, watching me as I search for the last buttonhole. Her lips curve, and she reaches for the bottom of my shirt, undoing the first misaligned button and refastening it with a kiss. My hands fall away as she works her way back up, until at the end she tips my chin down and plants a final kiss on my lips.

"I should get packing," she says, but she doesn't move.

"I'll clean up." The words are automatic. Of course I will, that's what I'm here for.

She kisses me again, then turns away. The lamplight throws her silhouette into relief for one last moment before she vanishes into the darkness, leaving me alone with the crumpled towels. The door to the main room closes with a dull click.

I scrub my hands over my face. *It wasn't supposed to be like that.* I turn off the lamp and sink to the ground. In the darkness, I close my eyes, willing the fantasies that have tormented me all these years to return. My laces are still undone. I push them aside, wrapping my hand around my half-hardened erection as I lay back. The twists and turns are familiar, mechanical even, but every imagined joining slips from my grip, replaced with the starkness of metal shelves and disappointment.

I convulse, habit pulling the quick out of me into the roughness of a towel. That's what should have happened. I lie there, attempting to shoehorn the sensation into the memory of Nareen on top of me.

Would it have mattered? The thought pierces me. I roll to my feet, switching on the light, and gathering up the soiled cloths. In the safety of the washroom, I drape them over the side of the sink as it fills. Wet patches gleam in the light.

I dump the towels into the soapy water, attacking the marks until they finally rinse clean. A beaker stares at me from the counter nearby, the first of an endless procession of things to clean, items to carry, bottoms to wipe, broken things to repair.

No. I wring a towel out and drape it on the drying rack before plunging my hands back in for the next, twisting the hapless cloth until it chafes against my skin. *It won't be like that.* The image of Nareen at the feast comes back to me, holding up her prize as people toast her success. *That will be me someday.* I finish the towels and reach for the beaker, then hesitate. *I'll show them.* The glass is cool against my palm. I set it back down with a click. I am the one who generates tools to be cleaned. I am more than a meaningless fumble in a storeroom. I am more than a pledgeless failure.

Not quite pledgeless. An image of Andeshe probing the data terminal swims before my eyes. *But he knows nothing.* It's almost a joke to have someone like me sent to work with someone like him.

I straighten. It may be a joke, barely a pledge at all, but if this is the hand I've been dealt, then it's the hand I'll play. He's been hesitant to spell out exactly what he wants, instead asking me questions that wander from the trivial to the impossibly complex in the way that only novices can, but no matter. Whatever I find to do will be the most impressive achievement anyone has ever presented. When the Wanderers' pledge is up at the solstice, I'll have so many families clamoring for me that Orzea-lun will kick themselves for passing me over.

I stalk into the main room of the lab, past where Nareen is packing her workstation into a box. Everyone expects her to do amazing things. Wait until they see me.

Chapter Nine
Andeshe

"So, do you know what you want to do?" Auntie Haveo asks. Our footsteps clatter on the wooden stairs that lead down from our temporary settlement on top of the ridge to the partially finished cave that will eventually be our home. "Negotiating for one of the most prominent families on the ridge to send us an assistant for you was a good excuse to build a connection, but I'd like something useful to come out of it as well."

I take a deep breath. "I think so." I follow Haveo inside. Lamps stationed at intervals flicker in the cool air, turning our shadows into rippling giants as we pick our way among carefully stationed tools.

My aunt makes an encouraging noise and switches on a headlamp as we duck into a tunnel at the back. None of the cave complex is habitable yet. I'd have thought there'd be more progress in the months since I was last here. The wooden buildings on the clifftop above were meant to be public spaces, not dwelling places. As soon as possible, Auntie Haveo wants the family to live down here like the Uplanders do.

"Auntie Haveo?" says a voice from behind us.

We turn. Velemeth is framed in the archway, a dark shape against the light.

"Has the work crew been here?" He shades his eyes as the beam from Auntie Haveo's headlamp illuminates his face.

"Not yet." My aunt switches off the light and motions us both toward the front of the cave.

Velemeth lets out a low hiss. "No one I've talked to has seen hide nor hair of them here in days."

"I saw them earlier today," I say. "A handful of people hauling rubble past the settlement, right?"

"But not coming from here?" My cousin's voice is tight.

"No." We step out onto the rough balcony in front of the cave. There's no railing yet, though the wooden walkway wends its way along the cliff around the granite protuberance that separates this cave from the others carved under Ikmeth. Velemeth presses his back against the stone wall, and I step between him and the drop below until he braces himself against his fear of heights enough to move again. I wave at the greenery peeping over the precipice far above our head. "They were coming from the path through the forest."

"Work does sometimes stop for a few days," Haveo says mildly. "Was there a rest after the festival?"

A muscle jumps in Velemeth's jaw. "I heard they dropped us to work for someone else."

"*What?*"

"That Uleu Asheveran family, the one whose daughter won the festival prize—"

"Nareen?" I put in. "I've met her."

"Everyone has. They're expanding their cave—it's a

last-minute thing. Showing they're wealthy enough to expand even just before the storms come."

"We have a contract." A line appears on my aunt's forehead.

"And those are never broken?" Velemeth asks bitterly.

Frowning, Auntie Haveo picks their way along the wooden walkway, running a stabilizing hand along the yellow sandstone. The stone changes to gray as we work our way around a curve in the wall to where we can see Ikmeth's northern cliffs. From this angle, the platforms at the top of the cliff hide the stone buildings that perch on the ridge itself, but the intricately carved openings to the dwelling caves in the cliff itself are clearly visible, as are the stream of people scampering around on the network of wooden walkways and stairs that the platform we're standing on should eventually connect to.

Haveo stops. "This was supposed to be finished by now." In front of us, the freshly sawn wooden treads trail off into a skeleton of beams anchored into the rock. A large gap separates us from the nearest platform.

Velemeth inhales sharply and points. "Look!" Among the newer caves near the bottom, a stream of ant-like workers are hauling baskets of broken rock up the stairs. "That's them, isn't it?"

Auntie Haveo's breath hisses from between their teeth. I don't know which family's cave they're working on, but it's not ours.

"The liars!" Velemeth seethes. "They told us we had to build over here because the rock in the main cliffs couldn't handle any more disturbances. What is that, then? Carving someone else's expansion by magic?" He spits on the wooden boards at our feet. "I told you, they were never planning to finish ours."

"It will be finished," Auntie Haveo says tightly. A jerk of their chin sends us back the way we came. The opening to our own cave looks even rougher by comparison. "And when it is, we will be at the highest level of the cliffs, same as the oldest and most prestigious families on this ridge. No matter if we're a little farther away."

"Which is only right. Our family is older and more distinguished than any of theirs." Anger colors Velemeth's voice. "They'd have nothing without us flying from ridge to ridge. Let them see how much they like hauling everything up and down the mountains on their backs!" Dust puffs up around his sharp footfalls as we start up the switch back trail to our current settlement.

At the top, Auntie Haveo stops and squeezes his shoulder. "Thank you for bringing this problem to my attention. I'll take care of it." They stride off.

Velemeth looks after them, lips still drawn in a tight line. "Maybe."

"Has this been happening a lot?" I turn my steps toward the pteradon roost, and he follows.

"Yes, though the Uplanders will never admit it. There's always some excuse, some reason why it's me who's wrong for even considering that they might be two-faced, double-crossing liars." He glowers. "We'll show them."

The hurt radiates from him, festering and unresolved.

"Have you talked to them about it?" I ask.

"It does no good. They won't even *argue*. You'll see once you've been here."

Footsteps make us look up. A trio of dusty figures strides toward us on the worn path that connects the rubble dump beyond our settlement with the forest trail leading back to Ikmeth. Empty baskets are strapped to their backs.

"Hey!" Velemeth hails them. "Where are you going?"

The man in the lead slows, and the two younger men behind him draw together reflexively. All three are tall, covered in gray dust except for the rivulets of sweat that trace gleaming lines of pink or brown down their faces.

Velemeth advances on them. "You should be working for us." He waves a hand at the side path we just came up. "We have a contract."

The man in the lead ducks his head. "Sorry, sir, we have to be at the other site." He detours around Velemeth, aiming for the opening in the trees that leads back to Ikmeth.

Velemeth darts forward and grabs his arm. "We won't be disrespected like this! You can't break a contract and expect to get away with it."

The man goes stiff, the muscles of his broad shoulders bunching. "We're not breaking any contract. We go where we're told."

"Well, I'm *telling* you that we have an unfinished cave and an unfinished walkway!" Velemeth's voice rises, and he waves his free hand sharply. "Your job is to go down there and finish it! We were first."

The man makes a surreptitious shooing motion at the two younger workers, and they slip away into the trees. He turns back to my cousin, his body language more placating.

"I'm sorry, sir," he says. "You'll have to talk to the boss about that."

Velemeth's face contorts. "It's always something with you people. Some excuse!"

"Velemeth!" I warn. It's one thing to be angry, but

that was uncalled for.

Both of them turn to look at me, and the dust-covered man's eyes go wide with alarm as his gaze shifts to something behind me. I turn. Fizz's head peers up over the crest of rock at the top of the roosting hill, attention drawn by the sound of my voice. With a shiver of her wings, she hops up, eyeing him with curiosity.

He jerks backward, breath coming in ragged pants. "I'm sorry, I can't—"

Velemeth's grip on the man's arm tightens. "There's nothing preventing you from walking down that trail, picking up the tools that are lying *right there*, and finishing your job! Don't think you can just break your promises and walk away!" He points upward, snapping his teeth.

"*Velemeth!*" Words desert me for a moment. I wheel back toward the man. "Fizz would never hurt you! Don't worry—"

The man tears his arm free and dashes for the path through the trees, veering around a handful of people emerging from the woods. Velemeth glares after him, arms crossed on his chest.

A few steps take me around to face my cousin. "How could you?"

Fizz nudges me with her beak, and I rein in my temper. "It's all right," I tell her. "I'll take care of it. Go back to sleep now." I dig my fingers into the rudimentary, feather-like filaments on her neck and give them a vigorous ruffle until she blinks, satisfied, and trundles back to her roost.

"What happened?" Auntie Haveo asks from behind me. The stress line still creases their forehead, and a roll of paper is clutched in their hand.

Velemeth fixes me with a tight-lipped glare. "They don't listen when we ask politely."

"And so you acted like we'd feed him to a pteradon if he didn't cooperate?"

Auntie Haveo's eyebrows rise, and they pin Velemeth with a disapproving look.

Velemeth looks back and forth between us, and a muscle in his jaw twitches. "We need every advantage we can get."

"Not that advantage. You know how much work we do to convince people *not* to be scared of them."

His eyes slide away from mine. "The pteradons will be gone soon enough. You don't need to worry about ingratiating them anymore."

"That's not the point." I search my cousin's face. He's been wary of pteradons ever since the long-ago flying accident that left him with his fear of heights, but threatening that Fizz will eat someone? "What happened? This isn't like you."

"Nothing happened. We just need people here to know they can't renege on their promises to us."

There's more to it, but I can tell he needs time to cool off before being pressed. After a long moment, I turn back to my aunt. "Besides, maybe we don't have to send the pteradons away. That's what I wanted to talk to you about. The goats we saw at the festival. They glow because they've been engineered to metabolize phosfoz differently. With enough modifications, we may be able to turn them into a food source the pteradons can eat." Hope flares in my chest once more. "If we work with the goat herders to build up the stock before the wild animal herds run low, we won't have to send the pteradons away after all. There are enough large caves nearby for them to duck into during the worst of the storms, it's always been food we were most worried about."

"Wait." Velemeth seizes my arm. "You're not working with *that* family, are you? Not the goat herders." He waves back toward the out-of-sight cliffs of Ikmeth. "The ones who just stole our chance to get our cave carved?"

"Not mostly. I've only met one of the women."

"You can't, Andeshe." His voice is low, urgent. "We're allies with *Isel's* family. They're the ones who helped us build the flier. They're the ones who have welcomed us and advocated for us. We can't give any impression that we're abandoning them. Not with things the way they are." His eyes flick to Auntie Haveo's grim face and back to me. Both of them have lines of strain around their eyes.

"What's going on?"

His brow furrows. "Isel's family should have been elected to the council a long time ago—or at least gotten closer than they have." He ticks off points on his fingers. "A family that's *that* wealthy? That's part of the clan that runs the mines? Who makes the machines other people rely on? If anyone else did something that important, they'd be heroes. But our allies have never been fully accepted, not when everyone thinks of them as outsiders."

I've never thought much about Uplander politics, but now that he mentions it, other impressions come back to me. Although Isel's family has caves here, they've always been different from the other Uplanders. Looser, louder, with closer ties to their clan's complex of workshops and refineries near the mines than to the insular families that never leave their ridge. More like us.

"We thought that was changing, though," Velemeth

continues. "Everyone expected Isel to win the best-in-show prize when she presented the flier at the festival. Her family would finally be recognized for what they do, they'd be a shoo-in for winning the election for the open seat, and then maybe other outsiders like us would have a chance of being welcomed. But now it's all up in the air. Did you hear what the priestesses said at the festival when they awarded the prize to those goats you're so enamored of?"

"The usual platitudes about discoveries and being proud of what the ridge can produce, I thought."

Velemeth snorts. "Try over-the-top praise for how superior biological sciences are and how those arts saved us after we fled a planet *stripped and poisoned by machines*. They weren't talking about why they picked the goats; they were slapping down the flier project as hard as they could without breaking their supposed 'neutrality.'"

I turn to Auntie Haveo. "I thought the priestesses helped you get the information for the project in the first place."

Auntie Haveo grimaces, running a hand over the stubble on their shaved head. "Some of them did. But the priesthood has its disagreements and divisions like anyone else. They simply never let outsiders see them. My contacts are as friendly as ever."

"They snubbed us." Velemeth's voice is hard. "Everyone knows mechanical flight will be a lifeline during the storms. There's no reason other than a deliberate snub that they would favor a minor advancement in genetics over it. And now the family they awarded the prize to is leveraging that win into a bid for the open seat themselves. If they pull it off...Isel's family has been here forever. If they can't win respect, what chance do we have? Especially in the face of the priestesses' disapproval. You haven't been here, Andeshe. You haven't seen how hard we have to struggle to get them to keep their bargains." He waves toward the half-completed cave. "Nonsense like that can't keep happening. We need their respect. We can't end up as beggars who barely cling to our foothold on the cliff, not if we want to survive the scarcities of the solar storms."

"It won't come to that," Auntie Haveo soothes.

Velemeth doesn't calm down. "We need to act now. We need to counteract what the temple said. Double down on showing everyone that the flier is indispensable. Throw our full weight behind making sure our allies win. That's why none of us can be involved with these goats. If we, of all people, act like we've lost confidence in either the fliers or our allies, what is everyone else going to think?"

"Or maybe keeping the pteradons could win back the priestesses' approval," I counter. "They're not mechanical."

Velemeth puts his hands on his hips. "And if this scheme of yours doesn't work? We don't have time to go elsewhere and try again. We'd stab our allies in the back and then end up with nothing. We can't afford to turn away from the one family that actually wants us here. They're more like us than anyone else. The more they succeed, the more we can follow in their footsteps. Too many other people on this ridge would be just as happy to see us gone."

Auntie Haveo stirs. "How likely is this to work, Andeshe?"

I shrug. "It seems easy enough to modify animals. Whether any of those modifications will be successful? There's no way to tell. It would allow us to hedge our bets."

Velemeth hisses through his teeth. "We can't afford to

hedge our bets. It's fine to work with whoever that man is that you found—his family already has one council seat, and they're staying out of the political fight for the other one—but you have to work on something else. These goats are too closely tied to the people trying to take our allies down. We can't look like we're boosting them. Especially not when our allies are mobilizing against these upstarts—and paying attention to who else does. We need to show them we're committed."

I take in his tight shoulders, the lines of tension radiating across his narrow face, and I blow out a calming breath. I'm willing to accept that there will be some differences about living here. I won't even argue with the way they stir up unnecessary antagonism by having two candidates put themselves forward for leadership and then forcing everyone else to choose a side. But some things are just wrong. "We can't afford to go around threatening the people we're going to be living with, either. Acting like Fizz was going to bite him, Velemeth? Really?"

My cousin has the grace to look embarrassed, but his jaw still tightens. "They can't treat us like that. If we don't insist on respect, we'll be nothing."

"Regardless, you need to apologize. That was wrong."

Velemeth straightens. "No."

I rock backward.

He presses into my space. "We have to demand they treat us right. We can't pack up and leave if things get bad anymore."

"But *that* wasn't right." I wave my hand toward the trail of broken stems in the woods. "There's adjusting to a new place and there's abandoning who we are." I look to my aunt for confirmation.

Haveo's face is distant, eyes focused on calculations only they can see. "The more options we have, the better," they say at last. Their eyes refocus on me. "I won't make sacrifices for this long of a shot, Andeshe, but it's worth investigating. Velemeth, yes, we will press for fair treatment." They waggle the rolled-up contract. "But we have avenues to try before we antagonize anyone. No threats. That needs repair."

I draw a breath of relief. Not everything has changed.

Velemeth's lips press together. "They need to go first. I've tried. I'm done taking what they dish out."

"Velemeth!" My shock triggers nothing more than an angry glare, and I peer closer at him. "Are you all right?"

"I'm fine. Is that all?"

I open my mouth, but Auntie Haveo inclines their head. Velemeth turns on his heel and strides toward the settlement, back stiff with tension.

I turn to my aunt. "How have you let him build up that much hurt?" The rawness of his anger lingers like a trail behind him.

The strain lines around Haveo's eyes deepen as they watch Velemeth's retreating form. "There's only so much I can do, Andeshe. You're used to a hundred people in a family—we all are—where we can sit everyone down and talk things out if need be. It's different here, where twenty-five thousand strangers are all jostling for position." The contract rolled up in their hand twitches. "If we had more time, things would be easier, but we don't."

"I'll do whatever I can, you know that."

My aunt's mouth curls in a tired smile, but it doesn't reach their eyes. For the first time, I wonder what they're giving up to be here.

"I can do the apology," I add. "I'm the one Fizz came looking for."

"Thank you. I do appreciate that." My aunt gives my shoulder a tiny squeeze. "And your project binds us closer to the family that holds the other seat. That can't hurt." They heave a sigh, then roll the tension out of their shoulders. "Was there anything else?"

I shake my head. With a final touch, my aunt departs. Even before they reach the tree line, they've unrolled the contract, attention absorbed in the hundreds of details of responsibility.

I take a deep breath and turn back toward the roost. *I hope this project works.*

Chapter Ten
Ya'shul

The bag of vials and syringes clinks against my hip as I walk along the path from the gardens at the edge of town through the scrubby forest to where the Wanderers have cleared away enough trees to perch their wooden buildings. I hitch the bag higher on my shoulder, then scrub the nervous sweat off my palm again. At least I know Nareen has never taken blood samples from a pteradon, not like I'm about to. A bubble of nervous laughter rises in my chest. *I may be about to get eaten by a giant flying monster, but hey, it's a once-in-a-lifetime experience!*

Andeshe promised this would be entirely safe. At least, that's what I told Nareen in my best nonchalant tone when she asked if I was free today: that pteradons only eat things they're fooled into believing are fish. I should have said more. *No, I'm not free. I'm not free until I prove myself. You can stop looking at me like you pity me.* Could have said, should have said. But what I actually said was almost nothing. She might have expected everything to go back to normal, but it's not possible, not with so much hanging in the air between us.

I hitch the bag up onto my shoulder again. This is my chance. Andeshe hoped that one of the strains of mice I already modified would be enough to overcome the pteradon's bad reaction to eating Earth-derived mammals; after a bucket of pteradon vomit proved otherwise, it was my idea to take Fizz's blood and tease out what exactly the pteradons are reacting to. This discovery will be all mine, a story I'll casually drop into conversations. *Oh, didn't you know? Yes, that was me.* Assisting Andeshe might not be quite the same as the formal pledges I was looking forward to among my own people, but I can make this work.

The Wanderer's settlement peeks through the trees. Flimsy wood and hide buildings dot the tromped-down clearing, their gaudy decorations echoing the colorful clothing of the Wanderers chattering and gesturing among them, but no giant monsters are in sight. Only Andeshe waits for me, sitting with relaxed confidence on a rock next to the path.

"Where are they?" I ask. My palms are still slick. When I first proposed this, I hadn't realized the creature would be awake for the procedure. Anyone who lives on a sheer cliff face knows the difference between impressive and suicidal.

"The pteradons? Over there." He waves toward a break in the ring of trees off to the right, past some Lowlanders who are trudging by with buckets. "Over the hillside."

He turns the other way and strides toward the wooden buildings.

"Wait, where are we going?" I hurry after him, catching up when he stops at a door and calls out that he's about to enter.

"We need to change," he replies, ushering me into a room that's covered in carpets and cushions. Bedrolls are tucked neatly against the wall between chests and sets of shelves, and the corners of the room are curtained off, although the curtains are drawn back now.

I catch his arm. "Into protective gear? I thought you said this wasn't that dangerous."

"Oh, it's not, but only women work with pteradons." He bends to rummage in one of the chests.

"I'm not a woman."

"Neither am I right now," Andeshe says. "That's why we need to change. Here." He tosses me a rolled-up bundle, and I stumble at its unexpected weight. It's a leather shirt and trousers, but the surface is mottled and oddly bumpy, with an unusual, sharp scent that pierces straight through to the animal recesses of my brain. I almost drop it. There's only one large animal the Wanderers raise.

Andeshe has disappeared behind a curtain. Bracing myself, I duck behind another and steel myself to pull on the stiff leather. When I rub my palms against the leggings, they don't absorb the sweat.

Will it think I'm one of the flock? I'm not hyperventilating. Really, I'm not. The leather presses oddly against my body as we emerge once more into the sunshine.

Andeshe leads the way across the clearing toward where the cliff gentles into a steep hillside interrupted by protruding boulders. Two figures stand in the gap in the treeline waiting for us. I stop. *Is she*—yes, the leather-clad woman leaning on a crutch is *missing a hand.*

A muffled squeak escapes my lips. "Is that—I thought you said this was safe!"

Andeshe turns back to me with a puzzled expression. "Is what—oh! No, Illeab didn't lose her hand to a pteradon. Don't worry."

It takes me two tries to swallow. "Oh, good."

The two figures turn. The woman has a Goddess-blessed *eyepatch* too, snaking around her face like an extension of her salt-and-pepper braids. I can feel the blood draining from my cheeks.

"Ah!" the zoman next to her exclaims. "Here's Andeshe and her assistant." They extend their hands to me with a warm smile. "Welcome again."

Cool, calm, collected. I manage an appropriate greeting. *I know what I'm doing. I'm here to assist—her?* I blink. Andeshe corrected me when I said that, but no correction is forthcoming now.

"Ya'shul, this is Illeab. She's one of the foremost experts we have on handling pteradons." Any wider a grin and Andeshe's face will split. "Illeab, I didn't realize you were coming!"

"Haveo told me what you were up to. I thought one of my favorite relatives could use the support."

Tension I hadn't even realized was present leaves Andeshe's body. *You said you weren't nervous about this.* Carefully, I calm my breathing, but it doesn't slow my racing heart. The leather still does nothing more than smear around the sweat on my palms.

"This is Ya'shul," Andeshe continues, drawing me closer to where the Wanderers have been standing at the crest of the rocky hillside. "She's one of the Uplanders, and she'll be helping me take samples."

What the hell? "I'm not—"

The words die in my throat as a giant eyeball rises

above the top of the hillside in front of me.

"Dear Goddess!" I clutch Andeshe's arm. A golden disk the size of my head pulses in front of me, bisected by a dark chasm. The disk flexes, and the slitted pupil focuses on me. Animal instincts shriek at me to run, but my feet are frozen to the ground.

Andeshe disengages my hand with a gentle squeeze, then gives the creature's beak an affectionate slap. "How's my favorite Fizzy Fizz?"

The pteradon blinks in a long, slow motion. Its gigantic head plops onto the path in front of us, throwing up a cloud of dust. The enormous eye squeezes closed.

I start breathing again with a gasp. My heart smashes against my ribcage as my eyes travel from the bulge of that eyelid down to the tip of its beak. All the way down. *Three paces, four? How long is that beak?* A small bush used to grow on the edge of the path. Now only squashed foliage peeks out from under the beast's chin. Farther up, the bony red crest on the top of its skull towers above me.

The pteradon cracks one eyelid, then closes it again.

"Oh, all right." Andeshe climbs up the last of the path and starts scratching vigorously above the eye ridge.

I let out a long, shuddering breath and clutch my trembling hands together.

A shape crosses between me and the pteradon. The other Wanderer, Illeab, blocks my view.

"If you're going to help with this, youngster, you need to carry yourself more confidently than that. You staying calm is what keeps the pteradon calm."

I force air into my lungs, trying to calm my racing heart. A sharp, alien scent slams against my nostrils, piercing across planets and millennia to the deepest recesses of my brain where a frantic prey animal lifts its head and screams.

Illeab adjusts her crutch, braids falling over her shoulder, and reaches out to take one of my shoulders. "You've never flown before?" Her expression is compassionate.

I shake my head.

"Follow Andeshe's lead. She knows what she's doing. All you have to do with a pteradon is pretend you're her mother. You're the one who fed her and nurtured her from the moment she hatched. You're the one responsible for giving her life. All pteradons need is to know they'll be taken care of."

I nod. *She*, because of course the Wanderers who work with pteradons are women.

"Breathe," Illeab adds.

I take a deep breath. The scent is still there, but it's echoed and humanized by Illeab's perfume.

"I've dealt with many dangerous animals," she continues. "Pteradons are too tame to even make the list."

"I—I've never seen one up close," I croak.

Illeab launches into an explanation of pteradon traits and breeding, but I barely catch the words. I've only ever seen them at a distance, cargo carriers unloading on the fairground, or once a trio of sleek and haughty militia pteradons from the capital. I inhale again, trying to focus on Illeab's words. The Wanderers fly lumbering gliders, the ones who have been bred for their size, ability to carry more than just the lightest adults, and—thank the Goddess—docility. Behind Illeab, Andeshe slaps a hand against the side of the pteradon's crest. The gigantic eye opens and rolls to look at her with what I can only call a mournful expression.

I told Nareen I was going to do this. None of the Wanderers show any hesitancy. Illeab gives my shoulder a reassuring thump, then stumps over to the pteradon's head and lays her crutch down. With practiced ease, she catches onto a network of leather straps that spiderweb across the back of the gigantic head and pulls herself up until she's perched at the base of the pteradon's skull.

"Come on up," she says, anchoring metal clips onto thick loops in her clothing. She gathers up the lines that lead to the creature's beak with her single hand. "Andeshe, the skin on her neck in front of the main saddle would be best. There's less tension there, and it'll be easy to bandage and monitor."

There's more? For the first time, I let my gaze travel past the pteradon's long neck to the body and wings that are still below the edge of the hillside, crouched next to a large boulder that has a top at the same level as the ground we're standing on. *There is more. Oh Goddess.* Of course there is. No creature consists only of a head and neck.

Andeshe jumps up onto the pteradon's neck and runs lightly along it, arms out for balance, confident as only a woman in her element can be. When she reaches a second saddle mounted where the neck merges into powerful shoulders, she stoops to unroll a rope ladder, then jumps back to the top of the boulder in front of me and pulls it taut to make a sort of rope bridge across the gap between the hilltop and the pteradon's shoulder. Fizz doesn't move.

"Come on." Andeshe anchors the ladder and beckons to me.

"Are—you sure? I could just...stay here."

She shakes her head. "This is the best way to do it. That way, if she twitches, we can ride the motion out.

Don't worry," she hastens to add. "Fizz would never *hurt* you. It's just that if she's startled and flips open a wing or something, it could knock you over."

Right, I gibber silently. *Right, perfectly safe.*

Fizz rolls an eye back to look at me, and her beak scrapes along the dirt, its slight motion scoring a meter-long furrow in the ground.

Yes. On her back. Very good place to be. I'm not hyperventilating. I'm not.

Andeshe is next to me, taking the bag gently from my hands and guiding me to the ladder. "If it's too much, you don't have to stay," she says in a low voice.

"No," I insist, mustering my courage. "I've always wanted to touch a pteradon." I wonder if the creature knows we're about to stick a giant needle in its neck.

Somehow, I cross the ladder-turned-rope-bridge. Somehow, I end up sitting in the back of the double saddle, safety clips firmly attached to the loops tightly sewn to my clothing, trying to ignore how the hillside next to me falls steeply away to the valley floor. Gingerly, I let my legs rest against the pteradon's sides. Up close, its hide is rough, almost pebbly, with a thin layer of not-quite-hair that reminds me of rudimentary feathers. I press a cautious hand against it. When the creature doesn't move, I risk a careful stroke. The filaments looked like they would be wiry, but they're soft to the touch.

Andeshe settles into the forward saddle and passes the bag back to me.

"Look." She shows me a spot just before the filaments thicken on the long neck and holds out her hand. "I'll draw the sample from here and pass it back to you. Have the bandage ready, and I'll slap it on. We'll be done in a moment."

With clumsy fingers, I fumble the needle and syringe out of their case and hand it to her. It had seemed huge when Andeshe asked me for the largest I could find, and I'd smugly packed the rest of the bag with sizes I thought more reasonable. Now I wonder if the big one will be long enough to even pierce the animal's skin. Under my legs, warmth radiates from the massive shoulders. A tiny bunching of muscle nudges my foot aside. Andeshe waits until I strip the adhesive off the bandage, then flips a switch on the battery pack at her waist and calls something up to Illeab. She cocks her head for a moment, listening, then pushes the needle against Fizz's shoulder. The supple hide resists for a moment, then the needle punches through.

The saddle bucks under me, flinging me upward as safety straps bite into my thigh. I scream. Andeshe sways with the motion, attention still focused on the syringe, which is slowly filling with blue blood. The tremors beneath us slow. I look around wildly. Fizz's head is still resting on the ridge. Illeab sits there with reins loosely held in one hand.

Was that—just a twitch? I try to slow my panicked breathing and convince myself that this isn't a prelude to a giant beak whipping around to snap my head off.

"Got it!" Andeshe exclaims. She withdraws the needle, and blood wells up, turning into a trickle of blue. "Bandage," she reminds me.

I scramble to stuff it into her hand, trying not to stab myself with the needle she passes back. Hands shaking, I snap the case closed while she coos over the bandage. With a final pat, Andeshe unclips herself from the harness and jumps lightly across the gap to land with a puff of dirt on the ridge. About to rush off to the pteradon's head, she instead pauses and turns back to look over at me.

"You can unclip and come back across," she says. "We're all done."

I don't move.

"Do you need help?"

"No," I croak. "I—I can do it." Carefully, I fumble for the fasteners. It takes a few tries before I can force my fingers to undo them. The wobbling ladder sways under my weight as I crawl back across it. When my hands touch the soft grass, I want to collapse onto it. Instead, I follow Andeshe back to Fizz's head, where she assists Illeab down and then showers the pteradon with a plethora of murmured endearments and eye-ridge scratches. When Fizz shows no signs of biting her in half in retribution, my heart rate finally slows.

I was on a pteradon. I look up at the enormous creature again. *I really did it. I got samples from a pteradon.* Nareen has never done any such thing. I stand a little straighter.

At last, Andeshe encourages Fizz to curl back up in the rocky depression for a well-earned rest, and the three of us walk back toward the Wanderer settlement. As the pteradon's visage slides behind the top of the boulder, the last of the tension leaves my body. Illeab bids us farewell, and Andeshe leads me once more to the room where we left our normal clothes. My hands are only shaking slightly as I change.

While Andeshe changes, I rummage through the bag. The sampling case is sealed and safe. I lift it out, marveling at the vibrant contents, then rearrange the padding that protects it. As much as it will impress everyone back home to hear what I've done, I have no desire to do it again.

Andeshe emerges, dressed once again in cloth trousers and a buttoned-up shirt, and picks up my neatly folded bundle of borrowed clothes. *Flying leathers really are nothing like our men's garb.* The thought hits me as I watch Andeshe kneel to tuck them away in a chest, vivid colors standing out against blue-black hands and white sleeves. My earlier confusion wells up once more.

"I—that woman back there," I venture as Andeshe and I start back toward the lab. "She called you 'she.'"

"Of course. I always go by 'she' when I'm a woman."

"*When* you're a woman?"

Andeshe waves me out the door and down one of the streets. "Yes. Just like I go by 'he' when I'm a man."

No wonder I've been so confused! Andeshe really has been using different pronouns at different times. I huff out an exasperated breath. "You can't just switch!"

"Of course you can." Andeshe glances at me as we near the tree line. "You wouldn't want to be stuck as—oh I don't know—a teenager or something all the time."

I blink. "Stuck as a teenager?"

"Yes. You know, the gender that gets sent out to gather food and raw materials, hunt, that sort of thing?"

Slowly, I shake my head. "There are only four genders: zomen, women, men, and children."

The Wanderer's eyebrows rise. "We have eight."

I know my mouth has fallen open, but I can't seem to close it.

Andeshe ticks a few off. "Teenagers, like I said. And we do have the others. Women travel and trade and do anything related to pteradons. Men take care of all the daily needs of the community—food, laundry, community events, anything that needs building or repairing or beautifying. Zomen provide leadership and resolve conflicts and handle anything out of the ordinary. But then there are parents, who do childcare and teaching and nursing. And lifegivers, who are the ones who actually bring new babies into the world—you don't have those as separate genders?"

I shake my head. "No. They're part of being a man or a woman."

Andeshe blinks at me without saying anything.

"You really just switch from one gender to another?" I ask.

"Of course. Any time you change jobs, you have to. Only women can do women's work." A brief hand wave indicates the hill of pteradons we just left.

It takes me a moment to find my voice. "But what gender are you really?"

"Right now?" Andeshe tugs at the cuff of one long sleeve. "'He.' I changed back when I changed out of my riding leathers." His eyes shadow with question. "In your culture, men are the ones who go into other people's homes, aren't they? I thought it only polite."

"No, I mean permanently." I wave my hands, reluctant to spell it out. "Your body."

A frown etches itself across the Wanderer's face. "Bodies have nothing to do with gender."

The place where I usually find my words is empty. My feet, of their own volition, have stopped carrying me along the path.

"Well," Andeshe adds, turning back to where I've come to a halt, "other than the youngest two genders, I suppose. Babies are too young to do anything for themselves. Children aren't mature enough to take on other genders' tasks."

Thank the Goddess. The thought of children being assigned an adult pronoun and sexual role makes my gorge rise. Andeshe looks at me, and his brow furrows as if he's putting together pieces of a puzzle he's not sure he wants to complete.

"After that, though... I know you Uplanders tend to stay one gender for a long time, but you're not saying it's assigned to you based on your *body,* are you?"

"Yes," I say firmly. I start walking again, and he follows, the dappled light of the trees flickering over his face. "People who bear children are women. People who deliver sperm are men. Anyone past menopause is a zoman."

He blinks. "But you can switch, right, if the gender you're assigned doesn't fit?"

"No, of course not."

He recoils. "*Why?*"

"Why? Because gender is based on reproduction, of course. People who bear children, quicken children, have finished bearing children, and can't reproduce yet. Four genders."

He draws back, startled. "That can't be right. That's not even all the options. What about adults who don't want to reproduce? Or who can't?"

"They go by 'en,' same as children."

He flinches. "But they're not! That's completely different."

I look away from his distress. There are always a few people who refuse to bear or quicken children, but I've never understood it. "That's the point of having genders, though, to know what everyone's reproductive role is."

Andeshe closes his mouth with a click. "The point," he says crisply, "is to clearly mark who does what work. Without that clarity, there are no boundaries around what it's acceptable to ask someone to do. If you know someone is a parent, you don't ask them to fly off and do a woman's work. Even people who take on two genders at once still get to have their limits."

Every interaction I've had with a Wanderer takes on a new cast. "But—but if anyone can be anything, how are you supposed to keep track of who you can reproduce with?"

Andeshe's head tips to the side. "You insist on knowing that all the time? Why?"

"Why?" The answer should be obvious. *How can he not—*

"I know why lifegivers would care—they're the gender devoted to reproduction—but everyone else?" He shakes his head. "And why organize people's entire lives around it? Even the people doing pregnancies, and certainly those of us contributing sperm, are lifegivers for only a handful of years out of an entire lifespan. Though I suppose people who love midwifing stay as that gender for longer."

"Sperm deliverers and child-bearers are the same gender?" I can't have heard that right, but he nods.

"Yes. Anyone who's ready to participate in creating a child transitions to being a lifegiver, as does anyone who will be coaching them through it. Then they figure out how to work together from there."

I shake my head helplessly. "But how do you tell who's who?"

"We...*ask*." He's definitely giving me the side-eye,

now. "The same as if someone wanted a particular trait in a sexual partner. Narrowing down who's ready to reproduce in the first place is a much bigger step, honestly."

"You really just ask?" My stomach churns at the thought.

Andeshe looks at me worriedly. "You are an advanced biologist, right? You can figure out way more complicated things about people than what reproductive systems they have?"

"Certainly," I reply, stung. "But we don't talk about people's private parts. It would be rude."

He gives me a long look. "Lifegivers discuss far more intimate things than the shapes of their bodies—fertility, pregnancy, postpartum complications. They must in order to help each other. That's the whole point of having a gender, to have a supportive group of people who understand."

"I just—it's not—" I scrabble desperately for something that makes sense.

"Your genders do have that, don't they?" he asks. "The way that being part of a group of people going through the same things creates camaraderie and support and its own way of being together?"

The stone buildings of Ikmeth come into view in front of us. Memory comes back to me of building the new room of the lab with other young men, of our boisterous shouts as we wrestled stones into place and our shared commiseration and ointments as we stretched sore muscles at the end of the day.

"I—yes."

Andeshe relaxes slightly. "And then, if you want to be

part of that group and participate in its tasks, you have to become that gender, right? That's how you show respect for the culture that's been built and signal that you want to be included."

I blow out my breath. "No! You can't just switch!"

He stares at me as if I'd objected to something as small as switching one shirt for another. "What's stopping you?"

"You just—you don't."

Andeshe says nothing for a long moment. "You're locked in, then," he says slowly. "From puberty. Even becoming a zoman, it's not really a choice the way genders are supposed to be. It's just a thing that happens to women?"

I nod.

His eyes go distant at some unknown memory, and he winces. "That explains…some things." He scrubs a hand across his face, then squares his shoulders as we turn onto the street leading through the stone buildings of Ikmeth to the auxiliary lab. "All right, so you do things differently here. I can—I can make this work." He looks about as excited as someone who has swallowed a live spider. "Tell me the rest of it. Once people are divided up here, who's allowed to do what?"

"It's not as big a deal as you think." I usher him toward the street that leads to the lab. Despite our differences, we can make this work. "We don't have rigid gender roles here. Men—you *are* a man, right?"

He hesitates. "By your rules."

A knot unwinds in my shoulders. I can guide another man through this. "You'll be fine. Men can do anything women can do now. Well, except nursing and things we physically can't do, but—"

"I've nursed."

"What?" I miss a step. He *said* he was a man. "How?"

He gives me a sideways glance. "Almost everyone has dormant milk glands. It's just a question of taking the right hormones to turn them on. I thought it was fun, if a little tickly. There are always bottles, too." He shrugs. "I had a few months when one of my younger cousins wanted Fizz for her first solo circuits. I thought I'd give being an auxiliary parent a try. Even when lifegivers want to continue as parents, there's always more than enough work to go around: night feedings, teaching children to read, giving primary parents a break."

Our steps slow. The door to the auxiliary lab comes into view in front of us. Next to it sits the stone bench where my sister Kiu likes to show off nursing her youngest, pride in her unique ability to give life etched into every line of her body.

"Well," I forge on, "women are the only ones who can *give birth*, at least, so traditionally their tasks were the ones that involved creation: inventing, making art, feeding everyone, developing new knowledge, teaching, those sorts of things. Whereas men were supposed to support and clear space for creation. Clean, lift, recycle, keep children out from underfoot and clean up their messes, etc. Zomen are the ones who created all of us, so they're the leaders who run things."

His lips move silently. "All right. I think I've got it," he says after a while, but he frowns at the bag on my shoulder. "If this project is supposed to create new knowledge, though, then doesn't that mean we should be women?"

"No!" My skin prickles at the thought. "We don't do

things that way. Besides, things aren't so rigid anymore. Men can do anything women can do now."

He tips his head, eyes narrowing. "It didn't look that way at the festival."

I wave the comment away, my cheeks heating. "Oh, no," I insist. "It's not that we can't, it's just not everyone wants to—or is good at—you know… But no, anyone can do anything. Really."

He looks skeptical. "Except switch genders?"

"Except that," I admit.

He doesn't say anything for a long moment, just stares at the door to the lab. "Well," he says finally, "this will be different." He takes a deep breath.

"You'll get used to it." I clap him on the shoulder reassuringly, then knock on the door to the lab. "Come on, we've got samples to analyze."

***

"What are you doing?" Perched on the stool next to my work bench, Andeshe rests his head on one hand, watching my every move as I squeeze the last pipette full of liquid into the test tube and gently agitate it up and down.

My mouth is dust. I only stopped narrating my actions for a moment, but evidently that was too long. "Adding the lysis mix," I tell him.

"Ah." He nods. After a moment, he asks, "What's that?"

I shake the last drop off the pipette and start the timer. "You saw me mixing it up earlier." Specifically, he followed me around, poking his nose into everything while I rooted in the storeroom, discovered we were out of one of the components I needed, and tracked down an alternative formula that would still work with cells evolved on this planet. "It breaks open the cells so we can get the DNA out of them."

"Oh, yes. Then what?"

Dear Goddess. I don't do well with hovering, even at the best of times. I do even less well while struggling to remember the subtle variations in procedure needed to compensate for the different ways life evolved on this planet. The first thing I do with any new sample is sequence it. It wasn't supposed to be such an ordeal.

"Well, it needs to sit for a while…" I trail off. I know I found the correct set of instructions, but I haven't been able to review the later stages, not with him breathing down my neck. "You know what?" I tell him. "These next few steps are rather tricky. Would you mind…?" I wave my hands toward anywhere else in the room.

"Oh, certainly." He wanders off to peer at something on another bench.

"Don't touch anything."

He carefully clasps his hands behind his back. After a moment, I let him fade from my awareness, replaced with soothing routines of pipettes and vials and the slow purification of DNA.

I finish the last step and stretch, coming back to the room and the soft murmur of voices. The clink of glassware sounds behind me. Andeshe is standing next to the genome sequencer talking to Nareen. She pops the lid and reaches in as Andeshe peers over her shoulder.

I sit bolt upright, almost elbowing my brother, who has climbed onto a stool to retrieve a box from an upper shelf.

"What is she still doing here?" I hiss at him. "She's

supposed to be in her own lab!"

Ya'kinem sniffs, freckled nose twitching. "That's what I said, especially after the way she treated you—that was crap, by the way—but no, Kiu said she's always welcome here." He lowers his voice. "Between you and me, I think Nareen's family overextended themselves trying to act like they're rich enough to start a major cave expansion right now. Half of Nareen's other pledges were about getting equipment and support for her new space, but I don't think she'll be able to do even a fraction of what she can do here. Certainly not before the storms come." He glances around the lab. "Kiu is even helping her revise things to present at the capital. She'll still be coming in as much as she can get away with."

I blink. "It's not like Kiu has nothing to do." I'd have thought my sister would be too busy taking over as the head of our lab to spend much time with her former mentee. Mother is taking retirement seriously.

"I told her we should stay out of it, and you know what she did? She *laughed* at me. She said that while I may be 'enamored with Isel'—which I'm not, I just believe in what she's doing—the rest of the family would be happy to have Nareen's family pull off an upset." He huffs. "It's not fair. No offense to your project, but the flier should have won. The priestesses just don't like Isel's politics. They don't get that not all traditions are worth keeping. If we want to thrive during the storms, we need to do what works *now*."

Mention of the festival makes something in my heart collapse all over again, but he doesn't notice. I take a deep breath. Being buried in misery is no excuse for ignoring the constant thrum of politics that is part of belonging to one of the ridge's most prominent families.

"Is Grandmother taking sides?" Last I'd heard, they hadn't been happy about the likely elevation of a family that has so little respect for tradition, but they'd been reluctant to antagonize a likely council member.

Ya'kinem shakes his head. "Isel's family is still the clear favorite." His eyes glint in satisfaction. "And it should stay that way. If the flier's test flight to the capital just *happens* to be on the day of the solstice festival when all the prizewinners are at Treverel presenting, and if Isel just *happens* to be flying it and willing to answer questions… Well, everyone will see who should have won."

"She's going to upstage Nareen? In front of everyone?" I look back toward where Nareen stands by the analyzer, talking animatedly with Andeshe. *See if you like how it feels*, a vengeful part of my heart murmurs. The other half twinges in sympathy. Only someone who knows her as well as I do would be able to spot it, but there are already tiny signs of strain around her eyes. Despite the confidence she routinely projects, it's not easy always being in the spotlight. And my family is used to it. Hers isn't.

"Unless Nareen manages to come up with something even more impressive. In—" he wiggles his 'glove to check the date— "less than three months." He looks satisfied at the impossibility. "It'd be hard to top being the only ridge that's still able to fly reliably during the storms."

He's right. The goats were impressive for debutantes, but neither of us expected to win. Our hope had been that future modifications might continue to make them marginally healthier. Most of her ideas for the next round of modifications had involved testing whether different colors were more effective, nothing transformative, nothing even as significant as Andeshe's quest to make it possible to expand pteradons' food source.

My mouth goes dry. Nareen is standing next to the analyzer talking animatedly *to Andeshe*. I shoot to my feet. "Put these away." I push the prepared samples toward him. Ignoring his protestations, I scramble across the room to join the other two.

"So that's what this does," Andeshe is saying in a satisfied voice. He peers at one of the tubes Nareen has removed from the sequencer. "Thank you for answering my questions. Now I don't have to bother Ya'shul so much."

"Any time," Nareen says warmly. "What is it that you're working on?"

"The sample's ready," I cut in as Andeshe opens his mouth. "I thought—I thought, since you're so interested, Andeshe..." I cast around for something to divert him. "Everything's so mechanized now that it doesn't look like much. I thought you might like to see where our techniques come from. They're—the early versions. They're really fascinating."

He nods amiably.

"This way." I catch his elbow and steer him—not toward the bench, where the blue blood would elicit too much interest—but toward the conference room. I pull the door open. "Wait here for a moment. I'll just need to grab a few things." I close the door again before he can respond.

Nareen is watching me. *Mine*, I think at her. *Haven't you gotten enough?* But before she can say anything, her attention shifts to Kiu's arrival. I breathe a sigh of relief. I've had enough credit stolen for what I've done. This is all mine. Careful not to draw their attention, I slip into the storeroom.

Chapter Eleven
Andeshe

The door opens, but it's not Ya'shul. Instead, an unusually tall man ducks his head under the lintel. He's at least a head-and-a-half taller than I am, neatly dressed with a muscular build and a trim beard. He halts when he sees me, and his face blanks.

I straighten. "It's you!" Without the coating of gray dust, he's the same golden-brown as some of the other lab members I've been introduced to, though with a dusting of freckles across a longer and narrower face.

A wary expression slides into place, the same unmistakable stiffness that I saw when he was trying to placate Velemeth.

"It *is* you." I'm sure of it now. I'd looked for him after the mess that happened by the cave, but without a name and with only the most general description, I'd been unable to locate him. "I'm sorry." I turn my palm upward and the words tumble out. "I looked for you to apologize, but I couldn't find you, and it didn't seem right—" I cut myself off. He has drawn back against the door frame, chin tucked, eyes narrowed.

"You were looking for me?" His voice is flat, unfriendly.

I take a deep breath. Suspicion radiates from him, as if he'd expected me to chase him down and berate him further. Not an entirely unreasonable assumption, given Velemeth's outburst.

"I've messed this up," I tell him. "Can I try again?"

"Try what?" If anything, the wariness worsens.

"Apologizing."

That wins me an almost imperceptible loosening. "For what?"

"My cousin used my pteradon to intimidate you, pretending that Fizz would bite you if you didn't work on our cave. That was wrong. He shouldn't have scared you like that, and I should have stepped in faster to stop him."

"I wasn't scared."

I note the hunch of his shoulders, the way his eyes dare me to contradict him. "All right."

We watch each other. His defensiveness bristles out of him, active and quivering in anticipation of danger. I take a breath and let it out in a slow exhale. *I'm no danger, or at least, I don't want to be.* When I say nothing, the hunch of his shoulders slowly lessens.

"You were really looking for me to apologize?" he asks. "To me?"

I nod. "I didn't mean for you to think it was something else."

"No, no, how could you…" He expels his breath in a sigh and glances away. "Apology, yes."

"I'm sorry I didn't stop my cousin from trying to intimidate you with my pteradon," I repeat. "None of them would ever actually bite someone—they're fish eaters—but that's no excuse."

"I—yes." He ducks his head. "All right."

The silence stretches out as if he's not quite sure what comes next.

"Is there anything you'd like me to know?" I prompt.

His brow furrows. "I *can't*." His eyes refocus on me, urgent and troubled. "I really *can't*. If I walk away from what I've been assigned, I don't have a job anymore. It's not like I have a choice. Tell your cousin that."

"I can do that. Are you worried it'll come up again?" Auntie Haveo's complaints to the rock carving family means work on our cave has resumed, but not at the rate it was going before. I don't know if he's personally working at the site.

He looks into the distance. "No," he says at last. "I'll deal with it."

I want to press, but something warns me off.

"If you need anything," I finally offer, "I'm Andeshe. I'll put right what I can."

For the first time, the faintest glimmer of a smile plays around his eyes. "Et'elark." He taps his bracelets together, and I do the same. With a faint whisper of sound, he disappears through the door to what looks like a washroom.

I sag back into my seat. As minimal as it was, that softening is more progress than I've been able to make with Velemeth. Sometimes, the people we're closest to are the hardest to be patient with.

The transition hasn't been easy for him. Auntie Haveo's voice echoes in my memory. *You know how much he was looking forward to coming here.* It was a cruel twist of fate that Velemeth's love of culture and sophistication became paired with a bone-deep fear of the only means to travel to it. I've always tried to bring back to him my observations about people and fashions on other ridges—anything to fill in the gaps that the people he corresponds with wouldn't think to describe—but it's not the same.

You know what they think of us? he'd asked me bitterly when I'd last tried to talk to him. *They think we're barbarians. Because we don't have what they have.* He'd twitched the crisply pressed folds of his shirt, pristine even in the growing heat. *I'd thought it would be different—I don't know—that I'd finally get to be around people who like the same things I do.* He'd shaken his head. *Is it so wrong to want to enjoy nice things instead of trading them away and eking out the barest level of survival? There are so many opportunities here, if only we can get to them.*

If only we can get to them. I rub my temples. I thought I knew a lot about Uplanders. It's only now that I've started living here that I realize how superficial my visits have been. *I can't believe I missed the absence of four whole genders.* I always thought they were simply out of sight.

The door opens and Ya'shul appears, juggling a vial of Fizz's blood and a handful of bottles and test tubes. He deposits them on the table, then slips away, returning with a piece of thin cloth and what appears to be a bottle of soap. He rolls his head, shaking tension out of his shoulders, and sits across the table from me. He gazes at the materials on the table for a moment, then looks into my eyes and smiles.

I blink, an answering smile drawn reflexively out of me. The tightlipped frown he wore earlier is gone, replaced by an openness that lights up his entire face.

"No matter how stressed I am, I always love this demonstration," he confesses.

"What is it?" The sparkle in his eye pulls me forward.

He raises a finger to his lips, and the spark of mischief deepens. "Watch and see," he tells me. "Or rather, *do* and see."

Mystified, I follow his directions, pouring a little blood into a test tube, adding salt and soap and alcohol, then gently swishing the tube around. Finally, I set it in a rack to rest and he bends forward, chin practically on the table, watching the test tube with parted lips. Slowly, layers form, blue on the bottom, clear on the top.

"What exactly are we doing?" I ask him.

The grin that lights up his face makes me blink. He gestures to the test tube, eyes never leaving it. "Everyone thinks that what we do is magic. And I understand why, because we work on such a tiny scale, manipulating things that no one else can perceive. All anyone who comes to visit us encounters are machines and test tubes and then there's this little pinprick—" he mimes injecting something into his arm— "and they're cured. But here's the thing." He raises his head. "The heart of what we work with is really very simple. Look here." He points to the test tube. White strands rise above the blue blood, reaching through the clear liquid toward the surface. "DNA," he breathes.

My breath catches. The delicate filaments hover between us, a tiny forest of thin strands.

"Amazing, isn't it?" Ya'shul murmurs. "No matter how many times I do this, I never get tired of it. The stuff that makes us who we are, that makes us humans or—or pteradons...it's right *there.*"

Fizz's DNA. All the breeding we've done, all the genetic legacy we're losing in the storms, distilled into its essence. The edge of the table bites into my hands.

Ya'shul hands me a wooden skewer, and I lower it into the liquid. The strands wind themselves around it eagerly. *Yes*, I imagine them saying, *take me. Find a way.* My hand trembles as I lower it into the vial of alcohol he holds out for me.

"What can you do with this?" I ask. My voice doesn't tremble.

He lifts a shoulder. "Anything. Change their wing length, change their metabolism. It's all right there, all the instructions for what makes them what they are. Edit those, and they can be anything."

A shiver runs down my spine. "Anything?" Longing burns through me. All of a sudden, I want to learn everything, to suck Ya'shul dry and plunge myself deep into the heart of whatever I can find. *What else can be done here?*

He smiles. "As is always the case, implementation is harder than theory. We can change anything we want. Knowing what to change is harder." He picks up the vial and peers at it. "We've—" a shadow crosses his face— "I've spent a lot of time in the guts of what exactly phosfoz does and what it binds to. Even though pteradons are different, I'm hoping there are enough similarities that once the computer has Fizz's DNA, it can reconstruct key proteins she makes and model how they interact. We have almost a complete library for goats and mice, so modeling changes is relatively straightforward. But who knows what might pop up for pteradons?" His face is alight with enthusiasm.

"How—how long will it take?"

His smile dims. "If I were trying to analyze the pteradons from scratch? Too long. But we don't need to know that much. There are only so many sequences for proteins that will bind a phosfoz molecule. We can look for those." He looks at me, his face a request for understanding. "It's just...the more we know about what they need, the more we'll know about what else to feed them. You know?"

Hunger for knowledge radiates out from him. I find myself nodding.

"I need a solution before the storms hit, though," I remind him.

"Of course." His lips tighten for a moment. "Don't worry, I need one well before that, too."

A rising arpeggio sounds in the other room, and a crease appears on his forehead. "Excuse me, I should check on that." He starts toward the main room, then turns back, gesturing the test tube. "I just wanted to show you this. It's where it all comes from, and it's all so simple, really. Once we *understood* that, we could do anything."

The door thumps closed behind him, and I stare at the coiled strands in the bottom of the glass. What Ya'shul showed me is so simple but so unlikely to be guessed. Wild fantasies spin out from it—shrinking the pteradons for a few generations and popping them back to life size at the end, turning them vegetarian entirely, speeding ahead the breeding projects that currently take decades to bring to fruition. *Stop it.* Ya'shul seems to take for granted his effortless mastery over the very code of life. I, however, am the veteran of many things that were more challenging than they should have been.

The door opens and closes again behind me.

"Are you done with those?"

I start. Et'elark's voice is warmer this time, a hint of

musicality in its looser tones.

"I—yes." I sit back. "At least, I think we are. Ya'shul was showing me something."

"He's the one who sent me." The neutrality is back, but his long fingers scoop up the glassware without hesitation.

"Then yes." I gather up the other remnants. "Where do these go?"

He looks at me in surprise. "This way." He bumps the door I haven't been through open with his hip and ducks under the lintel. It opens onto a room dominated by a wide sink and its attached countertop.

"Are you an apprentice here?" I ask as he shows me how to dispose of the liquids. I hesitate, but there's no good way to keep Fizz's DNA as a souvenir. *Maybe I can just keep her.*

"Hardly." His lips twist in an ironic smile. "Apprenticeships are for Uplanders."

"You're not one?" I could guess that he's not related to Ya'shul's family—despite having the same wavy hair and general skin tones, his nose is thin and narrow rather than broad, his eyes more closely set—but he's dressed impeccably in Uplander clothes. Unlike when we first met, they're clean and crisp.

"You couldn't tell?" He waves a hand back and forth above his head.

I look up into his face. Brown and gold-flecked eyes crinkle in faint amusement. His black hair is pulled back in a neat queue.

I shake my head slowly. "I'm sorry. Should I have?"

"No, no." The amused look on his face deepens. "It's all right." A smile hovers at the corner of his lips. "It's just...that's a new one. No, I'm one of the custodians here."

"Ah." I try to reconcile this with the stone I saw him hauling before.

His eyes slide away from mine. "When we met before, that's one of my other jobs. *This* is my main one." His lips compress.

"What do you do here?" Perhaps focusing on that will set him at ease.

"Manage the batteries that supply the lab and coordinate the different energy sources that feed them." He waves toward the ground beneath our feet. "Maintain their shielding and baby them along as much as possible. The energy draw from the computers is enormous."

I murmur my appreciation. Even just cooling and circulating the air of an entire building strikes me as extravagant. Habit guides my hand to my belt to wind the charging crank on the battery pack for my earpiece, then the same for the synthaglove I'm still getting used to wearing.

"And I clean things," Et'elark adds. "In my spare time." His smile fades.

"Well, thank you for your help," I tell him. "I appreciate it."

He stops moving, a test tube cradled in the towel in his hands. For the first time, his eyes really focus on me. "You're welcome," he says. This time, when he smiles at me, it feels real.

I smile back. A knot of tension in my belly loosens. One thing, at least, has been set right.

"Et'elark?" Ya'shul's voice calls. He pokes his head into the room. "There you are. The bio-waste container is almost full."

Et'elark's expression smooths back into blankness, but he ducks his head and slides past Ya'shul. Ya'shul turns to me with a blinding smile. "The analyzer's available." He rubs his hands together. "Ready to read your pteradon like a book?"

His glee is infectious. When he beckons me forward, I follow.

Chapter Twelve
Ya'shul

There. I close my eyes. Under my 'gloved hands, a receptor on the cell I'm studying locks onto a phosfoz molecule. Its wall bulges inward, cutting the molecule off from the outside with an almost palpable snap. I sit back, a smile spreading across my face. *Gotcha.*

Disentangling my hands from the manipulation box, I stretch, cracking two vertebrae in my neck. I know the sensations of the 'gloves are just simulations, a reconstruction of what the instruments have been able to sense, but nothing compares to the feel of digging my fingers into an experiment. Even my awareness of Nareen talking in low tones with my sister Kiu on the far side of the room can't diminish the glow of success. At least Se'jan is off at some martial arts competition of his today. I can pretend things are as they used to be.

I slip my own 'glove on and message Andeshe. *Phase two is go!*

His reply is a long time coming. I putter about, returning the eukaryotes to their incubating station and cleaning the machine. Andeshe's problem is that something in Earth animals' metabolism is binding the phosfoz mineral that is so common here into a compound that makes the pteradons throw up their entire meal. The details of how that happens are turning out to be ridiculously complicated, but at least I realized we could sidestep the entire issue. The phosfoz uptake genes I'm adding to microbes from the mice's digestive tract should trap the mineral and lead to it being excreted instead of being absorbed into the animal's bloodstream, where the toxic transformation seems to take place. If tests show that the microbes do successfully intervene before that process happens, I should be able to introduce them into any animal a pteradon might eat. It isn't elegant—certainly nothing as impressive as modifying mammals—but Andeshe won't care, not as long as having herds of genetically modified animals for the pteradons to snack on means that they can stay during the storms.

Seating myself at one of the data terminals, I pull up what I'm *really* excited about. My microbes may be enough for now, but Andeshe says pteradons don't simply get rid of phosfoz when they eat it; they *need* it. If they don't get enough of it in the right form, their hide starts to blister and degrade, its normal healthy suppleness replaced with lesions and swollen patches and painful growths that spread throughout their body. I can modify their food to get rid of phosfoz entirely, but that won't solve the need for supplements or reveal why they need it. The computer fans whir as a representation of the pteradon genome ripples out in front of me, the portions I've marked tingling in sharp contrast to their neighbors. I wave everything else away, and the proteins they code for spring to life, coils and textures slithering under my fingers as I start the simulations again. There's only so much a machine can tell me, but it can at least reveal if my hunch is plausible. We've always wondered about the natural protection that so many creatures here seem to have against the solar radiation that damages us so badly. Is this why? Is this compound lying in plain sight, the one we've always tried to get rid of as a nuisance, the key to thriving here?

The hum of the fan transmutes itself into the hum of imaginary voices discussing the implications of my work. *Can I have something by the solstice?* Even something preliminary would be enough, wouldn't it? Enough to make up for the awful humiliation of the festival. This time, I won't pretend to be less than I am.

On the table next to me, my 'glove buzzes. I extract myself from the data terminal and pull it on.

??? is Andeshe's reply.

I sigh. He can read, but not easily.

The cell I was modifying. It did a good job.
What it do?

I hesitate. I've explained receptor-mediated endocytosis to him before. Verbally.

Never mind, I reply. Any attempt to explain will only annoy us both. Getting the pteradons' prey to stop producing harmful forms of phosfoz is only a stopgap, anyway. What I really want to know is why pteradons need the natural form of it so badly. The data terminal beeps at me, and I pull up its results. Nothing promising related to their skin, but there are some tantalizing clues about other possibilities. I download the key results to my 'glove and wipe the display smooth, replacing it with my notes. I run a finger over the lumps and valleys of the symbols in amazement. I would never have thought the list of what pteradons use phosfoz for would grow so long.

The knock pattern I taught Andeshe raps against the door, jerking me from my reverie. When I open it, he bustles inside, discarding his sunshade at a crooked angle next to the others, and fishing a messy sheaf of papers out of a satchel slung over his shoulder.

"Were you talking about the eukaryotes or the bacteria?" he asks without preamble. His voice is, as always, overly loud. Across the room, Kiu raises her head.

"This way." I guide him over to the small desk that I've claimed as my own.

Here, our heads bent together, his voice softens. He spreads out the pile of paper, pulling a few pages of handwritten notes out of what I recognize as one of the introductory texts on genetics. The mechanically embossed surface of the temple's text has held up better than his notes. Their puffy, wax-like ink is chipping in a few places, unintentionally turning the double helix symbol for DNA into the symbol for RNA instead. I point it out to him wordlessly, and he fumbles with an uncooperative pen before giving up and borrowing one of mine.

"You could just read them on the 'glove." All the Wanderers I've seen around have had one. I don't know why he doesn't use his more.

He shrugs one shoulder. "It's easier when I can see the symbols. I'm not used to reading everything purely by feel."

A baby squeals and I jerk upright. My brother appears in the washroom's doorway, bouncing a fussing infant, U'kylay trailing in his wake. I let out a breath. He's the one in charge of the baby, not me.

"Bring the baby over here." Kiu settles herself at the data terminal behind us, shifting her still-rounded stomach. "Nareen," she continues, "let's go over the details of what you're thinking about again. Something's not right, but I can't quite put my finger on it." She waggles her fingers toward Ya'kinem, one breast already dripping milk. I dig a cloth out of my pocket and hurry to wipe up the spill.

Nareen takes her place beside Kiu, watching her enviously. She catches my eye and looks away, but her hand comes up to rub her belly. A lump rises in my throat. It's too early for her to know anything, only a few weeks, but for all that my family was one of the five pledged to her, I know I had no part in it. I look at the rag in my hand, the nearby benches, the data terminal, anything but her face.

The data terminal. My stomach flips. I didn't clear it before I answered the door for Andeshe. If either of them glances down, they'll see the entire overview of what I think phosfoz has the potential to do. My fingers itch to erase it, but Nareen is blocking the access port, holding a bottle up so my sister can express milk from her unoccupied breast.

"Pump?" Nareen asks Ya'kinem. He scrambles back toward the washroom to get my sister's breast pump. Nareen's eyes fall to the sculpted sand in front of her, but they're unfocused. I don't breathe. "I suppose it's too much to hope that Isel will literally crash that flier, not just use it to crash the solstice festival."

Kiu snorts, setting one dark brown hand on the paler woman's shoulder. "Just because her side's being petty, don't let what they're saying about you get to you."

"It's not." Nareen's denial is almost reflexive. "I know what I've got is better than what she does."

Oh? Confidence is one thing, but I've heard what she's come up with so far. It's not impressive. A pattern-less knock at the door interrupts them.

"I'll get it!" My brother bounds back into the room, drops Kiu's pump on the table, and skids to a halt at the door. U'kylay follows in his wake, chortling. He opens the door, and daylight spills into the room, framing a stocky, middle-aged woman who stands planted in the entrance.

Everyone in the lab freezes. Despite being dressed like anyone else, the woman's presence radiates from her. The bare muscles of her arms flex as she collapses her sunshade and steps inside, planting the tip of the sunshade on the floor and folding ruddy brown hands on top of its handle. Waves of deep mahogany hair tumble below her shoulders as she shakes it back, seeming to relish our discomfort.

"Isel." My sister breaks the silence, voice carefully neutral. She shifts the baby on her breast to a more prominent position.

"We're going to watch Se'jan's ijendra competition," Ya'kinem announces, popping up by the woman's side. He spreads a fresh layer of sunscreen onto one pink arm, his movements almost mincing in contrast to her solid presence. I start to stir, then stop myself. Grandmother has warned him off spending too much time with strange women before to little effect. The look he shoots at Kiu almost dares her to object to the excuse he's given this time. "Isn't it nice that Isel isn't too busy to come out and show support for our family?" he adds, eyeing Nareen. "You know how important martial arts are to Se'jan."

Nareen straightens. "Some of us have important work to do." Frost coats every word.

An amused smile twitches the corner of Isel's lip. Her

eyes roam over the lab, lingering on every exposed object. Her gaze lands on me, and a tiny shiver runs up my spine at the sense of coiled power that underlies her veneer of civility.

"So good of you to stop by." Kiu cuts through the tense silence. She pats a bead of milk on her breast with a cloth. I inhale as Isel turns her attention away from me to nod graciously at my sister. Her eyes drop to the data terminal, then flick back to Nareen.

"Is this what you're working on?" Her voice is low and gravelly. "I thought you were supposed to have your own lab by now."

Nareen bristles. "I do. There's no shame in working with alliance partners."

"Mmm. I suppose your family *wouldn't* have the energy budget for something like this."

Nareen's stool scrapes back. Even Ya'kinem winces. "U'kylay!" he interrupts, thrusting his hand at the child. "Are you coming with us?"

U'kylay's head turns back and forth. "I want to stay with Nareen," the child announces. Nareen gives Isel a tiny, triumphant look.

"Ya'shul?" My brother turns to me.

I feel trapped. He'd talked me into coming along before, but Nareen is watching me, chin raised, lips tight. I shake my head.

"Surely *you're* coming, Andeshe." A second voice speaks from the doorway, coming from a more slightly built woman I hadn't noticed. She's dressed like a wealthy Uplander with earrings and bracelets in the latest style, but the shape of her face and eyes reminds me too strongly of Andeshe to make me think she's one of us. For all that the

Wanderers are blending in more here, none of them have quite dropped the extravagant gestures and voluble speech that marks them as outsiders.

Beside me, Andeshe stirs. "I suppose," he says amiably. He shuffles his stack of papers back into order and rises, waving his farewell. The door closes behind the four of them with a click.

"Of all the nerve!" Nareen exclaims. "Coming in here like that."

In the vacuum left by Isel's absence, I can finally breathe again. "It's Ya'kinem," I say almost apologetically. "You know he never thinks things through." I wonder if she'll catch the lie. He knows exactly what he's stirring up.

"Still." For all that Nareen sounds slightly mollified, she continues glaring at the door.

"Ya'shul…" My sister's thoughtful tone raises prickles on my arms. "What is this?"

Slowly, I turn. She's looking at the molded sand of the data terminal. My heart sinks.

Nareen turns her attention to peering over Kiu's shoulder. "What's what?"

"It's nothing." I send up a brief, fervent prayer.

Kiu hands me the pump, shaking off a few extra drops of milk, and lifts the baby onto her shoulder. She connects her 'glove to the controls, then flicks through them, eyes growing distant. Carefully, methodically, I disassemble the hand pump, not daring to watch.

"'The Potential for Metabolizing Phosfoz as a Nutrient?'" My sister reads the title of my notes aloud, then twitches her 'glove, rifling through my other recent work. I close my eyes, heart sinking. As head of the lab, she has access to everything stored in its computers.

"What?" Nareen moves closer to the display.

Kiu's 'glove is still twitching. She pauses, quirking an eyebrow in my direction. "'Phosfoz: Ya'shul's Miracle Research that Beat the Sun.'"

I squirm to hear her read it aloud, doodled fantasies I'd imagined presenting while I sat here waiting for the computer to chirrup. Even Nareen struggles to suppress an incredulous look.

"I've just been doing some preliminary analyses," I mumble. "I would have double-checked everything if I'd known anyone would look at it."

Kiu pins me with a look. "So *that's* why the computers' power draw spiked." She starts her 'glove scrolling again, shaking her head. "We don't have infinite electricity to use on vanity projects, you know."

My face burns. I knew I was bending protocol not to ask. I just thought I would have something to show for it before it became an issue.

"Explain," she prods when I say nothing.

Haltingly, I summarize what I've found so far while she pokes at the models in front of her. I finish, and silence descends, broken only by the creaking of wire.

Creaking? I turn. U'kylay is balanced on a stool, tugging at the latch on one of the mouse cages.

"U'kylay!" I'm by the child's side before I realize I've moved, catching the cage before it can teeter.

"They're so pretty." U'kylay gives me a pleading look. "Take them out, Ya'shul! Can I play with them? Please! Pretty please!"

Gently, I swing en back down to solid ground.

"No, U'kylay, these are special mice. They aren't allowed to come out and play."

The child's lip sticks out in a pout. "Why not?"

Across the room, Kiu manipulates the display again and points out something to Nareen.

"Come on, U'kylay, let's go play over by your mother."

En's arms cross. "But I want to play with the mice."

I can't leave en here, not with glassware and chemicals arrayed so temptingly at eye level, but Kiu and Nareen are talking about my project. Without me.

"I promise I'll be good!"

I suppress a shudder. I remember the last time en promised that. And where's Ya'kinem? I can't believe he left and dumped this on me. U'kylay's voice rises to a whine, and Kiu glances up long enough to give me an irritated look.

"Here," I cast around for a distraction—any distraction—from the brewing storm. A few stray pieces of flower are caught in U'kylay's hair. I tug one out and hold it up. "Let's look at this under a microscope. You can be just like a real scientist."

My most cajoling tone is swept aside by a full-throated wail. "I. Want. The. Miiiiiice!" U'kylay flings enself on the floor, feet drumming.

Both women look up. *Please, Goddess, not now.* The last thing I need is for everyone to think I'm incompetent at my most basic responsibilities.

"Behave!" I hiss at the child.

"No." En glares up at me.

I cast an agonized glance back toward the table.

"Listen," I tell U'kylay. "If you calm down and sit quietly, I'll—I'll make you some cookies when we get back home."

Don't reward bad behavior, my uncle's voice

admonishes me. *You're teaching children that if they throw a tantrum, you'll give them a treat.* But what else am I supposed to do? Nareen is nodding along with my sister's words. I need to be over there, but there's nowhere in this room I can safely leave a child unattended.

"Okay." U'kylay jumps up and scampers to the microscope nearest Nareen, perching on the stool in front of it with angelic calm. I grit my teeth as I close the fragment of blossom in the chamber and a gigantic version molds itself up out of the display board on top of it. I've been outmaneuvered by a five-year-old, and we both know it.

With all the dignity I can muster, I turn back to the two women. "It seems like a massive undertaking," Nareen is saying. "Would it be feasible in a few months?"

"Would what be feasible?" I interject.

"Nothing so grandiose," Kiu replies to Nareen. A flick of her fingers, and most of my work goes skittering off the edge of the display into oblivion. I flinch. "But something preliminary, something actually methodical…" She slides her fingers away from each other, and my list of all the different ways pteradons use phosfoz expands. "That would be possible. A tantalizing tidbit to add to your solstice presentation, the possibility that phosfoz isn't something to get rid of, but something to harness. Something to get people excited about the future. That's what you want. You want people excited about your potential."

"Her potential?" The words burst from my lips. "This is *mine*."

Kiu turns slowly toward me. "Yours?" Her voice fills with warning, for all that she pats the infant on her shoulder gently. Nareen looks back and forth between us, then takes the excuse of U'kylay's frantic beckoning to give us privacy.

"Tell me," my sister continues, "what conclusion have you proved that you're claiming is yours?"

"Nothing, but these are my ideas. You can't just take them!"

She snorts. "As if squirting ideas around willy-nilly and then walking away is enough to create life." She rubs her stomach. "You have to actually do the work."

"I was going to. I just—"

"Right." Skepticism laces her voice.

I clench my fists. "I was."

A crow from U'kylay interrupts us. "Look what I've discovered!" The child's fingers skid over a spiky ball of pollen that the magnification reveals. "I'm a scientist just like you!" En scrambles down from the stool and latches onto Nareen's hand.

Nareen's lips twitch. "Of course you are, U'kylay." My cheeks flame. The child can't hear the adult condescension, but I can.

Kiu sighs. "You're not going to try to be selfish about this, are you Ya'shul?"

Everything in me recoils. "I'm not selfish! I just—"

"Want to keep everything to yourself." She makes a tsking noise. "Nareen's family is relying on her to impress everyone at the solstice. And think about the boost in our prestige if someone we've trained does well. Think what it would mean for our lab and our family if people were vying to apprentice with us." She indicates U'kylay and the baby with a jerk of her chin. "What we do now will determine their opportunities when they come of age after the storms.

You want those to be good, don't you?"

"Of course."

"Then what's the problem?"

U'kylay bounces over to me, followed at a more sedate pace by Nareen. The child grabs onto my leg and peering up at me. "Cookies now? You promised!"

I pull the child closer, willing en to silence, all too aware of Kiu's judgmental expression. "I just—I just want credit for what I've contributed." Even that much of a compromise tears at me. I'd wanted this to be mine alone.

"I'm sure Nareen will mention you in her presentation." Condescension fills my sister's voice.

"Of course." Nareen sounds almost offended that anyone would think it necessary to ask.

"There." Kiu sits back. "Problem solved." Nareen turns back toward the terminal.

The ground feels as if it's dissolving away under my feet. "I—"

My sister's nose wrinkles, and she pulls the baby away from her shoulder. "Diaper," she announces, handing en to me. My arms fold around the child before I even realize what I'm doing.

"Can't you take care of it?" I ask Kiu desperately. With every gesture Nareen makes, I can feel my work draining away from me to curl around her fingers.

Kiu's voice goes dangerously soft. "Did you tear yourself apart to give life to that child?"

Warning thrills across my nerves. Warily, I shake my head.

"Then why are you complaining?"

My mouth goes dry. This is no longer the sister I plagued in my youth. This is the newly elevated head of the lab, its principal investigator. Every request for materials that I make, every work assignment that eats into my precious time, is approved or declined at her sole discretion. I gulp and pull the child back to my chest.

"Take U'kylay down, too," Kiu adds. "It's nearly lunch time." She drops me from her attention with an almost-audible thump.

I swallow and hold out my hand to U'kylay. Docile for once, en follows me toward the door.

It swings closed, and I sag against it. *Damn it.* I tip my head back against the door. *Damn it, damn it, damn it.*

Chapter Thirteen
Andeshe

Se'jan's opponent sends him rolling across the dusty ground of the ijendra circle in a pinwheel of legs. He lands with a thump that makes everyone around me groan. The blur of action—too quick for me to follow—resolves itself, and he's on his feet again, shaking out his arm. I cringe. This looks far more painful than the display of martial arts skill I was expecting.

"Don't worry," Velemeth murmurs to me. "It doesn't hurt as long as everyone knows what they're doing."

"Good," I reply faintly. We've watched several pairs of competitors over the course of the morning, and I've been able to enjoy most of the bouts, but for whatever reason, this one has me on edge. The crowd cheers, and I shake the feeling off.

The baby in Velemeth's arms wriggles fretfully, and latches onto one bared breast, winning approving looks from the spectators who have gathered around several competition circles drawn on the northern side of the fairground.

"How are you enjoying being a woman?" I ask turning to her. Velemeth is one of the few people I know who has never been one before, but she has flung herself into the Uplander version of womanhood wholeheartedly. As odd as it is to see her nursing while wearing their loose, undyed trousers instead of the brightly colored wrap that marks someone as a parent, she does seem more at ease. The confidence I'd noticed when she came with Isel to fetch me and Ya'kinem from the lab hasn't faded.

"Better." Her smile flashes whitely. "The people here revere nursing, you know."

"In some people." I remember Ya'shul's reaction when I mentioned having done it myself. I'm still having trouble wrapping my brain around who they allow to do what.

She shrugs and makes a cooing noise at the baby. "Take what you can get. At least here having given birth counts for something."

"You seem like you're settling in." She seems less raw than in our last conversation. Perhaps the steady progress on our cave over the last handful of weeks has assuaged some of her sensitivity to slights.

"Somewhat." Her eyes narrow. "You have to insist on what you deserve here, but I understand better how to do that now. Too many of us need reminders of that to keep from getting taken advantage of."

"Are you happier, though?" I press. There's a standoffishness here that several of my relatives have mentioned. It wasn't until I realized Uplanders never leave their birth family that I realized how much practice our tradition of fostering between families has given us at welcoming newcomers. It may not always have been easy, but I never felt excluded, not even when I first arrived in Auntie Haveo's family.

Velemeth sends me an amused look. "Yes, Andeshe,

I'm fine. I've made a few friends." She tilts her head toward her far side, where Isel and Ya'kinem are shouting encouragement at Se'jan. "Now that Isel is in town more, she's been introducing me around."

I try to remember if Isel is one of the Uplanders Velemeth has corresponded with over the years. Their closeness seems like more than just our families' shared connections making us welcome in Isel's social circles, perhaps more even than Velemeth's thrill at burrowing into the heart of Uplander politics. Her familiarity hints at a longer friendship.

Se'jan goes down in a whirl that ends with him flat on his stomach, his opponent standing over him to apply the shoulder lock that signals the end of the bout. He taps out, but she leans in a little extra. I glance over at the referee. We've watched numerous bouts, and in the others, tapping out has triggered an immediate release.

"He should have known better than to try to use all that muscle." On my other side, two women have been commenting on every match. Apparently, ijendra focuses on *not* meeting an opponent's attack directly, but deflecting and redirecting it with skill instead of strength. "Using too much muscle" has been their main critique so far.

"The taller they are, the harder they fall," the other agrees. Her voice oozes with a satisfaction that makes my skin crawl. When we arrived, Velemeth pointed the two women out to me as members of the family that has lost too much prestige to retain its council seat, and they and Isel's party have been studiously ignoring each other ever since. I'm sure Velemeth is more sensitive than I am to the tension created by Isel's and Nareen's families competing for the council seat, but even I can tell that the community is abuzz with gossip and jockeying for position.

With one last press, the victor finally releases her hold and steps back. Se'jan gets to his feet, shaking out the arm.

"He is hot, though," the first woman adds. "I'd roll around with him on a mat any day. Do you think he'd struggle if I pinned him down? I don't like it when they go all limp."

The second woman laughs, but there's an ugly edge to it.

"Hey!" Ya'kinem leans around Velemeth, his freckled face radiating outrage. "That's my cousin. You can't talk about him that way!" He has the same wide cheekbones and rounded face as Ya'shul, but in place of his brother's self-conscious restraint, Ya'kinem's mobile features broadcast his every emotion.

She peruses him from head to toe with a lazy grin. "Says who?"

Ya'kinem's grip on his sunshade tightens, but he doesn't look away. "It's bad enough that the refs are being unfair. You don't need to be piling on." He gestures to Se'jan, who is limping toward the water jug as a new match begins.

"Unfair?" Amusement tinges the woman's voice. "He's just losing. He's not as good as the real competitors."

Ya'kinem draws himself up to his full, gangly height and glares at her. "He's not 'just losing.' He's always getting paired with people above his skill class, and the refs are calling their pins faster than his. And when he won anyway, everyone teased his opponent mercilessly, and she fouled him on the next round. And the ref didn't call it! You can't tell me that's fair."

That's what it was. I knew something was subtly wrong.

"Excuses, excuses." The woman waves a dismissive hand.

Ya'kinem's nostrils flare. "They're *not*," he insists. "It happens over and over."

She leers at him. "You know what *I'd* like to do over and over?"

His hands turn into fists by his sides.

"I saw the same thing Ya'kinem did," I interject. Leering is no way to respond to someone's concern.

The woman's gaze transfers to me, flicking over the clothing Velemeth has told me repeatedly is unfashionable, no matter how comfortable it is. "And you're an expert on ijendra?" Her voice is distinctly unfriendly.

Isel stirs, taking notice of our conversation. "Andeshe is my guest, Jamerol." Her words are quiet, but they drop into a space of sudden silence that ripples out around us.

"Isel saw it, too." Ya'kinem turns to her for confirmation. "Didn't you? The way they were treating him."

"Of course." Isel looks Jamerol up and down, and I can almost see the moment when she abandons the odd habit Uplanders have of refusing to talk openly about obvious things. "It should surprise no one that certain families have trouble thriving when they refuse to let all their members develop their full talents."

Jamerol's complexion is light enough to show the red that stains her cheeks as she stares at the woman whose family is supplanting her own. Isel holds her gaze until it becomes clear Jamerol won't respond, then turns dis-missively back to the competition. Ya'kinem smirks. Jamerol eases away with an attempt at nonchalance that fools no one.

Is that it? I look back and forth between the two women, Jamerol retreating in flushed humiliation, Isel watching the competition with arms folded. Nothing at all has been resolved. I hurry after Jamerol. "Excuse me," I say, tapping her on the shoulder. She turns, and I cup my hands palm up in front of me. "Ya'kinem's concerns haven't been addressed. He named that Se'jan isn't getting the chance to participate in the competition the way everyone else is and is being treated unfairly. Then you belittled him instead of talking about it." Surely that can't be what she means to do, at least not after it's pointed out to her.

Hostility radiates from every line of Jamerol's body. Neither she nor her companion even glance at my open hands. I hold them higher and give them a little shake. This kind of casual cruelty should be easy enough to make right.

Jamerol's gaze finally drops to my hands. "You want an apology?" she asks scornfully.

An apology? That's the least of what it means to cradle hurt in your hands in the company of others. She should have raised her own hand in turn, joining me in creating a space for us to listen to each other. I wait another heartbeat, but she doesn't.

"You *should* apologize." Ya'kinem appears next to us, glaring at Jamerol. "Keep your mouth off Se'jan!" He doesn't raise his hands either.

Do they...not do this here? I look at Jamerol's companion, but there's no sign of recognition on her face either. *Oh, this is not good.* The ritual of holding harm exists to guide people through the most difficult conversations about hurt and restoration. Without it, I feel as if I stepped onto the cliffside stairs only to have them crumble under me.

Jamerol smirks. "Wouldn't you like to know what I've done with my mouth?"

Ya'kinem begins to retort, but a smooth baritone cuts him off. "Did I hear my name?" Se'jan pauses just outside our group, a glass of water in one languid hand. He tosses back his curls, then raises the glass in a salute. "I trust we were all toasting my *incredible* skill and waxing appropriately superlative?"

"The refs weren't treating you fairly!" Ya'kinem exclaims. "I told her that, but she just mocked me!"

"Do you really think that?" Jamerol asks Se'jan. A smirk plays across her face.

"*I?*" he asks, heavy-lidded eyes widening in his olive face. "Now, why would I concern myself with a little thing like that? No, I'm more interested in how the refs would treat you." He smirks back at her. "I haven't seen you out there for a long time. Still claiming to be too injured to compete?"

Jamerol's face shutters. "I could compete if I wanted to. I have other priorities."

Se'jan nods knowingly. "Mmm, very important. That's why you spend all your time hanging out on the edges of ijendra matches critiquing everyone else but never daring to set foot in the circle yourself. It has nothing at all to do with that one time…" He taps his lip and looks at her with narrowed eyes. "What was it that happened?" He eyes Jamerol as she compresses her lips. "It was utterly humiliating; I remember that much." When she doesn't move, he clicks his fingers as if remembering. "Oh yes—"

"Come on," Jamerol snaps, catching her companion's arm. "There's nothing to see here. All the good matches are already over."

"Indeed!" Se'jan agrees. "I'm done for the day. There's *definitely* no point in staying around to watch anyone else." Jamerol shoots him a look of pure distaste before steering her friend away. Her disgruntled murmurs fade with the distance. Ya'kinem glares after her, then flounces back to Isel's side, leaving me and Se'jan alone.

"That was...disturbingly effective," I tell him. It also has nothing in common with anything I've been taught about how to repair relationships and knit together a community. If that was even his goal.

He gives me a tiny, yet somehow still flamboyant, bow. "Ah, sweet reason." He blows on his fingernails, then polishes them on his shirt with a satisfied expression.

I study him. His round face and broad nose are similar enough to Ya'shul's and Ya'kinem's to be a brother, not a cousin, but his expression radiates ironic detachment instead of their earnestness. He raises his glass to his lips and watches me from behind the rim.

"That seems like it could be fun," I say, indicating the ijendra circle. "When you're not getting picked on."

He snorts with laughter and almost spits out his mouthful of water. With mock surprise, he asks, "What? It's not obviously fair for us big, hulking brutes to get clobbered all the time? We're the ones trying to substitute brawn for cleverness and flexibility." He shows off a well-muscled arm.

I cock my head. "You don't believe that."

"It's harder to put a joint lock on someone who's double jointed." His eyes are alight with challenge and, oddly, enjoyment.

"Right, because *that's* what was going on." I match his breezy tone.

He laughs. "I'm Se'jan." He's not wearing bracelets, but he taps his wrists together as if he were.

"Andeshe." I mimic his gesture. "So, what did happen with the match?" I incline my head back toward the circles as one competitor dodges out of the other's reach. "I'd have thought being tall would give you more of an advantage."

His face goes blank, ironic mask falling away. "I'm not tall."

He's a full head taller than I am and noticeably taller than almost everyone around us. I tilt my head back to look into his face.

"*She's* tall." He stabs a finger toward a woman standing near us. "I'm not." There's no lightness in his voice now.

"Oh." The woman he's pointing to is clearly shorter than he is. I don't understand.

"Those are the tall people: him, her, her…and him." Se'jan's finger stabs out again, pointing to four people who are, I suppose, above average height for this group. Maybe. Almost everyone here is taller than I am. "The rest of us are short," he continues. His eyes bore into mine, as if me acknowledging this the most important thing in the world. "Except for him," he adds, pointing to a genuinely tall man who is attempting to pass out fliers.

I force myself to nod. That's enough cultural differences for today. Awkward silence descends.

"At any rate," Se'jan says, reassembling his mask of indifference, "ijendra's fun. You should try it sometime."

I stretch my lips slightly.

"It's not all getting picked on," he continues, "just us interlopers."

Right. One of the women entering the ring in front of

us says something to the other, who laughs and claps her on the back. What must it be like for Se'jan to watch that easy camaraderie extinguish rather than be extended to him?

"Why do you do it?" I ask him. "If it means you have to put up with that?"

His expression slips just the tiniest fraction. "I'm not one to be driven out. They'll have to try harder than that to get rid of me."

"Have they?" I'm almost afraid to ask.

He curls his arm in an exaggerated flexing motion again. "Nothing I can't handle." But the smile that stretches his lips doesn't soften the wariness in his eyes.

The competitors in front of us clash, then draw apart again. It's a relief when the end of the match gives me an excuse to retreat.

Chapter Fourteen
Ya'shul

T he eldest experimental goat bumps its head against the post of the fence around its pen and gives an irritable bleat.

"Patience," I tell it, dumping a second bucket of kitchen scraps over the railing. "You're getting the good stuff." The goatherd Nareen's family pays to care for the goats has clearly already been here, but I'm the one who brings them treats, even if it does mean trudging all the way across the ridge from the southern cliffs that house my family's cave. The goat buries its face in the scraps, and I reach over the fence to scratch its ears. In the dawn light, its glow from the prior day has faded, leaving it nothing but a normal farm animal.

Somewhere in the orchard beyond the pen, a ptercel calls, its whistling chirp answered by another farther away. It alights on one of the branches that extends out over the edge of the cliff, then flares its wings as the branch bobs under its weight. Its song warbles across the lightening sky.

A shape at the base of the tree stirs, and my breath catches in my throat. Lightly blanketed in the predawn mist, Nareen's familiar profile turns to peer upward into the branches. She stretches her neck, rubbing at a tense muscle, then she settles back against the tree once more, face turning toward where Treverel's distant mountain peeks through a gap in the ridge to our north, the capital buried in its heart.

A surge of anger scatters my tenuous calm. *Don't you have everything now?* All I want is a few moments of my old peace. Without her here, I could pretend that the clock had rewound, that the mists are about to part on a different sequence of days, ones when everything goes right.

She scrubs her hands over her face, then drops her head into them. The normally proud lines of her body slump with dejection. Despite all my anger, something twinges in my chest as she wraps her arms around her knees. For all that she claims the backbiting of politics doesn't get to her, I know her too well to believe it. The backlash to her unexpected elevation by the priestesses took us all by surprise. It's only belatedly that the other families that live lower on the cliff face have begun to rally around her. She sighs and rearranges her limbs, rubbing at her stomach. In the faint light, an ear-stud that marks a confirmed pregnancy twinkles. She's said nothing about the challenges of that either.

The goat bleats, butting its head against the now empty bucket. Nareen looks up with a start and goes still when she sees me. Her back straightens as much as it can, armor falling back into place.

"Ya'shul. I didn't see you there."

I know how much she wants to be strong for the people around her, but I can't help feeling a little hurt. Once she would have opened up more to me, at least. The goat butts the bucket again, and I pull it away, approaching

Nareen with tentative steps. The ptercel's tail ripples, and a long-buried memory tugs at me. I know better than to ask if she's all right, but in the liminal space of dawn, I can't quite let go of our past.

The ptercel lashes its tail again, then snaps its wings out, gliding out into the canyon like a kite.

Oh. Oh, that. Memory spools out behind it like the string of the old kite I found tucked in the closet I was cleaning. I'd been maybe seventeen, desperate to prove myself too old for toys, but still young enough to find the break in the clouds during the rainy season irresistible. Nareen had been at her desk when I'd clomped through the lab's main room, her head bent to expose the nape of her neck. Tickling it with the tail of the kite had been more temptation than I could resist, even when she batted it away.

I don't remember what I asked her, hitching my hip onto the edge of her desk and swinging my free leg, only that she'd leaned back, running her hands through her hair, revealing the same shadows under her eyes that I've seen too often since the festival. She's always been driven, acutely conscious of the unusual honor of getting to apprentice with another family and too stubborn to let anything get in the way of making her family proud.

Somehow, I lured her out under the open sky, far away from buildings and responsibilities, far away from the carafes of caffeine she's always tempted to substitute for the midday rest. As we wrestled the kite into the sky, her face cleared until, by the time I managed to get the kite stuck in a tree, she'd relaxed enough to laugh at the mishap. She insisted I boost her up into the tree to get it, and when she shimmied down again, her eyes were sparkling with mischief.

"I said I'd get it," she told me. "I never said anything about giving it back." She darted off, waving it at me, until I belatedly gave chase. We'd dodged among the trees until a lucky swipe snagged me the tail of the kite and I'd managed to reel us together. Her face lit in a smile so different from her normal expression that it took my breath away. She shifted, and the length of her body pressed against mine, chest still heaving from our exertions.

"All right." She let go of the kite. "But now that your hands are full…" A playful gleam in her eye was my only warning before she launched herself at me, fingers wriggling on my sides. Where I, unlike her, am not ticklish.

"Never attack your own weakness," I breathed in her ear as she doubled over, giggling and clutching her ribs to protect them.

Still laughing, she hooked a foot behind my ankle and barreled into me, knocking me flat on my back in the soft grass as she sprawled on top of me. Her gaze slid to my mouth, and her laughter faded. She shifted her body against me, and a surge of desire pooled in my groin. She'd said my name, voice rough with desire, and I'd tipped my head back, opening myself up to her. Her breathing had quickened, and her fingers had moved up to entangle in my hair.

"I—I should let you up," she'd told me, but she'd made no move to rise. Instead, her eyes focused on my lips again, and she licked her own. Ever so slowly, she'd peeled herself off me and straightened, holding out her hands to grasp mine. We'd stood there for a heartbeat, under a similar tree to this, fingers intertwined. We never spoke of that moment, but ever after that, each accidental brush of her hand against mine sent fire thrumming through my veins.

I close my eyes. Other memories crowd in, of laughter and playfulness, of our heads bent together working on a thorny problem. Of her body sliding against mine, and the bitter taste of defeat.

"I miss you." The words fall from my lips. I know they don't make sense, not when we see each other almost every day, but after a moment, she nods.

"I wish we could talk the way we used to," she answers.

I feel every brick in the wall that has sprung up between us. "About what?"

"I don't know. Everything."

We never talked about everything. Not when too raw of an emotion would send her scurrying to change the subject. But at least we used to talk about everything else.

She reaches out, slipping her fingers into mine. It's the first time we've touched since the storeroom. Some of the old warmth still thrums there.

"Why did you stop talking to me?" she asks quietly.

I don't remember choosing to, but I suppose I did.

"Because everything I tell you gets stolen from me." The truth is too blunt, but I don't have it in me anymore to prevaricate.

Her fingers twitch in mine. "I didn't—"

I shake my head sharply. I don't want to hear it.

"It'll be different this time," she says instead. "When I go to the capital, I'll tell everyone what you did. And that you're a scientist in your own right, not just an assistant."

I raise my eyes to the mountain in the distance. She means well. If only she thought I deserved more than a pittance.

"It's not the same," she coaxes. "Not without you."

I know. I've missed it, too, the way we would bounce ideas off each other, the full focus of her attention as she pondered something I said, her face lighting up when a concept clicked into place. And the lab has missed me, though they don't realize it. For all that Kiu dismissed my wilder speculations, I'm sure there's more to phosfoz than slow, plodding effects on digestion that they've explored so far. Andeshe has brought me a remarkable number of samples from different native creatures. No one else has thought to do a brute-force comparisons of their genomes to determine what the more sun-resistant creatures have in common.

Should I tell her this? I've had to quash the urge to tell Nareen every twist and turn of the process. I never used to think about what I do the way a zoman does, as a bargaining chip to leverage for the greatest advantage. Our old closeness hovers just past my fingertips. Once, I would have trusted her. Do I still? I hesitate. I'd thought to wait until I was done, until there was no chance that someone could claim I'd done less than everything, but that will be ages from now, long after the solstice.

I square my shoulders and look her in the eye. "There's more to my idea, something I haven't told you."

She makes an encouraging noise.

I take a deep breath. "But I want something for it. If it works out, I want to go to the capital with you."

She does a double take. "Am I even allowed to share the prize?"

"You can't present what I'm going to tell you unless you take me with you." I've never been to the Treverel, but I can imagine the striations of the distant mountain growing larger and larger until the cave entrances nestled among them welcome me into the heart of power and sophistication. If only I'd thought to bargain earlier, before handing my work over to Kiu.

She searches my face, curiosity etching hers. "Something that impressive?"

"Promise me," I insist. "I'll show you what I have, but no one touches this data until there's a spot secured for me. If that doesn't happen, nothing." The results from this, at least, are stored on my 'glove and nowhere else.

She blinks. "Fine. If it's good enough, there should be a way to persuade someone."

A knot unwinds in my shoulders. I can make this happen. I can make things turn out the way they should have been.

"Come on." I scramble to my feet and reach out my hand to her. The dawn light gilds the edge of my outstretched fingers, reminding me of another hand, another dawn. "When we get back to the lab. I'll show you."

***

The lab door opens on a bustle of activity. There's no sign of Nareen's earlier vulnerability as she strides into the room. Se'jan is at the data terminal, and he looks up as we come in. She steers me over without hesitation, making shooing motions at him. He gestures at the molded sand and says something, but after a brief exchange, she waves him away. He unplugs his 'glove, bowing me toward the now blank terminal with exaggerated courtesy.

"What was it you wanted to show me?" she asks me.

I edge around where Se'jan now lounges against a

table with his arms crossed. *Don't look*, I want to tell him. He's Nareen's real guarantee, the one our families deemed good enough for her, the one whose connection to his politically prominent mother shows how seriously my family is supporting Nareen's. I shake my nerves away. *It's good enough. It has to be.* I plug in my 'glove, and the sand molds upward until the key portions of the pteradon's chromosomes are arranged in neat rows, tagged with similarities found in other creatures. I wait for the speculative look to kindle in Nareen's eyes as I describe the ways we might track down the key that would allow us not to depend so much on huddling underground for our safety. I've missed working with her, the excitement that coils in her shoulders when she pursues new knowledge, the way she listens to me as if I'm the only person in the world. I try not to look at Se'jan. I know what I've produced isn't perfect, but I'm not sure I can take any of his biting comments. *Let me prove myself*, I plead with him silently. *Let me get back on my feet before you have your fun.* My palms grow clammy as the silence stretches out.

Nareen leans past me to skim 'gloved fingers over the display, eyes unfocusing as the computer vibrates additional information against her hand. With a few taps, she calls up something from the central computer. The ridges and valleys of the chart shift, settling into more precise peaks, emphasizing subtly different locations.

"Some of those *are* the areas the original planetary gene survey identified," she says. She taps at the display, and a handful of other sites rise into relief. "Ah, I thought there were secondary sites."

Cold coils in my stomach. "The…original planetary gene survey?"

She nods. "Once things stabilized enough after the Landing, the Founders catalogued native flora and fauna. Part of that was recording all their different genomes as well. The starship had the capacity for it, and back then there was enough fuel that people were still traveling back and forth from the surface." Her gaze refocuses on me. "Did you not know? My ancestors were involved in the survey, it's part of the reason my family thought to apprentice me here."

Words stick in my throat. "Did—did they find anything?"

She shrugs. "Nothing much. There was another big push to reanalyze the data after everyone realized how damaging the solar storms are—trying to determine how the animals here survive at all—but nothing came of it. I mean, it's still interesting, but the people who have tried in the past haven't found anything useful."

Her words hit me like a blow to the gut. She swipes my analysis back into visibility and I wince. It looks like a child's scribbles in comparison to the real one.

"You said you'd collected samples from several different creatures?" she asks me.

"Andeshe did," I mumble.

She purses her lips. "That might be useful." She's straining to come up with something positive to say. "You might investigate if anything has changed in the last several hundred years," she suggests at last. Her tone is kindly, but my entire face burns. A child could do that.

Nareen asks Se'jan something, but I can barely make out the words through the roaring in my ears. I know better than to embark on a project without querying my family and the temple about past research. I *know* better, but I'd been so desperate to prove I could succeed on my own. The sound of their conversation fades into meaninglessness until all that's real to me is the sight of them. Nareen sits straight on her stool, explaining something to Se'jan, then stopping to absorb his reply. She moves her fingers against the sand, and all my work fades away, replaced with something better.

I push back from the counter, mumbling some excuse, and stumble across the lab as if I know where I'm going. The aisle ends in front of the mouse cages. *I—I can do better. Please, Goddess, tell me I can do better.* I grip the cage. Never mind going to the capital, I don't want to be nothing. I don't want to languish here, buried under the knowledge that I'm not good enough.

Below me, the pups crawl feebly through their shavings. Somewhere in their guts, microbes are multiplying, giving me one last chance to prove I'm more than everyone thinks I am. The wires of the cage bite into my palms. *Please, Goddess. Just one more chance.*

Chapter Fifteen

Andeshe

Peeling off my Uplander men's garb feels like sloughing off a too small skin. I take a breath, stretching my arms up and rolling my head in a slow circle that sends a line of crackles down my neck. Changing into my riding leathers feels like putting back on my old self, the woman who was confident and content and knew she had a valued place in the world. I fly too few errands these days, too busy trying to build connections here.

I approach Fizz, nodding to the women who are loading bales of fabric onto her back. The pteradon wriggles and twists her head toward me, abandoning her careful stillness as if she can sense my excitement about being in the air again. Only when one of the women chivvies her back into calm can the crew finish loading. They step back, and Fizz cocks her head at me, giving her wings a tiny flip.

"Feeling frisky today, huh?" I ask, climbing into the shoulder saddle and performing the last safety checks. Her energy is a relief. She gives a hop, none of her recent stiffness constraining her movements. Her upward launch is strong, her wings snapping outward in a powerful downward beat that sends Ikmeth tumbling into the distance, turning it into nothing more than a handkerchief of color that is overwhelmed by the massive folds of the mountain range around it. I urge her into a spiral, her wings cupping a rising column of air as we ride it up as far as we can go. Other cities glimmer on the tops of distant ridges, shrinking in comparison to the deep river valleys that separate them from each other. I can finally breathe again.

As the air thins, Fizz gives another flap, as if she can sense my desire to leave the Uplanders behind. Giving into impulse, I turn her, not northeast toward the settled area near the river's mouth, but into a long glide west toward where the heart of the range thrusts up into sheer, barren stone.

After a while, a chime sounds in my ear. "The shipment does need to make it to the capital *sometime*, Andeshe," says Auntie Haveo's amused voice.

"Yes, Auntie." Obediently, I signal Fizz to wheel. The narrow stream that cuts through the rocks beneath us must inevitably, like all its cousins, merge into the mighty river that spills out past the Uplander capital into the great inland delta beyond.

It's probably only my imagination that Fizz's wings beat slower as the signs of civilization become visible: terraced rice paddies that stair-step their way down a mountain upstream from Ikmeth, the distant clear patch in the forest that is our settlement, Ikmeth's clustered buildings. Seeing the gray stone again weighs on me all the more for my brief moment of freedom.

I'll make this work somehow. Fine, Uplanders don't

have a good way to talk about harms and restore abraded relationships. They have other things going for them. I swallow away the unpleasant taste in my mouth.

Fizz chirrups, and I return my attention to her. Whatever is coming, I'm in the air now. Ikmeth's canyon looms in front of us, and Fizz shimmies the tiniest amount, a faint purr vibrating below me. A slow smile spreads across my face. I'm in the air now, and that canyon would be *perfect* for speed twirls.

I give Fizz the signal she and I practiced perhaps too many times when we were younger. She pulls in a wing, and suddenly our flight path turns into a dizzying spiral that shoots us down the length of the valley. The sky, cliffs, and river flash overhead in rapid succession. Screaming with laughter, I signal her to pull up. I haven't let loose like that in *ages*. I pat my safety straps, rechecking them, then twist to look backward. A loose strap flaps in the wind. The blood freezes my veins. *The cargo's not breakable*, I remind myself, trying to calm my racing heart. *It'll be okay.* Dropping a bale of fabric in the river would be a hassle, but a fixable one, not like the accident that made me so compulsive about securing passengers. Still, the women who helped me load this shipment should have checked the strap. Irritation floods through me. I look around for a landing spot. I've followed the canyon nearly back to Ikmeth, but I'm coming in far below the clifftops. At least this part of the river runs calmly through a flat expanse of pebbles, and there's substantial distance between the walls of the canyon. It's not ideal for a pteradon to take off from, but it's possible as long as I can keep Fizz's downdraft from showering river water all over the cargo.

Wait! There. I direct Fizz to a large, uneven pillar that

is connected to the base of one of the steep walls of the canyon by a handful of boulders. The top is flat and provides at least a little height to launch from. I brace myself, keeping one eye on the loose bale, as Fizz flares her wings and brings her hind feet under her, catching the rock face and ensconcing us—and the bale—safely on the top of the pillar. At my direction, she delicately picks her way down the jumble of rocks to the riverbed. I glance upward. The wooden walkways that adorn Ikmeth's southern cliff face are almost directly above us, but if we scramble back up the pillar for launch, we shouldn't embarrass ourselves too badly in front of everyone.

I unhook myself from my harness and clamber back along her rigging to tighten the upper straps. Around me, dry trenches meander through the flat, pebbled plane marking the shifting course of the river that currently flows placidly through a narrow channel. Upstream from us is a cantilevered bridge of wood and rope, moveable if the stream changes its course. On the other side of the bridge, a cluster of unusually tall people are standing and watching me.

I stop. Behind the group is a stone fire pit surrounded by baskets of food and piles of plates. Someone crouches next to it, but they've paused in their task of arranging wood and kindling to stare at me. Cave openings dot the base of the cliffs behind them, and rope ladders and pulley systems descend from several of them.

Oh, crap. There are no caves on this side of the river, but the rock column I landed on has steps carved into it. *Did I just land in the middle of the Lowlanders' settlement? I did. I landed on their Goddess-blessed stage.* The group in front of me stands absolutely still, ranks stiff and closed against danger. Behind them, a parent snatches a child into the safety of one of the caves.

"Stay still, Fizz." I put all the emphasis I can muster into the accompanying hand signal, and she freezes. I slide down her haunch and crunch my way across the pebbles toward the group, pulling off the headgear and goggles that protect me from the wind and sun. Several more fire circles dot the valley floor behind them, radiating out from carved stairs that lead to a switch back path that wends its way up the hill. A handful of other people sit by them, watching me warily.

"Hullo," I call when I'm within shouting distance. "I'm sorry to disturb you. I had a bale come loose and needed to stop and re-secure it. I'll be on my way again momentarily."

The woman in front sends a meaningful look back up the valley that I came barreling down. She calls back, "So I see."

I raise an open palm. "Did I damage anything?" I glance around. I didn't think I did.

"No." But the tension doesn't lessen.

"Is there something that you need from me?" I venture.

"No. Just go."

I hesitate. That isn't closure. It's not forgiveness, nor is it the clearing up of a misunderstanding. It's the limbo of being unable to make repair for a harm I haven't caused. I force my neck to bend in acknowledgement of her wishes. *Fizz isn't dangerous!*

"Andeshe?" From the back of the crowd, another tall figure steps forward.

I squint. "Et'elark?" He's wearing a loose, emerald-green tunic utterly unlike the skintight garments I always see him in up-slope. His hair is unbound, and his movements are loose and relaxed.

The woman who greeted me, a leader of some sort, turns to him with a questioning look.

"This is Andeshe," he says to her. "We've met before." He turns to me. "Do you always fly like that?"

His relaxed curiosity eases something in the crowd.

"Not normally." I barely dare to breathe.

He jerks his chin at the bale, still precariously tilted. "Perhaps I should help get everything sorted out."

I know a peace offering when I hear one. "Thank you." I send a last look at the woman in charge. "Fizz is tame. She won't cause any problems."

The woman is still frowning, but Et'elark strides toward the bridge, and as if at his signal, the people at the back of the group start to drift away. The woman in charge stays where she is, tawny arms crossed in front of her chest.

"I didn't realize you were still flying," Et'elark says as he approaches me. His gaze roams over Fizz.

"Not often," I reply, "but it's nice to take a break sometimes."

The corner of his lip twitches upward. "Understandable."

"Am I taking you away from something?" I ask as we crunch back across the gravel. "I don't mean to impose if you're busy."

"No, not at all. It's my day off. And besides—" his eyes narrow— "I've never seen a pteradon up close, not properly. I'm not afraid of them."

I recognize that determination. "Would you like to meet her?"

His eyes widen marginally. "If it's not inconvenient." The words can't disguise the nerves in his voice.

"Fizz, flat!" I call to her, and she sweeps her head down to the valley floor. Et'elark inhales swiftly. "Fizz, still!" I remind her, and she ceases all movement except for the massive eye that rolls to examine us as we approach.

"Fizz, this is Et'elark," I tell her. "I work with him up top. Et'elark, this is Fizz, she's the pteradon I fly most often."

I reach up and scratch her eye ridge. "Would you like to touch her?" I ask Et'elark.

He swallows. His mouth opens, but no sound emerges. Slowly, he comes to stand next to me, and I take his wrist. His arm is solid with muscle, wiry hairs brushing against my palm. Under my fingers, his heartbeat races.

"She loves this," I tell him. I guide his hand to Fizz's eye ridge. Tentatively, he scratches. Fizz's eye closes in pleasure.

Unguarded awe spreads across his face. "Incredible," he breathes.

I hadn't realized how closed his expression normally was. "That means she's happy," I tell him softly. He strokes Fizz's leathery skin, then reluctantly pulls his hand away. My heart gives a little flip.

"I should secure the bale," I say, but neither of us moves. Impulsively, I turn to him. "Do you want to come flying with me?"

His eyes widen. I hold my breath, then a slow grin splits his face.

"Seize the day," he says. "Why not?"

I let out my breath, then show him how to mount the ladder up to Fizz's pillion saddle. His movements, though slow, are far less nervous than most of my first-time riders. He listens while I give him the standard safety lecture I give all passengers.

"I don't have riding leathers for you," I say, "but since I'm in front, that will protect you from the wind." I hand him the leather hood and goggles I was wearing earlier. "You can wear the face protection. I'll be fine without it for a flight." I've done it before, but I wouldn't subject a neophyte to watering eyes and a wind-burnt face—poor souvenirs of their first flight.

He pulls the gear on while I scramble along Fizz's back to refasten the bale. It's the work of a moment, then I make my way back up to her shoulders, working my way around him with a murmured apology to settle myself in the front saddle. I fasten Et'elark's safety straps, but then guide his arms around my waist anyway. His torso is solid against my back, hands firm against my stomach.

The woman is still watching us from across the bridge. "Could you warn your kin to shield her eyes? Fizz will kick up a substantial breeze this close to the ground."

His arms loosen for a little, and I see his 'glove wiggle by my waist. After a moment, he takes hold again.

"Ready?" I ask. His breath is warm against my ear as he murmurs his assent.

His arms become a vise around me as Fizz clambers back up the pillar, then he gasps as she flings herself into the air. I glance back—the loose pants the woman is wearing flap around her legs while she shields her eyes. Behind her, a basket goes flying, spilling food as it rolls, and I make a mental note to send something in recompense.

With labored beats, Fizz flaps to gain altitude until

we're once more high above Ikmeth. After one convulsive clutch, Et'elark loosens his grip to a gentle clasp. Fizz levels out into a slow glide, and I twist my neck back to catch an expression of pure exhilaration on his face.

"How do you not spend all your time doing this?" he shouts in my ear.

"I wish I could," I yell back. A dart of sorrow lodges itself under my breastbone. I shake it off and urge Fizz to surge forward. Behind me, Et'elark laughs with delight.

The flight to the capital is too short. We follow the meandering path of the river as it curves away from Ikmeth, becoming broader and deeper as other tributaries rush out of the network of mountain valleys to merge into it. Fizz banks around one last curve, and an isolated peak looms in front of us. At its foot, the last tributary thunders over a waterfall to roil the more placid waters of the main river before the combined waters begin their final trip out through the gap in the mountain range toward the desert beyond. A handful of boats are moored at the foot of the mountain.

"Is that Treverel already?" Et'elark breathes behind me.

I nod. The peak that holds the capital towers above its surroundings, separated from most of the rest of the range by the rivers that come together at its base. From this angle, we can see the layers of rock that have been thrust upward, tilting to form stripes that cut diagonally across the mountain's face. Wind and water have sculpted the great limestone band that bisects the mountain into a set of rocky spires that strain toward where the brighter of the two moons is visible in the daytime sky. Trees nestle in the cracks between them, vegetation clinging to what footholds it can before the harder rock at the mountain's peak rises too steeply for anything large to grow.

"Where do we land?" Et'elark asks in a hushed voice. The spires in front of us are carved into elaborate shapes that are echoed at every turn in the rock and vegetation. Even though I've seen it before, the effect is imposing, a display of extravagance that showcases the people socializing among them, the sun glinting off a wealth of chimes on their clothing. Each of the few dozen ridges sends only two formal representatives to the ruling council, but far more people are drawn to the lure of power and luxury that permeates the place. Even the austerity of the head branch of the priesthood, quartered deep in Treverel's heart, has done little to restrain the glitter of the lifestyle above them.

I bank Fizz around the mountain until the gentler slope on the far side becomes visible. Here the plantings and carvings are no less elaborate, but they frame wide shelves of rock that double as both landing pads and places for outdoor gatherings. Toward the base of the mountain, the decorations become more utilitarian, mostly ignored by tiny figures that swarm like ants around piled bags and boxes, hauling them one by one into the depths of the mountain.

I tap my earpiece onto the landing channel and state my identity and cargo. A crackly voice directs me to a pad on the mountain's lower slopes. Delicately, Fizz sets us down and flips back her wings.

"And that's that," I tell Et'elark. "That's flying."

He pushes back his goggles and swivels his head around him. With visible effort, he tries to resume his air of nonchalance.

"I'll just get these unloaded," I tell him, unbuckling my straps, "then we can head back via the scenic route."

He laughs. "Because that wasn't scenic?"

"Fizz can fly much higher without cargo." I unroll the ladder and start to clamber down.

"Do you need help unloading?" he asks.

I would never ask such a thing of a guest, but I do know how awkward it can be to sit there while everyone else bustles about. "If you like. There's no need, though." Tentatively, I smile at him.

An answering smile creeps across his lips before he drops his eyes to fumble with the safety straps. "I'm happy to," he says. "Thanks for the ride."

The head porter emerges from a nearby opening, and by the time I've finished consulting with him, Et'elark has already set to—scrambling back up to unfasten the bales. He blends seamlessly in with the other porters as they wrestle the awkward bundles off Fizz's back. Despite their height, the porters still need ladders. I'd never quite realized how precarious they were until I watch Et'elark balance on one only to have one of the more experienced porters wave him off to help haul the unloaded bales into a neat pile by the entrance.

After settling accounts with the head porter, I gather the loose cargo straps into their carry sack. Et'elark stands on the edge of the landing pad, staring off toward the plain beyond the mountains. Below, the slope falls away, with only a few low foothills interrupting the descent. Scrubby trees and brush coat the skirts of the mountain range, giving way at their base to parched sand. A strip of greenery traces the path of the river until, in the distance, it widens into a verdant inland delta that spills out across the desert in the wet season. Soon, the baking sun will evaporate it all, and life will go dormant again, but for now it gleams like a jewel.

"Spectacular, isn't it?" I murmur as I join him.

He jumps. "I was looking at the fields."

Closer to us, where the river flattens out beyond the trees, geometric strips of green and gold line the waterway. Tiny figures waver in the heat, working their way across a field of wheat that is slowly turning from grain to stubble.

Et'elark's golden-brown face is pensive.

"Have you ever seen anything so flat?" I ask him. Beyond the delta, the desert seems to stretch to the horizon, so different from the crumpled folds of the mountain range where I spend most of my time. "Every time I come here, I'm awestruck."

"I've worked there before," he says, jerking his chin toward the fields below us. Abruptly, he turns away. "I've seen it. Just not from the air."

He's quiet as we remount Fizz. A moment before I'm about to give her the signal to launch, he puts a hand on my arm.

"Do you know where the mines are?" he asks.

"The mines?" I say in surprise. "More or less. They're out of our way, though."

"Could you...could you point them out to me as we go?" He sounds oddly vulnerable.

"Sure," I tell him, mentally sorting through a route that will curve us north and west without taking us too much out of our way. Fizz launches, spiraling up a thermal and flapping her way even higher when it gives out. I pat her neck gently, silently promising her extra eye ridge scratches for working so hard. She settles into a steady rhythm of wingbeats as we arc north, Treverel fading into the distance as our shadow ripples over the jagged land below. It's lush for now, the moisture that the mountains force up to create the winter rains still lingering, but soon everything except the deepest-rooted trees will turn golden brown in the heat. A lump rises in my throat. The dry season is already getting longer as the storms approach. If this project doesn't work out, it won't be long before I'll have to send Fizz winging her way far beyond the mountain streams where we used to take respite from the heat. Alone. I breathe out, reminding myself to enjoy the time we have.

In the distance, sunlight glints off water. "There," I say, pointing. Rainbows dance in the spray of a waterfall that tumbles down a sheer rock face. At the top, a hydroelectric dam perches, backing up the river into a massive lake that nestles between two peaks. I've flown to the cave complex that houses Isel's clan's workshops a few times. The dam they draw power from is unmistakable. The mines should be in the mountain across the lake from them.

Et'elark doesn't say anything. I glance back at his face, but it's expressionless. He cranks his head back for a long time even after I turn Fizz and the sight of the dam is replaced by the rapids in the canyon below the waterfall.

"Any particular reason you wanted to see it?" I ask.

He hesitates. "I have a relative who's there."

"Oh, who?" I've met a handful of people from the workshops, but they've all been Isel's relatives.

For a moment, I think he hasn't heard me, then he replies, "My mother's sibling."

"What is…" I want to ask what his relative's role is

there, but I hesitate on the pronoun. "What gender are people when they're there? Or," I catch myself, "what gender is your relative permanently?"

He goes very still behind me. "Cee doesn't identify with any of the genders," he says. "Or use pronouns." His voice is guarded.

Easy enough to remember. "What's Cee doing there?" I hope the innocuous question will set him at ease.

His arms relax, then stiffen again. "Working," he says shortly. "I haven't been able to visit in…a long time."

He sounds like he doesn't want to talk about it, and I let the conversation lapse. Fizz's wingbeats start to labor, and I direct her into a calmer glide that dips us back under the level of the highest peaks until she finds a thermal that allows us to rise above them high enough to glide the rest of the way back to Ikmeth.

"Is it all right if I drop you off up top?" I ask Et'elark. "Fizz is getting tired, and the riverbed is a tough take off." The long path down to the base of Ikmeth's southern cliffs is a bit of a hike, but I don't want to overstrain Fizz, not when her good days are getting rarer.

He nods his acquiescence, and Fizz back wings into a delicate landing on the cleared ground adjacent to our settlement. I help Et'elark down, clucking at Fizz when she tries to make her way over to her roost with her harness still on. She settles down to wait patiently for me to strip off her gear.

I look around and sigh as all the worries I left on the ground reach out to suck at me again.

"Thank you for taking me flying." Wonder softens Et'elark's voice.

"Of course," I say, my spirits rising. "I enjoyed it. I

was just wishing I could spend all day up there."

His lips twist. "Ready to be gone from here?"

I wish I had that choice. Fizz nudges me, blissfully unconcerned about the future. "I'll do what I have to do," I tell Et'elark.

"Don't we all," he murmurs back. He tugs at his clothing, and I realize that it looks out-of-place outside of his village. Et'elark's body language is constricting, too. For all that we're alone on the landing field some distance from even my family's temporary settlement, his movements are tighter and more careful than those of the confident man who strode across the bridge over the river.

"Do you…find it difficult being in Ikmeth sometimes?"

His lips stretch, but it's too tight to be called a smile. "Only sometimes?"

I snort.

"It's not a place where I can be myself," he says at last.

My breath puffs out. "Yes," I say, "that's exactly it." The more I'm there, the more cautious I become about acting in ways I would never have thought twice about at home.

I raise my eyes to his. *He knows.* Relief surges through me. Someone here gets it.

Silence lapses, but he doesn't turn to go. His eyes are warm. "Come to dinner with me." His offer sounds impulsive. "Next Restday—no, I'm working then—the one after that."

"I'd like that."

His teeth flash whitely as he smiles. "Good." He reaches over and claps me on the shoulder. "In the meantime, carve out a space where you can be at home in your own skin. You can't thrive if you're tiptoeing around everyone's judgment all the time." He gestures to the settlement behind us. "Do you have that here?"

"Yes," I tell him. *For now.* Despite the ongoing construction, Auntie Haveo moved the first of us to the handful of completed caves a few days ago. My eyes range over the traditional structures of carved timber and painted leather. I volunteered to be one of the last to abandon the familiar whisper of wind and glow of light for caves that will always seem lifeless and austere, no matter how many carvings eventually adorn them.

"That's good."

He bids me farewell, and I watch him disappear toward the woods. It's only a matter of time before the last of these buildings are disassembled and our transition is complete. A shiver runs down my spine. I strip the rest of Fizz's tack off her, then lean over to hug her neck, praying that one thing, at least, doesn't have to change.

CHAPTER SIXTEEN
YA'SHUL

I clutch the cage of sacrificial mice under my arm as I stride along the path to the Wanderer settlement. *This will work.* Modifying a single celled organism isn't as dramatic as I'd hoped for, but it means something. It means that I will be the one who made it possible for pteradons to stay here. Surely that counts for something.

Ya'kinem's voice echoes in my memory: *I don't see why you have to prove yourself. Everything Nareen is doing was your idea.* He'd set the beaker down with more force than he should have.

Even his honest outrage hasn't been enough to salve the burn of humiliation. I've been overhearing snippets of the careful work Nareen's team has been doing to pin down what phosfoz does. My own efforts were paltry in comparison. Ya'kinem may have protested otherwise as he helped me double check the eukaryotes I bioengineered into the guts of these mice, but that doesn't change reality.

This, however—this will work. I shift the mouse cage to my other arm. The modified cells absorb phosfoz, binding it into a harmless compound that passes right through the mice. There won't be anything in their flesh for the pteradons to react to, I'm sure of that. Ya'kinem and I checked everything we could think of.

Andeshe and Fizz are waiting for me on the far side of their settlement, down the path by the pile of rubble that's the dumping ground for the waste from carving caves. The Wanderer is dressed as a woman again, not only outfitted in flying leathers, but also accompanied by everything else she might need to handle the pteradon: goggles, thick gauntlets, and a wheelbarrow with a shovel sticking out of it. For cleanup, I presume. I hope it won't be needed. The pteradon seems unconcerned, cocking its head to eye me with its usual curiosity.

I thrust the cage at Andeshe, then retreat out of splatter range. Andeshe waves me back to put on my goggles.

Here goes nothing. I wrap my arms around myself and avert my eyes as Andeshe kills the mice as humanely as possible, pausing briefly in prayer over each one. Fizz swallows the first one in a single gulp, the tiny body disappearing into its maw like a crumb. We wait.

When nothing happens, Andeshe tosses in another and, after an additional wait, another until the last of them is gone. I hold my breath, but no torrent of sickness seems imminent.

"Do you think that was enough for the trial?" I call across the distance. The quantity of mice seemed excessive in the lab, but it's hardly anything in comparison to the pteradon's great size.

Andeshe nods, eyes staying on Fizz. More time passes.

"I think...I think that might have worked." Andeshe sounds like she doesn't quite believe it herself. She gives Fizz a considering look. "She's keeping them down.

Pteradons have very sensitive stomachs. Normally, if she's going to react, she'll vomit them back up immediately.

Pride fills me. There are more tests to do, of course. Getting calories is one thing, getting proper nutrients is another, but it's a start. This work matters. I push up my goggles.

The pteradon gives its head a sharp shake. Its beak clacks open and closed a few times, then it shakes its head again.

"Fizz? What is it, girl?" Andeshe reaches for the pteradon.

Fizz's beak opens, and its tongue lolls out like a bloated worm. It shakes its head again, so violently that Andeshe is forced to retreat, then swipes at its neck with a wing claw. A choking noise emerges from its mouth.

"She can't breathe!" Panic edges Andeshe's voice. The giant beak gaps again, but all that emerges is the gasping whistle of obstructed breath. It claws at its throat.

"No, you'll hurt yourself! Stop!"

The pteradon pays her no heed. Its thrashing worsens, wings half opening, head thrown back in a frenzied pant. Andeshe shouts something into a dislodged earpiece, then drops it, scrambling for Fizz's harness. She pulls herself up just as the swipe of a wing claw opens a gash in the pteradon's neck. Blood splatters over her as she clings to its neck.

The beast collapses, its sides heaving in futile gasps for air. Andeshe slides down and cradles the giant head where it lies sprawled in the dust, beak open, swollen tongue twitching out. The great beast's wheezing becomes a choking noise, the only sound in the clearing. Its blood turns the ground into mud. I grope at my hip, searching for the injection pen I used to carry before Ya'kinem got old enough to manage his allergic reactions for himself. There's nothing there.

Andeshe looks up, frantically searching the clearing. They land on me where I stand—hands empty. As if a human-sized dose could have stopped anaphylactic shock in such a gigantic creature to begin with.

Oh, Goddess, I killed it! Andeshe opens her mouth, and my nerve breaks. I sprint for the path, scrambling over rubble, pumping my legs as if speed will allow me to outrun whatever accusation Andeshe is about to voice. A group of Wanderers appear in my path, hands full of bandages. I dodge around them and then I'm gone, past the Wanderer settlement, past the orchard, out into the dusty, sun-hot, scrub-covered slopes. Finally, my legs give out and I drop to the ground, breath coming in heaving gasps. *What have I done?*

Chapter Seventeen
Ya'shul

The eye of the sun stares down at me, unblinking and merciless.

You killed it. The accusation Andeshe didn't voice reverberates through my head, anyway. I writhe away from the thought, but the sun offers no respite and no escape. *You killed it because you're not good enough. That's why you weren't given a real pledge. That's why Nareen is the one going to the capital. You're not good enough. You've never been responsible for something on your own, and this is why. You don't know what you're doing. You never have.*

I curl inward, but I can't run from myself.

I didn't mean to! I was trying to help.

Were you? the inner voice jeers. *Just like U'kylay tries to "help" light burners in the lab. Face it: What you've had is all you deserve. This is what happens when you try to reach for what you're not.*

No! No! I try to push the voice back, but it beats down as inexorably as the sun's rays.

You thought this project would change everyone's mind, the voice continues, *that it would get you a real pledging ceremony at the solstice, where everyone acknowledged you as her equal. Too bad that everyone was right about you in the first place. You're nothing. Good for a quick fumble in the storeroom, nothing else.*

My eyes burn. I swallow around the lump in my throat.

Go ahead and cry, the voice mocks. *Women go through childbirth dry eyed, but you can't even handle reality.*

Enough. That's enough. I push the thoughts away. Grass stems crinkle as I dig my fingers into the soil beside me. I tug one of them free of the earth, then another, until the thoughts start to recede. A line of weedy bodies spirals out from where I'm sitting, and finally I stand, ripping up handfuls of the drying grasses, relishing the sharp edges against the skin of my palms. Panting, I yank up another, then stop to suck on my abraded thumb. In the distance, a puzzled goat stops chewing to look at me.

I'm not useless. I fling myself down onto the dirt and stare back at the unblinking sky. *I did impressive things once, didn't I?* I plead. It gives back no answer.

Crunching sounds disturb the whisper of the grass in the breeze. The footsteps come closer, and Se'jan's face wavers into view. I close my eyes. He's the worst person who could have found me. Except for all the others.

"You have dirt on your face," he tells me.

I swipe at it, but from the feel, I suspect I simply added more. I must be a mess, sprawled in a frenzy of torn-up grass stalks.

He rustles through the grass, then lowers himself to sit by my shoulder. "It's not dead."

The words don't register for a moment. I push myself up on one elbow. "It's not?"

"No. Though not for your lack of trying."

Years of experience mean I barely even twitch at the jab.

"Then I didn't kill it."

"So I said. It just flopped around in terror until the reaction passed. It's mostly recovered. It's resting now."

"That's good." Relief turns my limbs to water. *I didn't kill it.* Breath enters my lungs again. "Thank you."

He says nothing. I stare up at the sky, too wrung out to move. My awareness returns. Insects buzz in the grass, a wisp of cloud drifts across the sky, gradually reshaping itself. The fact of Se'jan's presence. Knowing to tell me this. A thread of unease coils itself in my stomach again.

"How—how did you know to look for me?"

"Oh, I don't know. All the field hands who saw you running like your life depended on it? The giant trail of crushed vegetation that you blundered through?"

I sit up. A trail of broken stems and branches leads right to me. I hadn't even noticed the stinging on my face and arms. One of my sleeves is ripped.

"No, I mean…" I think of the scene I left, and the words fade away.

"Ya'kinem was looking for you. The Wanderers were in an uproar."

Oh, shit. Everyone knows, then. Ya'kinem can't keep his mouth shut to save his life. I moan and bury my head in my hands. Andeshe hating me is going to be just the start. Images of my family's reaction flash through my head. *Oh, Goddess. I am never getting pledged out.* Not to Nareen, not to anyone. It's only as hope dissolves that I realize how hard I've been clinging to it. Maybe someday. When I'm fifty. When the storms are a distant memory and people can afford to make mistakes again.

If only the ground would swallow me. The future crumbles like dust. I can't even muster the energy to brace myself for Se'jan's next cutting comment.

"Do you need a drink?" he asks.

Drinking is his solution to everything. I shouldn't encourage him.

"Yes," I say at last. "That sounds better than anything I've come up with."

He stands there looking down at me. When I don't move, he extends a hand. I flop one of mine up into his, and his firm grip pulls me to my feet.

"Come on," he says. "This way."

Chapter Eighteen
Ya'shul

Drinking doesn't fix anything. I knew that even before I woke up with my head throbbing and my eyes sticky.

"Up from your beauty rest?" Se'jan's voice is light and mocking in the darkness of our room. I wince. He goes quiet while he's drinking. It's the day after that his tongue is sharpest. I roll myself up tighter in my blankets. Maybe if he goes away, I can never come out again.

He prods me with a toe. "Get up. You have a visitor."

My eyes snap open. "Who?" The time on my 'glove still says early morning.

"Andeshe. You know, the one whose pteradon you nearly killed."

I push myself upright. Even the spears lancing through my head aren't enough to distract me from the hollow feeling in my gut.

"Come on." Se'jan hauls me to my feet. "Let's get you bathed and presentable before you go take your lumps. The family has a reputation to maintain. Grandmother may not care very much about this contract, but that doesn't mean you can ruin it entirely."

The damage I've done goes without saying. I squeeze my eyes shut, but he marches me down the hall to the mercifully empty baths. The hot water and the hangover remedy he presses into my hand clear my head, but that only allows my thoughts to pick up where they left off. In the dim light, he lounges by the edge of the sunken pool, watching me as I duck my head under and sputter again to the surface.

"Did you have to screw everything up?" His words drop into the silence like rocks.

I duck under again, but I can only stay under for so long before the need to breathe forces me up to the surface again.

"I realize it's perhaps overly generous to assume you were thinking anything at all," he says when I emerge, "but I have to ask: What *were* you thinking?"

I'm too numb to do more than twitch at the needling. "The bacteria—the ones that concentrate phosfoz. I put them in mouse guts to intercept it. I thought—I thought if that worked, we could do the same thing in other animals and that would make them okay for the pteradons to eat. The modified phosfoz Earth animals create is what's causing the problem." It seemed so sensible at the time.

His head comes up. "And where exactly did you think the phosfoz would go once it was concentrated?"

I blink. "Out."

"Or in. The biology of digestion is ridiculously complicated. Almost as complicated as immunology. What were you *thinking?*"

I sag back into the water.

"Have you worked with any of the biology of this planet before?" he asks.

"Yes! The bacteria. That was the start of my whole project with Nareen."

"Bacteria." He snorts. "You lucked out and discovered one gene, then spent all your time working with Earth animals that we have *millennia* of data about. Do you know how long it takes to make any headway with a creature that's almost completely new to you? *Years.* At a minimum."

"But it was just—"

"But it was just!" he mimics. "You never did realize how extraordinarily lucky you were on your first project. You can't luck out like that all the time."

A lump rises in my throat. "I didn't—"

"What did you tell that poor Wanderer? That you'd have something by the end of the season?"

I don't say anything.

"Ya'shul." Exasperation drips from the word. "If the entire lab worked on it and we were extraordinarily lucky, we *might* have something viable before the storms hit. Maybe."

A lump rises in my throat. That can't be true. "I thought—" My voice comes out in a whisper.

"You *didn't* think," he corrects.

I close my eyes. Clothing rustles, then Se'jan drops his feet into the water with a faint splash. Tiny waves lap at my neck.

"Why didn't you ask me?" he presses. "Or Mother? Or anyone other than your fool of a brother who wouldn't know an immune response if it bit him in the ass?"

"Mother's retired. And you're..." He's sarcastic, blunt, insightful, pushy.

"I'm what?"

"You're pledged to Nareen." The truth forces its way out of me. I look away from his wiry silhouette, crisply put together even after a night of dissipation. The living example of what I've failed to be.

"You think I wanted that?"

My skin prickles despite the warmth of the water. I never know what Se'jan wants, not when he hides himself behind mockery and sarcasm. But this? "Of course. Wouldn't anyone?"

"Of course," he mocks. "Because my highest goal in life is to be an interchangeable prick in the darkness." His voice drops. "I don't know about you, little cousin, but when I have sex with someone, I want them to know it's me. I don't want nothing to matter except my family name and my mother's position on the council."

I close my mouth with a click.

"Why do you *think* I try to avoid First Pledges?" he asks with uncharacteristic bitterness. "I did my best to queue this one up for you, but no, you had to go and screw it up."

"I—you what?"

He snorts. "Who talked you up? Who told Orzea-lun about how excellent his cousin in the next booth was? Who warned you to think about your Goddess-damned *audience* instead of just saying whatever came to your head like you always do? I did what I could, but no one can do your presentation for you. You were the one who needed to close the deal."

"But—but Orzea-lun picked you. They thought your presentation was better." A lump rises in my throat. *It was better.*

Se'jan's voice is hard. "I'm not going to pretend to be

less than I am, cousin, even for you. It's bad enough that the one time I exert myself to praise someone else's work, Orzea-lun comments on how *docile* I've become." He snorts. "As if. I should have kept my mouth shut. Maybe they'd have remembered my youthful shenanigans instead."

"You really didn't want to be pledged to Nareen?" I haul myself out of the water and reach for a towel.

"What did I just say? If I'd been able to find a way, I would have snuck you in there in my place." My jaw drops as he continues, "Then you'd just have had to deal with the woman you've been mooning after for ages thinking she was making love to someone else."

"She would have known!" I struggle to pull my clothes on over my still damp skin as he rises and drapes the towel over the rack.

"All of us smell the same in the dark."

"Nonsense!" I pursue him down the hall and up the stairs. Nareen and I have always been special to each other.

"I bet you." We reach the entry chamber, and he pulls open the door to the outside.

A squat Wanderer stands on the ledge, hands folded against the stomach of the flying leathers that mark her as a woman. I freeze. Despite cleaning, the morning light bouncing off the canyon behind her highlights an irregular discoloration blotching the left side of the garment.

"Andeshe." I force the word out.

"We need to talk." Her voice is soft, matter of fact.

Oh Goddess. What do I even say? Se'jan steps to my side, and I clutch at him for support, my fingers biting into the muscle of his forearm.

"Accidents do happen," my mother cuts in from the

other side of the ledge. "I've told you we can't make guarantees." Their voice is clear and sharp.

Andeshe flicks her fingers in acknowledgement, but her eyes are still on me. "You owe me an explanation." She doesn't look angry, only expectant. And firm. Her hands reach out. "Come for a walk with me."

Se'jan and my mother exchange a look. For all my sins, I can feel the moment my family closes ranks, protecting me against this outsider. The urge to duck back inside surges over me, to vanish back into the depths of the family and let my kin form a wall between me and the world. The world that I will never be allowed to try myself against again.

I take a deep breath and step forward. "All right." What other option is there? Cower at home forever? My mother stirs, but I shake my head. This is my responsibility.

I follow Andeshe off the ledge and along the series of wooden walkways that connect our dwellings to where the cliff turns into an irregular hillside shallow enough to support grass and scrub and a dusty path. We climb upward in silence, alone but for the herd of grazing goats and their shepherd in the distance. Moving loosens my muscles, and the still gentle sunlight warms my back as Andeshe turns off the path and pushes through the grass to the foot of a large tree that overlooks the grassy slope. She settles herself under it and motions me to sit next to her as she looks off across the valley. I follow her gaze to the distant cliffs. Despite everything, a tiny bit of their serenity seeps into me.

"What happened?" Andeshe's voice is gentle, but implacable. Her hands are cupped together in front of her in an oddly formal gesture.

I drop my eyes to where my own hands twist around each other in my lap. "I'm sorry."

"For what?" There's no accusation in her voice, only a gentle insistence that I confess.

Do I have to spell it out? A lump rises in my throat. "That I almost killed your pteradon." I know what Fizz means to Andeshe. "I didn't mean to. I didn't think it would do that."

She sits silently for a moment. "I was scared as hell," she says finally. "When Fizz was flopping around like that, I thought she was going to die."

I squirm. "I know, I'm sorry."

She looks faintly surprised, then raises a hand. "Let me finish naming the impact first, that's most of what I need."

I nod, looking down at the grass, its seed pods swaying in the wind. I clench my hands together rather than picking at it.

"I'd wondered about this risk," she continues. She waves at the distant goats. "I asked Nareen and her family and the people who herd the goats for them about what goats eat and what happens to them. Reactions like this are a possibility."

I squeeze my eyes shut. Of course, Andeshe has been talking to everyone.

"What happened?" Andeshe's voice is low, intent. "I thought for sure that if I knew about the need to test for severe reactions to new foods, that you would know to do so, too. I thought that when you reassured me things would be fine, it was because you'd already done those tests, not that you were brushing me off. You broke that trust. Why?"

Her words sear a path down my spine to lodge until they lodge in my gut. I curl inward. Some of Andeshe's hundreds of questions had brought up something about this. I'd been too caught up in how close we were to success to bother with them.

You broke my trust. "I'm sorry," I whisper. Haven't I said that enough?

A finger on my chin tips my head up until I meet Andeshe's puzzled eyes.

"I know you're sorry," she says. "But what I'm asking is for you to help me make sense of what happened."

I turn my head away, looking off across the sloping grass.

"I thought I could do it." The words pull themselves out of me like shards of glass. "By myself. I thought it would impress everyone." *So much for that*, the voice in the back of my head whispers. *You're useless. A failure.* I swallow against the lump rising in my throat.

"And that was important to you?" Andeshe's voice is gentle, curious.

"Of course." I look up in surprise. "After the festival—it was a disaster."

"How so?" She cocks her head.

"No one was impressed by what I did. They saw it as Nareen's accomplishment only." Her insistence that I downplay my contribution still burns. "Nareen's family head didn't even think I was good enough to be pledged to her."

That's because you're not, the voice whispers. My fingers clench. *See what happened? You're not good enough.*

Andeshe's head tilts. "But everyone was impressed with Nareen's presentation, yes?"

I nod.

"And you did the same thing."

I nod again.

"So what was different about yours?"

I hesitate a long time before responding. "She did do more with the actual goats." Truths I've never admitted force themselves to my lips. "They're the more complex organisms. I just isolated the gene from bacteria."

She cocks her head. "'Just?' Is there so little credit to go around? Neither one of you could have accomplished what you did without the other."

I glance away. "I didn't talk myself up the way she did," I mumble. "I should have, and I *didn't*." Anger swells within me. At myself or Nareen, I don't even know.

"Why not?"

Excavating an old wound is just as raw and painful as when it was fresh. *Do I even know anymore?* "I just fucked up," I mumble. The layers of hurt are too tangled now to even sort through. "I should have told people what I could do," I say, finally. "I promised myself I would going forward. That I would never pretend to be less capable than I am."

Andeshe's head tilts in a long, considering look. "How is that working out for you?"

I stare at her, then bitter laughter gushes out of me like fluid from a lanced wound. "Not so well," I tell her. "Now I'm just running around killing pteradons because I think I can do more than I can. People still don't respect me." I thump my forehead against my hand. "Orzea-lun wouldn't have picked me, anyway. It's unseemly to boast."

Andeshe sits there for a long moment, watching me wrestle with my thoughts. "It sounds like there was no right choice," she says finally, "only wrong ones."

My gut rebels at the thought. "There must be something I can do. Some way to succeed."

"And if there isn't?"

"There must be. I just have to be good enough to find it." The alternative stirs menacingly in the back of my mind. *This can't take years.* I raise my eyes beseechingly to hers. "No more mess-ups. I promise." *I can do this.*

Andeshe doesn't nod. Instead, she purses her lips, expression unreadable. "That's not what I need from you," she says at last.

What?

"You can't promise you'll never make mistakes," she continues. "You can only become so afraid of them that you're paralyzed."

Her words make no sense. I shake my head.

Her forehead creases. When I say nothing, she leans in. "Listen, has Nareen ever made mistakes?"

I blink. "Of course." The last time I was in the lab, Se'jan was talking her out of a truly terrible research plan.

"Big ones?"

"I—I suppose. I mean, there was that time when she was a new apprentice when she tripped the electrical circuit one of the refrigerators is on, and one of my sister's experiments was unrecoverable. My mother was furious." I'd forgotten that.

"And yet, she's still the 'most promising apprentice your mother has ever had.' She gets to be wrong and bounce ideas off other people and get feedback and correct them, and everyone still thinks she's an amazing scientist. Why does making one mistake turn you into a permanent failure?"

"You don't think I am?"

"No."

"But I almost killed Fizz!"

"Yes. And what I want from you is to make amends, not collapse in shame. Not to double down on the habits that caused you to make the mistake in the first place." Her eyes bore into mine.

"What kind of amends?"

"Fizz is all right. I know you weren't trying to hurt her, but you were careless. It was in your power to prevent this from happening, and you didn't. Why?"

Her bluntness scours my raw edges, but it also braces me, demanding blunt honesty in return.

"I could have told other people in the lab what I was working on and gotten feedback." Se'jan, Nareen, certainly my mother. They would all have known. "I didn't because Nareen has stolen all my projects, and I didn't want her to get this one, too." There, that's honest. A final piece of the truth forces its way out. "I thought I had to prove myself by myself, or I wouldn't be as good as she is."

"Ah." Andeshe draws the word out, filling it with understanding. "That's what I need you to work on, then. Whatever stopped you from getting the help you needed to succeed, I need you to put Fizz's wellbeing ahead of it. Can you do that?"

I open my mouth to say I will, then close it again. That is much harder than a mere apology.

Andeshe is watching me closely. "What's stopping you?"

"Getting help…" I'm reluctant to even say the words. "It means I'm not good enough to do it on my own."

She cocks her head. "Does anyone in your lab actually

do major projects by themselves? It doesn't seem like it."

"Of course, they—" I stop. The memories that grate at me are ones of Nareen with other people, surrounded by the affirmation and support that should be mine. "My grandmother." But even as I say the words, they ring false. My grandmother got *sole credit* for the life-extension therapies that solidified our place as one of the most respected families on the ridge. That's different. I'm old enough to know how many people must have worked on that behind the scenes.

Andeshe is still watching me.

"No," I confess to her. "There's no way anyone could expect to pull off something like this on their own. It's completely unreasonable." Bands of tightness loosen around my chest. My first deep breath in weeks floods into my chest.

"Then that's what I need you to change. And when you can't, because that will happen, I need honesty. I would rather you confess that you are ashamed of not doing something than that you cover it up."

Like I did. She doesn't need to say it.

"Like I did." The words release something I hadn't known I was clinging to.

She nods, but there's no accusation in it, only acknowledgement. "Like you can choose to do differently in the future. We're all works in progress, Ya'shul. I don't expect you to be perfect. I expect you to tell me what's going on. The rest of it we can work through when the time comes."

"I don't—I don't know if it's possible to engineer something." The confession bursts out of me. I look away. "It may take years."

Disappointment slides across Andeshe's face. She sits back.

"I know that's not what I told you," I add. "I'm—I'm sorry. I've discussed it with Se'jan."

She takes a deep breath and lets it out. "If that's how it is, that's how it is. Better to know than to have false hope. What I ask of you is that you try to the best of your ability. And that you're honest with me."

The tension slowly drains out of me. "Yes, I can do that."

Andeshe turns her palms upward again, like a butterfly opening, and reaches out to clasp my hands. "Then let what was broken be made whole and stronger for it."

I duck my head. It sounds like a ritual benediction, but I don't know the response. She hesitates a beat, then pats my hands.

"Are we good?" she asks.

The phrase rings oddly in my ears, but the more I sit with it, the more it feels like it fits. The shame that crushed me earlier has drained away, replaced with a determination to do better this time.

"Yes," I tell her. "Thank you."

She smiles. The warmth of it feels like balm on my abraded psyche. "Then we're good." She rises and stretches, shaking out her hands. "Give yourself time to process that, then we'll talk again. You don't need to know the entire journey to take the first step."

I push myself to my feet and turn back toward the stone buildings where our lab is. My emotions are still tender, but I can face it. Time to do what I should have done in the first place. Maybe Se'jan is wrong.

CHAPTER NINETEEN
ANDESHE

What are they doing to their people? I watch Ya'shul's slender form retreat through the scrub. I know the agonizing stab of guilt all too well from when I made my own mistakes at his age, but this is something different, tangled layers of hurt that strike at the core of what bothers me most about being here. I shake the unsettled feeling out of my arms. I wanted to seize his shoulders and shake them until they loosened, letting the contorted knot of self-loathing uncoil and pass. *Why, in the Goddess's name, would anyone cling to shame that hard?* It certainly doesn't do me any good. Or Fizz.

A lump rises in my throat, and I scrub away the tingling around my eyes. I'd always known it was a long shot, but I hadn't realized how far I'd let myself get my hopes back up. *Years. If ever.* I tip my head back against the tree, letting its rootedness ground me. Old grief tears at my chest, all the sharper for its brief hiatus. I let it wash through me, and I breathe in the scent of sun-baked hay until the pain recedes into its normal dull ache. *I still have her for a little while, at least.*

With a sigh, I pick myself up and dust off my leathers.

My family has been here long enough that there's a faint trail worn between the meadow and our settlement. Eventually, we'll finish moving to the cave, and this trail will fade. What else will vanish along with it?

My footsteps kick up the tiniest bit of dust. This close to the ground, the heat of the unmoving air sends sweat trickling down my back, making the inside of my flying leathers slick. The Uplanders' airy garb seemed flimsy and ridiculous when I got here. Now it seems only sensible. Will abandoning the skies seem sensible soon too? Will the children dodging between buildings now even remember that we once flew? Grief tightens my throat. *Who else am I supposed to be here?*

Back in my rooms, I shuck my sweaty leathers. Changing back into being an Uplander man cools me, but for all that I can pull on the clothes, the more restrained gestures, the quieter voice, no answers come with them. *Who am I if I'm not flying?* I suppose that's what I'm here to find out.

The sunshade twirls against my shoulder as I walk back along the main path. It's not necessary under the trees, but as soon as I step into the gardens, the sun is relentless. The sunshade makes sense, too, I suppose. If only I were so sure about everything else. Ya'shul's anguished face swims before my eyes. *All I wanted you to do was explain what happened and fix the problem.* I don't understand what makes that so hard.

"Andeshe!" The whisper draws my attention to the field of gourds on the north side of the path and the people bent among the rows harvesting them. Et'elark straightens from a crouch long enough to beckon me over and wipe his face on a grimy sleeve. With a glance toward a half-visible figure in the shade of the trees at the far side of the field, he motions me to furl the sunshade and bend down next to him.

"What happened?" he asks. "Rumors are flying." Leaves sway as his swift fingers pluck gourd after gourd from the row in front of him and place them gently in the basket next to him.

"You're picking the yellow ones?" At his nod, I tug one off and add it to the basket. "What rumors?"

He swipes at his forehead again. The cloth tied around his head is already soaked through. "I didn't think the stories of a pteradon foaming at the mouth and attacking people were true."

"*What?*"

He motions me to keep my voice down and drags an empty basket into place. "Like I said. Rumors. What happened?"

"Nothing like that! Fizz had an allergic reaction to something we tried to feed her. She never put anyone in danger—she just had some trouble breathing. And flopped around a bit."

"The mice?"

Of course he would know. I hesitate. Ya'shul and I have sorted things out, but I don't know how garbled the gossip might get if I add more information to it. "Between you and me, yes. But I'd appreciate it if that weren't noised around too widely. The details get complicated."

Et'elark raises a finger to his lips. "Allergic reaction it is, then."

"It's true!" The way he says it feels too much like a conspiracy of silence.

"I didn't say it wasn't."

"It's just—I wouldn't lie to you. Or ask you to lie for me."

He twitches his shoulder, almost as if he's dislodging an insect. "It's not a problem. You do what you need to do." A sudden grin flashes across his face. "But it's nice to know where I stand."

I pull another few gourds off their vines. "Do I want to know what other rumors are going around?"

He shrugs. "Nothing much involving you. The political families are just seizing on this as the latest weapon against each other. Apparently Nareen deliberately tried to poison Fizz because you Wanderers are supporting her rival."

I can't even find words for that. He looks at my expression and his lips twist.

"That's ridiculous," I sputter at last. "She had nothing to do with any of it. Nothing."

"As if the rumor mill cares." He ticks a few more off on his fingers. "Or that she's incompetent and poisoned it by accident. Or that she's a fraud who's still in the Lefmin lab because she can't make it on her own and has been taking credit for other people's work. The list goes on. There are a few on the other side. Those fliers are dangerous and going to explode, you know." His sardonic expression doesn't change.

I recoil. "None of that is true! What sort of vile—"

A shout cuts across the field. "Hey, no socializing on the line!"

Et'elark bends back down, hands flying.

I start to turn, but he motions me back down with a murmur to wait. Furiously, I yank squashes off the vine, though even my anger-fueled picking can't match his pace.

"I know," he says after a few minutes. "I work for the lab, remember?"

He's so unobtrusive that I wonder how many people realize how much he knows. It's odd how someone so tall can fade so completely from the awareness of the lab's other workers. We reach the end of the row, and I trail after him back toward the path.

"Thank you for telling me," I say when we reach it.

He shrugs, almost embarrassed. "Folks have to watch out for each other up here. All the Uplanders are talking about it, but I thought you might not know." He picks up a stack of empty baskets for the next row, and I retrieve my sunshade.

"Do you…do you need this?" I offer it to him. There's no shade to speak of, and even wearing Uplander garb, I'm soaked.

He shakes his head. "I have a break soon. I don't have the hands for it."

I nod my understanding, and his work draws him down the row until he's out of earshot.

What a mess. And here I thought I only had to sort out what I would do here. I'm used to rumors—no one grows up in a tight-knit community without them—but the speed and viciousness of these prickle the hairs on the back of my neck. Despite my hesitation, I turn my steps toward the one person who I'm sure will know everything that's going on.

***

"So, you don't think the pteradon project is going to work out after all?" Velemeth says when I finish telling her. She shifts on the rock bench near the temple entrance where we sit while she nurses.

Odd that she would pick up on that first. I thought she'd be more interested in the rumors. "Probably not," I finally admit, then pause while a young man with the air of an eager assistant pops out of the temple entrance to ask if she needs anything. I watch him carefully, but he adjusts her sunshade with no sign of the resentment that some of us have encountered here.

"I'm sorry for your disappointment," Velemeth says after he departs.

I let my lips stretch in an almost-smile. It's as honest as she can be.

"Well," she gives the distinct air of dusting off her hands despite her stillness. "There's a simple enough solution. I said from the beginning that you'd be better off working on the fliers. You'd be an excellent pilot. The controls may be different, but everything you know about air currents and maneuvering—that's half the knowledge. And it's harder to teach."

"Mmm." I'm no more enthusiastic about it than I was the last time she brought it up. "Let me have some time to let go, first."

"We can't wait for you forever, Andeshe. I told you at the outset this project wasn't a good idea. We need to adapt to being *here*, not clinging to the old ways. I've at least managed to turn most of these rumors away from us, but you haven't made it any easier."

"Turn the rumors? They're acting like Fizz is dangerous!"

"Pteradons are gigantic, Andeshe. Do you think anyone's ever really going to believe they're harmless?" Her voice takes on a brittle edge, and my breathing goes shallow. For all that we've worked things out, neither of us has forgotten the accident that threw Velemeth off Fizz's back to dangle screaming below. It took weeks for her leg to heal from being caught in the tangle of broken safety straps that stopped her fall.

"All they need is empathy and attention. They're no more dangerous than people." The accident happened because of me, not Fizz.

"How long have we danced attendance on them?" The hardness in Velemeth's voice makes me go still. "On you?"

"On me?" I repeat slowly.

A glitter in her eye cuts straight through me. "Always flying around everywhere, getting admired, having everyone trip over you—over any woman—to give you what you need." She puts one hand on her hip. "Just because I can't handle heights anymore doesn't mean I want to be stuck as one of the lower status genders all the time."

Reflex turns my palm upward before my conscious mind even catches up with her words. I thought our slow and painful conversations all those years ago had resolved her resentment over the panic attacks that stole her ability to tolerate flight. "Do you really feel that way?" I ask. "I never thought of them as lower status." I'd been aware that Velemeth hadn't always enjoyed the day-to-day grind of being a man or a parent, but no one loves what they do all the time. Her pregnancy as a lifegiver had been unpleasant but, I thought, respected.

"You wouldn't have noticed. You were hardly ever anything but a woman." The baby lets go, and she gestures to me to hold up the tiny pot of chaffing cream on the bench next to her. "I like the way they do things here. They understand what it means to give birth, to *give life* to another human being." She fingers the top of her ear, where she's wearing the metal studs I've seen on Nareen and many Uplander women and zomen. "And they honor the cost of it." She taps her ear studs again one by one. "Tearing, prolapse, joint damage—they mark them with badges of honor. Wanderers treat the injuries we suffer in childbirth as *normal*." Her voice hardens. "As *expected*. We risk our lives and sacrifice our bodies to manifest the Goddess's miracle. It's only fair for the rest of you to make it up to us. Not that anything really makes up for being torn apart and permanently injured, but you can at least *try*."

The unexpected heat in her voice knocks me back a step.

She plunges a finger into the pot and smears the cream on one reddened nipple. "Try it," she says tightly. She pauses and hooks a pinkie briefly at the corner of her mouth. "Try taking your fingers and stretching your lips as hard as you can. Feel how much that hurts? Now do it for thirty hours. Do it until your mouth literally *rips apart*. That's the price to me of creating the next generation."

"Weren't the other lifegivers there to support you?" I had known Velemeth struggled with complications after birth, but that's the point of having others who understand.

She shrugs. "To the extent that they could, but that doesn't make up for everyone else. After all that, I should have been *done*, not expected to plunge back into the misery of doing the same thing over and over because getting food on the table has to happen or playing another mind-numbingly boring round of a child's favorite game."

She rubs her temple with one hand. "Even the zomen back home spend all their time thinking about flying and basic survival and how to eke out a living in those awful wooden boxes everyone calls houses. Have you *seen* what the Uplanders have here? The art, the caves they live in, the things they do in their free time?" Velemeth's breath puffs out with a pained noise. "Which they actually have because they've had the sense to build up wealth over generations instead of feeding it straight into a pteradon's gullet. I made the best of what I had available. That doesn't mean I was happy with it."

I have no idea what to say. I would never have guessed that coming here would crack open old trauma like this. I wiggle my fingers. "What do you need?"

She glances down at my cupped palm, then shakes her head. "It's not something you've done. It's just… I didn't realize until we came here that there was another way."

"If you feel that we don't acknowledge birth injuries enough, I'm sure we can do a better job."

Gently, she curls my fingers closed. "It's more than that. The Uplanders make sure everyone *understands*, even if some of them will never really get it. Our culture…it's just different, you know?"

I don't know. Not really. I only know that her words deeply unsettle me.

The silence stretches out. The stone of the bench digs into my thighs.

"At any rate," Velemeth says in a more normal tone, "I'll help pull your fat out the fire, cousin—I'll talk to a few people, see what more rumors I can tamp down—but next time I warn you that something is not a good idea here, remember that I know what I'm talking about."

Past conversations echo in the air between us. I promised after the accident to listen better when she objected to risks I wanted to take. Does that promise still hold? By the time she rises, I still haven't said anything. Silently, I screw the lid back on the pot and help gather up her items. I do know that she understands the people here in a way I don't, but every instinct in me rebels at her words.

Velemeth disappears into the pitch blackness of the tunnel with the confident strides of a born Uplander. Hesitantly, I take one step in and then another, brushing my fingers along the wall for guidance. I've been in these halls before, or similar ones at least. Enough to know that the carvings under my fingers have been added layer upon layer for generations. I click my tongue experimentally, and the flatness of the sound makes me think that the antechamber I've entered is…small? Maybe? I take a cautious step forward. I could pull on the 'glove tucked into my belt, allow its sensors to vibrate the direction and distance of objects against my hand, but instead I just listen to the sound of distant running water and even more distant, the rhythmic thump of an eternal drum.

How many generations? My hand finds the wall again, sweeping up over carvings that reach higher than my fingers can stretch. How many generations did it take to carve something this complex into the mountain's bones? The wood and leather I grew up with seem flimsy in comparison. Above me, the mountain's weight above me grows heavier and heavier, compressing the air around me until it feels as if the thump of the drums and the prayers carved into the walls are the only barrier holding it back.

My nerve breaks, and I stumble back toward fresh air

and the freedom of a limitless sky. But as I turn the corner to the entrance, all I can see is the blinding glare of the ever-intensifying sun.

Chapter Twenty
Ya'shul

"Did you try this?" my brother asks, looking up from the desk next to mine. His 'glove twitches, and his message buzzes against my hand.

"Yes." I skim my fingers over the unfolding text. "That was one of the first things we looked into, remember?"

Ya'kinem slumps back, almost vanishing behind the piles of notes that teeter on the wooden work surface. "We'll find *something*." He reaches for another pile.

Normally, I find his eternal optimism energizing, something to cheer my spirit through the long twists and turns of research, but today I need realism. I have a problem to fix. The only good news is that Andeshe's pteradon is okay, and there are tenuous leads for how to modify Fizz's food source. But I need a sober assessment of how long the work will take, not a breezy reassurance that surely it won't be *that* hard.

The door to the lab opens. "I'm not going to just sit here and take this." Nareen's voice is low, almost a growl.

As raw as my emotions are, I still have my dignity. I congratulate myself on not flinching.

"You don't have to take it," my sister soothes. "All I'm saying is to be patient and let us handle the rumors. We've done this before. Charging off isn't always the best option."

"I'm not a plagiarist!"

Plagiarist? I turn. Beside me, Ya'kinem's head comes up as well.

"What happened?" I whisper to him. *That* would be a scandal for the ages. No one trusts someone who pretends to an intellectual fertility they don't have. Or any other kind. My brother hesitates, then shakes his head, expression troubled.

Nareen finally notices us and stops short. "Ya'shul."

"What happened?" Despite my reluctance, I can't help asking.

Her lips go taut. "Nothing I can't handle," she says tightly. "It's just backbiting and—" She puts a hand on her stomach, lips going pale. "I'll be right back," she chokes out. With as much decorum as she can muster, she hurries to the washroom. The sound of her heaves is audible even through the closed door.

Kiu jerks her head, and Ya'kinem follows after Nareen.

"You'd think with morning sickness that bad, she'd have proved she can create life." Kiu frowns after Ya'kinem. "But no, *some* people don't have proper reverence for the way pregnancy boosts creativity. *Some* people would rather spread ridiculous rumors than fight fair." At my murmur of inquiry, she adds, "Nareen's family has been making a stronger showing for the council seat than anyone thought they would. I should have anticipated that their opponents would stoop to dirty tricks." She seats herself at the terminal and plugs in her 'glove. "Rumors, nasty insinuations, people claiming she doesn't deserve the recognition she's getting. Our family will push back, of course. It's one thing to stay neutral, it's another to let someone smear the reputation of a protégé of *our* lab."

I nod. It's not as if we haven't closed ranks to do damage control before. The familiar format of talking points stares up at me as she brings the display to life, sorting snippets of text into different corners of the display.

"This one's yours." Kiu taps one, and it expands. "Your job is to make them look ridiculous."

"About what?" I hope it's not trying to explain *again* to non-scientists that research inevitably has ups and downs. Nareen's most recent project getting stuck doesn't really mean anything, though it's left me oscillating between mean-hearted satisfaction at her struggles and a niggling doubt as to whether I could have done better. I shake the feeling away.

"The rumor that Nareen stole your work. What else?"

My blood congeals.

"The other side is targeting her festival presentation." Kiu's lips writhe in disgust. "Of all the underhanded blows. Riling people up with how Nareen supposedly stole credit for a man's work, and how *Isel*'s family respects men and would never do such a thing." She points to the note. "The least you can do is deal with that. If any of the rest of us try, they'll just howl about how 'oppressed' you are that we're not letting you speak for yourself." Her nostrils flare. She's never had much patience with things that get in her way. Or people. "We need to get ready for the storms; we don't have time for this."

Slowly, my eyes drop to the display. I run my fingers over the glyphs as if touch will change what my eyes tell me. *Festival presentation plagiarism accusation. Work is all Nareen's. Have Ya'shul say so.* My fingers dig into the sand.

"It isn't." I thought I'd gotten over the festival, but the terse summary brings it all back. "Some of what she presented is work I did. Those were my ideas."

Kiu makes a throw away motion. "That doesn't matter right now. Clarity. Conciseness. Messaging. There is no nuance in damage control, only which side you're on." She pushes my hand away from where I'm twisting the display, pinning me with a look. "Which side *are* you on?"

"The family's. Of course." I grit the words out.

She forms her fingers into a command, and my 'glove buzzes with a copy of the note. Ever so slowly, I twist my hand to open it.

"As for this…" She taps another into prominence.

The silence stretches out too long. When she speaks again, her voice is dangerously quiet. "Would you care to explain how, exactly, Nareen ended up blamed for attempting to poison a pteradon?"

"I don't know." Shame flushes my body, but I fight it back, fumbling for the dignity I felt talking to Andeshe.

"First," she continues, voice harsh, "you used the lab's resources without telling me—protein modeling, really? Do you know how much energy that takes?"

"It was for a contract." My sister has always been able to make me feel small, her tight face and rigid posture channeling a miniature version of my grandmother.

"And then you careened off on your own and made a mess of things." She pushes the note across the display toward me. Despite myself, my eye picks out a few words. *Excitable young man…thought he could do more than he could…exaggerated.* My breath whooshes out as if I've been punched in the gut.

Andeshe forgives me. I cling to the thought with all my might. *I can redeem myself.* I take a steadying breath. I said I would do this. "I know I should have consulted with more people. I'm working on that now. I need help with Andeshe's project. Some way to do better testing ahead of time and to figure out what went wrong."

Kiu crosses her arms, looking at me as if she can't believe I would be so dense. "You're going to be too busy making sure the fallout from that misses Nareen." She indicates the note with a flick of her hand, then turns her attention to sorting through the display again. The two sets of talking points stare malevolently up at me, one stripping me of recognition and the other piling on blame.

Is there so little credit to go around? Andeshe's words come back to me. *Neither of you could have accomplished what you did without the other.*

"Other people have messed up before." I press my fists against my thighs. "We promised we'd do this project."

"We promised to try. Contracts always state that we can't guarantee success." She doesn't lift her eyes from the display.

"We haven't tried, not fully."

"And whose fault is that?"

I flinch. I should just take my penance and slink away, anything to end this excruciating conversation. That's what she expects. She expects me to be too wrapped up in my own shame to notice that I am being asked to become less, not more.

But I am more.

"No." The word comes from deep in my core. "I messed up. One mistake doesn't make me worthless." I clench my 'glove. "I'm not going to lie about what I did."

She spears me with a look. "You'd do that to Nareen?"

Guilt reaches up to suck at me. I bat it back.

Kiu leans forward, tapping the display for emphasis. "They're saying she's getting credit for work she didn't do, Ya'shul. You know what that means for her."

Old emotions break open, a clot still as raw and ugly as the day of the festival. "What about what it means for me? Did you think what it cost me to bite my tongue while everyone around me dismissed what I'd done? For her to walk away with a prize and *five* pledges, and me with nothing?" Rage surges up, white hot in my chest. "She did get credit for work she didn't do. That's the truth!"

A door closes, and I look up. Nareen stands just outside the washroom, staring at me. Ya'kinem hovers behind her. I almost take the words back.

Wrapping my dignity around me, I sweep toward the door instead. "You did," I tell her. "Don't blame me if someone else noticed."

I'm nearly to the door when my sister's words freeze me. "You think you're going to use the family's resources when you're not willing to do your part?"

I turn to face her.

Her eyes glitter. "Go. But don't expect to come back. Not until you're ready to do what you need to do."

Turning on my heel, I stalk out of the lab.

***

Footsteps patter on the path behind me, too quick and light to be Nareen's or my sister's.

"What happened?" Ya'kinem pants when he catches up with me.

As I recount the whole interaction, his fists clench. "Why should you have to clean everything up?" He shakes his head. "I can't *believe* Kiu did that. Or rather, I can believe it. That's the problem." He grimaces in distaste. When he turns to me, his eyes are wide and earnest. "Isel would never do something like that."

"Enough, Ya'kinem. Give it over." I'm not going to be dragged into whatever his latest scheme is.

He hurries to keep up with me. "I know you're skeptical—you think I'm all passion and no brain, like everyone says—but hear me out. Anything's better than that, right?" He jerks a thumb back the way we came.

I stop abruptly, anger surging again. *How could Kiu do that to me?*

He stops, too. "Why isn't your work important, huh? Why are you the one who always has to take the fall? It's not fair. That's what I've been telling you. That's what Isel is all about. We men should be treated better, not stuck always being treated like less."

I have never had the least interest in politics, but for once, his words have resonance.

He tugs at my hand. "Everyone's like, 'Oh, her family doesn't respect tradition,' but that's not the point. Why should we do things the way we always have if it's not working? Why shouldn't men get equal access to apprenticeships? Or get the same respect as zomen when we're done with our reproductive years? Or—or—get to do the other things women do." He flings his arms wide. "Isel's family believes in equality. For everyone. That's what I've been saying. I believe in them, and so should you."

He had me until the last. "I'm not going to break with the family."

"But have they broken with you?"

I pace down the path, away from the question. "Leave it, Ya'kinem." He can get away with dashing off after whatever strikes his fancy. No one takes him seriously, not since his promising early debut dissolved into increasingly irrepressible troublemaking. As long as he keeps his trousers buttoned, even Grandmother has given up trying to sit on him for long. I, on the other hand, haven't given up on winning my family's respect.

"Haven't they?" He scrambles after me. "That was utter crap back there, and you know it." He waves behind us.

"Don't push me. Not right now. Just because I'm not doing that, it doesn't mean—Nareen didn't even do anything. I'm not going to turn on her."

"Why not? It's not like Nareen is there for *you*."

Bands tighten around my chest. "Go away."

"What people are saying is just the truth. It's not their fault if the truth makes Nareen look bad."

"Go away, Ya'kinem."

Something in my tone finally penetrates his thick skull. He slacks his pace. "All right. I'm just saying—"

"I know." As if I need him to rub in how impossible my situation is.

"Just think about it." Ya'kinem falls back, and I take a shuddering breath. Think about it? My sister is *banning me from the lab*. I promised Andeshe I'd do what it takes to help Fizz. I promised myself I'd never pretend to be less than I am. Am I supposed to make myself into nothing in order to keep my access to the one place where I can do my work? My footfalls slap against the street. If only going fast enough would let me outrun my own thoughts.

CHAPTER TWENTY-ONE
ANDESHE

My 'glove buzzes with Et'elark's message. *Are we still on for dinner?*

Yes. I'm so ready for a break that I practically snatch at the 'glove, eager for something other than forcing myself to learn about flier controls and hating every second of it. Velemeth persuaded me to more seriously consider alternatives to throwing all my energy into pteradon biology, but so far it has only reenforced my longing for my original plan to work out.

I'm almost done here, Et'elark responds. *Meet me at the lab when you're ready. I'll walk you down.*

I hesitate. Last I heard, Ya'shul was still trying his hardest to track down what went wrong with his attempt to create something Fizz could eat. I want to give him the space to feel like he's trustworthy, not breathe down his neck. I sigh and stretch out my shoulders. *I could just check in. Ask him how things are going.* Surely that wouldn't be too intrusive. Besides, after an afternoon spent yearning to think about anything other than fliers, I also want to know if there's hope. I stuff the last few items in the basket I'm bringing and turn my steps toward the lab, messaging

Et'elark that I'm coming. I'm wearing the best of my Uplander clothes. It's too colorful by their standards, but I doubt Et'elark will mind.

Soon enough, the lab's polished wooden door looms in front of me, set against the careful joins of ancient stonework. I trace my fingers over the sun-bleached wood. It has been sanded and refinished so many times that the hinge fixtures protrude from its worn surface. The new coat of varnish is already bubbling and cracking under the sun's punishing rays.

I draw a deep, shuddering breath. *There's still time.* Nothing's going to happen tomorrow. No matter how much I might dread the future, it hasn't come yet. *Does it hurt more to hope or to not?* I knock on the door. Maybe there's still a chance to make my peace with the way things have to be.

Kiu answers the door. Past her shoulder, Nareen's short, plump form hunches over a desk. In the back, Et'elark's tall figure turns from a panel in the wall to look toward us.

Meet you in five. Et'elark's message buzzes against my hand, and he turns back to the panel.

I chime my bracelets at Kiu, waiting for her to invite me in. "Is Ya'shul here?" I ask her. "I wanted to ask him something."

"No." She's more curt than I've ever heard her. The door starts to close.

"Wait!" Normally, the head of the lab is courteous, if distant. I can't imagine what changed.

She opens it again. Partway.

"What's the matter?"

"Nothing." Her expression dares me to contradict her.

The hell it's nothing. "Is he okay?" I heard from him recently, but not for a few days.

"Yes. I'll tell him you came by." The door closes in my face.

I'm still standing there in shock when it opens again and Et'elark steps out. He makes an inquiring noise as he falls into step beside me, guiding me down one of the myriad of stone paths.

I take a slow, deliberate breath. "Sorry. That was just…odd. I thought I'd ask Ya'shul if anything was seeming promising. Kiu shut me down completely."

He snorts. "Of course she did. She basically banned him from the lab a few days ago."

The news collapses something inside of me. I'd messaged him. I'd asked him to keep me updated on progress *and challenges*. And he hadn't seen fit to mention a wee insignificant detail like *being banned from the lab*? A curse escapes me, and I close my eyes in a brief prayer for patience. "He promised he was going to ask for help!"

"He did, from what I heard." Et'elark shrugs. "It'll blow over—their arguments always do. Give them a few weeks and everything will be back to normal."

I'm appalled. "Weeks?" I count the time until the solstice marks the end of the time Ya'shul's been assigned to assist me. Before then, I need leads promising enough that I can persuade Auntie Haveo to negotiate for further work on them. The rest of what Et'elark says penetrates. "Blow over? Without resolving anything? Without talking about it?" As if anyone is going to do good work with that sort of unresolved tension hanging over them.

Et'elark eyes me skeptically. "You're a great believer in

talking things over, aren't you?"

We pass the last platform on Ikmeth's south side and keep going to where the cliffs give way to a scrubby hillside and a steep switchback path that leads down to the Lowlander settlement. I rub away the tension in my forehead, reminding myself to be here with him rather than lost in my own worries. "It works." Our footsteps stir up puffs of dirt as we start the climb down.

He looks across the valley toward the distant cliffs, face growing pensive. "I suppose. Sometimes." An odd note in his voice catches my ear.

"And other times?" I prompt.

He picks his way down the slope in silence for so long that I don't think he's going to answer. "You're an optimist," he finally replies. "I admire that about you."

Admire. Despite my lingering irritation, a tiny flush of heat warms me. "You're not?"

He shrugs one shoulder. "When I can be. Here, watch your step." His fingers close around my elbow as a sharp turn reveals a crumbling stone step. He's close enough that I can feel the warmth radiating from his body, see the sweat glistening on the curve of his neck before it slips underneath his collar. I glance back down at the path before he notices me eyeing him. Even through my sleeve, his fingers trail heat as he lets go.

"There." We turn another corner, and he jerks his chin at the pebbly ground of the valley floor below us, where rings of stumps and logs have been arranged in a loose circle a few rows deep with a stone oven at their center. "If you'll give me a moment?" He picks his way nimbly along a separate path that runs horizontally along the cliff, then scrambles up a rope ladder into one of what

I realize is a series of unevenly spaced caves set high on the rock wall. Occasional carvings decorate them, but far more sporadically than the regimented precision of the entrances at the top of the cliff. After a moment, he reemerges, dressed in a jewel-toned purple tunic and shaking back his freshly unbound hair. I'm suddenly glad that I wore my best.

"This is for you." I hand him the basket from my arm as he returns, and he accepts it with a murmur of thanks. He guides me down the rest of the path and across the pebbly ground to where a short queue of people are lining up to receive food from the group of—I guess they're women here—in charge of the bubbling pots. Et'elark produces a pair of bowls and spoons from somewhere on his person and hands one to me, steering me into the center of the circle. He introduces me to the women in charge, who welcome me warmly. I follow his lead, holding up my bowl to them with murmured thanks, then stopping to spoon a tiny amount into another bowl that is resting alone on a flat rock near the oven.

"Offering for the departed," he explains at my curious look.

"Ah." I follow him as he finds us seats on a pair of small stumps near the back of the circle and introduces me to the people around us. They all loom over me, I'm the shortest adult here by at least a head and a half, but the unpretentiousness of the setting and the Lowlanders' casual chatter remind me powerfully of gatherings of my own clan. I can feel the muscles in my back unwind.

"Is everyone here your family?" I ask. There are maybe seventy or eighty stumps in the circle, but only half of them are filled. I've never been to a meal with the Uplanders, but

I thought families here were closer to a hundred or a hundred fifty at full capacity.

He shakes his head. "We collaborate with three other families for meals."

"Three?" I count again. "Your families must be tiny." Even as the stumps fill, there are far fewer zomen and women than I would expect.

He shrugs. "Forty-ish. Not everyone can make it here at the same time. And some of those are children." He points his spoon toward a group of youngsters who are chasing each other around the outside of the circle. "The caves are smaller down here, which limits family size." He waves to a cousin who looks vaguely familiar, and another round of introductions begins. Slowly I relax. Without a pteradon in my wake, the people who greet me are far more open and quick to smile.

As the shadow of the cliff lengthens, a bonfire crackles to life beyond the circle. With a whoop of delight, the youngsters spring to their feet, hauling log seats into a semicircle in front of it, then assisting their elders over to the new seats. Et'elark disappears into the darkness with my bowl, then reappears with it as I find a place at the edge of the new seats. I take a cautious sip of some sort of sweet liquid. The larger, dimmer moon peeks its face over the rim of the canyon, warming the scene with its rosy light.

The jangle of a tambourine calls my attention back to the center of the semicircle. A trio of zomen have arranged themselves between the audience and the fire, two of them seated with a drum and a set of wooden flutes while the third stands in front of them, long braid swaying as they shake the tambourine.

"Set down your worries," the zoman croons, tapping

the tambourine again. "Listen to the tale of Zetiya and her sisters."

Next to me, Et'elark makes a pleased noise in his throat and starts up from the log. "My favorite."

I look up at him.

"Here," he says, pressing his own bowl into my hands. "Hold this for me while I go up, would you?"

Mystified, I start to stand as well. "Should I…"

"No, no, there's nothing you have to do." He presses a hand to my shoulder. "Not unless you want to. Though you're welcome to sing along. The chorus is easy to learn."

Behind him, the zoman begins a call and response that quickly resolves itself into the refrain of a song. Et'elark looks down at me with an inscrutable expression on his face.

"You can't talk everything out," he tells me when quiet descends again. His eyes are intent. "Expecting that you can—you can't burden yourself with that much weight all the time. Sometimes you just have to set it down." Before I can respond, he disappears into the crowd, reappearing again next to the fire with a handful of other people.

The quality of the group's silence changes, and then the singer's voice spirals upward in an achingly beautiful prayer for loved ones far from home. I suck in my breath as unexpected longing pierces my heart. Home is gone. Rolled up and dismantled, unfolded here into something that will never be the same. *Is this what he means by 'set it down?'* What rolls through me feels more like a redoubling. A lump rises in my throat. Other voices join in, rising from the throats of the people swaying in their seats around me.

The last note trails off into a hushed silence. A few

people wipe their eyes. Then the tambourine shakes, and the flute starts the cheerful, lilting melody from before. *No, this.* The first was just an opening prayer, I realize with relief.

The singer launches into a lighthearted tale of the increasingly ridiculous mishaps of a young woman and her sisters all attempting to woo the same man. The youngsters closest to the fire jostle each other to claim masks before each new character is introduced, eliciting gales of laughter from the onlookers as they add over-the-top embellishments to their reenactment of the singer's words. The young man playing the lover closes out a verse with a series of handstands ending in a flourishing bow that sends his loosened mask flying. Et'elark snatches it up to hoots from the audience and struts into the next verse, fingers catching in his hair as he reties the ribbons that hold the mask in place. The firelight gilds his throat as he throws his head back, half-unbuttoned shirt slipping off one shoulder.

Oh. My mouth goes dry. I shift the bowls in my lap to hide my inevitable reaction. Freed by my anonymity in the crowd, I let my eyes trace the line of his body as he arches backward and his companion leans in for a pretend kiss.

I'd be happy not to pretend. The thought lances straight to my groin. Auntie Haveo has always admonished us to keep our trousers buttoned when we're away from our own people. Too many misunderstandings. Too much that gets garbled into rumors that I have to bat down. *No, we do not have sex with just anyone!* How they got that out of us not having pledging ceremonies is beyond me. *Yes, children are old enough to practice other genders at four or five, but that doesn't mean they have sex!* As if something as important as readiness for that would ever be conflated with gender. *Yes, some people do pair bond for life, but that does* not *mean we screw our own blood kin. We know perfectly well who has been fostered in and who hasn't.* The queries still rankle, as does the defensiveness and tossed-off apologies I got when I named that they did. Of all the ways for the Uplanders' growing comfort with my family living here to manifest, did it have to be invasive questions about sex?

Sometimes you just have to set it down, Et'elark's voice whispers in my mind.

That's not how we do things, but I'm not at home anymore. I'm here, where thousands of people bounce in and out of each other's lives without ever knowing the impact they have—or even wondering. I'm here, where I'm too bound up in the past to appreciate the sensual pleasure of watching Et'elark doing something that brings him joy.

The song ends in applause, and Et'elark returns to my side, a wide smile on his face and eyes sparkling with pleasure. My heart gives a little flip. I've never seen him like this up top. I clap along to the next song, picking up the refrain as Et'elark belts it out at the top of his lungs. Stomps and cheers and shouts from the crowd buoy me upward until my worries finally fall away in the catharsis of laughter. The musicians and singer rotate out for other groups until exhausted dancers have had their fill and second moonrise has come and gone. Finally, the music winds down with a lullaby, and the crowd begins to disperse, leaving a guttering fire and the musicians putting away their instruments.

"Enjoy yourself?" Et'elark murmurs in my ear. His

voice is low and throaty.

I turn to him, breath catching in my throat, but the glow of celebration is all I see in his eyes.

"Very much. Is it always like this?"

"Sometimes. Some weeks it's poetry or dance—"

"That wasn't dance?"

He chuckles. "Everyone dancing all at once. Something to lay our worries down." He looks at the fire and a little of his exhilaration falls away. "To the extent that we can."

Two men are standing next to the fire. One tosses something into it with a jerk, wiping away tears while the other wraps an arm around his shaking shoulders. The two stand there, heads pressed together, for a long time.

Et'elark's throat bobs, then he jerks his chin. "For the rest...we would say let the smoke take it up to the Goddess."

The tide that buoyed my emotions starts to ebb, leaving a creeping bleakness in its wake.

He takes a deep breath. "Do you think talking things out works?"

I open my mouth, then close it again. "I...don't know. I'm trying to adapt to how things are. You know, up there."

He digs in the gravel with his toe, then scoops up a handful of pebbles. They trickle through his fingers with soft clinks. "I used to want to be an apprentice up there once." His voice is soft. In the firelight, his face is only half visible. "I started helping out in the Lefmin's lab in my early teens." His eyes slide to me and then away. "We always assign tasks to one person who's an expert at it and one person who's learning. That way there's always someone who can fill in if needed."

I nod. I'd wondered why he seemed to come and go.

"Cee was the expert there when I was learning," he continues.

I blink. "Cee, your relative in the mines?"

He dips his head, casting his face in shadow. "I thought for a while that maybe I could learn to do what the Lefmin do. A few of my distant relatives have apprenticed with Uplander families. But apprentices don't get paid…and that's if I could even get an opportunity." He shrugs. "And then things happened, and eventually I realized what it would cost." He scoops up another handful of pebbles. "Even if I could now, I don't think it would be worth it. To become one of them, that is."

I press my lips together, looking at the vibrancy of the community around me. "You're assuming I have a choice. Once the solar storms come, the old ways are gone."

"So I've heard."

"I have to find something," I continue, "some way to still be me, to still have work that's respected even after everything changes completely. I don't mind finding something new—well, I do, but I've reconciled myself to it. It's just that I never realized how differently they lead their entire lives. They're hurting each other constantly, and they don't *do* anything about it."

"There's hurt and there's *hurt*. They're treating each other with the tenderness of ptercels to their chicks compared to what they could be doing."

"But they're building up so much unresolved conflict and shame and humiliation and tension." I rub the back of my neck. "How does it not explode?"

"You're assuming it doesn't."

Dropping my head into my hands, I rake my fingers through my hair.

Et'elark's voice is soft in the darkness. "If you could keep one thing, what would it be?"

"The pteradons." My answer is immediate. "Fizz." She's recovering from her ordeal, but I'm less and less convinced her aging body will have the stamina to make it to the sea.

"And if not Fizz?"

I close my eyes. I always knew it was a long shot. It's only getting longer. Fizz's swollen tongue flashes before my eyes, her useless wingbeats as she writhed. Even if we can find a food source, nothing lives forever, no matter how beloved. I open my eyes again, staring into the fire's dying glow. *Let it go.* Have I grieved enough yet? I imagine feeding my grief to the flames, letting its smoke rise up to the distant stars. Does it help?

I tip my head back, gazing at the cliff face far above us. Moonlight cuts across its top, illuminating the web of walkways. From this distance, they resemble spider's lace, such delicate strands to wrap me in bands that feel like iron.

"I want to be free," I say at last.

"From what?"

"Shame." The word comes to me immediately. "Their shame. Over everything." The words spill out of me. "The slightest mistake, the thought that they might need to do better—they react as if the entire town is about to drive them out." Ya'shul's impulse was to collapse into a puddle of guilt rather than claim his power to make repair comes back to me. "It's as if their only choices are to pretend no harm was done or to utterly crush the person who did it." Is that why so many of them have been so defensive? They think collapsing is the only alternative? "I don't understand."

"Do you not feel shame, then?"

"It's not that." Old grief twinges at me. Some sorrows we only become more practiced at bearing, no matter how much time passes. "But shame points toward something else. Toward grief at not living up to who you wanted to be. Toward something damaged that you didn't realize was precious to you. Toward fear of loss or broken connections." I take a deep breath, drawing on long-ago lessons. "It's not supposed to be a lash to flay your spirit."

A shudder runs through him.

"Tell them that." His voice is ragged.

"Tell who what?"

He waves to the cliffs above us. "Teach them that."

"Me? But it's so—"

"It's not obvious. No more obvious than how to use a 'glove was to you."

He witnessed my struggles with that. He's the one who showed me how to interpret the technical manuals.

"Does your work have to be physical?" he asks.

"No," I tell him slowly. "I suppose not. But any of my family could teach how to hold harms." I cup my hands in front of me. "That's who we are. We built our lives around creatures who can kill with the snap of a beak. Shaming them does no good, only empathy and paying attention to their needs." I search for words to explain. "You can't blame a pteradon. You can only work together as a community to stop whatever went wrong from happening again."

He's silent for a long time. "Is anyone else teaching those lessons?"

His words make me pause. The men back in the settlement have little more contact with the Uplanders than before we moved. Of those of us who have ventured out to find apprenticeships, how many have even noticed what I've noticed? And how many are like Velemeth, made starry-eyed by the glamor of a new, more comfortable life? Many more of the latter than the former.

"No," I admit. "They're not." My sense of who I am relative to my new home slowly reorients itself. I've been so focused on what I will lose when Fizz dies. I never thought about the legacy she might leave.

"Well?" He tilts his head, raising one hand, palm up, with a shrug of his shoulder.

I laugh. "That's the gesture for telling someone you want to repair a harm you've done, actually."

His smile flashes in the firelight. "See, you've already taught me something."

I smile back, feeling lighter. "Thank you," I tell him. "You've given me a lot to think about." Something deep within me realigns itself. I know who I can be here.

"I'm glad I could help you think things through."

The sounds around us grow quiet as I look into his eyes. In front of us, the fire has dimmed into coals. It's only the way that my eyes have adjusted to the darkness that allows me to see when his tongue darts out to lick his lips. My breath hitches.

He looks away. "I—I have a favor to ask you."

"Yes?" I shift my gaze back up to his eyes.

"Does your flying ever take you out to the mines?"

"The mines? Not exactly. They're near the lake above

the dam, though. Someone in my family flies there often enough."

"You do? Why?"

"Ferrying people to and from the workshop complex. The pteradons love the lake, too, it's a popular flight. That and the family that runs the workshops—they've always treated us well."

His shoulders tense, but he doesn't say anything.

"Why do you ask?"

He looks down at his hands. "It's Cee," he says reluctantly. "I haven't—we haven't seen each other in over a year. I'm allowed to visit, but only if I find a way to get there myself." His hands twist around each other. "Even if I had enough time off of work, boats don't go up that tributary much, not when they can't get past the waterfall."

"Oh, you need a ride." From his sudden tension, I'd have thought there was something more. "I can ask if there's something that needs to be delivered out there. Fizz isn't solely mine to fly, but if there is, I can probably make room for a passenger."

The hope on his face is almost painful to behold.

"I can't make promises," I caution him, "but I'll do my best. Surely I can find something." My mind is already sorting through possible excuses that I could turn into a reason to go.

His voice is rough. "That's all I can ask. Thank you."

Silence falls until I finally, reluctantly, straighten. "It's getting late."

He rises, holding out his hands to help me up. He draws me to my feet, then stands looking down at me, face hidden in the shadows.

"You wanted freedom," he tells me. "You have it. Just

don't lose it." We're standing just the tiniest bit too close, but neither of us step back. Behind him, a log breaks, and the fire crumbles to coals. "Let me walk you up," he says.

It's a long, cold climb even in the moonlight. It would be an even longer and colder one coming back down.

"Only as far as you want to," I reply.

He stays with me the entire way to the top.

Chapter Twenty-Two
Ya'shul

I need to talk to you. It takes me three tries to send the message.

Where are you? Andeshe's response is immediate.

Above me, the leaves of the ancient tree rustle softly. I've come back to the spot where Andeshe and I talked, hoping that it would bring me clarity. It hasn't. I message Andeshe where to find me, then drop my hands to my lap, tugging at the fingers of my 'glove. Another gust of wind ripples across the grassy slope.

Maybe I should just give in. Kiu is adamant that she won't let me back in the lab until I grovel sufficiently and promise to "do my part," but I can't bring myself to do it. I tip my head back against the tree trunk, looking up through the leaves at the fragments of sky. *All I want to do is keep my promises and be myself. Does it have to be this hard?*

Something nudges my foot. A half-grown goat butts the sole of my shoe again and bleats. A collar around its neck peeks out through its long hair. I reach forward and hook my fingers through it, tugging the animal closer. It's one of the experimental ones, not needing the bulky sensors that so often fail to keep goats out of the areas with the heaviest phosfoz concentration. I eye it critically. It seems healthy, but the sun is too bright to tell whether it's glowing. In the distance, I see the tall form of one of the goat herders that works for Nareen's family, but she seems in no rush to recollect this one.

"I thought I saw it come this way." Nareen's voice filters through a patch of scrubby bushes. She steps out from behind the concealing branches, then stops short. Se'jan follows her around the edge of the bush carrying a clipboard. He looks back and forth between the two of us.

"That's the last one," he prompts.

Nareen starts moving again, but her eyes are fixed on me, not the goat. She runs a cloth measuring tape between her fingers.

"I'm no plagiarist," she tells me.

So we are going to talk about this. We haven't spoken since my sister banned me from the lab.

"I didn't say you were. I said—"

"You said, 'She did get credit for work she didn't do.' What do you think that means?"

"I mean—" I take a deep breath. "The festival. You got credit for our work, while I—"

"*Our* work." She glares at me. "*Ours.* I have a right to it. You've heard what they're saying about me. I can't believe you'd side with them!" She snaps a lead rope on the goat's collar and tugs the animal toward her, passing it to Se'jan to hold. With jerky motions, she wraps the measuring tape around the goat's barrel, calling out measurements to Se'jan.

I press my lips together. I have heard. It's vicious. My family put out a statement of support, but it has done little to stop the wildfire spread of the rumors. And now, Nareen is looking at me as if I started them myself. All I want is to be recognized as her equal.

"I'm not siding with the others."

"How could you?" She stands up, wrapping the measuring tape around her hand.

Why does the truth keep retreating farther and farther from my grasp? Why is this only getting harder to untangle? I push myself to my feet and turn to go. I'm sick of trying to explain myself. Kiu and the rest of the family are bad enough.

Se'jan snorts. "How could he? How could *you*?" His voice is light and mocking.

Nareen rounds on him. "How could I what?"

"Nothing." He jots a final number on the clipboard with calculated insouciance, the goat's lead still in his hand.

Nareen fists her hands on her hips. "If you have something to say, spit it out. You've been making snide comments for days, and I'm sick of it!"

My heart leaps in my chest. Has he really been standing up for me?

"Are you sure?" My cousin's careless slump, the one Marin-lun has always hated, takes on an edge of warning. The hairs on my arms prickle. This is different from the verbal sparring they've always seemed to enjoy, more personal somehow.

A muscle in Nareen's jaw twitches. "Spit. It. Out." Her eyes flash with an anger even hotter than the temper she worked so hard to contain as a youngster, the one that led my mother to coach her in breathing exercises and the patience needed to calm down when she was thwarted. Reflexively, I fill my lungs with air and let it out slowly, the way my mother taught us both.

"Very well." Se'jan straightens, twirling the clipboard on one finger. "Every equinox, judges from the capital invite the person with the *best* new discovery in each village to present at the solstice festival. Normally, that sort of invitation is the capstone of someone's career. To get to go so early... It's the boost of a lifetime, hmm?"

Nareen's eyes narrow. "It is." She knows him too well not to be suspicious of conceding a point to him.

"*The* best, the person who had the *single* best discovery goes. So...why are you taking Ya'shul's place?"

My breath goes shallow. "Se'jan—I wasn't—"

"How dare you!" Nareen's face contorts as her tenuous hold on her anger snaps. "I won that prize fair and square. Nothing—not Isel, not these rumors, not you, *no one*—gets to undo that!"

Se'jan leans in. "Really? Because I saw who was in here on rest days doing the splices and preparing the samples and checking the results. I also saw who got to have an idea and say, 'Ya'shul, implement this,' versus who put in the hours and hours of labor to make it happen. I saw who made it *possible* and who got to waltz in and out whenever she wanted."

"I did plenty! Regardless of what they say."

"Who did *more*?"

"Anyone could have carried out the steps," she grits out. "The real work is thinking of what to try."

His normally heavy-lidded eyes narrow. "Anyone could have done it, but you didn't have to. Tell me, how much less 'real work' would you have done if the men in your life hadn't cleared everything else away to give you time to sit and think? You *think* you deserve to go because you don't believe all the extra work he did really counts." He opens a hand toward me.

Nareen's eyes dart to me, widening briefly as if only now remembering that I'm here. "That's not true," she insists.

"Isn't it? Tell me, did you even consider that Ya'shul might be your rival for the festival prize, or did you assume that you could get credit for anything he'd done?"

"It's not like that," she backpedals. "I never thought I would get it at all."

"Really? No inkling? No heads up? No one in your family grooming you extra carefully because this might be the opening they needed?"

She opens her mouth, then closes it again. Even in her anger, she's honest to a fault.

"Those prizes are never a complete surprise," Se'jan says softly. "The inquiries start months ahead of time, along with negotiations for which would be the most auspicious festival to present at. The people who are truly under consideration know they're being scrutinized."

They do? I wait for Nareen to deny it, but she says nothing. *They do.* My hands clench into fists. I was never in the running at all. All that time at the festival when I agonized over how to present. All that time afterward that I kicked myself for not doing things differently, for not reaching the heights that Nareen did.

"You knew." I don't recognize my own voice. "Is that why you told me to tone my presentation down? You thought it might detract from yours? How long ago did you know?"

"No! You were worried about whether your pledge would work out. So was I. That was all." She says it as if speaking firmly is enough to make it true.

Se'jan's reply is soft, but implacable. "That's the real secret to success. Make sure your competition is too busy scrabbling for the things you take for granted to have time to beat you at the rest of it."

She turns toward him with a hiss.

"You never even considered that you might not get pledges, did you?" he continues. "No more than you've had to worry about finding time to keep working after you give birth." He circles her. "No, it's Ya'shul who has to drop everything when a bottom needs to be wiped. It's your brother who will stay up half the night bouncing your screaming baby. And then you'll come in having had a good night's sleep and never wonder why you get so much more 'real work' done."

"It isn't like that!"

"Isn't it?" He raises an eyebrow. "Don't think I haven't seen you. Maybe—*maybe*—if Ya'shul does everything perfectly, if he pulls off by himself what you can do with an entire team, perhaps you'll deign to recognize him as your equal. For you, equality is the floor. For him, it's the ceiling."

Her lips have gone white around the edges. "I didn't. I deserve—"

"So does he."

She whirls to face me. "What was I supposed to do?" she asks, voice ragged. "Was I supposed to turn down an invitation to Treverel itself? Think what that would have done to my family!"

Words tangle behind my lips. I don't know what she sees in my face, but alarm comes into her eyes.

"I know you do a few things more around the lab, but

it's not really *that* much, is it?"

My whole body recoils. The image arises, as fresh as the day it happened, of her and Kiu sitting together, deep in conversation, as I shooed children out the door. How many times have I dropped everything because their work was too important to interrupt—and mine wasn't?

I can't speak. I can't not speak. Feeling like a coward, I back away and flee.

***

My traitorous feet take me to the fairground. I stare up at the outthrust stage, fists clenching. I can almost see my old self kneeling there, my shoulder under Nareen's hand, never imagining what was coming.

You knew, I think at the ghost of Nareen. *You knew even then.* And here I thought we were equals. Across the field, a handful of younger women laugh and shove each other as they cross from one side of the ridge to the other. *I don't want to be here.* I turn away, automatically taking the first few familiar steps toward the lab before I stop myself. I can't go there, but I can't stand going home, either.

A message buzzes through my 'glove: *I'm headed over to you now.* It's Andeshe.

Nausea twists my stomach. Without replying, I pull the 'glove off and tuck it in my belt.

Overhead, a ptercel trills. It pulls out of a dive and flares its wings to alight on the cluster of rocks around the temple's entrance. The dark opening below it burrows into the mountain, a stark reminder of how things should have been.

I take a tentative step forward. I haven't been here

alone in years, not when Restday services are always a jumble of families putting in their appearances and my grandmother ensuring a strict rotation of the rest of us doing our duty. If the world were fair, I should have come here the evening of the festival, not completely alone, but acknowledged and elevated. Chosen. A group of Wanderers passes me, their chatter overly loud and jarring. I duck into the temple entryway, removing my shoes and socks and placing them on the shelves just around the corner from the sunlight.

The light fades as I go deeper, each step taking me down the route I should have walked. I can never be the focus of a pledging ceremony, but I should have been a part of Nareen's. I don't care what Se'jan says, she would have known. She would have recognized me as much as she could.

Are you sure? a little voice whispers, and I sigh. My fingers find the wall, prayers whispering under my fingertips the hope that finding rest and rejuvenation in the darkness will give me strength to face the light once more. The prayer above it asks for healing. For redemption.

The hallway opens into the central sanctuary. Soft drumbeats echo in the round chamber, an eternal heartbeat that thrums even now when the temple is occupied only by acolytes going about their duties and the occasional supplicant praying at one of the alcoves that ring the room.

Am I a supplicant? Habit bends my limbs until I'm kneeling, bowed forward to touch the floor of the first alcove, reaching for the carved symbol that starts its opening prayer. It's a prayer of thanksgiving. Thanks for the blood that still beats in my veins, for the breath in my body, for the muscles that arch my back as I stretch forward, tracing the text that leads across the floor and up into a carved scene that stretches higher than I can reach. The Goddess, represented as a zoman, gently binds a deep gash across a woman's abdomen, but the scene isn't smoothly carved. Instead, each shape is created out of prayers that curl themselves into the appropriate shape, textured fillings bringing the scene to life. Supplications for healing adorn the curves of the Goddess's robes. Prayers of gratitude are infused into every limb of the supplicant. Prayers of grief for hurt loved ones puddle in the spilled blood that pools at the base of the scene. There are even prayers of repentance dripping from the fingers of a figure in the background.

Rising, I run my fingers over the scene. The prayers of supplication are the most well-worn, except for the occasional one whose lines have been more recently refreshed. I let my fingers trail over the largest of them. The Goddess's hand never shows itself. No prayer will lead to the world wrenching dramatically back into place, only to the subtle miracle of flesh knitting to wholeness under a bandage.

Behind me, priestesses begin one of the meditative chants that punctuate the day. I could join them, anyone is welcome to seek communion in the swaying and chanting, but instead I find myself trailing my fingers along the wall, making the solitary pilgrimage around the wall to pray at each alcove.

Fertility. My fingers skim over the plaque by the next opening in the wall. In the alcove, the Goddess's rounded stomach protrudes gently from the wall, the rock worn smooth by generations of hands that have stroked it in wordless prayer. The deity smiles benevolently at the nestled form of a sleeping child while other children gambol amid fruit trees and sheaves of grain.

This can't be all there is. My questing fingers stretch upward, to where the Goddess's thoughts radiate outward, drawing into being starships and cities and the breath of imagination.

There. I can create that kind of life. I lower my hands. Does it really matter that I'll never give birth? I remember the flash of Nareen's pregnancy earring in the sunlight. Se'jan's words echo back to me. It never occurred to me that I might deserve more recognition than Nareen. All I've been fighting for is the remote possibility that I might be her equal.

Like a thunderclap, rage fills me. What could I have done with the support she's received? My imagination spins outward, surrounding me with a team of people charged with turning my ideas into reality. Outward still to my sister mentoring me through every step of the process. Outward still to the people tripping over each other to make sure nothing disturbs my concentration. My breath hisses between my teeth. I'm not inferior. I'm not inferior *at all.*

The next alcove is dedicated to childbirth. The one after that to children, whose handmade offerings are tucked into tiny niches flanked by simple carvings and simplified prayers. The alcove after that is for men.

I stop. I've never prayed here before. Not before the festival, before I had the right to, and not in the chaotic time since. Cautiously, I step inside.

It takes me a moment to find the representation of the Goddess on the wall. Flowing robes wreathe a figure that covers the entire background, smiling beatifically at industrious figures cradled in the mantle's folds. Prayers for strength and stamina shape men who are hauling stones for what I suddenly realize is a half-completed Ikmeth. Figures play with children, muck out stalls, carry an ancient zoman up a trail. There are more prayers—for patience, for safety, for the wellbeing of family. More carvings—of men clearing trees, turning over compost, picking apart a worn-out shirt.

Where am I? My fingers move faster and faster across the carvings. It's not that I don't like physical work—I do—but that's not all I am. I skim over prayers for guidance, for humility, for the blessing of being of service to others. I don't disagree. But what I'm searching for more and more desperately is something different, something to guide me in my current dilemma.

I don't want to be content with how everyone thinks I should be. I flinch from prayers for chastity, modesty, and obedience to the zomen in my family. Here, an ancient story glorifies a man who lies on his death bed, having sacrificed all his food so that his sister's children could eat. There, a spiral of text lists the virtues of an ideal man—the uncomplaining, self-effacing helpmeet who cleans up messes so that others can pursue glory unencumbered.

I step backward, groping along the wall for the next alcove. A corner of jagged rock is my only warning before I stumble into a narrow cleft where swirls and chaotic lines of symbols wind back and forth without pattern. My fingers trace a broken line of text that asks what lies beyond death. Fragments of poetry raise the hairs on the back of my neck even as their full meaning evades my grasp. Unformed prayers grapple with mystery beyond human comprehension.

Is there a prayer here for me? Warm air flows upward, and I stretch after it, wishing I could float upward in its wake, away from all my confusion and turmoil. My hands fold into first one rocky depression and then another, as if I might climb up them toward the echo of distant water that trickles deep into the mountain's heart.

It's only when I take the first step that I realize they *are* handholds, carefully carved into this natural chimney in the rock. I peer up into the darkness, but no light is visible. The echoes suggest a narrow, vertical tunnel, but nothing else. I hesitate for a moment, then set my bare feet to the stone and climb.

It's not an easy climb, but it's not a dangerous one either. Midway up, a second shaft splits off, but the handholds carry me away from the sound of trickling water. I wiggle around a bend, and faint light starts to pick out the remains of a winch that must once have been used to raise and lower materials into the main cavern. The light grows brighter until I round another bend and emerge, blinking, to sit on a sheltered ledge high on the promontory that forms the prow of the ridge. A narrow path leads up to the array of instruments that monitor the sun and communicate with neighboring ridges. Below me, the stone buildings of Ikmeth spread out in their careful lines, giving way in the distance to forest and grass-covered slopes and the majestic peaks that eventually tumble in foothills to the sea.

It takes me a moment to realize that artisans have carved prayers here as well. Prayers for new perspectives, for other options, for different ways of being. Prayers, I realize wryly, that might appeal to people inspired to climb the hard way out the back exit of the temple. I trace one, and my breathing slows. I'd been told there are ways we've always done things, ways the world has to be. But here I am surrounded by sunlit sacred carvings and a world that stretches farther than anyone can grasp. I run my fingers over the prayers of my ancestors, wondering who else has sat here, the breeze in their face, seeking a new perspective on the life unfolding beneath them.

I lie back in the shade of the overhang and look up into the cloudless sky. Here, we keep our heads down, knowing that the sun's rays are too harsh, that they can damage and kill. I stare up into the blue. *What would I do if I weren't afraid?*

It's only as I ask the question that I realize I *am* afraid. Afraid of contradicting my family. Afraid of being cut off from the work I love. Afraid I don't deserve what I've reached for.

What would I do if I weren't afraid?

Something unfolds within me, rumbling with the built-up determination of magma that has been waiting for the rock containing it to crack. The fabric of my 'glove pulls against my fingers as I curl my hand. *All right*, I message my brother. *Tell Isel I'll meet with her.*

CHAPTER TWENTY-THREE
ANDESHE

Finally. I trudge through the woods toward where Ya'shul told me to meet him. Et'elark has been keeping me updated on the minuscule progress my project has been making while Ya'shul has been practically banned from the lab, but I've been hoping against hope that Ya'shul will follow through on his promise to tell me himself. Even so, I wasn't able to come immediately when Ya'shul messaged me. I can only hope that his lack of response to my replies doesn't mean he's lost his nerve.

At the edge of the forest, the ancient tree Ya'shul told me to meet him at stands in its isolated majesty, but Ya'shul isn't there. Instead, Nareen and Se'jan stand in its shade glaring at each other with such concentration that neither of them notices my arrival. The only other creature present is a small goat whose lead tangles in a bush as it strains to reach tender leaves on the upper branches. I message Ya'shul again, but he still doesn't respond. Frustration fills me. I told him the one thing I wanted was for him to talk to me honestly about what's going on. As much as I want this project to succeed, I can handle the disappointment if it fails. Even if everything goes perfectly, I know Fizz won't live forever. It's the way she has taught me to be in the world that I truly don't want to let pass away.

Nareen and Se'jan haven't moved. It's not uncommon for them to bicker, but something about how they're standing makes me think they've been arguing for a while. Se'jan's face is twisted with genuine anger, his normal edge of teasing gone. "'I know you do a *few* more things around the lab.'" His imitation of her higher pitched voice is scathing. "You said that and you're wondering why he stalked off?" He stabs a finger toward the village. Whatever Nareen replies is lost in the back and forth of their argument.

How does the tension not explode? I'd asked Et'elark.

You're assuming it doesn't.

"And don't even get me started on sex!" Se'jan launches the hurtful words at Nareen with clipped precision. She flinches.

Should I step in? I may not know where Ya'shul is, but the two of them are here, flinging verbal knives at each other. I finger the cuff of my long-sleeved shirt. For all that my conversation with Et'elark clarified what I can offer my new community, it's still difficult for me to believe how bad Uplanders are at talking through hurt feelings. Why can't I shake the feeling that there's something missing, some reason grown adults are stumbling over skills a child should have mastered?

Auntie Haveo believes I can do this. I'd told my aunt that I wanted to try helping the Uplanders learn to hold harms, and an affectionate smile had lit their eyes. They'd risen and rummaged in a chest in the corner of their room.

"I think this is yours, then," they'd said, holding out a folded bundle of cloth.

I'd unfolded the top, and they'd let go, allowing the wrappings to fall to my feet as a zoman robe unfolded in my hands.

"Me?" I'd looked up in shock to meet the head of my family's eyes. For all our flexibility in moving between genders, being a zoman is special. There are always a few younger people mature enough to handle murky situations that demand new ways of being, but most zomen are elders, people who have the wisdom of long experience and the perspective to handle the most complex and difficult circumstances. "But—are you sure I'm ready? I'm not even sure this is what I want to do." I had an idea, but that doesn't mean I feel qualified to guide other people through the messiest portions of their lives. I remember the zomen who supported me through my most difficult times. They were far more serene and collected than I'll ever be.

Haveo's mouth had quirked in rueful memory. "Is anyone ever ready? We all grow up faster when times are changing."

My hands had trembled as I refolded the robe. "Thank you."

Auntie Haveo had taken my hands, giving them a gentle squeeze. "Nothing's set in stone, not yet. Give it a try. You might not realize it, but you have a lot to teach."

Now, I exhale another breath, grounding myself in the present. My aunt believes I can do this. So do the people who smiled at me when they saw me in my new robes and brought me practice conflicts they could just as easily have resolved themselves. There's something steadying about the weight of a role with so much history behind it.

Velemeth's warning echoes in my mind. "You can't be a zoman here," she'd told me as I twirled in front of her, swishing the robe's unfamiliar skirt. The weight had felt heavy on my shoulders, but also somehow bracing.

"Why not?" I'd stopped, the long sleeves bumping against my arms.

"You haven't gone through menopause."

"That again." I'd put my hands on my hips. "That's not how we do things. They haven't had a problem with the rest of it." Uplanders may not always notice when my clothing choices indicate that I've changed gender, but so far the worst I've encountered are blank looks and the occasional intrusive question.

"They've indulged you," she corrected, "because you've never tried to present yourself as an Uplander woman. But a zoman?" She'd shaken her head. "You haven't heard what a scandal it is here when a woman tries to pretend her menstrual cycle has stopped before it has."

The words crawled across my skin like the footsteps of a venomous rock-fly. I hadn't been conscious of it, but she's right. I've always flown as a Wanderer. In the Uplander settlement, I've been a man.

"You want this to succeed, don't you?" she'd pressed. "You're off to a good start, working with one of the most prominent families on the ridge. If they speak well of you, you have a chance that they'll recommend you to others. But only if it goes well."

I'd hesitated, smoothing a hand over my front. Untangling knots of conflict is zoman's work. That's the point of the interlocking patterns on the robe, to slow the eye down and create space, to trace unexpected paths to other destinations. Yet what does it mean to be a zoman except to be flexible and creative when the normal rules are no longer enough?

"You really think so?" I'd asked, and she'd nodded, softening as she recognized my disappointment.

I'd had to take a deep breath. I still don't like how they blur boundaries here. That's half of what is causing Ya'shul so much anguish: trying to do all of women's work and all of men's work at once. No one can. Not well.

Velemeth had continued more gently, "It's not that you can't teach the Uplanders to handle conflict better, you can. But you have to let me help you with how to be accepted while you do it. Things are different here. Being a zoman won't work."

That's why I'd turned to Velemeth in the first place. We may not always agree, but she understands Uplanders in a way that I don't. I suppose it is a freedom, of a sort, to simply act without needing to decide what gender your actions fit into. Nonetheless, I'd shivered as I'd taken the robe off, missing the weight that had hung so oddly on my shoulders such a short time ago.

Back in the woods, I tug at the sleeve of my men's garb again. *I can do this.* I feel off balance without the support of the robes and their whispered connection to the people I've seen handle difficult situations with such grace, but I can do this. Nareen and Se'jan are well past the point where most people can recover on their own. Someone needs to intervene.

I raise my hands, traditional words hovering on the tips of my tongue, then stop. Meaningless words to them. I think they would value learning the rituals and containers that hold conflict within productive bounds, but they definitely don't have them to draw from now. I lower my hands.

No, wait. "Hello?" I interject as Se'jan stops to draw breath.

Two heads turn to me, Se'jan's eyes narrowing, Nareen's nostrils still flared with outrage.

"Do you both do ijendra?" I continue. They do have structures and rituals here that contain conflict, just different ones.

Se'jan's eyes flick back to Nareen in an assessing glance. Almost reflexively, she shifts her stance, one leg sliding back into a more stable position.

My surprise almost erupts as a laugh. I'd only meant to prompt reflection. But what I said must have struck a chord. I suppose trying to hit each other might hurt less than what they were doing before.

"Do you want to clear the rocks first?" I ask, waving a hand at the ground near their feet. A few stones peek out of the grass.

Almost reluctantly, the two Uplanders peel their eyes from each other and glance at the ground. Nareen is the first to straighten.

"This is ridiculous. Why are we even doing this?"

"That," I put in softly, "is an excellent question. Why *have* you been doing this?" A wave of my hands tries to encompass their whole conversation.

They both turn to me, Nareen's forehead furrowing while Se'jan's face goes blank. After a moment, his lips twist, and ironic amusement seeps back into his expression. "Touché." He gives me a tiny salute. With a nod to each of us, he strides away into the woods.

"Where's he going?" Nareen exclaims. "He can't just say all that and walk away!"

"There's something to be said for cooling off."

She makes a disgruntled noise, but doesn't disagree, only crossing her arms over her chest as she stares after him.

I wait, letting her fury settle. "Why *were* you arguing?"

"He was being completely unreasonable."

I make an encouraging noise and settle myself in the shade at the base of a tree, patting the ground beside me. Instead of sitting, she paces in front of me.

"He said—he said I don't deserve to present at the capital. That Ya'shul does." Her lips crimp. "I thought they were both on my side."

"Ouch." I wince. "That must hurt."

She turns to me. "No, of course not. He's just being a—" She cuts off, shaking her head. "All I did was ask Ya'shul—and honestly, I just *asked*—if he really did that much extra work. That's no reason for them both to come after me!"

There's so much to unpack there, but her entire body is as tight as a rope straining to hold a load suspended over the edge of a cliff.

"It's okay to acknowledge that you feel hurt," I tell her.

She paces back the other way. "It's just—of *course* he's going to do the childcare and things. It's not like I'm any good at it." The self-deprecating smile that briefly stretches her face feels like a concession. "And Kiu, can you imagine? It's only fair that the Goddess gave men a natural edge in *some* child-rearing skills to balance out not being able to give birth."

She can't be this deeply in denial of her own feelings, or of the impact her words must have had on Ya'shul. "The people who know you best told you that you don't deserve the recognition you're getting for the work you're most proud of," I push gently. "Anyone would feel hurt by that."

Her shoulders twitch. "You men are naturally better at childcare, though, aren't you? That's just fact."

As if. I can't quite stop myself from getting drawn into the argument she would so clearly prefer to have. *No one's good at it at first. It's just a question of who's allowed to give up when things get tough.* "Anyone gets better when they have to practice," I say instead. I cast about for some way back to the heart of what's going on. "You've known Ya'shul for a long time, right?" I ask, finally settling on something neutral.

She looks thrown by the change of subject, then gives a cautious nod.

"When did you first meet?"

"When we were children, I suppose." I make an encouraging noise, and the corner of her mouth quirks. "He would tell you it was when I first came to apprentice at the lab, but it was years earlier. You know how children are. He always had this blanket tied around his shoulders to pretend he was a pteradon, and he'd go 'flying' around the village, jumping off things." She puts her arms out to the sides and pretends to soar. "I thought I was older and *much* too mature for that sort of game, but he's always had this way about him…. He jumped out of a tree and landed *on* my sandcastle, and by the time I finished scolding him, I was chasing him around, pretending to be a pteradon, too. I don't think he even knew who I was. He was just always that enthusiastic and would draw people into his play. Then puberty took us our separate ways, of course, and once I became an apprentice…" She leans in. "His intensity. Have you seen it? The way he pours his whole attention into things? He didn't even have to say a word, and I was transfixed."

"It sounds like you really care about each other."

"Of course." Her smile fades, replaced by strain around her eyes. "Or at least I thought he did."

"Have you asked him about how he's been feeling?"

"I know what he wanted; he wanted recognition at the festival. But now he's taking not getting it out on me, and how is that fair? I was trying to help!"

I hold up a hand to cut off the torrent of words. "Have you *asked* him? And then really listened to what he says? Half of what people want is to feel heard."

The expression fades from her face. "I...suppose not."

"What would happen if you did?"

Something flares in her eyes, too quickly suppressed for me to read.

"Breathe," I remind her. I don't think she realizes how shallow her breathing has gotten.

The effect is instantaneous, tapping into something deeper than my words alone. Her shoulders drop, though she still stands across from me in the grass instead of coming to sit beside me. "Hashing things over won't help. It never does."

"What are you afraid would happen if you tried?"

"I'm not afraid." But her voice is sharp.

"Everyone's afraid of being vulnerable," I tell her gently. "Everyone's afraid that if we lower our defenses and really listen, we might let in something we can't bear to hear."

She's so still now that I'm not sure she's breathing at all.

"It takes a lot of strength to face that," I add gently.

"Strength?" She fixes me with a penetrating look.

I nod. "To sit with hurt—with any difficult

emotion—and not run away."

"I've never run away from anything!"

"Not even emotionally? Changing the subject? Insisting on moving on? Jumping straight to action, instead of leaving time and space to feel?" Now that I know what to look for, the tricks so many Uplanders use to flee from even the faintest potential for guilt are obvious.

The silence stretches out until she finally looks away. When she speaks again, her voice is flat. "Do you think he's the one who started the rumors?"

"Ya'shul?"

A short jerk of her head is all she can manage.

I let out my breath in a long sigh, letting the tension unspool. "Come, sit." I pat the ground beside me, and after a moment, she joins me. "Is that what you're afraid of?" At her reluctant nod, I continue. "Tell me more."

Her hands open and close in her lap. "I thought he knew me better than anyone, but it's like I don't even know who he is anymore. Does he really think—I didn't steal his work—I *didn't*. The old Ya'shul would never have said something like that, much less tried to turn the whole ridge against me, but this new one?" Hurt flashes in her eyes. "These rumors came from somewhere."

I hesitate. "They came from your conflict with Isel," I point out. "That's what's driving them." I've been surprised by the vitriol that has accompanied the contest for the council seat—and by the way the Uplanders let it spread like wildfire, instead of taking steps to rein it in. Suspicion and hard feelings are natural in any conflict, letting them get out of hand is a community's choice.

She shakes her head. "Isel wouldn't know half the

things that have shown up in the rumors. Someone's been telling her."

"Have you tried talking to her, though? If the two of you toned things down, you'd have the breathing room to sort out everything else." I've seen conflicts dissolve into bad blood before, but never with so many bystanders lining up to take sides rather than intervening. I can't be the only one on the ridge relying on collaboration between people who have stopped talking to each other.

Nareen looks at me as if I asked her why she doesn't flap her arms and take flight. "Tone things down? And leave those of us who live on the lower levels to keep struggling while the storms make everything harder?"

I blink. She must mean the lower levels of Ikmeth proper. As far as I know, the Lowlanders who actually live at the bottom of the cliff haven't taken sides.

"We don't want to tone things down," she continues. "We want to win."

I can tell when someone is not willing to be moved. "Ya'shul, then. He is someone you need to talk to. Not doing so is tearing you both apart."

Nareen's shoulders sag slightly, but she doesn't disagree.

"Is what he'd say if you talked to him worse than what your imagination is tormenting you with now?" I cajole.

She barks a laugh. "Fair enough."

"Listen to him," I urge her, "and sit with the feelings that arise instead of getting defensive or running away."

"That doesn't sound so hard," she says dubiously.

An unexpected stab of pain lances through me. "On the contrary, it's probably the hardest thing I've ever done." Memories come back to me of trembling with shame as I took my place in a circle filled with people harmed by my actions. Not only Velemeth, injured leg sticking out awkwardly after the accident, but also the relatives of the other friend who had been with us on that flight, the one whom the safety straps hadn't caught, the one who had plunged to her death after a push I had meant to be playful. "To let down your defenses and listen while someone you care about tells you how badly you've hurt them?" I rise to my feet and hold out my hands to her. Only the faith of the people supporting me those many years ago had kept me from bolting entirely. "But sometimes it's the only way to move forward. If you have the courage for it."

"You think I don't?" She takes my hands and levers herself to her feet.

I consider what I've seen of her defensiveness, of the way she bridles at the merest hint that she may have erred. Do I think she could handle a fraction of what I've gone through? "Not yet," I admit. "Not without help."

"I don't ask for help."

"I know. Being able to do that is its own type of strength."

She snorts, then cuts off when she sees my face. "You're serious."

"Very. Would you rather ask for help or put yourself in physical danger?"

She gives me a long, considering look.

I hesitate, torn between what I think she's ready to hear and my desire to pass along lessons that would have saved me so much heartache. "Maybe the people around you don't want you to pretend to have no weaknesses," I say at last. "Maybe they want you to open up, even when you're feeling vulnerable or uncertain. You and Ya'shul are both hurting. Someone has to listen first."

She studies me for a long time before her chin jerks infinitesimally upward, and she strides off into the woods.

Chapter Twenty-Four
Ya'shul

Isel is late. I sit in the stage's shadow with my brother, trying not to jiggle my leg in impatience like a child.

"When did she say she'd be here?" I ask Ya'kinem. We nod to another group that passes, chattering, on their way to the ijendra circles.

He wiggles his 'glove. "Soon."

There is no reason for me to feel this anxious. It's not like I'm doing anything wrong. I have every right to meet with anyone I please. There's no reason for me to jump every time a swirl of trousers or a flash of an arm reminds me of Nareen or Kiu. They're in the lab. Like they always are. Unlike me. Just because the woman I spotted out of the corner of my eye walks with the same firm stride as Nareen, that doesn't mean—

"Ya'shul."

My heart skips. Nareen's greeting is stiff and uncomfortable. "Ya'kinem." She includes my brother in the greeting and shifts her weight on her feet. "I was wondering…"

"Yes?" It comes out more curtly than I intended. I don't have time to puzzle over her unusual reticence. Isel is going to be here any minute.

She waves tentatively at the grass beside me. "Listen, can I join you?"

"Oh!" I scramble to my feet, heart galloping in my chest. "No! There's no need."

Hurt flashes in her eyes, quickly concealed.

"That is—I was just getting up." I nod firmly. The fairground is devoid of the woman I'm waiting for, but for how long? "What was it you wanted?"

"Can I talk to you?"

"Now isn't really a good time." I stop myself from looking around the fairground again.

"Oh." Her face shutters. She starts to turn away, then looks back. "I didn't mean to hurt you. That's all I wanted to say. And to listen."

What? I blink. It's not that she never apologizes, but as I look closer at her, something seems different. An edge of uncertainty, perhaps, has crept into her usual confidence. She turns away, and I stare after her, disconcerted.

"There's Isel." Next to me, my brother points at a stocky form pacing across the grass, loose trousers slung low across her hips. I hold my breath, but Nareen doesn't look back.

"Come on." Ya'kinem levers himself to his feet and turns to me. "Shall we go?"

***

The flier Isel created crouches in front of me, its windows watching me like baleful eyes in the small clearing near the edge of town. I rub my palms on my trousers. "We're going to your workshops?" I'd thought that we would just talk here.

"Of course." Isel opens the door and casually swings herself up into the flier's interior, as if casting free of gravity itself is no more noteworthy to her than taking a breath. Ya'kinem climbs up behind her, then turns to offer me his hand. I glance back. The carefully cultivated crops of Ikmeth ripple gently in the breeze, their roots anchoring them safely to the ridge. In the distance, stone buildings squat, planted and steady. Only the promontory above the temple thrusts its way into the sky. In the front seat of the flier, Isel manipulates an instrument panel, her movements quick and confident.

"Come on," my brother says. "You'll love it. This is what freedom feels like. I get Isel to take me with her every chance I get."

Does Grandmother know that? Oddly, the thought steadies me, pulling me back into the familiar realm of family politics and running interference for my little brother. I take a deep breath and pull myself into the flier, the ginger and metal scent of Isel's family wrapping around me. Nothing's going to change if I don't take some risks. Isel has been respectful, solicitous even, treating me with the courtesy due someone important. We should be fine. Besides, with Ya'kinem along, there isn't even any impropriety.

With a roar, the blades above us spring to life, thunderous even through the ear protection my brother shows me how to don. The flier lurches, then the ridge falls away, trees and buildings shrinking to mere toys as I clutch the arms of my seat.

"Amazing, isn't it!" Ya'kinem shouts, barely audible over the motor and the pounding of my pulse in my ears. I manage a jerky nod, barely able to peek at the landscape rippling so far below us. He jostles me with an elbow, and I sit up, forcing myself to turn my full attention out the window. Majestic upthrusts of rock frame valleys where slashes of greenery line streams that tumble into churning waterfalls. Slowly, my racing heart calms as the awe that keeps Ya'kinem's nose glued to the opposite window starts to seep into my soul. *Could I get used to this?* Other members of our family fly regularly, but normally neither Ya'kinem nor I would ever be important enough to travel with them.

The flier banks gently, then descends toward a lake that fills the valley between two peaks before spilling over a dam into an enormous waterfall. A trio of pteradons splash at the far end of the lake. With only a few slight bumps, Isel settles the flier on a flat outcrop of rock near the water and cuts the power. In a few moments, we're back on solid ground, staring up toward an unadorned cave opening while Isel unrolls a cable and plugs it into a hatch in the flier's side. Finished, she raises her 'glove to her ear, listens to the ring of a call, then frowns when no one picks up. Her fingers writhe and she listens again, before exchanging brief comments with someone whose voice is inaudible amidst the thunder of the waterfall.

"He's this way." She beckons us not up toward the entrance I saw, but toward the side of the landing pad, where another path leads around a curve in the mountain. "I thought you'd like to see what men can *really* do," she tells me.

The fall's rumble diminishes as we turn a corner, replaced with a new, crackling noise. Another turn, and a blast of heat greets us as the pathway widens into a shelf of rock. At the far end, a huge metal door is rolled up, creating a portal into the mountain. A gigantic cylinder of metal and tubing squats there, sparks cascading in fountains from its top. I step backward, not needing the warning arm Isel puts out to stop me from stepping closer. Silhouetted against the flying sparks, two figures stand, their backs to us, silvery protective suits glinting in the sun. One moves a lever on a control box, and the sparks fade away. The other plunges a long pole into a fiery opening near the cylinder's base, scraping globs of molten metal out of its maw.

"Are they—" I don't even know what I'm asking, only that my heart is in my mouth as the glowing mass oozes out of the opening into a blackened metal container.

Isel spares me an unconcerned glance. "Removing the slag? Yes. The purified metal is tapped inside the mountain." She gestures to a second, person-sized doorway I hadn't noticed. Down a short tunnel, orange light flickers, blocked by the sudden emergence of a third figure, also bulky in its protective gear. A distorted image of myself warps briefly across the darkened face shield before the figure passes us and touches the shape with the control box on the shoulder. Heads bend in an inaudible conversation, then the control box changes hands, and its original owner turns to us, pulling off a hood to reveal tousled brown hair that frames a man's tan face.

"Here you are." Isel greets him with both hands outstretched, and he strips off his gauntlets to take them. Isel tilts her head toward me. "I wanted Ya'shul to see your demo." With a flash of a smile, the man ducks into the tunnel, and Isel turns back to me. "The future!" She flings her arms wide, a gesture that has always seemed too large and wild in Ikmeth, but which now echoes the rawness of the elemental forces behind her. The breeze steals a strand of her hair away from her head, and she rakes it back.

The man emerges again, cradling a tiny version of the flier in his hands, and guides us back around the corner to where he can explain its workings to me without shouting over the roar of the furnace. As he launches into a clearly practiced explanation, it's not lost on me that despite his deference to Isel, a man is the one showing us how *he* developed the drones that were the flier's precursors. The coated metal flashes in the sun as he toggles a control box and maneuvers the drone away from the mountain's face, curving it in tighter and tighter arcs that show off its nimbleness. While Ya'kinem oohs and ahhs, I study the man. Freed from his protective gear, the muscles in his arm ripple with the same vitality as Isel's, their family resemblance visible in the shared roundness of their faces and wide-set eyes. Isel didn't say if he was a brother or a cousin, but in either case, her pride in him is clear.

The demonstration ends, and Isel and Ya'kinem and I climb a narrow set of stairs to a shaded alcove, where a small, low table laden with refreshments overlooks the lake. A tunnel at the back echoes faintly with mechanical clanks and rhythmic hammering.

Isel gestures me to the position of an honored guest on the middle seating cushion and serves me with her own hands, savory flatbreads and a delicate fish paste that complement tart fruits that must have been flown in from distant foothills. *See*, the spread whispers to me, *this is how you could always be treated.* I murmur my appreciation. Dry, warm air breathes from the tunnel behind me, battling against the cooler breeze blowing off the lake.

"So," Isel says, setting down her glass, "why are you letting Nareen steal your place at the capital?"

I close my eyes, the bluntness of the question spearing me through the gut. "I'm not." I force my eyes open again. "She—a lot of the work is hers. She deserves to be honored for it." What my family would want me to say keeps getting harder and harder to mouth.

"And you don't deserve to be?"

Out of sight, the noise of the furnace starts up again, fainter now, but echoed through the tunnel behind us. The breeze on the back of my neck feels like warm breath, as if some giant beast in a cavern below is grumbling and straining against the mountain that holds it in. Despite the heat, a shiver runs up my neck.

"We worked together." The words are all I can find to say, ones whispered to myself too many times in an attempt to salvage my sense of self-worth.

"Did that stop her from ditching you?" Ya'kinem demands hotly.

No. I look away, unable to deny the truth. "It's not so simple as that," I grind out. "The priestesses chose her. I don't get to overrule them. None of us does."

Ya'kinem trades a glance with Isel, and she stirs, leaning toward me. "That's what they want you to think. That doesn't mean it's true."

"You don't have to put a good face on it," Ya'kinem adds. "Not with Isel on our side."

Under the table, my fingers dig painfully into my thighs. "What would you do?" I croak.

Isel settles back. "The priestesses are powerful, yes, but they're not immune to public pressure. They don't want the embarrassment of sending a plagiarist to Treverel to represent Ikmeth."

I flinch at the word.

"So far," she continues, "your family's clout has been enough to brush any rumors under the rug, and without someone knowledgeable—such as the man whose work was stolen—being willing to stand up and say anything…" She shrugs. "Well, there's only so much we can do. But if that were to change?" Her eyes bore into mine. "All my allies would back you up. This isn't just about you. It's about every man who has been deemed less than, whose work has been taken for someone else's glory. This is about *justice*."

Her words vibrate deep within me, resonating with something long buried. I can almost smell the air of the capital, stories I've heard about its delicate artwork of perfumes merging into the aromas of the delicacies in front of me. I've heard of rooms so carefully sculpted that ever-changing sounds tease the senses, of the elaborate carvings that adorn the council chamber, of all the places I've never been.

"Grandmother would never let me." Se'jan's mother and a few other high-ranking zomen visit Treverel regularly to lobby for what our ridge needs and to grow our family's influence. I can't imagine them looking happily on anything that disrupts their careful dance of power.

Isel tilts her head. "Marin-lun hasn't held onto power this long without developing the ability to know which way the wind's blowing. They'll cut loose rather than go down with the losing side. Especially if it means your family ends up presenting at the capital. For all your prominence, it's been awhile."

At her side, Ya'kinem nods vigorously. I have no faith in his judgment, but what Isel says rings true.

"What would I need to do?" Everything I've always

wanted hovers tantalizingly close.

Isel refills my glass. "Claim your work," she says simply. "Go public with who *really* deserves credit—and who doesn't."

And who doesn't. The ugly reality slides around until I can no longer avoid staring it in the face. All I have to do is tell everyone who will listen that my closest collaborator, the woman I've loved for years, is a fraud.

"I need to think about it." I don't even recognize my own voice.

Isel smiles over the rim of her glass. "Take your time," she says. "But not too long."

***

I can't stop thinking about it. Not on the flier ride back. Not while my feet take me unthinkingly to the lab I can no longer enter. Not when I retreat to the goat pens that should be empty, only to find Nareen already there. It takes everything in me not to crank my head toward the landing pad for Isel's flier, not that far distant through the trees. The muscles in Nareen's back flex as she bends to check a bandage on the leg of one goat that hasn't gone out with the others. Memories cascade around me, my head bent next to hers, me tossing out ideas that nobody else grasped, but that made her face light up like starfire. The times when she would come to work rolling her eyes about some irritation at home and we would trade commiserations until the world fell away around us and all that was left was our awareness of each other, of the way my palms itched to graze against her skin. Am I really going to throw away everything I've had with the woman who used to be as close to me as my own breath? I still remember her taking the fall for me over the improvised still Ya'kinem and I roped her into making in the storeroom, her face completely straight as she tried to persuade my mother that was all part of a project she'd thought up.

The glow of memory sours abruptly. *All part of a project she thought up.*

She catches sight of me and straightens. "Ya'shul? You're here. Does that mean you're ready to talk?"

"About what?" It comes out more hostile than I meant it to. I brace for her irritated retort, but it doesn't come. Instead, she shifts her weight as if forcing herself not to walk away.

"I'm trying to listen." She almost flings the words at me, then stops and takes a deep breath. "Not jump to conclusions, not to get defensive. I just want to know what's going on. For you. With your feelings."

What the hell? I've never heard her like this. I look around the mostly empty pen, but the pile of feed and the contentedly chewing goat offer no clues. *Maybe she's trying to be a decent human being.* Isn't that some of what I've wanted from her? My shoulder blades itch with an awareness of Isel's flier.

"Did you have anything you wanted to tell me?" she prompts.

Maybe you don't deserve that prize. The thought bubbles up, angry and raw. *Maybe I do.* But I can't say that, not yet, not with her standing here in front of me, dark eyes wide with a mixture of hope and determination. Maybe I can't say it, ever.

"I'm sorry." Her abrupt words break the lengthening silence, feeling as if they've been pulled out of her.

"For what?" I can think of any number of things, but I wouldn't have expected her to be able to.

She opens her mouth, but nothing comes out. She licks her lips, then closes it again. "Perhaps…you should tell me?" she deflects.

Why not say it? How much hurt does it take to shatter years of memories? How much does it cost me to hold the silence in? *But she's trying to apologize*, a tiny voice protests. Shouldn't I give her a break for trying to do the right thing?

So? New thoughts rumble with the built-up potential of magma that has been waiting for centuries for its rocky prison to crack. *Has she ever censored herself for you? She's thought nothing of telling you what you don't deserve.* Hairs rise on my arms. If I truly thought back to those oh-so-idyllic years, what else would I remember? *Why should you hold back when no one else does?*

"Maybe I should take your place." My words drop like rocks into the space between us. "Maybe you don't deserve it."

She flinches as if I'd punched her in the gut. "How could you—" She snaps her lips shut, but her eyes are still wide with her objection. *Yes*, I think at her, *that's what it means to listen. That's what it means to sit there and hear everyone who claims to care about me agree when the priestess says I'm not as good as you are. Why should you be spared?*

I shrug. "It's just something I've been thinking about. Something I might mention to you before your festival presentation to warn you against reaching too high." Viciousness sharpens my voice, but I don't care anymore. "After all, you thought nothing of warning me not to believe in myself too much."

She wants to argue with me. The need practically

vibrates through her. But the goat interrupts, looking upward with a plaintive "maa" that draws her attention to a pteradon gliding in just over the treetops to land at the Wanderer's settlement. "Is there more?" she asks instead after it passes.

The magma pumping through my soul has breached the surface now, spilling its viscous buildup of hurt into the open. But I glance upward, too, remembering another conversation, another person desperate to make amends.

I inhale. "I felt awful at the festival," I tell her. It feels awkward to simply say it. "I'd worked so hard, and I thought I would be celebrated for what I could do. Your changes—they made me doubt myself. I spent all day blaming myself for not being good enough, thinking it was my fault."

She wets her lips but doesn't say anything.

"I never realized that the whole thing was stacked against me to begin with. And I'm angry about that." It feels so good to just say it. "I'm angry that everyone fawned over you and ignored me. I'm angry that you're deemed worthy of your own lab, and I get nothing. I'm angry that you got five pledges, and I got hardly even one. I'm angry that you're going to the capital, and I'm not. And yes, I'm angry at you. But mostly I'm angry at all of it. I wish I'd said what I had to say, and who gives a damn about the consequences? At least I could have been proud of *myself*." I look at her, really look at her. "I know you were trying to help me, but you *didn't*. You should have asked me what I wanted, not assumed you knew."

She ducks her head stiffly. "Is there more?" she prompts again when I lapse into silence.

I never thought about what would happen after I

spoke. The pressure has built up for so long, I'm not sure what to do as it pumps itself out. The goat butts my fingers where they're wrapped around the pen's railing, begging for scratches.

"I could do it." I don't know what prompts me to tip my hand. "I could take your spot." I doubt she'll hear the warning for what it is, but giving it feels only fair.

She cocks her head. Disbelief is writ large across her face, but worry shadows her eyes. "This is bothering you that much?"

Anger flares through me again. "Have you heard a word I said?"

"Of course." She raises placating hands. "It matters to you. Very much. Right. Yes. I didn't mean it that way. I just wanted to ask—" She hesitates, then dispels the unspoken question with a shake of her head. "Never mind. I'm trying."

She's trying. What would it be like to work with someone who didn't have to try?

"Try harder," I growl. Before all this, I might have had more patience.

She straightens as if poked with a pin. "I will. And—and I thought of just the thing." She searches my face. Whatever she sees there creases her forehead with apprehension. "Be patient. That's all I ask. I've got this." Watching me as if to make sure I'll stay put, she lets herself out of the pen and disappears down the path.

Chapter Twenty-Five
Ya'shul

I stare at the door to the lab, not quite able to bring myself to knock. For all my tossing and turning last night, I'm no closer to knowing what I should do. Every day that passes is another day that the projects I've worked so hard on are stalled, pushed ahead only fitfully by people to whom they don't matter. Kiu will do the minimum necessary to fulfill what we've promised Andeshe's family, but she won't prioritize it. I close my eyes, resting my forehead gently against the weathered wood. *Claim your work.* Isel's voice resonates in my head. Does she realize how much I ache to do just that? But memories of the visit to Isel's workshop fade into an image of Nareen's worried eyes. Isel wants me to lie. That's the crux of it. And Nareen is trying to do the right thing, but how long am I supposed to pat her on the back for finding the fortitude to bear a tiny fraction of what I'm expected to swallow without complaint?

The door opens, and I nearly stumble inside. Kiu blinks at me in surprise.

"There you are." She recovers immediately and pulls

me into the room. "Why am I being told to drop everything and report to the temple?"

"The temple?" I'm not sure I heard right, but she nods curtly. "Why would I know?"

"Because—" she skewers me with a look— "the message *specifically* says to bring you."

Cold prickles along my arms. "There's nothing I know of."

She gives me a searching look but pulls a sunshade from the collection by the door and opens it with a snap. I follow in her wake, tamping down an automatic surge of guilt. I haven't even *done* anything yet.

We hurry down the path, slowing only when a tight cluster of robed figures comes into view near the stage, their tense stance and low voices drawing curious looks from passersby. My mother, my *grandmother*, and…Nareen's family head? I blink, but Orzea-lun doesn't disappear.

We clink our bracelets, and the zomen turn to look at us. Orzea-lun's eyes rake over me, narrow with anger.

The zoman turns on Kiu. "Did you know Nareen was planning this?"

Planning what? I look around the group frantically, but there are no hints beyond general expressions of disapproval. My sister must be as mystified as I am, but unlike me, she doesn't show it.

"Perhaps we should find out what Nareen has to say?" Her recovery is smoother than I could ever have managed.

Orzea-lun looks at her for a long moment, then jerks their head toward the entrance. An acolyte waits for us to remove our shoes, then guides us into the midnight depths of one of the temple's side passages. The heartbeat of the central chamber fades as our passage curves, then veers sharply away and down a set of steps. The acolyte announces us at the doorway to a small chamber, and the scent of incense billows outward as Priestess Wekmet bids us to enter. Nareen, voice strained but defiant, announces her presence in the darkness as well.

"Now," Wekmet says in a clipped voice as the chimes of our entry die down. "Someone explain to me why Nareen saw fit to try to upend all the arrangements that have already been finalized for going to the capital?"

Puzzled silence fills the room.

"I told you." Nareen's voice is tight. "Ya'shul did just as much work on that project as I did. He deserves to present it with me."

Despite the dark, I turn toward her, air flooding into my lungs. *You really think so?* A mist-shrouded conversation curls up out of my memory. *Of course.* I deserved to go the entire time. Why should I have needed to bargain away doing something more?

"And *I* told *you*," the priestess replies, "that we send one person from each ridge, no exceptions. The displays at the capital are supposed to be sober presentations of the greatest minds the ridges have produced, not political favors handed out like candy." The iron in their voice is a slap in the face.

"There have been exceptions before," Nareen presses.

I hold my breath, willing her onward.

She continues, "The second time Marin-lun was chosen—"

"That was different," Priestess Wekmet snaps. "Those were established scientists who worked together from the beginning."

"So did we! There's no reason for this to be different."

"Nareen!" Orzea-lun's warning voice cuts through the darkness.

My heart hammers. *Don't fold*, I urge Nareen. She's the most stubborn person I know, infamous throughout our childhood for digging in her heels despite adults' patient efforts to teach her to bend. We have a chance.

"I won't go unless he does." Her words echo in the shocked silence of the room.

My indrawn breath is loud in the darkness. Despite the tension in the room, warmth kindles in my chest. *She's really doing it. She just defied the head priestess.* Gratitude floods me. I reach for her hand. It's dry and warm when she squeezes back.

Kiu recovers first. "Think of what that would mean for us." To anyone else, her voice would sound honey sweet, a mentor trying to use gentle reason to repair a breach that should never have come to the attention of the zomen. "It's not just your family whose prestige is riding on this. We've poured so much into supporting you. To refuse to go…" Only I can hear the warning underlying the head of the lab's words. *You're embarrassing me in front of the priestess. How dare you?* Reflexively, I flinch away from the danger.

Wekmet's voice is as sharp and cold as a diamond. "I have in no way authorized a second person from this ridge to present research at the solstice. I am not going to. I have made this abundantly clear, regardless of how hard certain other families try to demand that we endorse a second project." A disgusted snort conveys too clearly what they think of that endeavor. "I do not appreciate rumors that I might. I do not appreciate having my superiors in Treverel call me to ask what in the Goddess's name I think I'm doing."

"That has nothing to do with us," Nareen objects. "That's Isel's problem."

"Enough!" The priestess' voice cracks through the air. Tense silence reigns.

Should I say something? My brain races in frantic circles. But what would I say? I clutch Nareen's hand, breath coming in shallow pants. I've never been able to handle confrontation, not for very long. The weight of the zomen's combined disapproval feels like it's pressing on my chest.

"I guess I'll have to not go, then." Nareen sounds so calm.

"Do you want me to send Isel instead?" Wekmet snaps. "Enough people have lobbied for it." The priestess can't mean it, but they sound angry enough that I can almost imagine them doing just that. I cast around frantically for something to say, but my mind is blank.

"Of course not," Orzea-lun jumps in. A whisper of air passes behind me, and the zoman is next to us, hissing something almost inaudible in Nareen's ear.

"Then this discussion is over." The steel in the priestess' voice brooks no argument.

Nareen starts to protest, but Orzea-lun overrides her. "Yes, Priestess. We're sorry to have wasted your time." Nareen's hand is pulled away from mine. "We are, of course, grateful for the honor."

"But—" Nareen's objection is silenced by another hissed whisper from Orzea-lun.

"I *trust*," Priestess Wekmet cuts in, "that everyone in this room understands that the arrangements for the festival will go as planned. *Exactly* as planned."

Murmurs of acknowledgement echo around the room.

No. You can't do this. I grope for Nareen's hand again, but she's no longer next to me.

"Nareen?" the priestess presses.

The zomen's unified censure crushes in around us, all the more perilous for its absolute silence. Orzea-lun's robes whisper with some tiny motion.

"Yes, priestess." Nareen's voice is wooden.

The assent punches the breath out of me. Now, after all these years, she's finally learned to back down. I curl forward, invisible in the darkness.

Bracelets chime, the zomen falling over themselves to withdraw from the high priestesses' presence. I find myself herded out of the room and down the hallway until the semi-gloom near the entrance reveals Nareen ahead of us, Orzea-lun's hand clamped tightly on her shoulder. The zoman glances back at me, then whispers something to Nareen in an angry, low-voiced hiss. Nareen casts a look back as well, mouth tight with strain.

What happened? I mouth at her. Surely, she has a plan, some reassurance for me that she'll make this work.

She flinches, a gut-deep twitch of guilt that takes my breath away. The normally proud lift of her shoulders curls in on itself until, by the time she turns away, she's hunched against a blow. Cold washes down my body. *No.* My steps falter until I come to a halt on the grass outside the temple. *How could you?* Her retreating back provides no answer.

Only as she vanishes out of sight do the sounds around me filter back into my consciousness.

"I had thought, Kiu, that preparation for the first

major showcase of the lab under new leadership was going more smoothly than this." My grandmother's irritated voice is the first thing I hear.

Kiu's new responsibility for managing the lab hangs around her like an ill-fitting coat. "It will be sorted out, I promise."

"See that it is. I do not ever want to be called before the head priestess like that again." Their tone leaves no doubt of the consequences of failure. I cringe. Marin-lun's iron sense of propriety has kept them from intervening directly in the lab after their retirement, but it was their time leading the lab that built the family's prestige and fortune originally. Now that they run the family, there will be no mercy for anyone who damages that legacy.

After a long moment, my grandmother departs in a scuff of robes and strident footsteps. Only Kiu remains, her presence lingering at my back.

"How could you?" A hand grabs my shoulder and I jump. Kiu glares at me. "If you'd just kept your head down and done what you were supposed to do, none of this would have happened!"

"I had nothing to do with this!" Turmoil roils my gut as the mess Nareen has left me with slowly sinks in.

She gives me a scornful look, and sarcasm laces her voice. "No, Nareen just came up with this on her own. It had *nothing* to do with you stomping about, demanding privileges you never earned. It had *nothing* to do with the way you've been giving her the silent treatment after all these years of mooning after each other. What was the poor woman to do to try to get your attention?" Kiu's lip curls. "She's been far more patient than I would have been. I'd have dropped you the instant you started getting a puffed head about yourself. But no, I suppose every young woman at some point has to learn the hard way that it does no good to pander to a man's ego."

Is that what you think of me? I can hardly find the words to sputter a response. "That's not what happened! I never told her—She and I, we—*Is that what you think of me?*"

Her baleful stare doesn't change. "She's humored you long enough. You're not anything special. You're an assistant in the lab, and that's it. Nareen is going to Treverel because she deserves to, and you don't. The faster you adjust to that, the faster things can go back to normal."

Everything I could say slips away like mist. I blink back the burning in my eyes. She's my *sister*. Enough older than me to be distant, a mini copy of Marin-lun once she reached adulthood, but I'd thought she felt some pride in what I can do.

"Get it together," she grates out. "I'm not recommending you for pledging again until you get this through your head."

I'm too numb to even respond to the threat. My chances of a future pledge are ash, anyway.

Kiu gives me a hard look. "Or for working back in the family's lab. I have no interest in dealing with that attitude either."

Even the numbness can't stop ice from congealing in my veins. There is nothing that requires her to let me back into the lab. Ever.

"Do you understand?" she demands.

I nod, throat too closed to speak.

"I said, *do you understand?*" she demands again.

"Yes, Kiu," I whisper.

With a final sharp look, she turns and stalks off across the field. My trembling legs barely get me to the shadow of the rocks near the temple's entrance before I collapse at their base.

Eventually, the air stirs, and a warm shape lowers itself to the ground next to me. I don't look up.

"What happened?" my brother asks.

In a monotone, I give him a halting summary.

"How *could* they?" he sputters. "That was nonsense, utter nonsense! Of course you deserve to go. Even Nareen recognized that! You're awesome. Kiu doesn't know what she's doing. Losing you? That would be a disaster."

It's nice to have a partisan. I manage to raise my head. Earnestness suffuses his freckled face, his eyes round with outrage. "Kiu would cope," I say roughly. "I'm the one who would be done. It's not like there's another fully equipped lab lying around." Even in the open air, I can feel walls closing around me. I drop my head back against the stone. "Do you think I should fold?" Nothing short of abject capitulation will be enough for Kiu now, but what is that compared to the pain already radiating through my chest?

"No!" He sits bolt upright. "There's always Isel. She'll help. She believes in you."

I can barely muster the energy to turn my head in his direction. I had a hundred reasons why that was a bad idea. "She wants me to lie."

"And no one else does?"

I close my eyes, a headache starting in my temples. Nareen's betraying flinch replays itself in my mind. She tried. And failed.

"You can't give in," my brother coaxes. "What does it

mean for the rest of us if you fold? For the men who look up to you as an example?"

"What men? No one cares about what I do." Except the people who want me to be less.

Ya'kinem shakes his head. "Not true. You being you—you showing everyone what a man can do—that means something. Other men look at that and say, 'Well, if he could do that, then what about me?' You can't back down."

I never thought of that, that I might have inspired someone I never noticed. How many other men have so desperately looked for themselves in the alcoves of the temple? Even the carvings on the sunlit ledge above don't fully capture who we could be.

"Come on," my brother presses.

Reluctantly, I nod.

Chapter Twenty-Six
Andeshe

"Andeshe?" Nareen's voice sounds frayed. "Is that you?" She stops at the edge of the field where I'm helping Et'elark pull withered vines out of rows of mounded dirt.

I straighten, wiping the sweat from my forehead. I haven't intentionally made a habit of joining Et'elark in his work, but I keep finding myself seeking out the warmth of his smile and the way it sends a tiny shiver through my stomach. I may not be fast, but I'm competent enough that his work seems to go a little quicker and more enjoyably when I'm here. Quickly enough, at least, that the zoman who oversees the work doesn't shoo me off, despite their frown.

"Do you need something?" I ask her. The smell of loam fills my nostrils, rich and earthy. Around us, the rhythm of a work song fills the morning air.

She glances around, her sunshade and crisply pleated slacks out-of-place amid the industry of the fields. She hesitates, then jerks her head toward the path. "Maybe we could talk?"

I turn to Et'elark. "See you later?"

He raises his own hand in brief acknowledgement.

I dust off my hands. "Hopefully, I'll have heard more about flights by then." Fizz's flying schedule has been packed, especially as her need for rest between trips increases, and a recreational trip to the mines is the last thing on Auntie Haveo's priority list.

A smile flashes across his face anyway—all the thanks I need.

I fall into step beside Nareen, whose body practically vibrates with tension. I'd warned her, last time we spoke, that change isn't easy. I have to remind myself of that, too. No matter how impatient I am to prove that I have skills to offer here—or to save Fizz—some things can't be rushed. I wiggle the tension out of my shoulders and prepare myself to listen to her with my complete attention.

Nareen steers me into the orchard and down a side path so faint that I wouldn't have called it a trail. I'm unsurprised when it peters out amid dry leaves before she speaks. "I tried," she says finally, voice is clipped. "It was a disaster."

"Back up," I tell her. "What did you try?"

"I talked to Ya'shul. Listened, that is." Hurt flashes in her eyes. "These rumors, I still don't know if he's the one who started them, but he's jealous. The things he said—" She breaks off, shaking her head, then turns to me, eyes gripping mine urgently. "I thought I could fix it, though. I had this idea. If we shared the spot, then there'd be no problem. So I went to ask Priestess Wekmet, and—" she claps her hands together— "squished. Like a bug."

Something's missing from her story. "Did you talk to Ya'shul about sharing the spot?"

She shakes her head. "It's hopeless. It's not only the

head priestess, my family head came down on me like a mountain's worth of rocks."

"Did you ask him ahead of time?" I clarify.

The silence lengthens. "No," she says at last.

"Have you talked to him since?"

"What would I even tell him? I tried."

"The question is, what might *he* say? And what does he need in order to feel listened to?" I wait for her to put the pieces together, but she doesn't. "How do you think he felt," I prompt, "landing in the middle of a plan he knew nothing about and was never consulted on?"

She winces. "Oh." After a long pause, she adds, "Fuck, I messed that up, didn't I?"

I give her shoulder a quick squeeze of empathy. "Yes."

She deflates unexpectedly. "And so now I need to go back and listen to him," she says flatly. She rubs her forehead. "All right. I can take my lumps."

I start to reach out but hesitate at her odd reaction. Being able to make repair is a gift of grace. It's being unable to make things right that's soul killing. "It's not about you being punished for messing up," I explain. "It's about finding better ways to show him he's someone whose opinions and feelings matter to you."

A thoughtful crease furrows her forehead, then she nods slowly. "I can do that."

I clap her on the shoulder, feeling my way through the web of her reactions. "Be gentle with yourself. Habits take a long time to overcome. You're still a worthwhile person, even if you fail."

"Right." She exhales a long sigh, then straightens. "Thanks for the encouragement, Andeshe."

"Anytime. I appreciate your trust."

She looks up at me, startled. "You're easy to talk to. It's like, well, it's like you really listen." From the quirk of her lips, the irony isn't lost on her.

I incline my head. "My people have ways of coaching one another through conflict that go back generations. I'm just adapting them for what works here. If the pteradon project doesn't work out, I thought I might work more on that instead."

She tilts her head, a speculative expression taking over her face. "I can imagine you doing that."

Tension in my shoulders loosens. "Do you think families here would value it?"

Her eyes grow distant. "You might need to toss it in as a freebie in the pledging processes until people got a taste, but over time?" She nods slowly, her lips pursed. "Keep me updated on how it's going. I can put in a good word for you."

"Already?" I don't hide my surprise. I feel like I'm fumbling everything. Velemeth has been giving me advice, as have the zomen at home, but no new skill comes perfectly on the first try.

She gives an embarrassed shrug. "Who else can I talk to like this?"

The revelation in that statement makes my heart hurt. I know how they are to one another here, but I keep struggling to believe it. She seems like she's about to say more, but she stops, gaze sharpening as a figure crunches his way through the trees toward us.

"You weren't answering your 'glove," Se'jan tells her as he draws near.

Nareen's eyebrows knit. "How did you find me?"

He shrugs one shoulder. "If you don't want to be

found, you should turn the locator on your 'glove *off*." She claps a hand over her forearm, but he just gives her an acerbic look. "Anyway, you've been busy, but those results you've been pestering me about are in, and if you're that impatient to get your hands on sensitive files Kiu won't allow to be sent over the public network, then here." He pulls out a cable and connects his 'glove to Nareen's. "Don't say I never did anything for you."

I glance back and forth between the two of them. For all their surface cooperation, the air between them thrums with resentment. How are they supposed to accomplish anything if they won't address the heart of the issue?

"Do you think Nareen is stealing other people's work?" I ask him.

"Andeshe!" Nareen swings toward me, horrified.

Se'jan goes completely still, eyes boring into me. I watch him back, alert for signs that he's about to retreat behind his sardonic mask.

"No," he says at last. It feels like an admission.

"That's good, isn't it?" I turn to Nareen. "From what I've heard, half the town takes for granted that you did."

Nareen's lips compress, but she doesn't disagree. Instead, she darts a sideways look at Se'jan. "He doesn't hate me as much as he could."

"I don't hate you." The confession pulls itself from Se'jan's lips. "I'm just angry."

"Could have fooled me," she mutters. The transfer finishes, and she unplugs the cord, handing it back to him.

"About what?" I ask him.

He folds the cord more times than he needs to, then looks up, eyes flat. "A lot of things."

"Right now?"

Nareen stirs as if she's about to say something, but she doesn't. A bitter smile plays over Se'jan's mouth. "I'm used to things as they are. I'm used to not having a say over my own body. I'm used to playing the gracious assistant to people with half my talent."

Nareen flinches.

"But—" he pins her with a look, and his voice heats. "Do you know how much I've done over the years to make sure my cousins *don't* have that experience? I can absorb what comes my way, but I did not work this hard only to watch this feud you launched with Isel tear Ya'shul apart now."

"That *I* launched? I tried to fix it! She's the one who's dragging my reputation through the mud!"

He crosses his arms with a disbelieving look. "And you had nothing to do with trying to persuade everyone that Isel's family should be disqualified from the seat because their new lithium mine is going to poison the water and kill us all?"

I can't stop my eyebrows from rising. I hadn't heard that.

Nareen has the grace to look embarrassed. "They don't belong here. Everyone knows that. The seat should go to someone who represents *us*."

"And they don't?" I interject. Isel's family has lived on this ridge for generations.

"No." Animosity fills Nareen's voice. "You don't understand. They're not like us."

Neither is my family. I don't know if we'll ever be. "Surely there's room for variety in how people are. Just because they have strong connections to their clan or spend more time off ridge—they're still contributing to the community. The wealth from the mines, if nothing else." I would hope one conflict isn't enough to trigger trying to drive a family off the ridge.

Nareen glares at me. "Do *you* think my family should give up, too? That we have no business thinking we're as good as the families at the top of the cliff?"

I raise my palm. "What made you think I meant that?"

She runs a hand through her hair. "Nothing. It's just that things are getting to me, you know? The sideways looks and 'gloves that start twitching everywhere I go. The people who are supposed to be my allies who blame me for things I didn't do." She shoots Se'jan a look.

I hesitate. She shut me down when I suggested it last time, but— "I really think you need to talk to Isel."

Nareen snorts. "Like that would do any good. She's not reasonable."

The fact that these people don't know how to talk to each other is why I have something to contribute here. That doesn't make her disbelief any less frustrating. I have seen situations far more difficult than this resolved successfully. I look to Se'jan in mute appeal. At home, I wouldn't be trying to resolve something like this alone. For all the confidence my relatives have expressed in my plan to teach these people some of our ways, I can feel the chasm left by the absence of the traditional rituals and roles that should be here to support me.

He stirs. "And what's your alternative?" he asks Nareen. "Keep lobbing potshots at each other, regardless of the damage you do to innocent bystanders?"

"No!" She frowns at him. "This has gone on long enough. If they don't stop, my family's going to lodge a formal complaint against her *and* all her rumormongers.

That'll push your grandmother into finally taking a side. Isel needs to prove what she says, or else shut up about it." A vengeful look suffuses Nareen's face. "Enough evidence that she knew she was lying, and we'll have claim to fines as well. *Steep* fines."

"And you think they won't retaliate?" Se'jan asks incredulously.

Nareen shrugs, face stony. "Let them try. I'm sick of being gracious while they act like I'm a punching bag."

I can imagine the escalating tension and resentment. I trade a look with Se'jan. This is already worse than it should be. How long until simply having a close relationship with one of the combatants is enough to taint my family's overtures for half the ridge?

"But what will you do afterward?" I ask. "You all still have to live together when this is done."

"Afterward?"

"Yes, afterward," Se'jan echoes. "Did you think about that? You and Isel, you're both acting like this election is all there is, that the day will come, you'll win, and somehow that will magically transform everything. It doesn't work like that. The reality is you wake up the next morning and have to deal with all the same people and the same issues. Only now you all hate each other's guts."

"But if we win—"

"Then you win a council seat. One vote. You think that magically gives you the power to do everything you want to do?" He snorts. "You've told yourself the story that it will be a life changer, that anything is worth sacrificing because once you have that seat, all your problems will be solved." He shakes his head. "Take it from me; I've watched my mother manage our family's seat for years. It's mostly headaches and people expecting you to magically fix problems that are just as thorny as they ever were."

Nareen's eyes narrow. "Your family isn't doing too badly for themselves being on the council."

He shrugs one shoulder. "I'm not saying there are no benefits. I'm saying it's not the magic wand you think it is. If you scorch the earth to get what you want, what you have at the end is *a bunch of scorched earth*."

"And what should I do instead, oh wise one?"

All of his normal insouciance drops away, leaving only intensity darkening his eyes. "Andeshe's right. You need to call a truce. Before things get even more out of hand."

"You can't be serious! We're not going to knuckle under."

The odd phrase catches my ear. "Is that what you think talking to Isel would mean?" I ask slowly. I have to remember the difficulty they have holding complexity. "Treating her with dignity and working toward reconciliation doesn't mean sacrificing your own needs. You don't have to pretend you have no disagreements in order to find common ground. Just don't let what you oppose about each other turn into the entire story."

Nareen looks unconvinced.

"This conflict is hurting you, too," I add. "Do you really want to continue the way things have been going?"

"That's why we were going to file our complaint."

"Nareen." Se'jan leans forward. "What role, exactly, do you imagine Ya'shul will play during this complaint of yours?" When she doesn't reply, his voice goes so deadly quiet that it raises the hairs on my arms. "I won't let your ambitions tear my cousin apart. Not again."

Nareen goes still, caught by the menace in his tone.

"Give it a shot," he says, "like Andeshe suggested. What's the worst it could do, start another feud?"

It takes her a long time to reply. "All right," she says reluctantly. "One try. But if it doesn't work, I'm stopping this one way or another."

Se'jan inclines his head in regal acknowledgement. "We can talk about that if the time comes." Battle lines almost seem to shimmer into being around him. I shiver.

I hope this works.

CHAPTER TWENTY-SEVEN
YA'SHUL

The shallow cave and the table Isel leads us to are the same as before, though the temporary quiescence of Restday has stilled the sound of the workshop below. Other than us, the only movement is the dark shape of a barge puttering slowly across the lake toward the mines and refineries on the far shore. Once again, Isel is solicitous about getting me settled, but then her restraint peels away as she and Ya'kinem fall into a more and more animated conversation arranging my future. I wince as Ya'kinem mangles a description of the events in the temple, barely waiting for my correction before tumbling ahead with his enthusiastic planning. Heat rises in my face. Do I even want to know what garbled rumors Nareen's attempt to fix things is going to spark? The humiliating way Kiu confronted me about the last set of rumors hovers too close, scalded into my memory. Without that, where would I be now?

Unbidden, another memory rises, of Andeshe's forgiveness and quiet faith that I could do better. My heart sinks a little, the optimism I felt then tainted by the knowledge that in the chaos I haven't followed through.

What would have happened if things had gone differently?

I turn to Isel. "This plan that you're coming up with, what exactly would it do?"

"It's our chance." Her intensity radiates across the table. "There are too many families wavering about whom to support. You know we haven't always been accepted here. There are families who would like nothing better than an excuse to stay with the status quo. You'd think that with the storms coming, it would be obvious that we need every advantage we can get, but no." She shakes her head. "Nonetheless, the only reason our opponents are getting a serious second look is the priestesses' endorsement coupled with some shrewd follow up by Orzea-lun. If you make a splash, throw enough doubt on the validity of that accomplishment, interest in them will fade and our bid will be back on solid ground. No one admires that kind of scandal."

I turn her words over in my mind. "And what happens to me?"

"Once we have the council seat? What men have been wanting for ages." Passion fills Isel's voice. "Recognition. Equality. The right to use your talents. Why should you have to be content with men never winning the festival prize? With always being a mere adjunct to the women and zomen around you?"

I try not to let on how deeply that strikes home.

She leans forward. "You don't even get credit when your quick waters a child. The greatest act of fertility there is, and snip!" She makes a scissor-like motion with her hand. "You're cut right out of it."

"They used to call it being a *father*," Ya'kinem puts in, tongue awkward around the unfamiliar word. "I want to be one. Why shouldn't we get earrings? One at least."

My breath catches, and I stop myself from fingering the spot on my ear where an earring like Nareen's would go. The yearning I felt as I ran my fingers over the temple carvings reverberates again in my soul. I dart a glance at Isel. Would any woman really share credit for *that*?

Isel's eyes bore into mine. "*We're* the only ones fighting for all of that. You think Nareen's family will? They don't care about standing up for anyone but themselves. They're too busy trying anything to get to the top, no matter how many morals they have to compromise to do so. You deserve better than that. Especially when the stresses of the storms come. That's when things backslide. We have to make progress now, hold fast against the days when rape was considered nothing more than theft of a family's quick, not a violent crime against the man it happened to. We need someone on the council who will truly stand up for men."

Ya'kinem is practically applauding from his seat, face glowing with ardor. Given all the knocks I've taken, I should be just as moved. Why does something in me still pull back in unease?

"*After* you get the seat." I struggle to pin down that elusive sense of warning. "What about before?"

"What about it?" Isel shrugs the question away.

"If I get up in public and denounce Kiu's protégé—my *mother's* protégé—as a fraud, what do you think is going to happen to me? You think Kiu will shrug and let it go?" Ruthlessly, I quash the stab of pain that comes with imagining the look on Nareen's face at my betrayal.

"Isel's allies will protect you," Ya'kinem tells me earnestly. "If Kiu retaliates, they'll make a stink about it."

Isel nods in confirmation.

"'A stink,'" I repeat slowly. The step-by-step practicalities unfold in my mind. "Say I succeed. I get to present at the capital, but then I *come back*. Fame comes and goes. Kiu will be approving and denying requests in the lab long after everyone else's attention fades."

"She'll retire eventually."

I snort. "In a few decades, then I can look forward to having a zoman with even more influence who hates my guts."

"She doesn't hate you," he protests.

"Determination to crush me down into my proper place is better?" I try to imagine the very best-case scenario, attempting to do anything productive in a room filled with frozen resentment and a vengeful desire for me to fail. "This will never work. You can't protect me from my family. Force their hand, and I'll be paying for it for the rest of my life."

Isel's steady gaze is sympathetic, but unmoved. "It's hard throwing off your chains."

Whatever response I was expecting, it wasn't that.

She takes one of my hands in hers, her palm hot and dry. "Sometimes, progress requires sacrifice. Once we hold the seat, things will be better."

"Isn't it worth it?" Ya'kinem asks. "Think about the blow you can strike for justice! You're no coward." The look he gives me is filled with the starry-eyed admiration of the child who used to follow his big brother everywhere. I struggle not to look away. He has so little status in the family. To him, it's little more than a place to eat and sleep and dodge the tempers of his elders. Even back when he was praised and petted, it was because of the promise of his passionate starts, not because he followed through. If any challenge becomes too much, it costs him nothing to fling himself into something new and exciting. I'm not like that. The work I do in the lab is my life—the work that can be done nowhere else.

Nareen. She'll have a lab, if less well equipped. And after this, I'll never have a prayer of setting foot anywhere near it.

I stare out at the lake, trying to gather my thoughts. Is that what's holding me back? Cowardice? Memories from before everything went wrong flash before me. Camaraderie, laughter with Nareen, my mother's pride, the thrill of stretching my mind to its limits. Is it so wrong to want to feel that joy again? Sunlight bounces off the water, sending spots dancing across my vision. I look away. None of the options in front of me are palatable.

Downstream of the dam, a pteradon wheels, flaring its wings in a descent that ends on the sandy shore just below the main entrance to Isel's workshop. It folds its wings, revealing four riders clinging to its back, and Isel straightens, a frown creasing her forehead. The Wanderer at the reins unbuckles the first rider, who climbs down the pteradon's side with a languid nonchalance, then hands the next woman down. My breath catches as she pulls off her hood. Dark curls spring from the figure's head as she frees them from the confines of the leather.

What is Nareen doing here?

Chapter Twenty-Eight
Andeshe

The main entrance to Isel's family workshop stands open above us, practical and unpretentious in contrast to the ornately carved entrances to the cliff dwellings in Ikmeth. Nareen stands on the gravelly shore, head tilted back to stare up the short path that vanishes into the darkened interior. At her side, Se'jan slouches with apparent unconcern that doesn't fool me in the least. This won't be easy, but if I can help these families negotiate a resolution, not only will it show what I have to offer, it will calm some of the treacherous winds my family has to navigate to be accepted here. I reach around Et'elark to disengage the last of the safety straps. When Se'jan persuaded Kiu to request a flight to take us here, it was the best chance yet to get Et'elark to the mines.

A hand catches my wrist, and I look up. Et'elark's gaze is faintly shadowed.

"I couldn't help overhearing." A tiny jerk of his head indicates Nareen and Se'jan below. During the calmer parts of the flight, the three of us had discussed our plans for talking with Isel, but he'd remained silent.

"I always value your perspective," I tell him.

A brief smile crosses his lips, but it fades almost instantly. "You want them to talk things out with Isel, to work together instead of being at odds."

I nod. "The community needs that, don't you think? With the storms coming, we'll need everything we've got—machines and biotechnology. We need both families to thrive."

"I see." He releases my wrist, turning away to fumble with the straps.

"Et'elark?" It's my turn to touch his wrist. "What's wrong?" I know him well enough now to read through the first layer of his reserve, at least.

He's quiet for so long that I don't think he's going to answer. Finally, he looks up. "Isel's family...how well do you know them?"

Had anyone else asked me, I'd have said quite well, that the bonds between our families go back for generations, that they're the Uplanders I feel most comfortable around by far, but his wariness stops me. How well do I really know them? "I guess it's more that I know *of* them," I confess. "Auntie Haveo is the one who has worked most closely with them—creating the flier and battery, you know. And if they don't fit in here, I don't know how we will."

"And the mines?"

They exist, obviously, but for all that I've promised Et'elark to help get there, I realize that I've heard very little about them except for Haveo's excitement about the lithium deposit that made smaller and lighter batteries for the flier possible. Other half-remembered comments tickle my memory. There was something beyond just the raw resources the mines provide, something about the people there having the opportunity to contribute to the community.

"Aren't they necessary?" I say.

If I'd thought Et'elark's face was closed before, it's a wall now. His chin ducks jerkily, and he starts down the ladder to the ground. The bag of letters he brought with him bumps against his back. "Thanks for the ride." He reaches the ground and turns to stare across the lake toward the mountain that towers on its far side. He squares his shoulders and starts toward the water.

"Where are you going?" I scramble after him, the slap of him shutting me out vibrating through me.

He points toward a spot midway up the side of the mountain, almost directly above the dam. "That's the visitor's entrance."

I shade my eyes. Farther upstream from the dam, giant lifts ratchet their way slowly downward from gaping holes in the mountain's face to the beach below, but where he points there's nothing but a long switchback trail that starts at the barge's dock and climbs torturously up to a flat area with a barely visible tower. Inwardly, I curse. I promised Et'elark I'd get him to the mines, but when my family says the mines are "close" to the workshops, they mean as a pteradon flies.

"What you said just now…" I grind to a halt, looking back to where Nareen and Se'jan are waiting for me to go in. Et'elark is staring at the distant barge as if enough determination can change the fact that it seems disinclined to move anytime soon. "Listen, I'll take you up. Nareen and Se'jan can wait for a little. You don't have to try to get across on your own." That distance should be no more than a few minutes via pteradon. Enough time to talk briefly, then return to meet with Isel. I'm pretty sure Nareen and Se'jan's truce will hold that long.

He refocuses on me. "You won't be able to leave once we get there, not until I do. They don't let visitors split up. It could be hours." His eyes flit to where the two Uplanders are standing, heads bent in conversation.

I hesitate. My intuition screams at me not to let him walk away with those cryptic comments unresolved, but I'd wanted to be here for this negotiation. I look back toward Nareen, who stands running her thumb across the tips of her fingers. It was hard enough to bring her around to trying this at all. I'm not convinced she has the skills to do it on her own.

"Nareen?" I crunch my way across the sand toward her, Et'elark trailing behind me. "Something's come up. I'd meant to take Et'elark to visit someone in the mines, but they're farther away than I thought." Perhaps she'll have a solution we haven't thought of.

"The mines?" Nareen turns to Et'elark, shock widening her eyes. "You know someone there?" She scans his face as if this changes everything she knows about him. My skin crawls.

Et'elark's stiffens too. Despite his skill at concealing his emotions, I can feel embarrassment radiating from him. "Yes," he says flatly. A muscle jumps in his jaw.

I look back and forth between them, feeling like I've made a misstep. Frustration at what isn't talked about here fills me once more. Too many urgent tasks clamor for my attention. I've messed things up with Et'elark somehow, but do I have time to sort it out now? Back home, we would stop and slow down, giving little abrasions the time we need to address them before they fester, but Nareen and

Se'jan are eyeing the entrance to Isel's workshop anxiously. Velemeth would tell me to go with them, but they won't be willing to wait.

Behind me, Fizz shifts her weight, crunching the gravel below her. Automatically, I take a deep breath. *Patience*, her presence reminds me. No one can ever rush a pteradon. I let myself reconnect with all the different emotions welling up: frustration, an urgency to prove myself, and disappointment at my misstep. Underneath it all is the conviction of the values my ancestors passed down to me. *The urgency is a lie. Take the time to go slow and do things right.* The thought steadies me. If my presence at one meeting with Isel is the only thing that makes an agreement possible, then we haven't laid the groundwork that will allow what we build to last. I exhale. Nothing is going to fully resolve itself in one conversation. Whatever Nareen and Se'jan can do will be the starting point. Very few negotiations have only one shot at success.

"I need to go with Et'elark," I tell them. Conviction fills me. At this moment, this is what needs to be done right. "I'll connect with you later to hear how the conversation went and plan for what to do next." I hesitate, feeling like I should say something to shore up Nareen's confidence. "You'll do fine."

Nareen is already eyeing the cave entrance again. "We've got this," she says airily.

I can't tell if it's her self-assurance or her refusal to ask for help that's speaking, but either one is what we have to work with for now. I bid the two of them farewell and help Et'elark back into Fizz's saddle. At my signal, she launches us toward the enigmatic mines.

Chapter Twenty-Nine
Ya'shul

Isel leads us through the tunnel at the back of the alcove with the swift steps of someone intent on defending her territory. We turn a corner, and a vast, arching cavern opens up, spots of artificial illumination picking out machinery arranged on the cavern floor. The tang of metal and ozone is stronger here, intertwined with the scent of ginger. The harsh glare of sunlight falls like a curtain across the cave's entrance, but Isel strides through it without hesitation, the sunlight turning her form into a burst of color. I stop just inside the entrance, hidden in the gloom. Below us on the path, Nareen climbs her way up the slope, jaw set in determination. Next to her, Se'jan scans the darkness behind Isel, though neither I nor Ya'kinem are visible.

What are you doing here? I think at Nareen. I wrack my brain, but I can't come up with any reason that would bring her to the heart of her opponent's territory.

"Nareen." Isel plants herself on the path, blocking the way upward.

"Isel." Nareen's acknowledging nod is curt. She comes

to a halt, drawing herself up with all the dignity she can muster. "I came to talk."

The silence that follows is long enough to make me wonder if Isel is going to kick her off the mountain, but finally, Isel speaks, "Talk, then."

"Truce," Nareen says curtly, when it becomes obvious that, despite Nareen's clearly marked pregnancy, Isel has no intention of inviting her out of the sun. "This isn't how contests for the seat are supposed to go. We're tearing the town apart."

"Feeling the heat, are you?" I can't see Isel's face, but her tone is arch. "Playing hardball was fine when you felt you were winning, but once things start to turn, everyone else is supposed to back off?"

"No. We got into this to make the community better off. That's what I care about."

"The community." Isel prowls down the path, circling the younger woman with a predatory air. "I'd believe that more if you had more care for the part of the community closest to you."

"What are you talking about?"

"You can't think of anything? No one close to you that you've stabbed in the back in your quest for power?"

"No." Nareen's eyes narrow, her shoulders stiff as she tracks Isel's prowling movement. The puzzlement in her voice is genuine, and I flinch. I know exactly who Isel is talking about. I thought that after everything, Nareen at least understood a little of what she's done to me.

Isel stops behind Nareen and leans forward until her mouth is almost by the other woman's ear. "'I won't go unless he does.'"

Nareen jumps forward, swinging around until she's

facing Isel, fists clenched. "How do you know about that?"

"Taking his place, stealing his work..." An unfriendly smile plays across Isel's face. "Aren't you ashamed?"

"That's not—that's not what happened," Nareen spits out.

Isel leans forward. "If he's not going, you shouldn't be either. You admitted it yourself."

Nareen's breathing is ragged.

Isel's gaze slides toward where she knows I'm standing. She eases back. "Tell you what, though, maybe I'm being unfair. Maybe you were just humoring him." Her voice shifts into more sympathetic tones. "I'd understand that. You never really meant it—you were just trying to make him feel better, and it got out of hand." She lifts one shoulder. "I've been outraged because a gifted scientist wasn't getting credit. If that's not what's going on...well, perhaps we have more room to come to an understanding. Maybe I haven't fully appreciated your work." She pins the younger woman with a meaningful look.

The rock wall digs into my palms. It never occurred to me that Nareen might have said what she did only to placate me. The urge surges through me to cover my ears, to block out the next words that I will never be able to un-hear. Should I curse Isel or thank her for provoking Nareen into showing me who she truly is? At my side, Ya'kinem bounces on his toes, cheering Isel along as if this were a sporting match. I close my eyes, holding my breath.

"No." Nareen's voice is strained but determined. "He deserves it. We should go together. The priestesses just won't let us."

I let out my breath, hands trembling, and pry my

eyelids open. It's so little that I expect from her, but it's a start.

Next to Nareen, Isel seems faintly disappointed, as if she has gambled and lost. Ya'kinem groans, too.

What? I nudge him with my elbow, letting my confusion show.

"I wanted you to see what she's really like," he whispers back. "You've been contorting yourself into knots all this time to make excuses for her. She doesn't deserve you."

"Apparently she meant it. You shouldn't be disappointed by that. I don't want the person I've worked with most closely for years to secretly believe I'm worthless."

My brother wrinkles his nose. "She doesn't really mean it, though. You saw how willing she was to sacrifice you—how willing everyone was—when it would have helped fend off the rumors that really got to her."

The rumors. My stomach twists as memories scrape still raw nerves. Below us, Isel says something, and Nareen straightens in reflexive readiness to lash back before she visibly brings herself under control. The backbiting of politics has always felt like the weather to me, an impersonal rain burst beyond human control, but this isn't. From the start, this has been personal and intimate and nasty, people deciding to do what hurts the most.

Ya'kinem hisses, and the sound pulls my eyes back to him. The roundness of youth has finally faded from his freckled cheeks, leaving a man whose eyes are fixed on Isel, lips moving in silent encouragement. A man who, for all his flightiness, yearns to be important. My partisan, the man who knows *everything* I've ever attempted. The one who believes in what he does so passionately that he never stops to consider the consequences of jumping into the fray. My skin grows cold. I never stopped to think about it, but those rumors really were odd. My festival presentation was a disaster. I wouldn't expect anyone in the community to have more than a vague notion of who I am, much less enough awareness of my work to twist the truth into a wedge to use to tear Nareen and my family apart. But Isel did. My mind races, events that should have been obvious finally slapping me in the face. I sat here not an hour ago listening to him hand Isel the words she just wielded as a weapon against Nareen. No one who was in Priestess Wekmet's office that day would have said a word. No one aside from him has even *heard* me pour out the ins and outs of my conflicted feelings about Nareen.

I grab his shoulder, spinning him to face me. "What did you do?"

"Do what?" he protests.

"You told Isel everything!" I give his shoulder a tiny shake. "*That's* how I ended up getting torn apart in the middle of all this. Did you stop to think about what that would do to me? Or ask me if I wanted you to?"

Ya'kinem's eyes go wide. "What Nareen was doing to you was wrong. And you weren't doing anything about it!"

"And maybe I had my reasons! Did either of you think of that?" I let go of Ya'kinem and turn to pace across the entrance. For all Isel's talk about supporting me, what have I actually seen her do? She knows this conflict is tearing me apart. She sat with me in the alcove above not an hour ago, her calculating mind describing exactly how my story could be twisted to hurt Nareen the most. I hadn't realized that same mind had already twisted it to hurt me.

Ya'kinem catches up with me. "We had to! If Isel doesn't win, we're never going to make any progress."

I stare down at Isel and Nareen. "So I get to make the sacrifices? They're the ones competing for power." Anger brings me clarity. "Do you see either of them risking never being allowed to do the work they love again?"

Ya'kinem's mouth gapes. "But think of all the men who will be helped! That's worth it."

"Then why isn't it worth Isel supporting me *and* Nareen presenting at the capital?" That's what I wanted. That's the solution Nareen proposed. That's the option Isel quietly deflected me from the entire time we were talking. "The two of us presenting as equals, that's just as much of an inspiration as me presenting by myself. More so because Nareen's side would support it, too, instead of fighting it."

My brother blinks rapidly. "But Isel is the one who cares about men."

What *have* I actually seen her do? I've heard her rhetoric, but have all those high ideals justified actions that make my life better or reasons why she should hold power? I stare down at the two women again. *Congratulations!* a sardonic voice chirps in my head, *you get to choose between the side that says what you want isn't important and the side that just acts like it!* I clench my fists.

"Who else is going to fight for us?" Ya'kinem presses. "It's not just now, it's all the things she's going to push for in the future."

I don't have an answer for that. *Can't I have another choice?* There's no one else who even has a chance at the seat. I tug on my hair in frustration, my elbows flashing into the sunlight.

Below us, Se'jan's head comes up. His eyes narrow, the keenness with which he scans the entrance belying his apparently casual slouch. I stop moving. His insolence makes it easy to not take him seriously, but he's the sharpest political mind I know. I drop my arms, realization of who I've been overlooking all this time flooding through me. *Help,* I message him. *I don't want either of them to win.* Or maybe that's not quite true. *They're not the point,* I clarify. *I don't want to be a pawn. I don't want to be torn apart so one of them can triumph over the other.*

His 'glove twitches. *What do you want?*

Kiu's face rises in my mind's eye, contorted with anger while my blood freezes in fear. *I want recognition, AND I want to be able to do science again without retaliation.* I want to be able to breathe again.

Then come out. Se'jan's return message buzzes across my palm. *I'll soften them up for you.*

I turn to Ya'kinem. "*Isel* says the only way forward is for her to win—she may even believe it—but are the rest of us really so helpless?" I wave at all of us who have come here. "You, me, Se'jan—even Nareen. Are you telling me there's nothing we could do on any of those issues if Isel lost?"

He blinks. "It would be easier if she won."

"Easier." Muscles unlock all down my back, sending energy flooding through me. "Not the only way. Not worth any sacrifice. *Easier.*" But what other options are there? What would happen if I sat Se'jan down and truly talked instead of being put off by his armor of cynicism? If Ya'kinem has the power to do this much damage by charging off on his own, what could he do if I took him into my confidence? "Listen," I tell my brother, "I know you've been trying to help me, but this—" I indicate the scene below us— "this isn't what I need. I need you and me and Se'jan to put our heads together and find something that really works for us." A thought slips into my head, feeling like something Se'jan would say. *Power isn't choosing a side. Power is getting to define what the sides are.* "I need your help, but the kind where you talk to me, not where you do what you think I ought to want without consulting me. Can you do that?" He nods, and I brace myself, stepping out into the sunlight.

Nareen sees me first, cutting off mid-sentence as her eyes widen in shock. Her tongue darts over her lips, and I can almost see her replaying everything she has said. Isel sidesteps, turning enough to see me while still keeping her other eye on Nareen, and settles into a watchful stillness.

"Did either of you think to ask Ya'shul what he wanted?" Se'jan asks into the silence. He turns to Isel. "You act as if all you have to do is defeat Nareen, and you'll have defeated every force that's keeping him down." He snorts and spears Nareen with a look. "I know you think highly of yourself, but I hate to tell you—you're not a big enough deal to be the source of all injustice." He switches his censuring look back to Isel. "You claim you're trying to change a culture; destroying Nareen does nothing."

Isel draws herself up, voice frigid. "As soon as we hold the seat—"

Se'jan snorts. "You'll find out it's just as hard to get anything done as it is now. You're telling everyone this myth that you can't do anything until you have everything, and that all the damage you do now is justified because *someday* the glorious future will come when you finally have enough. *Then* you can start doing what you said you'd do." He shoots her a look of pure disgust. "I'd be more impressed if you were doing anything to benefit Ya'shul in the situation he's in now."

"We are—" Isel starts, but Nareen holds up a hand, turning to me.

"Has Ya'shul said what he wants?" She says the words awkwardly, but determinedly.

I wait until Isel trails off under the gravity of Nareen's attention to me.

"Neither of you really get it," I say into the ensuing pause. "Neither of you have to risk retaliation to claim what you can do. I do, and I want you to help protect me from that. Then I want Nareen and me to present at the capital together." There's more, but that's a start.

Isel stirs. "I'm afraid sending you both isn't an option."

"Why not?" I keep my voice carefully neutral.

"The priestesses said *one*." She turns to Nareen. "Now, if you were willing to let him go in your place…"

Slow outrage flushes my body as her real priorities reveal themselves.

"One project, not one person," Nareen murmurs. "That would let Priestess Wekmet save face."

Isel shakes her head, her face a picture of regret.

I fix her with a hard look. "You claimed you and your allies had enough clout to force the priestess to replace Nareen with me if I would only support your bid for the seat. That means your side plus Nareen's side plus my family ought to have the power to insist that Priestess Wekmet send us both. *If* you choose to use it."

Isel radiates sincerity. "We haven't come this far only to let someone who will uphold the status quo snatch power. This is the last election before the storms. Justice can't wait."

"Justice is what I'm asking for," I snap. "I want both Nareen and me to get exactly what we deserve, no more, no less. What you want is to use me as a cudgel against her family so that you can win while the blame and resentment for taking 'her' spot falls on me."

Isel looks faintly amused. "It's not like that. This is just how politics is. Are bruised feelings really such a big deal compared to the good we might do?"

Bruised feelings? My words dissolve in a sputter. Hastily, Ya'kinem jumps in, taking up the thread of the argument while I seethe. *Bruised feelings? I'm getting kicked out of the lab!* How can she be so righteous in her plans to save men yet be unable to take seriously the one standing right in front of her nose?

Ya'kinem's explanations have no more effect than mine. She seems to listen, only to turn around and appeal to him and Se'jan with the utter necessity of her getting what she wants. I would never have thought Nareen would be more ready for a way out than Isel. She seems too convinced that, given a pair of bad choices, I'll be able to talk Nareen into yielding her claim to me. A sour taste arises in my mouth. Isel, at least, would get everything she wanted.

Or would she? I straighten. "I don't think you've thought this through." I cut through the argument, my brain working furiously. "You assume that if I replace Nareen, it will prove everything you've been saying has been right all along." I lean forward. "But there's one thing you're forgetting about."

"And what is that?" Isel turns to me.

"Me," I breathe. Isel may have written a script, but nothing says I have to follow it. "When resentment flares about Nareen losing her slot, I won't take the fall. You assume I'll be grateful to you, but that wasn't what I asked for. I will be perfectly happy to tell everyone who will listen that I agree with them, that I wanted us both to go, and you're the one who refused to allow it. You plan to make political hay out of this. I will make damned sure you don't. Whose praises I sing are up to me. And they won't be yours."

Isel's face has gone completely blank. Whispers of danger thrum along my nerves.

"Think carefully," she says, "is that really what you want?" She sounds so like Marin-lun in that moment that it takes everything in me not to wipe at the sweat that has sprung up on my palms. *You don't want to be my enemy*, her expression whispers, and my breath catches in my throat. Power flexes under her veneer of restraint.

"I told you it's not what I want," I remind her sturdily. "But it's not what you want either. What I want is another way."

"Another way?" she asks. "Another way to choose between right and wrong?"

Se'jan makes a dismissive noise deep in his throat. "You're just jealous you don't get to go yourself."

She rounds on him, her calm and collected mask slipping into something more human. It's only as the mask cracks that realization hits me. Isel has always seemed so much larger than life, but she didn't get to go to the capital either. Behind all her soaring rhetoric, how much of what she's doing comes down to a human being who feels hurt and betrayed and wants to stick it to the woman who took what she thought was hers by right? Sudden empathy wars with impatience within me. I know how that feels. I look at her again, searching for the hurt under her anger. It's not that I want her to lose, necessarily, it's that I want a way out.

"Is there so little credit to go around?" I interrupt. At Isel and Se'jan's blank looks, I continue, "The priestesses control who does the formal presentation, that's true, but is that really what you need?" I point to the flier sitting by the lake, a plan taking shape in my mind. "What if you flew us to Treverel for the solstice festival? And once you're there? How much more would you gain if our families praised your work instead of everyone being at odds with one another? Whatever the priestesses have against your inventions, we have no such issues."

Isel's eyes narrow in suspicion. "You'd do that?" she asks Nareen.

Nareen hesitates, and Isel draws back.

"What are you two really gaining from this fight?" I press. "Sure, there's a council seat, but it's not like either of you will hold it. At most, you're going to struggle to persuade the zoman who does hold it to try to persuade the other council members to eventually support… something." The way Isel acted like her victory would magically fix everything was nonsense. I should have realized. "In the meantime, you're ripping apart everything you say you're fighting for. Keep competing, keep being rivals, that's fine. But remember that there's something more than that. Something that will last even after the political contests are over." Out of the corner of my eye, Nareen nods slowly. I wave a hand toward the workshop and all its wonders. "With all the creativity in there, surely you could find something that benefits both families? You may not be able to both hold the council seat, but that doesn't mean you can't both grow wealthy or—or gain prestige by collaborating." I scan the mountain across the valley where a giant lift is making its way slowly back to the opening of a mineshaft. Half remembered write-ups from ancient research tug at the edges of my memory. "Isel, maybe there's a way to make your inventions in ways that the priestesses condone. I know there are ways to use microorganisms to assemble materials. Or something else. Maybe drones would make goat herding easier and free up more of Nareen's family for everything else they do." I'm tossing out ideas now, but in their faces, I see the ideas getting traction. At heart, they're both innovators. Behind them, the ore-piled barge at the base of the mountain starts to plow its way through the water toward us. I remember the awe I felt seeing for the first time what Isel and her family can forge out of the raw rock from the mines. There must be some way for Nareen and me to build on that.

Isel turns to Nareen. "And would you give up competing for the seat if you got that?"

"There's no need to stop competing," I cut in. "Just keep the conflict from taking over everything."

"And if you don't," Se'jan adds cheerfully, "we'll show you what it means to really scorch the earth. So far, my family has stayed out of the fray. Do you want us to make the sides into *us* versus you, or will you take a bargain that makes us all better off?"

Isel snorts incredulously. "Marin-lun wouldn't break their neutrality."

"Kiu would," Se'jan replies. "She came *this* close to it the last time you attacked her protégé. Do you want to find out how many—or few—of us need to work together to do significant damage?" The teeth he bares are only superficially a smile.

Nareen steps forward. "Truce," she says again. "Take us both to Treverel, find new projects for collaboration, and we'll compete cleanly, instead of ripping each other to shreds. If all three of the most prominent families on the ridge ask the priestess for the same thing, we won't be refused, not when your faction almost had enough clout on your own." She holds out her hand, and her lips twist in a rueful smile. "Think of what else we could do with all the time and energy we're putting into trying to destroy each other."

Isel looks at the outstretched hand for a long moment. "Truce," she says finally and enfolds Nareen's hand in hers.

Chapter Thirty

Andeshe

From above, I wouldn't have guessed this was the entrance to a mine at all. A short tower squats in the middle of a flat area that juts from the side of the mountain. Garish pink hatching splashes the ground all around it, signaling "no safe landing." Only a single yellow circle near the cliff's edge shows that landing is permitted here at all. Fizz huffs in offense, then back-wings so delicately that not a single toe touches down outside the marked boundary. She wraps her tail around her feet with an air of injured dignity.

"Thank you," Et'elark says from behind me as the dust settles. He still sounds stiff and awkward.

"I said I'd get you to the mines," I tell him, "not that I'd abandon you halfway there."

He unclips himself, then hesitates. "I just want you to know. No matter what it looks like, you're safe. *You'll* be fine."

Safe? I give the area another sharp look. Beyond the hatched lines, the greenery I'd seen from the air resolves itself into an entire field of low-growing sneezeweed that reaches nearly back to the vertical cliff that has been hacked into the rock. I blink, but it's still there. An eye and nose irritant for humans without face protection, intolerable for our pteradons under any circumstances, who would plant a field of the stuff?

The tower door opens, and three women emerge. On the rocky ledge above them, one of the gray-brown boulders moves, flaring a set of pointed, triangular wings. A wedge-shaped head, smaller than Fizz's, lifts from the rock, peering suspiciously in our direction. Almost no pteradons can stand sneezeweed. While we bred our pteradons for cargo capacity and friendliness, the ruling council's militia bred theirs for speed, maneuverability, and a host of other characteristics that they've stayed ridiculously tightlipped about.

What is this place? Normally, I would unclip and slide down, but I hesitate. There's nothing on this ledge but the tower and the field and the landing spot, no safe paths marked across the ground nor any indication of the nature of the hazard. Only at the far end does the sneezeweed give way to bare ground and to mine shafts chiseled into the rock. Unlike everything I've seen in Ikmeth, it's devoid of carvings.

The three women come to a halt farther away from us than normal. The one in front gestures us to dismount with an unmistakable air of command.

"Name and business?" she asks once we're down. Her eyes are alert and unsmiling.

"Andeshe Kel-Orek Umolin," I tell her. "Delivering Et'elark, um…" I hesitate. I don't actually know his family name.

"Ell Hetlarth," he supplies, his voice a dry croak. "Visiting Cee Ell Hetlarth." He frees the bag on his back.

"And delivering letters."

The woman frowns, but gestures to her companion to take the bag from him. Only after the second woman rifles through it does the first address me. "Ground your pteradon and come with us, then."

I signal Fizz to lie down and she goes still, though one of her wingtips twitches in distress as I step out of the safety of the yellow circle. My skin prickles, but the ground seems solid.

"Your names?" I prompt the woman with the bag of letters, who falls into step behind me. I should know the family scents by now, but even under the sneezeweed, hers isn't one I've memorized.

She frowns. "Jamerol's the only one you need to concern yourself with." She jerks her chin at the woman walking ahead of us. With a start, I recognize the woman who was at the ijendra competition, but the other two are still unknown to me. I glance at Et'elark out of the corner of my eye. His face is pinched and drawn, but he gives no sign that this rudeness is unusual.

At the base of the tower, Jamerol presses her palm against a pad by the door, and it opens onto a small stone room with a desk and a single chair. She seats herself behind it while we stand awkwardly in front, the other two women still hovering behind us. Jamerol activates a terminal screen lying flat on her desk and skims her fingers over it without taking her eyes off us.

"Ell Hetlarth?" she asks at last. "Celdone?"

Et'elark flinches, and his jaw clenches. With effort, he unlocks it. "Yes." His voice sounds like gravel.

"You're not scheduled."

His eyes close, lines etching themselves into a face far

too young for them. "I wrote ahead. Surely—"

"Her shift is over in two hours. We'll bring her out then."

Et'elark sends me an agonized look.

"I'll wait with you." This doesn't feel like a place to be alone in.

He closes his eyes briefly, the strain he's under surfacing for just a moment. "Thank you," he whispers.

The other two women depart, and at Jamerol's gesture, we settle ourselves on the bare floor, backs against the stone wall. Talking is awkward in such a small space with a stranger working at her desk. I'm reluctant to break the silence.

Are you all right? I message him with my 'glove instead.

His 'gloved fist clenches and relaxes. For a moment, I think he's going to write back, but he just shakes his head in a minute motion.

I'd wanted to ask him about what he'd said earlier, but every instinct screams at me that this is not the time. *I'm here for you*, I message him instead.

He nods shakily.

It just...it gets to me, he finally messages back. *That isn't Cee's name. And Cee ISN'T a she.* His lips are pressed so tightly together that my own ache.

Can you correct it? I ask.

He shakes his head. *We've tried. Cee shouldn't be in a woman's encampment in the first place. Cee shouldn't be here at all!* The emphasis buzzes my 'glove audibly.

Jamerol looks up. "Anything electronic or metal needs to be left here before you visit." She picks up a basket from beside her desk and waggles it at us.

Et'elark bows his head. Finger by finger, he pulls the

'glove off, though the visit isn't for hours. "Don't argue," he murmurs, catching my look. "They can cancel it for any reason." He takes a few things out of his pockets and places them in the basket as well. With a last message to Nareen that I'll be out of contact, I do the same.

As we resettle ourselves in silence, I take his hand. His skin is cold against mine, rough with calluses. A wan grimace twitches briefly across his features as he squeezes back, then closes his eyes and lets his head fall back against the stone. I study his profile. A faint sheen of sweat coats his forehead. *What do you know about this place?* I'd thought it was a bustling community like any other—an extension of the thriving creativity that thrums through the complex across the lake—but instead it feels stifling and on edge, as if one toe placed out of line will send a person tumbling down the cliff under an avalanche. I cradle Et'elark's hand in mine. The single point of human comfort anchors us both.

***

It feels like more than two hours before Jamerol escorts us out of the tower, but sitting silently with no way to check the time has disoriented me. As we emerge, I cast my eyes up to the sun, seeking reassurance in its predictable motion. Jamerol leads us past the sneezeweed, but not to one of the openings in the cliff. Instead, she leads us around the side, where part of the mountain rises in a sheer face to three times Et'elark's height. A wide, shallow trench runs parallel to it, and behind it, a thin and stoop-shouldered elder sits on a cushion. White, wispy hair frames a face whose faded sepia skin is furrowed by deepening wrinkles. Et'elark's footsteps falter. Not yet aware of our presence, the person before us looks worn and fragile. Then Cee looks up, and an expression of pure joy revitalizes merely human flesh. Almost involuntarily, Cee starts to rise, unfolding to a height almost equal to Et'elark's.

"Remember," Jamerol breaks in, "no touching, don't cross the trench, no gifts, and keep your hands where I can see them." Cee sits back, and Jamerol gestures us to the two cushions on our side of the trench with a frown. Et'elark takes the one nearest Cee, and I settle on the one set behind him and off to the side. Positioned, I realize, so that I don't block the line of sight between Jamerol, who stands at the end of the trench, and Et'elark.

No touching? Et'elark is leaning forward, hands tight on his knees, vibrating with the suppressed desire to reach out. I curl my fingers into my palms.

"Et'elark." Cee's voice is rough, but also gentle and welcoming. "It's good to see you."

Et'elark raises a trembling hand to swipe at his eye. "You too." He clears his throat. "I've wanted to come, but I couldn't until Andeshe brought me. She's a Wanderer. She gave me a ride."

Cee taps bare wrists in my direction appreciatively. "Thank you."

I incline my head in return. "Et'elark is my friend. It's the least I could do." We both look at him, but he's struggling to hold himself together. Cee's hand twitches in an abortive gesture to reach out, and my own hand clenches in sympathy. *Can I touch him?* I glance questioningly at Jamerol, but she stands, face impassive, eyes fixed on the wall. The stone feels too close, closing me in. Questions build up on my tongue, but I bite them back. This is Et'elark's time.

After a moment, Cee turns back to me, giving Et'elark space to compose himself. Sharp, knowing eyes probe mine, and the corner of Cee's lip twitches. "Still, thank you." The words are clear and precise. "Not everyone flies their friend out to the middle of nowhere for prison visits."

Et'elark's flinch is almost violent. His panicked eyes dart to me. "They exiled you for political activism. It's not your fault that someone got hurt!"

Cee is still watching me. "And if it had been? Would that have stopped you from coming to visit?"

Et'elark looks away. "Of course not," he says in a low voice. "I just don't want anyone to look down on you." His shoulders coil even more.

Does he mean me? The shame that wraps around him is so tight I can barely breathe. "Why would I look down on anyone?" I look back and forth from him to Cee, who radiates graciousness that would be a credit to the most respected elders I know.

The lines at the corners of Cee's eyes crinkle. "Because I'm here to be punished, of course."

"Of course?" I repeat. There's no "of course" about it, but the bleakness of our surroundings whispers to me something I'm more and more sure I don't want to hear. "You did something that hurt someone—"

"Not really," Et'elark mumbles.

"Killed someone," Cee corrects.

"Killed someone," I repeat slowly, "and when that happened, they sent you far away from the community to a place where you couldn't do anything to make amends, and your absence ripped a hole in your loved ones' lives?" I look over at where Et'elark sits hunched over, radiating pain. A puff of breeze chills the sweat on my neck, and I'm suddenly back in the air, battling biting winds as I desperately try to bring Fizz in for a landing, Velemeth's unending screams drawing running figures out of buildings all over the settlement. My heart starts to pound. "Didn't the zomen call a circle?" My circle demanded the expertise of four of the oldest zomen we had.

"A what?" Cee blinks.

The blood drains from my face, leaving me lightheaded. Once more, I stand on the landing pad clutching Fizz's broken straps while a parent wraps a blanket around Velemeth, guilt slicing into my gut as I wait for someone to ask about our missing companion. "A circle," I croak. "To grieve and learn and make amends."

I know what Cee's response will be even before it comes, but the slow inevitability of it reminds me too much of the frozen moments after the push, as the damaged straps I'd failed to check stretched and parted and limbs pinwheeled inexorably out into space. Of course they haven't heard of such things here. I've seen that over and over in their little conflicts and abrasions. How could they possibly have the expertise to resolve something bigger? Hyperventilating breaths rasp harshly in my ears—my own.

"How long have you been here?" I demand raggedly.

"Nine years, ten months, and five days." Cee's response is immediate.

Pain lances through my chest. No place of healing would leave someone counting the days that precisely. "But how do you make restitution if you're out here like this? How does the community learn to stop the same thing from happening again?" I can hear the franticness in my voice, but I can't stop it.

"They don't." Cee's serenity doesn't waver, but the look I get probes my very soul.

"You have fifteen more minutes," Jamerol interrupts.

Questions pile up behind my lips, clambering over each other in the desperate hope that one of them will have an answer that changes all this. I bite them back. "This is Et'elark's time. I didn't mean to take it all up."

Cee nods. "You can always write. Et'elark has the direction. Letters are always welcome."

"Of course." It takes me two tries to swallow. I know what I'm capable of now, but I also know how much of that is due to the generosity and grace of those who supported me and helped me work through the ugly truths I'd tried to hide from myself. The ways that I *had* meant that push. The resentment I hadn't talked out but had let boil into anger during a fateful conversation on the back of a pteradon so long ago. The joking and shoving match that really wasn't. Who would I be if that tangle of guilt and shame and resentment had instead been left to fester, or worse, smothered in desperate lies to avoid punishment? Who would I be if my community hadn't supported me to make amends, painful as that process was, but had instead thrown me away as irredeemable? I examine the stoop-shouldered elder in front of me again. Could I have retained as much dignity here as Cee has?

Et'elark's movements are still stiff with shame and pain, but he leans forward, voice finally under control. "How are you doing? Is your cough any better? Did you get the medicine we sent?"

Cee waves the question away. "I'm fine, I'm fine. I got your letter, but no, there was nothing with it."

Et'elark's shoulders sag, but he forces them straight

again. "We'll…we'll just have to pay for more. Somehow."

"They'll confiscate it again," Cee replies.

Et'elark's hand tightens into a fist on his knee. "It got through the time before that. If only the rules didn't change all the time."

"I'll be fine."

"Have they let you see a medic?"

Cee looks away. "Don't worry about me."

It's answer enough. Et'elark's nostrils flare. "Cee," he chokes out.

Cee waves him off again. "Tell me, how is everyone back home? Has Ileria had her baby yet?"

Almost I think Et'elark will refuse to be put off, but he acquiesces with a slump, filling Cee in on the details of loved ones until Jamerol announces that our brief time is up. He rises, trembling with the need to reach out, eyes riveted on the last sight of Cee vanishing into the depths. A tear rolls down his cheek until he angrily swipes it away.

"We're done here," he tells me. He tries to take a deep breath, but it comes out in a jerky gasp.

I let him lead us, under Jamerol's watchful eye, back to the tower and then to Fizz's side. There's only silence as I help him up, check the straps, and settle myself into place. I should give Fizz the signal to launch, but I only sit there holding my goggles. A message on my 'glove from Nareen says that they've gotten another ride home.

"Et'elark?"

"Yes?" His voice is ragged.

"Do you want to go sit somewhere and talk instead of going straight back to Ikmeth?"

He's silent for a moment, but then his breath puffs out against my hair. "Yes, but not here."

"No," I agree, "not here."

***

There's only one place that feels right to take him to. Fizz wheels above the abandoned clearing where my family lived all those years ago, looking for space among the scrubby trees that compete for sunlight where buildings once stood. Only the old landing site is still clear, the slightly tilted rock whispering with ghosts and memories that time will never fully erase. I ease Fizz down and slide off her shoulder, steadying myself against her sun-warmed hide. In the dappled sunlight, vines and bushes press their way among the trees, clamoring with life that never ceases in its quest to grow and thrive. I take a deep breath. I'm no longer the impulsive youngster I used to be. I'm the woman whose legendary strictness about safety makes me one of the most trusted flying teachers in the clan. I cannot imagine what it would be like to stay static—trapped in the eternity of one mistake—for years.

Et'elark follows me as I push through the undergrowth to the overlook where I sat so often, alone or with a warm arm wrapped around my shoulders, wrestling with grief and anger and guilt and finally acceptance. It's still there, though time has chipped away at some of the rock, tumbling boulders into the chasm below. Across the valley, the waterfall still arches down in a spray that disintegrates into clouds of mist before it can hit the river below. Rainbows scatter among its remnants.

"It's beautiful," Et'elark breathes behind me.

"It was one of my favorite places to come when we lived here," I tell him. "A reminder that there's still beauty in the world even when the pain seems unbearable."

He settles himself onto a bare patch of rock, and I join him. I can almost feel the ghost of my younger self sitting, arms curled around knees, beside us.

Pain laces his voice. "I wish Cee could see this."

I don't say anything, just give him space to breathe.

"What happened?" I ask softly. I send up a brief prayer that there is some explanation, something that makes the pieces I've gleaned so far fit into something that is not horrific.

He glances at me out of the corner of his eye. "Where do you want me to start?"

"Wherever the story starts."

His breath puffs out. "Where it starts… You saw the fields. When we went to Treverel?"

I nod.

He continues. "Every harvest, every planting, four of us from every family have to go work there." He glances at me, then continues bitterly, "We're not like the Uplanders, we don't have the money to buy out of it, especially not when our families are so much smaller than theirs." He presses his lips together.

"Why is that?"

His gaze flicks sideways at me again. "Over the generations, they've dug their caves large enough to fit a hundred fifty people before they have to split into new families. Ours can fit maybe forty or fifty. We'd make them larger, but that costs money." He rubs his temples. "Do you know how hard it is to make ends meet when there's always something? My family almost saved up enough for an expansion—just a little one, but it was something. We were going to bring more people into the family, I was going to be freed up to go do an apprenticeship up top instead of needing to go serve the head tithe so much… But you have to have the whole payment in advance, enough to make it worthwhile to someone who knows how to plan around the instability of the rock." He bites his lip. "We were so *close*. And so, my uncle went to the harvest—even though we *knew* he had heart problems—because we were so close, and if I stayed at my job in the lab, then I would show I was committed to becoming an apprentice and wouldn't disappear for a month at a time for every planting and harvest."

He closes his eyes. When he speaks again, his voice cracks. "We found out later. My uncle had dizzy spells, but the supervisor accused him of malingering. They threatened to deny us our portion of the harvest if he wouldn't work longer to make up for it. So he did. He worked well into the day and collapsed from heatstroke." He draws a ragged breath. "He might have survived if he'd gotten medical care, but the supervisor insisted he was faking it. Until it was too late."

"They left him there?" I ask incredulously.

"They didn't care. They cut our portion of the harvest anyway, said it was our fault for sending someone so obviously infirm, and that our family hadn't worked our fair share." He gives a bark of something that bears little resemblance to laughter. "They're always looking for excuses to cut it—that we're not working hard enough, or we're being 'uncooperative'—but this was the first time I'd heard of it being cut for *dying*." His lips crimp in pain. "We protested, Goddess knows we protested, but there was a scuffle and an Uplander got hit with a scythe, and they exiled Cee as the one responsible for it, and on top of that they fined us the cost of flying my uncle's body home." He swallows jerkily, looking away. "And told us to be grateful. And that was that."

I stare at him in numb horror, his words refusing to coalesce into something that makes sense.

He swipes water away from his eyes with the side of his hand. "After," he continues, "do you know how expensive it is to have a relative in the mines? Visits, communication, making sure they have even the most basic necessities, medical care. Cee has a *lung disease* now. If we hadn't spent down the last of our reserves to visit in person, we never would have known. Now it's trying to arrange for some sort of medical care—and make sure it happens! And there's money for medicines and—" He takes a deep breath and scrubs his hands over his face. "And it's even harder because none of Cee's 'wages' even go to us, not like before the exile. They're all claimed as forfeit." He presses his fist against his mouth. "It's just…it's a lot to carry. All the time. Keeping it together for the youngsters, trying not to be a burden on the rest of my uncles." Strain lines age his face.

I fight down my own panic, willing support through the hand I'm holding in mine. There are no words that will make it better, but I can bear witness to his grief.

He swipes at his eyes again. "I don't mean to fall apart on you like this."

"It's all right," I tell him. "You shouldn't have to bear this alone."

Silence descends, interrupted only by Et'elark's occasional swipe at his face. Eventually, his breathing eases.

"Have you talked to anyone about this?" I ask tentatively.

He shakes his head in sharp negation. "You don't just

go around telling people you have a family member who's been sent away. Not everyone reacts well. Most people don't."

I remember Nareen's odd comment when she'd realized Et'elark's destination. "But Isel's family, surely. They're different from all the rest. If they knew—"

Bitter laughter pours from his throat. "You think they don't? They may not supervise the mines themselves, but they use almost everything extracted from them. They know exactly what's going on."

That can't be true. They're the family most like us, the people we could be if we settled here. I shake my head.

Et'elark's eyes spark with anger. "Yes. They. Do." He leans forward. "I've had to bite my tongue watching you run around all this time, so convinced that these are all good people and if you can just get them to talk to one another, everything will be fine. You have no idea what's going on." He straightens, all the emotion he normally hides blazing into life.

I rock backward. "You're the one who suggested it to me. That I might teach them how to resolve conflicts better."

His rictus of a smile has no humor in it. "I meant the ones that really matter. You've been trying to get the best-off families to talk about the smallest hurts they're doing to each other, and even that has been like pulling teeth." He tilts his head, eyes narrowing. "Do you really want to know why they refuse to talk about the little things?"

Trepidation fills me, but I nod. He's heard me puzzle over it often enough.

"Well?" His eyes bore into mine. "Where would it *end*? If they made a habit of talking about all little ways they've hurt people, then what excuse would they have for refusing to talk about the big ones? You think they want to face the fact that every bite they eat, every shiny new gadget they invent is built on someone else's suffering? Nonsense. Easier to convince themselves that somehow 'those people' deserved it, that they're not really human. Then there's no need to care."

"But how could they—they can't—" Words desert me. Destroying one's own empathy is *soul killing*.

"You haven't noticed? All it takes is one mistake, and then—" He makes a stabbing motion. "Everyone says you deserve whatever happens to you."

I clutch at his hand. "But no one can live like that. There's not a human being alive who can measure up to that level of perfection."

His lips take on a cynical twist. "Enough lying and they manage. Haven't you noticed how much time they spend desperately convincing themselves that *their* screwups weren't really screwups? Or weren't that bad?"

With grim inevitability, pieces click into place: Nareen's resistance to admitting mistakes, the Uplanders' puzzling hostility toward being asked to make repair, and Ya'shul almost collapsing with guilt. The tightness in my chest feels like a weight pressing down on me. I thought their obsession with assigning and deflecting blame merely an oddity. It never occurred to me to wonder what happens when it sticks.

I feel my way through my next words as carefully as if they're edged with broken glass. "You're telling me they can't admit to doing harm because if they do, they'll end up back there?" I jerk my thumb the way we came.

"No." He stares unseeingly into the valley below us,

eyes haunted by memory. "That's the excuse they give for sending *us* there. *They* can do whatever they want."

I shake my head, resisting all of it. The cruelty and senselessness.

"Pay attention sometime." Slowly, he folds back in on himself, packing his emotions away once more behind shuttered eyes. "Who do the knives come out for, and whose behavior gets excused as no big deal?" He shrugs and starts to turn away.

This can't be what we're becoming part of. It *can't*. "But surely if you talk to them they'd come around. No one really wants their only choice when someone is hurt to be eviscerating the person who did it or pretending it never happened."

He turns back, anger sparking in his eyes once more. "You think we haven't tried? They won't even acknowledge the harm they're doing to other *Uplanders*, never mind to us. Pay attention sometime to what happens to the families up there who can barely cling to their caves. Or are forced out. And they treat them well compared to us, even those of us who live upslope." He shakes his head. "It's a nice attempt, but you're on a fool's errand. They have too much riding on convincing themselves that they're innocent."

I want to tell him he's wrong, that I can teach them, that it's possible for me to make a place here.

As if he can read my thoughts, he pins me with one last look, challenge written in every line of his body. "Try it," he says. "Try it and see."

Chapter Thirty-One
Ya'shul

The chamber that has been set aside for Nareen's new lab is only a single room tucked away in a building that houses supplies for her family, but it gleams. Her other guarantees must have worked frantically in the days since Isel agreed to a truce to make it project this much pride and potential. I settle myself gingerly on a stool. We were right; the combined lobbying from the three families was enough to persuade Priestess Wekmet to approve sending Nareen and me as a single project. And if no one felt the need to ask permission for Isel to fly us there, well, what's done will be done. I think all the families are relieved to have a detente. If only it didn't feel quite so precarious. Se'jan and Ya'kinem and I have been working constantly to hold the two sides together and build a tenuous trust.

The door opens and Nareen ushers Isel in, Ya'kinem hovering in the background. Isel invited Nareen to her workshop, as much to boast as to extend a peace offering. Nareen is obligated to reciprocate. I hold my breath. The contrast between the two spaces could not be more stark.

"There's more at home," Nareen assures Isel, her chin

rising in a challenging tilt. "Not to mention everything else we produce. This is just the new public area for my lab."

Isel pulls a stool out from under a counter, seating herself with loose-limbed confidence that fills the space. She looks around. "Everyone starts from somewhere," she says, and I exhale. I've seen flashes of this, a generous spirit and dry sense of humor that I wouldn't have guessed at. Perhaps not needing to constantly be on the attack brings out her better side as well. "Now," she continues, "I'm intrigued by these possibilities you've mentioned for microbes that process and concentrate metals."

Nareen turns to me. I flex my fingers and pull up the overview of the relevant research from my family's archives—research that Nareen now tells everyone is *my* area of expertise. She's by no means perfect, but I won't forget her quiet insistence to Kiu that I be allowed back in the lab, nor her reaction when we and my sister had strategized over how to put our best foot forward with Isel. *No*, she'd told my sister when Kiu had offered up the documents she'd set her assistants scouring the archives for, *I don't think I should be the lead on that. I think Ya'shul should be.* Now here I am, presenting my findings while three sets of eyes look at me as if I'm someone to be taken seriously. For the first time in months, it feels like I can stretch without limits.

I glance at Nareen as I finish, catching a smile that's almost shy. As fragile as our relationship still feels, things are slowly righting themselves. I smile back. *We can do this.* What was Andeshe's little ritual blessing? *Let what was broken be made stronger for it?* Nareen is so tentative and fumbling in her attempts to ask after my feelings and what I would like that it's almost endearing. For now, at least. I hope she'll make progress as quickly as she's learned so many other skills.

The conversation turns to discussing what I've found so far, and I revel in using my brain and creativity once more. This is what I was meant to do. This is what I'm going to show off at the capital. Already, my festival clothes are getting additional adornments to make them into something that will show my family's pride. Despite the strain of the past weeks, excitement bubbles up in my chest. I did this. Nothing will take this away from me again.

A knock sounds on the door, Andeshe's pattern. Ya'kinem hurries to answer it.

"Andeshe!" I say when he steps in. I can finally face him. "We haven't forgotten you." I know I promised to keep him updated even when things were going wrong, but now I have something even better, promising ideas to fix the problem his pteradons are having. I glance at the others, then rattle off possibilities we've discussed. We'll continue exploring whether we can modify our herd animals into something that pteradons can eat, but that's always a chancy business. It may be more promising to use some of the longer-range drones Isel is developing to herd native animals into more viable ranges for hunting. Or else develop better sensors on the goats' collars that can actually warn them off of things that contain phosfoz. Something should work, especially by the time we work through potential modifications of native animals and fish stocks in the reservoirs behind the dams.

He smiles when I finish, but it's barely a twitch of his lips. A thread of irritation worms its way into me. I went out of my way to ensure his project wasn't lost in the shuffle.

"These projects," Andeshe says. "They're all made

with resources from the mines?"

I frown at the complete non sequitur. "Of course. What else? If you're worried about the lithium they'll need, I know it's expensive, but surely your family can afford some." After all this work to find something for him, the last thing I want to hear is that it won't work.

"It's not that. It's the people in the mines."

Relief floods through me. I thought he had a serious concern.

"You don't have to worry about them," Isel reassures him. "They can't get out."

His face is oddly expressionless, only his eyes sliding to her. "You know about them?"

Surprise makes me interrupt whatever Isel was about to say. "Doesn't everyone?" I know he's not from here, but still. "They're criminals. All the people who are too dangerous to be around the rest of us. At least in the mines they're doing some good."

Taut silence stretches out between us. When Andeshe speaks again, his voice is weirdly soft. "Dangerous? The mines are what's dangerous. I asked. Cave-ins, dust that damages the lungs, poor nutrition, overwork, poor medical care. Fieldwork, likewise, especially as the solar storms approach. People are getting hurt and dying to produce these metals and food."

The rest of us exchange looks. "It's unfortunate," Isel says finally, "but someone has to do it. If they didn't want to work hard, they should have followed the rules. They knew what the consequences would be."

Andeshe's throat bobs, and his eyes dart among us. "And if *you* mess up?" he croaks. "That's what happens to you?"

I recoil. "I'm not a criminal. *I* would never kill anyone. Or—or do any of the other things they get sent there for." I restrain my irritation. *He's not from here. He doesn't understand what he's implying.* I turn away, my earlier euphoria draining out of me. "Do you want to hear about ways to keep the pteradons or not?" I don't know why he's going on about this now. It's taken everything I have just to get this far. I'm done with letting anything come between me and what I deserve. I fix my eyes on the terminal, spinning the possibilities Nareen and Isel and I have brainstormed into life. "See, this is what we're working for."

Andeshe's hands twitch, the palms turning toward us before he slowly lets them fall to his side again. "Yes," he says faintly. "So I see."

Chapter Thirty-Two

Andeshe

I would never kill anyone. Ya'shul's words echo in my head, the loathing in his voice making me sick to my stomach. I've retreated to the rocks on the far side of the fairground, tucking myself among the boulders that spill from the base of the promontory toward the edge of the far cliff. A desiccating wind blows past me, an implacable reminder that the summer's brutal drought is only getting started. Before, I could have retreated to the mountains' upper slopes, where cooler temperatures and condensing clouds ensure that trickles of water, at least, cling to the rocks all year round. I've never been stuck here, feeling the hot winds inexorably draw the moisture out of me. *I would never kill anyone.* Would it have helped to point out that his plans already do, or would that simply have bounced off his bone-deep need to fend off blame? I shake my head, trying to clear it. It wasn't my personal guilt and apology that healed my community, it was the soul searching we all did to find the web of interconnections that led to that death and the alternatives that could stop such a thing from happening again.

Despite the heat, a shiver runs over me. How could anyone exchange that web of mutual responsibility for the false promise that packing guilt onto the shoulders of a few people will let the rest claim complete innocence?

"Andeshe?" Footsteps rattle the pebbles along with Velemeth's surprised voice. After a moment, she settles herself on the rocks beside me. "I didn't expect you to come watch."

"Watch what?" My voice barely sounds like my own.

"The latest flier test run." A casual wave of her hand draws my attention to a crowd gathered on the grass of the fairground below us, all peering off to the northeast. In the distance, a dark spot appears in the air. The faint whump-whump of rotating blades reaches our ears.

"This flight confirms the outer range it can go on a charge," Velemeth explains. "If it works, that means it can reliably make most three-ridge flights."

"People are dying to produce the materials to make those things." Out of the corner of my eye, I watch for her reaction.

Velemeth sighs but shows no evidence of surprise. My stomach sinks.

"Andeshe, they do things differently here." She runs her hands down the side of her loose Uplander trousers. "I know you're having trouble accepting that, but things won't be the way they were back home, and I, for one, think that's a good thing." She fingers the studs in her ears. "Look at what they've accomplished. We would never have been able to build the flier without their technology. Their *settled* technology that they've built over generations in ways we could never do."

My heart starts to hammer as I stare at the stranger

beside me. "And who pays the price so we can have our happy ending?"

"So the world isn't perfect. Would you rather we cease flying entirely and grub in the dirt instead? Better them than us."

My fingers dig into the gravel among the rocks, desperate for something to anchor me against her clear-eyed ruthlessness. "Hurting others wounds your own soul," I croak. I know that; I've felt it. Velemeth was *there*. I grope for the teachings of our youth, the ones so deeply woven into our souls that I can barely articulate them. "Think of who we were. Who are we becoming now?"

"Ultimately? We're becoming wealthy, powerful, and respected. You've never cared for anything but flying, Andeshe, but some of us were born to create life, and we have the responsibility to do what's best for *all* of our family." Her posture shifts, and the woman who sits next to me exudes an uncompromising authority. "Leave it to us," she tells me, rising. "Men like you wouldn't understand."

Her words punch me in the gut.

I curl forward. "Velemeth!" I call after her. My voice cracks. "*That's not who we are!*" Fists clenched, I will her to understand. "That's not who I am."

She turns back, silhouetted against the sun. "It is now."

"Who are you?" I gasp. The cousin I know would never put me in a box like that, would never have said any of it.

"Get with the times, Andeshe. The old ways are over." With grim finality, she turns her back on me and picks her way back down the rocks.

I bury my head in my hands, the stones around me

closing in like a vise. The urge seizes me to spring onto Fizz's back and escape home to somewhere—anywhere—that will put everything back the way it was. I try to calm my breathing, to reassure myself even as panic batters against the cage of my ribs. Surely Auntie Haveo would never agree to this. I raise my head, clinging to that hope. On the fairground below, the crowd waits, gathered Wanderers indistinguishable from the surrounding Uplanders. Memories force their way into my mind, conversations between zomen, Haveo's commitment to carve out a place for our family at the top of this village. Cold horror washes through me. *This is who we're becoming.*

Footsteps crunch on the gravel behind me again, but I can't bring myself to look.

"I thought I saw you come this way," Et'elark says. After a moment, he sits beside me.

"You were right." I can barely speak.

He lets out his breath in a long sigh. "I wish I weren't." He gazes off into the distance, where a black dot grows in size, the faint thump of propeller blades growing louder. It wallows in for a landing, and the blades spin to a halt. The door opens, and a tall figure steps down, towering over the crowd of shorter Uplanders. Someone else brushes past her, barely coming up to her shoulder, and climbs into the cockpit.

For a moment, my brain doesn't process the significance of what I'm seeing, then my stomach heaves with realization. *A Lowlander did the test flight*—the test flight that risked not returning. I close my eyes against nausea.

"What do you even do?" I whisper to Et'elark.

He gives me an unreadable look, then swivels to watch

the pilot below. The tall form edges through the eddying crowd until she can turn her back on it and stride away toward the far side of the fairground. Et'elark's gaze returns to me, and I can feel him weighing me with his eyes. "Are you sure you want to know?"

He asked me that before. Am I?

"I have to," I tell him finally. I can't bury my head and pretend none of this is happening. I have to face it.

He rises and holds out his hand. "Come with me, then, and I'll show you."

I set my hand in his, the warmth of his callused palm reminding me that, somehow, he has managed to stay alive and whole. He pulls me to my feet, and I follow.

* * *

Thank you!

Thank you for reading *Pledging Season*! If you enjoyed the story, please consider leaving a review. Reviews, long and short, are vital for authors' careers and help readers find the next book they'll enjoy.

***

If you'd like to know when the next book in the series becomes available, or to get announcements about preorders, you can sign up for my email list at **eemauthor.com** or follow me on Twitter **@eemauthor**.

Names and Pronunciations

As the reader, you are welcome to pronounce names however you like, but if you are wondering how they sound in my head, here you go! All characters' names follow the same format: personal name, family name, and clan name; therefore, Ya'shul Lefmin Quemzol would be part of the Lefmin family, Quemzol clan. Wanderers who have chosen to become part of a family other than the one they were born in hyphenate their family names, so Andeshe Kel-Orek Umolin is born into the Kel family, adopted into the Orek family, and part of the Umolin clan. Uplander zomen attach the suffix "-lun" to their names as an honorific, whereas Wanderer zomen names are preceded by "Auntie."

WANDERERS

Andeshe	ahn-DAY-shuh
Haveo	ha-VAY-oh
Illeab	eel-EH-ab
Velemeth	vel-eh-METH

UPLANDERS

Isel	ih-SEL
Jamerol	jam-er-OL
Kiu	key-OO
Marin	mar-IN
Nareen	nar-EEN
Orzea	or-ZEY-ah
Se'jan	say-JAHN
U'kylay	oo-KAI-lai
Viya	VIE-ya
Wekmet	Wek-MET
Ya'kinem	ya-KEY-nem
Ya'shul	ya-SHUL

LOWLANDERS

Et'elark   ET-eh-lark
Cee   SEE

FAMILY/CLAN NAMES

Umolin	oo-mo-LEEN	Andeshe's clan name
Kel	kel	Andeshe's birth family
Orek	OR-ek	Andeshe's adopted family, headed by Haveo
Quemzol	QUEM-zhol	Ya'shul's clan name
Lefmin	LEF-min	Ya'shul's family name
Asheveran	ah-SHEV-er-ahn	Nareen's clan name
Uleu	oo-LEH-oo	Nareen's family name
Hetlarth	HET-larth	Et'elark's clan name
Ell	el	Et'elark's family name

PLACES/OBJECTS

Iamar	EYE-ah-mar	dim, red moon
Ikmeth	ick-METH	city where Ya'shul lives
Kynthia	KIN-thee-ah	small, white moon
Treverel	TRAY-ver-el	capital city and mountain
oozmert	OOZE-mert	alcoholic beverage that is also a mild aphrodisiac
phosfoz	FOS-fohz	Phosphorescent compound common on this world
pteradon	TER-ah-don	giant pterosaur large enough to carry humans
ptercel	TER-sell	smaller cousins of the pteradons

Acknowledgements

Writing a book is a humbling endeavor, and I am deeply grateful to all the people who made it possible to bring this one to fruition. Thank you to my husband first and foremost for his unwavering support and encouragement and for making it possible for me to start writing full time. Thank you also to my parents and in-laws for hours upon hours of pandemic childcare, without which this book would still be slogging its way through the early drafts.

Thank you to my wonderful editor Sarah Cypher at The Threepenny Editor, whose ability to give feedback that is both encouraging and immensely clarifying leaves me in awe. Thank you also to everyone who critiqued all or part of the manuscript: all my readers at Spun Yarn, Veronica at Salt and Sage, Arley Concaildi (thank you also for the marketing advice and support!), Stitch, May Peterson, Erick Erickson, and my proofreader Neha at Salt and Sage.

I'd also like to shout out a few of the people whose work gave me the tools to become a writer at all. Thank you to Maggie Hogarth, whose transparency about what it's like to be an indie author made me realize that normal people can do that sort of thing—maybe even me! Rachel Aaron's book *2K to 10K* was invaluable writing advice for me as a baby author stumbling around the ideas that would eventually coalesce to form this world. I'm by no means a fast writer, but 0K to 2K is by far the most important step. Joanna Penn at The Creative Penn has been my go-to source for fantastic resources about the business of writing. I'm also deeply grateful to Jessica Denise Dickson and her Disrupt the Narrative group for invaluable coaching that has deepened my understanding of many of the issues I write about here.

Finally, thank you to James T. Egan at Bookfly Design for a beautiful cover, and thank you to Lorna Reid for interior formatting. Writing the words is only part of the challenge!

About the Author

Erika Erickson Malinoski grew up in Michigan and now lives in New Jersey with her multi-generational family. In between, she earned a Master of Public Policy degree from the University of Michigan, taught secondary math and sex ed in California, and realized that the universe is very strange. She is a devout Unitarian Universalist.

CPSIA information can be obtained
at www.ICGtesting.com
Printed in the USA
LVHW111256130522
718722LV00017B/96